Timeless Legends

These great stories from Greek, Roman and Norse mythology are the fountainhead of all literature. In them, the figures of antiquity come vividly to life.

Here are the gods of high Olympus—mighty Zeus, all too human, and Hera, prototype of the jealous wife. Here are the famous love stories of Cupid and Psyche, Pyramus and Thisbe, and Pygmalion and Galatea; the thrilling adventures of Jason and the perilous Quest of the Golden Fleece; the Trojan War, and the superhuman achievements of Odysseus and Aeneas. And here too, you'll meet the families whose turbulent histories formed the plots of the famous Greek plays—Agamemnon and his children; tragic Oedipus and heroic Antigone. And from Norse mythology come the stirring legends of Signy and Sigurd—tragic tales of love, death and heroism.

Renowned for her love and understanding of classic literature, Edith Hamilton has retold these great myths for modern readers in a way that preserves the flavor and excitement of the originals.

"Classical mythology has long needed such a popular exposition as Miss Edith Hamilton has given us in this volume, which is at once a reference book and a book which may be read for stimulation and pleasure."—*New York Times*

"Mythology as it should be written . . . She has the rare quality which is able to penetrate into modes of thought not our own and to transcribe the spirit of another age."—*Book-of-the-Month Club News*

MYTHOLOGY

By EDITH HAMILTON

Illustrated
by Steele Savage

A MENTOR BOOK from.
NEW AMERICAN LIBRARY
TIMES MIRROR
New York and Scarborough, Ontario

MENTOR TRADEMARK REG. U.S. PAT. OFF. AND FOREIGN COUNTRIES
REGISTERED TRADEMARK—MARCA REGISTRADA
HECHO EN CHICAGO, U.S.A.

SIGNET, SIGNET CLASSICS, MENTOR, PLUME, MERIDIAN AND NAL
BOOKS are published *in the United States* by
The New American Library, Inc.,
1633 Broadway, New York, New York 10019,
in Canada by The New American Library of Canada Limited,
81 Mack Avenue, Scarborough, Ontario M1L 1M8

  59   60   61   62   63   64   65   66   67

PRINTED IN THE UNITED STATES OF AMERICA

Foreword

A book on Mythology must draw from widely different sources. Twelve hundred years separate the first writers through whom the myths have come down to us from the last, and there are stories as unlike each other as "Cinderella" and "King Lear." To bring them all together in one volume is really somewhat comparable to doing the same for the stories of English literature from Chaucer to the ballads, through Shakespeare and Marlowe and Swift and Defoe and Dryden and Pope and so on, ending with, say, Tennyson and Browning, or even, to make the comparison truer, Kipling and Galsworthy. The English collection would be bigger, but it would not contain more dissimilar material. In point of fact, Chaucer is more like Galsworthy and the ballads like Kipling than Homer is like Lucian or Aeschylus like Ovid.

Faced with this problem, I determined at the outset to dismiss any idea of unifying the tales. That would have meant either writing "King Lear," so to speak, down to the level of "Cinderella"—the vice versa procedure being obviously not possible—or else telling in my own way stories which were in no sense mine and had been told by great writers in ways they thought suited their subjects. I do not mean, of course, that a great writer's style can be reproduced or that I should dream of attempting such a feat. My aim has been nothing more ambitious than to keep distinct for the reader the very different writers from whom our knowledge of the myths comes. For example, Hesiod is a notably simple writer and devout; he is naïve, even childish, sometimes crude, always full of piety. Many of the stories in this book are told only by him. Side by side with them are stories told only by Ovid, subtle, polished, artificial, self-conscious, and the complete skeptic. My effort has been to make the reader see some difference between writers who were so different. After all, when one takes up a book like this one does not ask how entertainingly the author has retold the stories, but how close he has brought the reader to the original.

My hope is that those who do not know the classics will gain in this way not only a knowledge of the myths, but some little idea of what the writers were like who told them—who have been proved, by two thousand years and more, to be immortal.

Contents

FOREWORD V

INTRODUCTION TO CLASSICAL MYTHOLOGY 13
    The Mythology of the Greeks 14
    The Greek and Roman Writers of
       Mythology 21

PART ONE:
   The Gods, the Creation, and the Earliest Heroes

1 THE GODS 24
    The Titans and the Twelve Great
       Olympians 24
    The Lesser Gods of Olympus 36
    The Gods of the Waters 38
    The Underworld 39
    The Lesser Gods of Earth 40
    The Roman Gods 43

2 THE TWO GREAT GODS OF EARTH 47
    Demeter (Ceres) 49
    Dionysus or Bacchus 54

3 HOW THE WORLD AND MANKIND WERE
   CREATED 63

4 THE EARLIEST HEROES 75
    Prometheus and Io 75
    Europa 78
    The Cyclops Polyphemus 81
    Flower-Myths: Narcissus, Hyacinth,
       Adonis 85

PART TWO: Stories of Love and Adventure

5 CUPID AND PSYCHE 92
6 EIGHT BRIEF TALES OF LOVERS 101
    Pyramus and Thisbe 101

Orpheus and Eurydice 103
Ceyx and Alcyone 106
Pygmalion and Galatea 108
Baucis and Philemon 111
Endymion 113
Daphne 114
Alpheus and Arethusa 116

7 THE QUEST OF THE GOLDEN FLEECE 117

8 FOUR GREAT ADVENTURES 131
Phaëthon 131
Pegasus and Bellerophon 134
Otus and Ephialtes 137
Daedalus 139

PART THREE:
The Great Heroes before the Trojan War

9 PERSEUS 141
10 THESEUS 149
11 HERCULES 159
12 ATALANTA 173

PART FOUR: The Heroes of the Trojan War

13 THE TROJAN WAR 178
Prologue: The Judgment of Paris 179
The Trojan War 179
14 THE FALL OF TROY 193
15 THE ADVENTURES OF ODYSSEUS 202
16 THE ADVENTURES OF AENEAS 220
Part One: From Troy to Italy 220
Part Two: The Descent into the Lower
World 226
Part Three: The War in Italy 230

PART FIVE: The Great Families of Mythology

17 THE HOUSE OF ATREUS 236
Tantalus and Niobe 237

      Agamemnon and His Children 240
      Iphigenia among the Taurians 248

18 THE ROYAL HOUSE OF THEBES 254
      Cadmus and His Children 254
      Oedipus 256
      Antigone 261
      The Seven against Thebes 264

19 THE ROYAL HOUSE OF ATHENS 268
      Cecrops 269
      Procne and Philomela 270
      Procris and Cephalus 271
      Orithyia and Boreas 273
      Creüsa and Ion 273

PART SIX: The Less Important Myths

20 MIDAS—AND OTHERS 278
      Midas 278
      Aesculapius 279
      The Danaïds 281
      Glaucus and Scylla 282
      Erysichthon 284
      Pomona and Vertumnus 285

21 BRIEF MYTHS ARRANGED ALPHABETICALLY 287

PART SEVEN: The Mythology of the Norsemen

      Introduction to Norse Mythology 300

22 THE STORIES OF SIGNY AND OF SIGURD 303

23 THE NORSE GODS 308
      The Creation 312
      The Norse Wisdom 314

GENEALOGICAL TABLES 316

INDEX 323

Illustrations

Greece first discovered mankind   *Frontispiece*

The Greeks, unlike the Egyptians, made their gods in their own image   15

Olympus   26

The rape of Persephone (Proserpine)   51

Pandora lifted the lid and out flew plagues and sorrows for mankind   71

The rape of Europa   80

Psyche gazed at the sleeping Cupid   97

Pygmalion and Galatea   109

The Harpies and the Argonauts   121

Bellerophon on Pegasus killing the Chimaera   136

Perseus holding Medusa's head   147

The Minotaur in the Labyrinth   153

Hercules carrying Cerberus   166

Atalanta and the golden apples   176

The judgment of Paris   180

The wooden horse   197

Odysseus and Circe   213

Aeneas and the Sibyl enter Charon's boat   229

Clytemnestra and Orestes   247

Oedipus and the Sphinx   258

Athena appears to Creüsa and Ion   277

Glaucus and Scylla   283

Sigurd riding through the fire to Brynhild   305

Introduction To Classical Mythology

> *Of old the Hellenic race was marked off from the barbarian as more keen-witted and more free from nonsense.*
>
> HERODOTUS I: 60.

Greek and Roman mythology is quite generally supposed to show us the way the human race thought and felt untold ages ago. Through it, according to this view, we can retrace the path from civilized man who lives so far from nature, to man who lived in close companionship with nature; and the real interest of the myths is that they lead us back to a time when the world was young and people had a connection with the earth, with trees and seas and flowers and hills, unlike anything we ourselves can feel. When the stories were being shaped, we are given to understand, little distinction had as yet been made between the real and the unreal. The imagination was vividly alive and not checked by the reason, so that anyone in the woods might see through the trees a fleeing nymph, or bending over a clear pool to drink, behold in the depths a naiad's face.

The prospect of traveling back to this delightful state of things is held out by nearly every writer who touches upon classical mythology, above all by the poets. In that infinitely remote time primitive man could

> Have sight of Proteus rising from the sea;
> Or hear old Triton blow his wreathèd horn.

And we for a moment can catch, through the myths he made, a glimpse of that strangely and beautifully animated world.

But a very brief consideration of the ways of uncivilized peoples everywhere and in all ages is enough to prick that romantic bubble. Nothing is clearer than the fact that primitive man, whether in New Guinea today or eons ago in the prehistoric wilderness, is not and never has been a creature who peoples his world with bright fancies and lovely visions. Horrors lurked in the primeval forest, not nymphs and naiads. Terror lived there, with its close attendant, Magic, and its most common defense, Human Sacrifice. Mankind's chief hope of escaping the wrath of whatever divinities were then abroad lay in some magical rite, senseless but powerful, or in some offering made at the cost of pain and grief.

THE MYTHOLOGY OF THE GREEKS

This dark picture is worlds apart from the stories of classical mythology. The study of the way early man looked at his surroundings does not get much help from the Greeks. How briefly the anthropologists treat the Greek myths is noteworthy.

Of course the Greeks too had their roots in the primeval slime. Of course they too once lived a savage life, ugly and brutal. But what the myths show is how high they had risen above the ancient filth and fierceness by the time we have any knowledge of them. Only a few traces of that time are to be found in the stories.

We do not know when these stories were first told in their present shape; but whenever it was, primitive life had been left far behind. The myths as we have them are the creation of great poets. The first written record of Greece is the *Iliad*. Greek mythology begins with Homer, generally believed to be not earlier than a thousand years before Christ. The *Iliad* is, or contains, the oldest Greek literature; and it is written in a rich and subtle and beautiful language which must have had behind it centuries when men were striving to express themselves with clarity and beauty, an indisputable proof of civilization. The tales of Greek mythology do not throw any clear light upon what early mankind was like. They do throw an abundance of light upon what early Greeks were like—a matter, it would seem, of more importance to us, who are their descendants intellectually, artistically, and politically, too. Nothing we learn about them is alien to ourselves.

People often speak of "the Greek miracle." What the phrase tries to express is the new birth of the world with the awakening of Greece. "Old things are passed away; behold, all things are become new." Something like that happened in Greece.

The Greeks, unlike the Egyptians, made
their gods in their own image

Why it happened, or when, we have no idea at all. We know only that in the earliest Greek poets a new point of view dawned, never dreamed of in the world before them, but never to leave the world after them. With the coming forward of Greece, mankind became the center of the universe, the most important thing in it. This was a revolution in thought. Human beings had counted for little heretofore. In Greece man first realized what mankind was.

The Greeks made their gods in their own image. That had not entered the mind of man before. Until then, gods had had no semblance of reality. They were unlike all living things. In Egypt, a towering colossus, immobile, beyond the power of the imagination to endow with movement, as fixed in the stone as the tremendous temple columns, a representation of the human shape deliberately made unhuman. Or a rigid figure, a woman with a cat's head suggesting inflexible, inhuman cruelty. Or a monstrous mysterious sphinx, aloof from all that lives. In Mesopotamia, bas-reliefs of bestial shapes unlike any beast ever known, men with birds' heads and lions with bulls' heads and both with eagles' wings, creations of artists who were intent upon producing something never seen except in their own minds, the very consummation of unreality.

These and their like were what the pre-Greek world worshiped. One need only place beside them in imagination any Greek statue of a god, so normal and natural with all its beauty, to perceive what a new idea had come into the world. With its coming, the universe became rational.

Saint Paul said the invisible must be understood by the visible. That was not a Hebrew idea, it was Greek. In Greece alone in the ancient world people were preoccupied with the visible; they were finding the satisfaction of their desires in what was actually in the world around them. The sculptor watched the athletes contending in the games and he felt that nothing he could imagine would be as beautiful as those strong young bodies. So he made his statue of Apollo. The storyteller found Hermes among the people he passed in the street. He saw the god "like a young man at the age when youth is loveliest," as Homer says. Greek artists and poets realized how splendid a man could be, straight and swift and strong. He was the fulfillment of their search for beauty. They had no wish to create some fantasy shaped in their own minds. All the art and all the thought of Greece centered in human beings.

Human gods naturally made heaven a pleasantly familiar place. The Greeks felt at home in it. They knew just what the divine inhabitants did there, what they ate and drank and where they banqueted and how they amused themselves. Of course they were to be feared; they were very powerful and very dangerous when angry. Still, with proper care a man could be quite fairly at ease with them. He was even perfectly free to laugh at them. Zeus, trying to hide his love affairs from his wife and invariably shown up, was a capital figure of fun. The Greeks enjoyed him and liked him all the better for it. Hera was that stock character of comedy, the typical jealous wife, and her ingenious tricks to discomfit her husband and punish her rival, far from displeasing the Greeks, entertained them as much as Hera's modern counterpart does us today. Such stories made for a friendly feeling. Laughter in the presence of an Egyptian sphinx or an Assyrian bird-beast was inconceivable; but it was perfectly natural in Olympus, and it made the gods companionable.

On earth, too, the deities were exceedingly and humanly attractive. In the form of lovely youths and maidens they peopled the woodland, the forest, the rivers, the sea, in harmony with the fair earth and the bright waters.

That is the miracle of Greek mythology—a humanized world, men freed from the paralyzing fear of an omnipotent Unknown. The terrifying incomprehensibilities which were worshiped elsewhere, and the fearsome spirits with which earth, air and sea swarmed, were banned from Greece. It may seem odd to say that the men who made the myths disliked the irrational and had a love for facts; but it is true, no matter how wildly fantastic some of the stories are. Anyone who reads them with attention discovers that even the most nonsensical take place in a world which is essentially rational and matter-of-fact. Hercules, whose life was one long combat against preposterous monsters, is always said to have had his home in the city of Thebes. The exact spot where Aphrodite was born of the foam could be visited by any ancient tourist; it was just offshore from the island of Cythera. The winged steed Pegasus, after skimming the air all day, went every night to a comfortable stable in Corinth. A familiar local habitation gave reality to all the mythical beings. If the mixture seems childish, consider how reassuring and how sensible the solid background is as compared with the Genie who comes from nowhere when Aladdin rubs the lamp and, his task accomplished, returns to nowhere.

The terrifying irrational has no place in classical mythology. Magic, so powerful in the world before and after Greece, is almost nonexistent. There are no men and only two women with dreadful, supernatural powers. The demoniac wizards and the hideous old witches who haunted Europe and America, too, up to quite recent years, play no part at all in the stories. Circe and Medea are the only witches and they are young and of surpassing beauty—delightful, not horrible. Astrology, which has flourished from the days of ancient Babylon down to today, is completely absent from classical Greece. There are many stories about the stars, but not a trace of the idea that they influence men's lives. Astronomy is what the Greek mind finally made out of the stars. Not a single story has a magical priest who is terribly to be feared because he knows ways of winning over the gods or alienating them. The priest is rarely seen and is never of importance. In the *Odyssey* when a priest and a poet fall on their knees before Odysseus, praying him to spare their lives, the hero kills the priest without a thought, but saves the poet. Homer says that he felt awe to slay a man who had been taught his divine art by the gods. Not the priest, but the poet, had influence with heaven—and no one was ever afraid of a poet. Ghosts, too, which have played so large and so fearsome a part in other lands, never appear on earth in any Greek story. The Greeks were not afraid of the dead—"the piteous dead," the *Odyssey* calls them.

The world of Greek mythology was not a place of terror for the human spirit. It is true that the gods were disconcertingly incalculable. One could never tell where Zeus's thunderbolt would strike. Nevertheless, the whole divine company, with a very few and for the most part not important exceptions, were entrancingly beautiful with a human beauty, and nothing humanly beautiful is really terrifying. The early Greek mythologists transformed a world full of fear into a world full of beauty.

This bright picture has its dark spots. The change came about slowly and was never quite completed. The gods-become-human were for a long time a very slight improvement upon their worshipers. They were incomparably lovelier and more powerful, and they were of course immortal; but they often acted in a way no decent man or woman would. In the *Iliad* Hector is nobler by far than any of the heavenly beings, and Andromache infinitely to be preferred to Athena or Aphrodite. Hera from first to last is a goddess on a very low level of humanity. Almost every one of the radiant divinities could act cruelly or contemptibly. A very limited sense of right and wrong prevailed in Homer's heaven, and for a long time after.

Other dark spots too stand out. There are traces of a time when there were beast-gods. The satyrs are goat-men and the centaurs are half man, half horse. Hera is often called "cow-faced," as if the adjective had somehow stuck to her through all her changes from a divine cow to the very human queen of heaven. There are also stories which point back clearly to a time when there was human sacrifice. But what is astonishing is not that bits of savage belief were left here and there. The strange thing is that they are so few.

Of course the mythical monster is present in any number of shapes,

Gorgons and hydras and chimaeras dire,

but they are there only to give the hero his meed of glory. What could a hero do in a world without them? They are always overcome by him. The great hero of mythology, Hercules, might be an allegory of Greece herself. He fought the monsters and freed the earth from them just as Greece freed the earth from the monstrous idea of the unhuman supreme over the human.

Greek mythology is largely made up of stories about gods and goddesses, but it must not be read as a kind of Greek Bible, an account of the Greek religion. According to the most modern idea, a real myth has nothing to do with religion. It is an explanation of something in nature; how, for instance, any and everything in the universe came into existence: men, animals, this or that tree or flower, the sun, the moon, the stars, storms, eruptions, earthquakes, all that is and all that happens. Thunder and lightning are caused when Zeus hurls his thunderbolt. A volcano erupts because a terrible creature is imprisoned in the mountain and every now and then struggles to get free. The Dipper, the constellation called also the Great Bear, does not set below the horizon because a goddess once was angry at it and decreed that it should never sink into the sea. Myths are early science, the result of men's first trying to explain what they saw around them. But there are many so-called myths which explain nothing at all. These tales are pure entertainment, the sort of thing people would tell each other on a long winter's evening. The story of Pygmalion and Galatea is an example; it has no conceivable connection with any event in nature. Neither has the Quest of the Golden Fleece, nor Orpheus and Eurydice, nor many another. This fact is now generally accepted; and we do not have to try to find in every mythological heroine the moon or the dawn and in every hero's life a sun myth. The stories are early literature as well as early science.

But religion is there, too. In the background, to be sure, but nevertheless plain to see. From Homer through the tragedians and even later, there is a deepening realization of what human beings need and what they must have in their gods.

Zeus the Thunderer was, it seems certain, once a rain-god. He was supreme even over the sun, because rocky Greece needed rain more than sunshine and the God of Gods would be the one who could give the precious water of life to his worshipers. But Homer's Zeus is not a fact of nature. He is a person living in a world where civilization has made an entry, and of course he has a standard of right and wrong. It is not very high, certainly, and seems chiefly applicable to others, not to himself; but he does punish men who lie and break their oaths; he is angered by any ill treatment of the dead; and he pities and helps old Priam when he goes as a suppliant to Achilles. In the *Odyssey*, he has reached a higher level. The swineherd there says that the needy and the stranger are from Zeus and he who fails to help them sins against Zeus himself. Hesiod, not much later than the *Odyssey* if at all, says of a man who does evil to the suppliant and the stranger, or who wrongs orphan children, "with that man Zeus is angry."

Then Justice became Zeus's companion. That was a new idea. The buccaneering chieftains in the *Iliad* did not want justice. They wanted to be able to take whatever they chose because they were strong and they wanted a god who was on the side of the strong. But Hesiod, who was a peasant living in a poor man's world, knew that the poor must have a just god. He wrote, "Fishes and beasts and fowls of the air devour one another. But to man, Zeus has given justice. Beside Zeus on his throne Justice has her seat." These passages show that the great and bitter needs of the helpless were reaching up to heaven and changing the god of the strong into the protector of the weak.

So, back of the stories of an amorous Zeus and a cowardly Zeus and a ridiculous Zeus, we can catch sight of another Zeus coming into being, as men grow continually more conscious of what life demanded of them and what human beings needed in the god they worshiped. Gradually this Zeus displaced the others, until he occupied the whole scene. At last he became, in the words of Dio Chrysostom, who wrote during the second century A.D.: "Our Zeus, the giver of every good gift, the common father and saviour and guardian of mankind."

The *Odyssey* speaks of "the divine for which all men long," and hundreds of years later Aristotle wrote, "Excellence, much labored for by the race of mortals." The Greeks from the earliest mythologists on had a perception of the divine and the excellent. Their longing for them was great enough to make them never give up laboring to see them clearly, until at last the thunder and lightning were changed into the Universal Father.

THE GREEK AND ROMAN WRITERS OF MYTHOLOGY

Most of the books about the stories of classical mythology depend chiefly upon the Latin poet Ovid, who wrote during the reign of Augustus. Ovid is a compendium of mythology. No ancient writer can compare with him in this respect. He told almost all the stories and he told them at great length. Occasionally stories familiar to us through literature and art have come down to us only in his pages. In this book I have avoided using him as far as possible. Undoubtedly he was a good poet and a good storyteller and able to appreciate the myths enough to realize what excellent material they offered him; but he was really farther away from them in his point of view than we are today. They were sheer nonsense to him. He wrote,

> I prate of ancient poets' monstrous lies,
> Ne'er seen or now or then by human eyes.

He says in effect to his reader, "Never mind how silly they are. I will dress them up so prettily for you that you will like them." And he does, often very prettily indeed, but in his hands the stories which were factual truth and solemn truth to the early Greek poets Hesiod and Pindar, and vehicles of deep religious truth to the Greek tragedians, become idle tales, sometimes witty and diverting, often sentimental and distressingly rhetorical. The Greek mythologists are not rhetoricians and are notably free from sentimentality.

The list of the chief writers through whom the myths have come down to us is not long. Homer heads it, of course. The *Iliad* and the *Odyssey* are, or rather contain, the oldest Greek writings we have. There is no way to date accurately any part of them. Scholars differ widely, and will no doubt continue to do so. As unobjectionable a date as any is 1000 B.C.— at any rate for the *Iliad*, the older of the two poems.

In all that follows, here and in the rest of the book, the date given is to be understood as before Christ, unless it is otherwise stated.

The second writer on the list is sometimes placed in the ninth century, sometimes in the eighth. Hesiod was a poor farmer whose life was hard and bitter. There cannot be a greater contrast than that between his poem, the *Works and Days*, which tries to show men how to live a good life in a harsh world, and the courtly splendor of the *Iliad* and the *Odyssey*. But Hesiod has much to say about the gods, and a second poem, usually ascribed to him, the *Theogony*, is entirely concerned with mythology. If Hesiod did write it, then a humble peasant, living on a lonely farm far from cities was the first man in Greece to wonder how everything had happened, the world, the sky, the gods, mankind, and to think out an explanation. Homer never wondered about anything. The *Theogony* is an account of the creation of the universe and the generations of the gods, and it is very important for mythology.

Next in order come the Homeric Hymns, poems written to honor various gods. They cannot be definitely dated, but the earliest are considered by most scholars to belong to the end of the eighth century or the beginning of the seventh. The last one of importance—there are thirty-three in all—belongs to fifth-century or possibly fourth-century Athens.

Pindar, the greatest lyric poet of Greece, began to write toward the end of the sixth century. He wrote Odes in honor of the victors in the games at the great national festivals of Greece, and in every one of his poems myths are told or alluded to. Pindar is quite as important for mythology as Hesiod.

Aeschylus, the oldest of the three tragic poets, was a contemporary of Pindar's. The other two, Sophocles and Euripides, were a little younger. Euripides, the youngest, died at the end of the fifth century. Except for Aeschylus' *Persians*, written to celebrate the victory of the Greeks over the Persians at Salamis, all the plays have mythological subjects. With Homer, they are the most important source of our knowledge of the myths.

The great writer of comedy, Aristophanes, who lived in the last part of the fifth century and the beginning of the fourth, refers often to the myths, as do also two great prose writers, Herodotus, the first historian of Europe, who was a contemporary of Euripides, and Plato, the philosopher, who lived less than a generation later.

The Alexandrian poets lived around 250 B.C. They were so called because, when they wrote, the center of Greek literature had moved from Greece to Alexandria in Egypt. Apollonius of Rhodes told at length the Quest of the Golden Fleece, and in connection with the story a number of other myths. He and three other Alexandrians, who also wrote about mythology, the pastoral poets Theocritus, Bion and Moschus, have lost the simplicity of Hesiod's and Pindar's belief in the gods, and are far removed from the depth and gravity of the tragic poets' view of religion; but they are not frivolous like Ovid.

Two late writers, Apuleius, a Latin, and Lucian, a Greek, both of the second century A.D., make an important contribution. The famous story of Cupid and Psyche is told only by Apuleius, who writes very much like Ovid. Lucian writes like no one except himself. He satirized the gods. In his time they had become a joking matter. Nevertheless, he gives by the way a good deal of information about them.

Apollodorus, also a Greek, is, next to Ovid, the most voluminous ancient writer on mythology, but, unlike Ovid, he is very matter-of-fact and very dull. His date has been differently set all the way from the first century B.C. to the ninth century A.D. The English scholar, Sir J. G. Frazer, thinks he probably wrote in either the first or the second century of our era.

The Greek Pausanias, an ardent traveler, the author of the first guidebook ever written, has a good deal to say about the mythological events reported to have happened in the places he visited. He lived as late as the second century A.D., but he does not question any of the stories. He writes about them with complete seriousness.

Of the Roman writers, Virgil stands far ahead. He did not believe in the myths any more than Ovid did, whose contemporary he was, but he found human nature in them and he brought mythological personages to life as no one had done since the Greek tragedians.

Other Roman poets wrote of the myths. Catullus tells several of the stories, and Horace alludes to them often, but neither is important for mythology. To all Romans the stories were infinitely remote, mere shadows. The best guides to a knowledge of Greek mythology are the Greek writers, who believed in what they wrote.

PART ONE

The Gods, The Creation, and the Earliest Heroes

1 The Gods

Strange clouded fragments of an ancient glory,
Late lingerers of the company divine,
They breathe of that far world wherefrom they come,
Lost halls of heaven and Olympian air.

The Greeks did not believe that the gods created the universe. It was the other way about: the universe created the gods. Before there were gods heaven and earth had been formed. They were the first parents. The Titans were their children, and the gods were their grandchildren.

THE TITANS AND THE TWELVE GREAT OLYMPIANS

The Titans, often called the Elder Gods, were for untold ages supreme in the universe. They were of enormous size and of incredible strength. There were many of them, but only a few appear in the stories of mythology. The most important was CRONUS, in Latin SATURN. He ruled over the other Titans until his son Zeus dethroned him and seized the power for himself. The Romans said that when Jupiter, their name for

Zeus, ascended the throne, Saturn fled to Italy and brought in the Golden Age, a time of perfect peace and happiness, which lasted as long as he reigned.

The other notable Titans were OCEAN, the river that was supposed to encircle the earth; his wife TETHYS; HYPERION, the father of the sun, the moon and the dawn; MNEMOSYNE, which means Memory; THEMIS, usually translated by Justice; and IAPETUS, important because of his sons, ATLAS, who bore the world on his shoulders, and PROMETHEUS, who was the savior of mankind. These alone among the older gods were not banished with the coming of Zeus, but they took a lower place.

The twelve great Olympians were supreme among the gods who succeeded to the Titans. They were called the Olympians because Olympus was their home. What Olympus was, however, is not easy to say. There is no doubt that at first it was held to be a mountain top, and generally identified with Greece's highest mountain, Mt. Olympus in Thessaly, in the northeast of Greece. But even in the earliest Greek poem, the *Iliad*, this idea is beginning to give way to the idea of an Olympus in some mysterious region far above all the mountains of the earth. In one passage of the *Iliad* Zeus talks to the gods from "the topmost peak of many-ridged Olympus," clearly a mountain. But only a little further on he says that if he willed he could hang earth and sea from a pinnacle of Olympus, clearly no longer a mountain. Even so, it is not heaven. Homer makes Poseidon say that he rules the sea, Hades the dead, Zeus the heavens, but Olympus is common to all three.

Wherever it was, the entrance to it was a great gate of clouds kept by the Seasons. Within were the gods' dwellings, where they lived and slept and feasted on ambrosia and nectar and listened to Apollo's lyre. It was an abode of perfect blessedness. No wind, Homer says, ever shakes the untroubled peace of Olympus; no rain ever falls there or snow; but the cloudless firmament stretches around it on all sides and the white glory of sunshine is diffused upon its walls.

The twelve Olympians made up a divine family:—

(1) ZEUS (JUPITER), the chief; his two brothers next, (2) POSEIDON (NEPTUNE), and (3) HADES, also called PLUTO; (4) HESTIA (VESTA), their sister; (5) HERA (JUNO), Zeus's wife, and (6) ARES (MARS), their son; Zeus's children: (7) ATHENA (MINERVA), (8) APOLLO, (9) APHRODITE (VENUS), (10) HERMES (MERCURY), and (11) ARTEMIS (DIANA); and Hera's son (12) HEPHAESTUS (VULCAN), sometimes said to be the son of Zeus too.

Olympus

ZEUS (JUPITER)

Zeus and his brothers drew lots for their share of the universe. The sea fell to Poseidon, and the underworld to Hades. Zeus became the supreme ruler. He was Lord of the Sky, the Rain-god and the Cloud-gatherer, who wielded the awful thunderbolt. His power was greater than that of all the other divinities together. In the *Iliad* he tells his family, "I am mightiest of all. Make trial that you may know. Fasten a rope of gold to heaven and lay hold, every god and goddess. You could not drag down Zeus. But if I wished to drag you down, then I would. The rope I would bind to a pinnacle of Olympus and all would hang in air, yes, the very earth and the sea too."

Nevertheless he was not omnipotent or omniscient, either. He could be opposed and deceived. Poseidon dupes him in the *Iliad* and so does Hera. Sometimes, too, the mysterious power, Fate, is spoken of as stronger than he. Homer makes Hera ask him scornfully if he proposes to deliver from death a man Fate has doomed.

He is represented as falling in love with one woman after another and descending to all manner of tricks to hide his infidelity from his wife. The explanation why such actions were ascribed to the most majestic of the gods is, the scholars say, that the Zeus of song and story has been made by combining many gods. When his worship spread to a town where there was already a divine ruler the two were slowly fused into one. The wife of the early god was then transferred to Zeus. The result, however, was unfortunate and the later Greeks did not like these endless love affairs.

Still, even in the earliest records Zeus had grandeur. In the *Iliad* Agamemnon prays: "Zeus, most glorious, most great, God of the storm-cloud, thou that dwellest in the heavens." He demanded, too, not only sacrifices from men, but right action. The Greek Army at Troy is told "Father Zeus never helps liars or those who break their oaths." The two ideas of him, the low and the high, persisted side by side for a long time.

His breastplate was the aegis, awful to behold; his bird was the eagle, his tree the oak. His oracle was Dodona in the land of oak trees. The god's will was revealed by the rustling of the oak leaves which the priests interpreted.

HERA (JUNO)

She was Zeus's wife and sister. The Titans Ocean and Tethys brought her up. She was the protector of marriage, and married women were her peculiar care. There is very little that is attractive in the portrait the poets draw of her. She is called, indeed, in an early poem,

> Golden-throned Hera, among immortals the queen.
> Chief among them in beauty, the glorious lady
> All the blessed in high Olympus revere,
> Honor even as Zeus, the lord of the thunder.

But when any account of her gets down to details, it shows her chiefly engaged in punishing the many women Zeus fell in love with, even when they yielded only because he coerced or tricked them. It made no difference to Hera how reluctant any of them were or how innocent; the goddess treated them all alike. Her implacable anger followed them and their children too. She never forgot an injury. The Trojan War would have ended in an honorable peace, leaving both sides unconquered, if it had not been for her hatred of a Trojan who had judged another goddess lovelier than she. The wrong of her slighted beauty remained with her until Troy fell in ruins.

In one important story, the Quest of the Golden Fleece, she is the gracious protector of heroes and the inspirer of heroic deeds, but not in any other. Nevertheless she was venerated in every home. She was the goddess married women turned to for help. Ilithyia (or Eileithyia), who helped women in childbirth, was her daughter.

The cow and the peacock were sacred to her. Argos was her favorite city.

POSEIDON (NEPTUNE)

He was the ruler of the sea, Zeus's brother and second only to him in eminence. The Greeks on both sides of the Aegean were seamen and the God of the Sea was all-important to them. His wife was Amphitrite, a granddaughter of the Titan, Ocean. Poseidon had a splendid palace beneath the sea, but he was oftener to be found in Olympus.

Besides being Lord of the Sea he gave the first horse to man, and he was honored as much for the one as for the other.

> Lord Poseidon, from you this pride is ours,
> The strong horses, the young horses, and also the rule
> of the deep.

Storm and calm were under his control:—

> He commanded and the storm wind rose
> And the surges of the sea.

But when he drove in his golden car over the waters, the thunder of the waves sank into stillness, and tranquil peace followed his smooth-rolling wheels.

He was commonly called "Earth-shaker" and was always shown carrying his trident, a three-pronged spear, with which he would shake and shatter whatever he pleased.

He had some connection with bulls as well as with horses, but the bull was connected with many other gods too.

HADES (PLUTO)

He was the third brother among the Olympians, who drew for his share the underworld and the rule over the dead. He was also called Pluto, the God of Wealth, of the precious metals hidden in the earth. The Romans as well as the Greeks called him by this name, but often they translated it into *Dis*, the Latin word for rich. He had a far-famed cap or helmet which made whoever wore it invisible. It was rare that he left his dark realm to visit Olympus or the earth, nor was he urged to do so. He was not a welcome visitor. He was unpitying, inexorable, but just; a terrible, not an evil god.

His wife was Persephone (Proserpine) whom he carried away from the earth and made Queen of the Lower World.

He was King of the Dead—not Death himself, whom the Greeks called Thanatos and the Romans, Orcus.

PALLAS ATHENA (MINERVA)

She was the daughter of Zeus alone. No mother bore her. Full-grown and in full armor, she sprang from his head. In the earliest account of her, the *Iliad*, she is a fierce and ruthless battle-goddess, but elsewhere she is warlike only to defend the State and the home from outside enemies. She was pre-eminently the Goddess of the City, the protector of civilized life, of handicrafts and agriculture; the inventor of the bridle, who first tamed horses for men to use.

She was Zeus's favorite child. He trusted her to carry the awful aegis, his buckler, and his devastating weapon, the thunderbolt.

The word oftenest used to describe her is "gray-eyed," or, as it is sometimes translated, "flashing-eyed." Of the three

virgin goddesses she was the chief and was called the Maiden
Parthenos, and her temple the Parthenon. In later poetry she
is the embodiment of wisdom, reason, purity.

Athens was her special city; the olive created by her was
her tree; the owl her bird.

PHOEBUS APOLLO

The son of Zeus and Leto (Latona), born in the little island of
Delos. He has been called "the most Greek of all the gods."
He is a beautiful figure in Greek poetry, the master musician
who delights Olympus as he plays on his golden lyre; the lord
too of the silver bow, the Archer-god, far-shooting; the Healer, as well, who first taught men the healing art. Even more
than of these good and lovely endowments, he is the God of
Light, in whom is no darkness at all, and so he is the God of
Truth. No false word ever falls from his lips.

> O Phoebus, from your throne of truth,
> From your dwelling-place at the heart of the world,
> You speak to men.
> By Zeus's decree no lie comes there,
> No shadow to darken the word of truth.
> Zeus sealed by an everlasting right
> Apollo's honour, that all may trust
> With unshaken faith when he speaks.

Delphi under towering Parnassus, where Apollo's oracle was
plays an important part in mythology. Castalia was its sacred
spring; Cephissus its river. It was held to be the center of the
world, so many pilgrims came to it, from foreign countries as
well as Greece. No other shrine rivaled it. The answers to the
questions asked by the anxious seekers for Truth were delivered by a priestess who went into a trance before she
spoke. The trance was supposed to be caused by a vapor rising from a deep cleft in the rock over which her seat was
placed, a three-legged stool, the tripod.

Apollo was called Delian from Delos, the island of his
birth, and Pythian from his killing of a serpent, Python,
which once lived in the caves of Parnassus. It was a frightful
monster and the contest was severe, but in the end the god's
unerring arrows won the victory. Another name often given
him was "the Lycian," variously explained as meaning Wolf-
god, God of Light, and God of Lycia. In the *Iliad* he is called
"the Sminthian," the Mouse-god, but whether because he
protected mice or destroyed them no one knows. Often he
was the Sun-god too. His name Phoebus means "brilliant" or

"shining." Accurately, however, the Sun-god was Helios, child of the Titan Hyperion.

Apollo at Delphi was a purely beneficent power, a direct link between gods and men, guiding men to know the divine will, showing them how to make peace with the gods; the purifier, too, able to cleanse even those stained with the blood of their kindred. Nevertheless, there are a few tales told of him which show him pitiless and cruel. Two ideas were fighting in him as in all the gods: a primitive, crude idea and one that was beautiful and poetic. In him only a little of the primitive is left.

The laurel was his tree. Many creatures were sacred to him, chief among them the dolphin and the crow.

ARTEMIS (DIANA)

> *Also called Cynthia, from her birthplace, Mount Cynthus in Delos.*

Apollo's twin sister, daughter of Zeus and Leto. She was one of the three maiden goddesses of Olympus:—

Golden Aphrodite who stirs with love all creation,
Cannot bend nor ensnare three hearts: the pure maiden Vesta,
Gray-eyed Athena who cares but for war and the arts of the craftsmen,
Artemis, lover of woods and the wild chase over the mountain.

She was the Lady of Wild Things, Huntsman-in-chief to the gods, an odd office for a woman. Like a good huntsman, she was careful to preserve the young; she was "the protectress of dewy youth" everywhere. Nevertheless, with one of those startling contradictions so common in mythology, she kept the Greek Fleet from sailing to Troy until they sacrificed a maiden to her. In many another story, too, she is fierce and revengeful. On the other hand, when women died a swift and painless death, they were held to have been slain by her silver arrows.

As Phoebus was the Sun, she was the Moon, called Phoebe and Selene (Luna in Latin). Neither name originally belonged to her. Phoebe was a Titan, one of the older gods. So too was Selene—a moon-goddess, indeed, but not connected with Apollo. She was the sister of Helios, the sun-god with whom Apollo was confused.

In the later poets, Artemis is identified with Hecate. She is "the goddess with three forms," Selene in the sky, Artemis on earth, Hecate in the lower world and in the world above when it is wrapped in darkness. Hecate was the Goddess of the Dark of the Moon, the black nights when the moon is hidden. She was associated with deeds of darkness, the Goddess of the Crossways, which were held to be ghostly places of evil magic. An awful divinity,

> Hecate of hell,
> Mighty to shatter every stubborn thing.
> Hark! Hark! her hounds are baying through the town.
> Where three roads meet, there she is standing.

It is a strange transformation from the lovely Huntress flashing through the forest, from the Moon making all beautiful with her light, from the pure Maiden-Goddess for whom

> Whoso is chaste of spirit utterly
> May gather leaves and fruits and flowers.
> The unchaste never.

In her is shown most vividly the uncertainty between good and evil which is apparent in every one of the divinities.

The cypress was sacred to her; and all wild animals, but especially the deer.

APHRODITE (VENUS)

The Goddess of Love and Beauty, who beguiled all, gods and men alike; the laughter-loving goddess, who laughed sweetly or mockingly at those her wiles had conquered; the irresistible goddess who stole away even the wits of the wise.

She is the daughter of Zeus and Dione in the *Iliad*, but in the later poems she is said to have sprung from the foam of the sea, and her name was explained as meaning "the foam-risen." *Aphros* is foam in Greek. This sea-birth took place near Cythera, from where she was wafted to Cyprus. Both islands were ever after sacred to her, and she was called Cytherea or the Cyprian as often as by her proper name.

One of the Homeric Hymns, calling her "Beautiful, golden goddess," says of her:—

> The breath of the west wind bore her
> Over the sounding sea,
> Up from the delicate foam,
> To wave-ringed Cyprus, her isle.
> And the Hours golden-wreathed
> Welcomed her joyously.
> They clad her in raiment immortal,
> And brought her to the gods.
> Wonder seized them all as they saw
> Violet-crowned Cytherea.

The Romans wrote of her in the same way. With her, beauty comes. The winds flee before her and the storm clouds; sweet flowers embroider the earth; the waves of the sea laugh; she moves in radiant light. Without her there is no joy nor loveliness anywhere. This is the picture the poets like best to paint of her.

But she had another side too. It was natural that she should cut a poor figure in the *Iliad*, where the battle of heroes is the theme. She is a soft, weak creature there, whom a mortal need not fear to attack. In later poems she is usually shown as treacherous and malicious, exerting a deadly and destructive power over men.

In most of the stories she is the wife of Hephaestus (Vulcan), the lame and ugly god of the forge.

The myrtle was her tree; the dove her bird—sometimes, too, the sparrow and the swan.

HERMES (MERCURY)

Zeus was his father and Maia, daughter of Atlas, his mother. Because of a very popular statue his appearance is more familiar to us than that of any other god. He was graceful and swift of motion. On his feet were winged sandals; wings were on his low-crowned hat, too, and on his magic wand, the Caduceus. He was Zeus's Messenger, who "flies as fleet as thought to do his bidding."

Of all the gods he was the shrewdest and most cunning; in fact he was the Master Thief, who started upon his career before he was a day old.

> The babe was born at the break of day,
> And ere the night fell he had stolen away
> Apollo's herds.

Zeus made him give them back, and he won Apollo's forgiveness by presenting him with the lyre which he had just invented, making it out of a tortoise's shell. Perhaps there was some connection between that very early story of him and the fact that he was God of Commerce and the Market, protector of traders.

In odd contrast to this idea of him, he was also the solemn guide of the dead, the Divine Herald who led the souls down to their last home.

He appears oftener in the tales of mythology than any other god.

ARES (MARS)

The God of War, son of Zeus and Hera, both of whom, Homer says, detested him. Indeed, he is hateful throughout the *Iliad*, poem of war though it is. Occasionally the heroes "rejoice in the delight of Ares' battle," but far oftener in having escaped "the fury of the ruthless god." Homer calls him murderous, bloodstained, the incarnate curse of mortals; and, strangely, a coward, too, who bellows with pain and runs away when he is wounded. Yet he has a train of attendants on the battlefield which should inspire anyone with confidence. His sister is there, Eris, which means Discord, and Strife, her son. The Goddess of War, Enyo,—in Latin Bellona,—walks beside him, and with her are Terror and Trembling and Panic. As they move, the voice of groaning arises behind them and the earth streams with blood.

The Romans liked Mars better than the Greeks liked Ares. He never was to them the mean whining deity of the *Iliad*, but magnificent in shining armor, redoubtable, invincible. The warriors of the great Latin heroic poem, the *Aeneid*, far from rejoicing to escape from him, rejoice when they see that they are to fall "on Mars' field of renown." They "rush on glorious death" and find it "sweet to die in battle."

Ares figures little in mythology. In one story he is the lover of Aphrodite and held up to the contempt of the Olympians by Aphrodite's husband, Hephaestus; but for the most part he is little more than a symbol of war. He is not a distinct personality, like Hermes or Hera or Apollo.

He had no cities where he was worshiped. The Greeks said vaguely that he came from Thrace, home of a rude, fierce people in the northeast of Greece.

Appropriately, his bird was the vulture. The dog was wronged by being chosen as his animal.

HEPHAESTUS (VULCAN AND MULCIBER)

The God of Fire, sometimes said to be the son of Zeus and Hera, sometimes of Hera alone, who bore him in retaliation for Zeus's having brought forth Athena. Among the perfectly beautiful immortals he only was ugly. He was lame as well. In one place in the *Iliad* he says that his shameless mother, when she saw that he was born deformed, cast him out of heaven; in another place he declares that Zeus did this, angry with him for trying to defend Hera. This second story is the better known, because of Milton's familiar lines: Mulciber was

Thrown by angry Jove
Sheer o'er the crystal battlements; from morn
To noon he fell, from noon to dewy eve,
A summer's day, and with the setting sun
Dropt from the zenith like a falling star,
On Lemnos, the Aegean isle.

These events, however, were supposed to have taken place in the far-distant past. In Homer he is in no danger of being driven from Olympus; he is highly honored there, the workman of the immortals, their armorer and smith, who makes their dwellings and their furnishings as well as their weapons. In his workshop he has handmaidens he has forged out of gold who can move and who help him in his work.

In the later poets his forge is often said to be under this or that volcano, and to cause eruptions.

His wife is one of the three Graces in the *Iliad,* called Aglaia in Hesiod; in the *Odyssey* she is Aphrodite.

He was a kindly, peace-loving god, popular on earth as in heaven. With Athena, he was important in the life of the city. The two were the patrons of handicrafts, the arts which along with agriculture are the support of civilization; he the protector of the smiths as she of the weavers. When children were formally admitted to the city organization, the god of the ceremony was Hephaestus.

HESTIA (VESTA)

She was Zeus's sister, and like Athena and Artemis a virgin goddess. She has no distinct personality and she plays no part in the myths. She was the Goddess of the Hearth, the symbol of the home, around which the newborn child must be carried before it could be received into the family. Every meal began and ended with an offering to her.

Hestia, in all dwellings of men and immortals
Yours is the highest honor, the sweet wine offered
First and last at the feast, poured out to you duly.
Never without you can gods or mortals hold banquet.

Each city too had a public hearth sacred to Hestia, where the fire was never allowed to go out. If a colony was to be founded, the colonists carried with them coals from the hearth of the mother-city with which to kindle the fire on the new city's hearth.

In Rome her fire was cared for by six virgin priestesses, called Vestals.

THE LESSER GODS OF OLYMPUS

There were other divinities in heaven besides the twelve great Olympians. The most important of them was the God of Love, EROS (Cupid in Latin). Homer knows nothing of him, but to Hesiod he is

> Fairest of the deathless gods.

In the early stories, he is oftenest a beautiful serious youth who gives good gifts to men. This idea the Greeks had of him is best summed up not by a poet, but by a philosopher, Plato: "Love—Eros—makes his home in men's hearts, but not in every heart, for where there is hardness he departs. His greatest glory is that he cannot do wrong nor allow it; force never comes near him. For all men serve him of their own free will. And he whom Love touches not walks in darkness."

In the early accounts Eros was not Aphrodite's son, but merely her occasional companion. In the later poets he was her son and almost invariably a mischievous, naughty boy, or worse.

> Evil his heart, but honey-sweet his tongue.
> No truth in him, the rogue. He is cruel in his play.
> Small are his hands, yet his arrows fly far as death.
> Tiny his shaft, but it carries heaven-high.
> Touch not his treacherous gifts, they are dipped in fire.

He was often represented as blindfolded, because love is often blind. In attendance upon him was ANTEROS, said sometimes to be the avenger of slighted love, sometimes the one who opposes love; also HIMEROS or Longing, and HYMEN, the God of the Wedding Feast.

HEBE was the Goddess of Youth, the daughter of Zeus and Hera. Sometimes she appears as cupbearer to the gods; sometimes that office is held by Ganymede, a beautiful young Trojan prince who was seized and carried up to Olympus by Zeus's eagle. There are no stories about Hebe except that of her marriage to Hercules.

IRIS was the Goddess of the Rainbow and a messenger of the gods, in the *Iliad* the only messenger. Hermes appears first in that capacity in the *Odyssey*, but he does not take Iris' place. Now the one, now the other is called upon by the gods.

There were also in Olympus two bands of lovely sisters, the Muses and the Graces.

THE GRACES were three: Aglaia (Splendor), Euphrosyne (Mirth) and Thalia (Good Cheer). They were the daughters of Zeus and Eurynome, a child of the Titan, Ocean. Except in a story Homer and Hesiod tell, that Aglaia married Hephaestus, they are not treated as separate personalities, but always together, a triple incarnation of grace and beauty. The gods delighted in them when they danced enchantingly to Apollo's lyre, and the man they visited was happy. They "give life its bloom." Together with their companions, the Muses, they were "queens of song," and no banquet without them could please.

THE MUSES were nine in number, the daughters of Zeus and Mnemosyne, Memory. At first, like the Graces, they were not distinguished from each other. "They are all," Hesiod says, "of one mind, their hearts are set upon song and their spirit is free from care. He is happy whom the Muses love. For though a man has sorrow and grief in his soul, yet when the servant of the Muses sings, at once he forgets his dark thoughts and remembers not his troubles. Such is the holy gift of the Muses to men."

In later times each had her own special field. Clio was Muse of history, Urania of astronomy, Melpomene of tragedy, Thalia of comedy, Terpsichore of the dance, Calliope of epic poetry, Erato of love-poetry, Polyhymnia of songs to the gods, Euterpe of lyric poetry.

Hesiod lived near Helicon, one of the Muses' mountains—the other were Pierus in Pieria, where they were born, Parnassus and, of course, Olympus. One day the Nine appeared to him and they told him, "We know how to speak false things that seem true, but we know, when we will, to utter true things." They were companions of Apollo, the God of Truth, as well as of the Graces. Pindar calls the lyre theirs as well as Apollo's, "the golden lyre to which the step, the dancer's step, listens, owned alike by Apollo and the violet-wreathed Muses." The man they inspired was sacred far beyond any priest.

As the idea of Zeus became loftier, two august forms sat beside him in Olympus. THEMIS, which means the Right, or Divine Justice, and DIKE, which is Human Justice. But they never became real personalities. The same was true of two personified emotions esteemed highest of all feelings in Homer and Hesiod: NEMESIS, usually translated as Righteous Anger, and AIDOS, a difficult word to translate, but in common use among the Greeks. It means reverence and the shame that holds men back from wrongdoing, but it also means the feeling a prosperous man should have in the presence of the unfortunate—not compassion, but a sense that the difference between him and those poor wretches is not deserved.

It does not seem, however, that either Nemesis or Aidos had their home with the gods. Hesiod says that only when men have finally become completely wicked will Nemesis and Aidos, their beautiful faces veiled in white raiment, leave the wide-wayed earth and depart to the company of the immortals.

From time to time a few mortals were translated to Olympus, but once they had been brought to heaven they vanished from literature. Their stories will be told later.

THE GODS OF THE WATERS

POSEIDON (Neptune), was the Lord and Ruler of the Sea (the Mediterranean) and the Friendly Sea (the Euxine, now the Black Sea). Underground rivers, too, were his.

OCEAN, a Titan, was Lord of the river Ocean, a great river encircling the earth. His wife, also a Titan, was Tethys. The Oceanids, the nymphs of this great river, were their daughters. The gods of all the rivers on earth were their sons.

PONTUS, which means the Deep Sea, was a son of Mother Earth and the father of NEREUS, a sea-god far more important than he himself was.

NEREUS was called the Old Man of the Sea (the Mediterranean)—"A trusty god and gentle," Hesiod says, "who thinks just and kindly thoughts and never lies." His wife was Doris, a daughter of Ocean. They had fifty lovely daughters, the nymphs of the Sea, called NEREIDS from their father's name, one of whom, THETIS, was the mother of Achilles. Poseidon's wife, AMPHITRITE, was another.

TRITON was the trumpeter of the Sea. His trumpet was a great shell. He was the son of Poseidon and Amphitrite.

PROTEUS was sometimes said to be Poseidon's son, sometimes his attendant. He had the power both of foretelling the future and of changing his shape at will.

THE NAIADS were also water nymphs. They dwelt in brooks and spring and fountains.

LEUCOTHEA and her son PALAEMON, once mortals, became divinities of the sea, as did also GLAUCUS, but all three were unimportant.

THE UNDERWORLD

The kingdom of the dead was ruled by one of the twelve great Olympians, Hades or Pluto, and his Queen, Persephone. It is often called by his name, Hades. It lies, the *Iliad* says, beneath the secret places of the earth. In the *Odyssey,* the way to it leads over the edge of the world across Ocean. In later poets there are various entrances to it from the earth through caverns and beside deep lakes.

Tartarus and Erebus are sometimes two divisions of the underworld, Tartarus the deeper of the two, the prison of the Sons of Earth; Erebus where the dead pass as soon as they die. Often, however, there is no distinction between the two, and either is used, especially Tartarus, as a name for the entire lower region.

In Homer the underworld is vague, a shadowy place inhabited by shadows. Nothing is real there. The ghosts' existence, if it can be called that, is like a miserable dream. The later poets define the world of the dead more and more clearly as the place where the wicked are punished and the good rewarded. In the Roman poet Virgil this idea is presented in great detail as in no Greek poet. All the torments of the one class and the joys of the other are described at length. Virgil too is the only poet who gives clearly the geography of the underworld. The path down to it leads to where Acheron, the river of woe, pours into Cocytus, the river of lamentation. An aged boatman named Charon ferries the souls of the dead across the water to the farther bank, where stands the adamantine gate to Tartarus (the name Virgil prefers). Charon will receive into his boat only the souls of those upon whose lips the passage money was placed when they died and who were duly buried.

On guard before the gate sits CERBERUS, the three-headed, dragon-tailed dog, who permits all spirits to enter, but none to return. On his arrival each one is brought before three judges, Rhadamanthus, Minos, and Aeacus, who pass sentence and send the wicked to everlasting torment and the good to a place of blessedness called the Elysian Fields.

Three other rivers, besides Acheron and Cocytus, separate the underworld from the world above: Phlegethon, the river of fire; Styx, the river of the unbreakable oath by which the gods swear; and Lethe, the river of forgetfulness.

Somewhere in this vast region is Pluto's palace, but beyond saying that it is many-gated and crowded with innumerable guests, no writer describes it. Around it are wide wastes, wan and cold, and meadows of asphodel, presumably strange, pallid, ghostly flowers. We do not know anything more about it. The poets did not care to linger in that gloom-hidden abode.

THE ERINYES (the FURIES), are placed by Virgil in the underworld, where they punish evildoers. The Greek poets thought of them chiefly as pursuing sinners on the earth. They were inexorable, but just. Heraclitus says, "Not even the sun will transgress his orbit but the Erinyes, the ministers of justice, overtake him." They were usually represented as three: Tisiphone, Megaera and Alecto.

SLEEP, and DEATH, his brother, dwelt in the lower world. Dreams too ascended from there to men. They passed through two gates, one of horn through which true dreams went, one of ivory for false dreams.

THE LESSER GODS OF EARTH

Earth herself was called the All-Mother, but she was not really a divinity. She was never separated from the actual earth and personified. The Goddess of the Corn, DEMETER (CERES), a daughter of Cronus and Rhea, and the God of the Vine, DIONYSUS, also called BACCHUS, were the supreme deities of the earth and of great importance in Greek and Roman mythology. Their stories will be found in the next chapter. The other divinities who lived in the world were comparatively unimportant.

PAN was the chief. He was Hermes' son; a noisy, merry god, the Homeric Hymn in his honor calls him; but he was part animal too, with a goat's horns, and goat's hoofs instead of feet. He was the goatherds' god, and the shepherds' god, and also the gay companion of the woodland nymphs when they danced. All wild places were his home, thickets and forests and mountains, but best of all he loved Arcady, where he was born. He was a wonderful musician. Upon his pipes of reed he played melodies as sweet as the nightingale's song. He was always in love with one nymph or another, but always rejected because of his ugliness.

Sounds heard in a wilderness at night by the trembling traveler were supposed to be made by him, so that it is easy to see how the expression "panic" fear arose.

SILENUS was sometimes said to be Pan's son; sometimes his brother, a son of Hermes. He was a jovial fat old man who usually rode an ass because he was too drunk to walk. He is associated with Bacchus as well as with Pan; he taught him when the Wine-god was young, and, as is shown by his perpetual drunkenness, after being his tutor he became his devoted follower.

Besides these gods of the earth there was a very famous and very popular pair of brothers, CASTOR and POLLUX (Polydeuces), who in most of the accounts were said to live half of their time on earth and half in heaven.

They were the sons of LEDA, and are usually represented as being gods, the special protectors of sailors,

> Saviors of swift-going ships when the storm winds rage
> Over the ruthless sea.

They were also powerful to save in battle. They were especially honored in Rome, where they were worshiped as

> The great Twin Brethren to whom all Dorians pray.

But the accounts of them are contradictory. Sometimes Pollux alone is held to be divine, and Castor a mortal who won a kind of half-and-half immortality merely because of his brother's love.

LEDA was the wife of King Tyndareus of Sparta, and the usual story is that she bore two mortal children to him, Castor and Clytemnestra, Agamemnon's wife; and to Zeus, who visited her in the form of a swan, two others who were immortal, Pollux and Helen, the heroine of Troy. Nevertheless, both brothers, Castor and Pollux, were often called "sons of Zeus"; indeed, the Greek name they are best known by, the *Dioscouri*, means "the striplings of Zeus." On the other hand, they were also called "sons of Tyndareus," the *Tyndaridae*.

They are always represented as living just before the Trojan War, at the same time as Theseus and Jason and Atalanta. They took part in the Calydonian boar-hunt; they went on the Quest of the Golden Fleece; and they rescued Helen when Theseus carried her off. But in all the stories they play an unimportant part except in the account of Castor's death, when Pollux proved his brotherly devotion.

The two went, we are not told why, to the land of some cattle owners, Idas and Lynceus. There, Pindar says, Idas, made angry in some way about his oxen, stabbed and killed Castor. Other writers say the cause of the dispute was the two daughters of the king of the country, Leucippus. Pollux stabbed Lynceus, and Zeus struck Idas with his thunderbolt. But Castor was dead and Pollux was inconsolable. He prayed to die also, and Zeus in pity allowed him to share his life with his brother, to live,

> Half of thy time beneath the earth and half
> Within the golden homes of heaven.

According to this version the two were never separated again. One day they dwelt in Hades, the next in Olympus, always together.

The late Greek writer Lucian gives another version, in which their dwelling places are heaven and earth; and when Pollux goes to one, Castor goes to the other, so that they are never with each other. In Lucian's little satire, Apollo asks Hermes: "I say, why do we never see Castor and Pollux at the same time?"

"Well," Hermes replies, "they are so fond of each other that when fate decreed one of them must die and only one be immortal, they decided to share immortality between them."

"Not very wise, Hermes. What proper employment can they engage in, that way? I foretell the future; Aesculapius cures diseases; you are a good messenger—but these two— are they to idle away their whole time?"

"No, surely. They're in Poseidon's service. Their business is to save any ship in distress."

"Ah, now you say something. I'm delighted they're in such a good business."

Two stars were supposed to be theirs: the Gemini, the Twins.

They were always represented as riding splendid snow-white horses, but Homer distinguishes Castor above Pollux for horsemanship. He calls the two

> Castor, tamer of horses, Polydeuces, good as a boxer.

THE SILENI were creatures part man and part horse. They walked on two legs, not four, but they often had horses' hoofs instead of feet, sometimes horses' ears, and always horses' tails. There are no stories about them, but they are often seen on Greek vases.

THE SATYRS, like Pan, were goat-men, and like him they had their home in the wild places of the earth.

In contrast to these unhuman, ugly gods the goddesses of the woodland were all lovely maiden forms, the OREADS, nymphs of the mountains, and the DRYADS, sometimes called HAMADRYADS, nymphs of trees, whose life was in each case bound up with that of her tree.

AEOLUS, King of the Winds, also lived on the earth. An island, Aeolia, was his home. Accurately he was only regent of the Winds, viceroy of the gods. The four chief Winds were BOREAS, the North Wind, in Latin AQUILO; ZEPHYR, the West Wind, which had a second Latin name, FAVONIUS; NOTUS, the South Wind, also called in Latin AUSTER; and the East Wind, EURUS, the same in both Greek and Latin.

There were some beings, neither human nor divine, who had their home on the earth. Prominent among them were:—

THE CENTAURS. They were half man, half horse, and for the most part they were savage creatures, more like beasts than men. One of them, however, CHIRON, was known everywhere for his goodness and his wisdom.

THE GORGONS were also earth-dwellers. There were three, and two of them were immortal. They were dragonlike creatures with wings, whose look turned men to stone. Phorcys, son of the Sea and the Earth, was their father.

THE GRAIAE were their sisters, three gray women who had but one eye between them. They lived on the farther bank of Ocean.

THE SIRENS lived on an island in the Sea. They had enchanting voices and their singing lured sailors to their death. It was not known what they looked like, for no one who saw them ever returned.

Very important but assigned to no abode whether in heaven or on the earth were THE FATES, *Moirae* in Greek, *Parcae* in Latin, who, Hesiod says, give to men at birth evil and good to have. They were three, Clotho, the Spinner, who spun the thread of life; Lachesis, the Disposer of Lots, who assigned to each man his destiny; Atropos, she who could not be turned, who carried "the abhorrèd shears" and cut the thread at death.

THE ROMAN GODS

The Twelve great Olympians mentioned earlier were turned into Roman gods also. The influence of Greek art and literature became so powerful in Rome that ancient Roman deities were changed to resemble the corresponding Greek gods, and were considered to be the same. Most of them, however, in Rome had Roman names. These were Jupiter (Zeus), Juno (Hera), Neptune (Poseidon), Vesta (Hestia), Mars (Ares),

Minerva (Athena), Venus (Aphrodite), Mercury (Hermes), Diana (Artemis), Vulcan or Mulciber (Hephaestus), Ceres (Demeter).

Two kept their Greek names: Apollo and Pluto; but the latter was never called Hades, as was usual in Greece. Bacchus, never Dionysus, was the name of the wine-god, who had also a Latin name, Liber.

It was a simple matter to adopt the Greek gods because the Romans did not have definitely personified gods of their own. They were a people of deep religious feeling, but they had little imagination. They could never have created the Olympians, each a distinct, vivid personality. Their gods, before they took over from the Greeks, were vague, hardly more than a "those that are above." They were THE NUMINA, which means the Powers or the Wills—the Will-Powers, perhaps.

Until Greek literature and art entered Italy the Romans felt no need for beautiful, poetic gods. They were a practical people and they did not care about "Violet-tressed Muses who inspire song," or "Lyric Apollo making sweet melodies upon his golden lyre," or anything of that sort. They wanted useful gods. An important Power, for example, was One who Guards the Cradle. Another was One Who Presides over Children's Food. No stories were ever told about the Numina. For the most part they were not even distinguished as male or female. The simple acts of everyday life, however, were closely connected with them and gained dignity from them as was not the case with any of the Greek gods except Demeter and Dionysus.

The most prominent and revered of them all were the LARES and PENATES. Every Roman family had a Lar, who was the spirit of an ancestor, and several Penates, gods of the hearth and guardians of the storehouse. They were the family's own gods, belonging only to it, really the most important part of it, the protectors and defenders of the entire household. They were never worshiped in temples, but only in the home, where some of the food at each meal was offered to them. There were also public Lares and Penates, who did for the city what the others did for the family.

There were also many Numina connected with the life of the household, such as TERMINUS, Guardian of Boundaries; PRIAPUS, Cause of Fertility; PALES, Strengthener of Cattle; SYLVANUS, Helper of Plowmen and Woodcutters. A long list could be made. Everything important to the farm was under the care of a beneficient power, never conceived of as having a definite shape.

SATURN was originally one of the Numina, the Protector of the Sowers and the Seed, as his wife OPS was a Harvest Helper. In later days, he was said to be the same as the Greek Cronus and the father of Jupiter, the Roman Zeus. In this way he became a personality and a number of stories were told about him. In memory of the Golden Age, when he reigned in Italy, the great feast of the Saturnalia was held every year during the winter. The idea of it was that the Golden Age returned to the earth during the days it lasted. No war could be then declared; slaves and masters ate at the same table; executions were postponed; it was a season for giving presents; it kept alive in men's minds the idea of equality, of a time when all were on the same level.

JANUS, too, was originally one of the Numina, "the god of good beginnings," which are sure to result in good endings. He became personified to a certain degree. His chief temple in Rome ran east and west, where the day begins and ends, and had two doors, between which stood his statue with two faces, one young and one old. These doors were closed only when Rome was at peace. In the first seven hundred years of the city's life they were closed three times, in the reign of the good king, Numa; after the first Punic War when Carthage was defeated in 241 B.C.; and in the reign of Augustus when, Milton says,

> No war or battle's sound
> Was heard the world around.

Naturally his month, January, began the new year.

FAUNUS was Saturn's grandson. He was a sort of Roman Pan, a rustic god. He was a prophet too, and spoke to men in their dreams.

THE FAUNS were Roman satyrs.

QUIRINUS was the name of the deified Romulus, the founder of Rome.

THE MANES were the spirits of the good dead in Hades. Sometimes they were regarded as divine and worshiped.

THE LEMURES or LARVAE were the spirits of the wicked dead and were greatly feared.

THE CAMENAE began as useful and practical goddesses who cared for springs and wells and cured disease and foretold the future. But when the Greek gods came to Rome, the Camenae were identified with those impractical deities the Muses, who cared only for art and science. Egeria who taught King Numa was said to be a Camena.

LUCINA was sometimes regarded as a Roman EILEITHYIA, the goddess of childbirth, but usually the name is used as an epithet of both Juno and Diana.

POMONA AND VERTUMNUS began as Numina, as Powers Protecting Orchards and Gardens. But they were personified later and a story was told about how they fell in love with each other.

2 The Two Great Gods of Earth

For the most part the immortal gods were of little use to human beings and often they were quite the reverse of useful: Zeus a dangerous lover for mortal maidens and completely incalculable in his use of the terrible thunderbolt; Ares the maker of war and a general pest; Hera with no idea of justice when she was jealous as she perpetually was; Athena also a war maker, and wielding the lightning's sharp lance quite as irresponsibly as Zeus did; Aphrodite using her power chiefly to ensnare and betray. They were a beautiful, radiant company, to be sure, and their adventures made excellent stories; but when they were not positively harmful, they were capricious and undependable and in general mortals got on best without them.

There were two, however, who were altogether different —who were, indeed, mankind's best friends: Demeter, in Latin Ceres, the Goddess of the Corn, a daughter of Cronus and Rhea; and Dionysus, also called Bacchus, the God of Wine. Demeter was the older, as was natural. Corn was sowed long before vines were planted. The first cornfield was the beginning of settled life on earth. Vineyards came later. It was natural, too, that the divine power which brought forth the grain should be thought of as a goddess, not a god. When the business of men was hunting and fighting, the care of the fields belonged to the women, and as they plowed and scattered the seed and reaped the harvest, they felt that a woman divinity could best understand and help woman's work. They could best understand her, too, who was worshiped, not like other gods by the bloody sacrifices men liked, but in every humble act that made the farm fruitful. Through her the field of grain was hallowed. "Demeter's holy grain."

The threshing-floor, too, was under her protection. Both were her temples where at any moment she might be present. "At the sacred threshing-floor, when they are winnowing, she herself, Demeter of the corn-ripe yellow hair, divides the grain and the chaff in the rush of the wind, and the heap of chaff grows white." "May it be mine," the reaper prays, "beside Demeter's altar to dig the great winnowing fan through her heaps of corn, while she stands smiling by with sheaves and poppies in her hand."

Her chief festival, of course, came at the harvest time. In earlier days it must have been a simple reapers' thanksgiving day when the first loaf baked from the new grain was broken and reverently eaten with grateful prayers to the goddess from whom had come this best and most necessary gift for human life. In later years the humble feast grew into a mysterious worship, about which we know little. The great festival, in September, came only every five years, but it lasted for nine days. They were most sacred days, when much of the ordinary business of life was suspended. Processions took place, sacrifices were held with dances and song, there was general rejoicing. All this was public knowledge and has been related by many a writer. But the chief part of the ceremony which took place in the precincts of the temple has never been described. Those who beheld it were bound by a vow of silence and they kept it so well that we know only stray bits of what was done.

The great temple was at Eleusis, a little town near Athens, and the worship was called the Eleusinian Mysteries. Throughout the Greek world and the Roman, too, they were held in especial veneration. Cicero, writing in the century before Christ, says: "Nothing is higher than these mysteries. They have sweetened our characters and softened our customs; they have made us pass from the condition of savages to true humanity. They have not only shown us the way to live joyfully, but they have taught us how to die with a better hope."

And yet even so, holy and awesome though they were, they kept the mark of what they had sprung from. One of the few pieces of information we have about them is that at a very solemn moment the worshipers were shown "an ear of corn which had been reaped in silence."

In some way, no one knows clearly how or when, the God of the Vine, Dionysus, came to take his place, too, at Eleusis, side by side with Demeter.

> Beside Demeter when the cymbals sound
> Enthroned sits Dionysus of the flowing hair.

It was natural that they should be worshiped together, both divinities of the good gifts of earth, both present in the homely daily acts that life depends on, the breaking of bread and the drinking of wine. The harvest was Dionysus' festival, too, when the grapes were brought to the wine-press.

> The joy-god Dionysus, the pure star
> That shines amid the gathering of the fruit.

But he was not always a joy-god, nor was Demeter always the happy goddess of the summertime. Each knew pain as well as joy. In that way, too, they were closely linked together; they were both suffering gods. The other immortals were untouched by lasting grief. "Dwelling in Olympus where the wind never blows and no rain falls ever nor the least white star of snow, they are happy all their days, feasting upon nectar and ambrosia, rejoicing in all-glorious Apollo as he strikes his silver lyre, and the sweet voices of the Muses answer him, while the Graces dance with Hebe and with Aphrodite, and a radiance shines round them all." But the two divinities of Earth knew heart-rending grief.

What happens to the corn plants and the luxuriant branching vines when the grain is harvested, the grapes gathered, and the black frost sets in, killing the fresh green life of the fields? That is what men asked themselves when the first stories were told to explain what was so mysterious, the changes always passing before their eyes, of day and night and the seasons and the stars in their courses. Though Demeter and Dionysus were the happy gods of the harvest, during the winter it was clear that they were altogether different. They sorrowed, and the earth was sad. The men of long ago wondered why this should be, and they told stories to explain the reason.

DEMETER (CERES)

This story is told only in a very early poem, one of the earliest of the Homeric Hymns, dating from the eighth or the beginning of the seventh century. The original has the marks of early Greek poetry, great simplicity and directness and delight in the beautiful world.

Demeter had an only daughter, Persephone (in Latin Proserpine), the maiden of the spring. She lost her and in her terrible grief she withheld her gifts from the earth, which turned into a frozen desert. The green and flowering land was icebound and lifeless because Persephone had disappeared.

The lord of the dark underworld, the king of the multitudinous dead, carried her off when, enticed by the wondrous bloom of the narcissus, she strayed too far from her companions. In his chariot drawn by coal-black steeds he rose up through a chasm in the earth, and grasping the maiden by the wrist set her beside him. He bore her away weeping, down to the underworld. The high hills echoed her cry and the depths of the sea, and her mother heard it. She sped like a bird over sea and land seeking her daughter. But no one would tell her the truth, "no man nor god, nor any sure messenger from the birds." Nine days Demeter wandered, and all that time she would not taste of ambrosia or put sweet nectar to her lips. At last she came to the Sun and he told her all the story: Persephone was down in the world beneath the earth, among the shadowy dead.

Then a still greater grief entered Demeter's heart. She left Olympus; she dwelt on earth, but so disguised that none knew her, and, indeed, the gods are not easily discerned by mortal men. In her desolate wanderings she came to Eleusis and sat by the wayside near a well. She seemed an aged woman, such as in great houses care for the children or guard the storerooms. Four lovely maidens, sisters, coming to draw water from the well, saw her and asked her pityingly what she did there. She answered that she had fled from pirates who had meant to sell her as a slave, and that she knew no one in this strange land to go to for help. They told her that any house in the town would welcome her, but that they would like best to bring her to their own if she would wait there while they went to ask their mother. The goddess bent her head in assent, and the girls, filling their shining pitchers with water, hurried home. Their mother, Metaneira, bade them return at once and invite the stranger to come, and speeding back they found the glorious goddess still sitting there, deeply veiled and covered to her slender feet by her dark robe. She followed them, and as she crossed the threshold to the hall where the mother sat holding her young son, a divine radiance filled the doorway and awe fell upon Metaneira.

She bade Demeter be seated and herself offered her honeysweet wine, but the goddess would not taste it. She asked instead for barley-water flavored with mint, the cooling draught of the reaper at harvest time and also the sacred cup given the worshipers at Eleusis. Thus refreshed she took the child and held him to her fragrant bosom and his mother's heart was glad. So Demeter nursed Demophoön, the son that Metaneira had borne to wise Celeus. And the child grew like a young god, for daily Demeter anointed him with ambrosia

The rape of Persephone (Proserpine)

and at night she would place him in the red heart of the fire. Her purpose was to give him immortal youth.

Something, however, made the mother uneasy, so that one night she kept watch and screamed in terror when she saw the child laid in the fire. The goddess was angered; she seized the boy and cast him on the ground. She had meant to set him free from old age and from death, but that was not to be. Still, he had lain upon her knees and slept in her arms and therefore he should have honor throughout his life.

Then she showed herself the goddess manifest. Beauty breathed about her and a lovely fragrance; light shone from her so that the great house was filled with brightness. She was Demeter, she told the awestruck women. They must build her a great temple near the town and so win back the favor of her heart.

Thus she left them, and Metaneira fell speechless to the earth and all there trembled with fear. In the morning they told Celeus what had happened and he called the people together and revealed to them the command of the goddess. They worked willingly to build her a temple, and when it was finished Demeter came to it and sat there—apart from the gods in Olympus, alone, wasting away with longing for her daughter.

That year was most dreadful and cruel for mankind over all the earth. Nothing grew; no seed sprang up; in vain the oxen drew the plowshare through the furrows. It seemed the whole race of men would die of famine. At last Zeus saw that he must take the matter in hand. He sent the gods to Demeter, one after another, to try to turn her from her anger, but she listened to none of them. Never would she let the earth bear fruit until she had seen her daughter. Then Zeus realized that his brother must give way. He told Hermes to go down to the underworld and to bid the lord of it let his bride go back to Demeter.

Hermes found the two sitting side by side, Persephone shrinking away, reluctant because she longed for her mother. At Hermes' words she sprang up joyfully, eager to go. Her husband knew that he must obey the word of Zeus and send her up to earth away from him, but he prayed her as she left him to have kind thoughts of him and not be so sorrowful that she was the wife of one who was great among the immortals. And he made her eat a pomegranate seed, knowing in his heart that if she did so she must return to him.

He got ready his golden car and Hermes took the reins and drove the black horses straight to the temple where Demeter was. She ran out to meet her daughter as swiftly as a Maenad runs down the mountainside. Persephone sprang into her arms and was held fast there. All day they talked of what had happened to them both, and Demeter grieved when she heard of the pomegranate seed, fearing that she could not keep her daughter with her.

Then Zeus sent another messenger to her, a great personage, none other than his revered mother Rhea, the oldest of the gods. Swiftly she hastened down from the heights of Olympus to the barren, leafless earth, and standing at the door of the temple she spoke to Demeter.

Come, my daughter, for Zeus, far-seeing, loud-thundering, bids you.
Come once again to the halls of the gods where you shall have honor,
Where you will have your desire, your daughter, to comfort your sorrow
As each year is accomplished and bitter winter is ended.
For a third part only the kingdom of darkness shall hold her.
For the rest you will keep her, you and the happy immortals.
Peace now. Give men life which comes alone from your giving.

Demeter did not refuse, poor comfort though it was that she must lose Persephone for four months every year and see her young loveliness go down to the world of the dead. But she was kind; the "Good Goddess," men always called her. She was sorry for the desolation she had brought about. She made the fields once more rich with abundant fruit and the whole world bright with flowers and green leaves. Also she went to the princes of Eleusis who had built her temple and she chose one, Triptolemus, to be her ambassador to men, instructing them how to sow the corn. She taught him and Celeus and the others her sacred rites, "mysteries which no one may utter, for deep awe checks the tongue. Blessed is he who has seen them; his lot will be good in the world to come."

. . .

Queen of fragrant Eleusis,
Giver of earth's good gifts,
Give me your grace, O Demeter.
You, too, Persephone, fairest,
Maiden all lovely, I offer
Song for your favor.

. . .

In the stories of both goddesses, Demeter and Persephone, the idea of sorrow was foremost. Demeter, goddess of the harvest wealth, was still more the divine sorrowing mother who saw her daughter die each year. Persephone was the radiant maiden of the spring and the summertime, whose light step upon the dry, brown hillside was enough to make it fresh and blooming, as Sappho writes,

> I heard the footfall of the flower spring . . .

—Persephone's footfall. But all the while Persephone knew how brief that beauty was; fruits, flowers, leaves, all the fair growth of earth, must end with the coming of the cold and pass like herself into the power of death. After the lord of the dark world below carried her away she was never again the gay young creature who had played in the flowery meadow without a thought of care or trouble. She did indeed rise from the dead every spring, but she brought with her the memory of where she had come from; with all her bright beauty there was something strange and awesome about her. She was often said to be "the maiden whose name may not be spoken."

The Olympians were "the happy gods," "the deathless gods," far removed from suffering mortals destined to die. But in their grief and at the hour of death, men could turn for compassion to the goddess who sorrowed and the goddess who died.

DIONYSUS OR BACCHUS

> *This story is very differently told from the story of Demeter. Dionysus was the last god to enter Olympus. Homer did not admit him. There are no early sources for his story except a few brief allusions in Hesiod, in the eighth or ninth century. A late Homeric Hymn, perhaps even as late as the fourth century, gives the only account of the pirates' ship, and the fate of Pentheus is the subject of the last play of Euripides, in the fifth century, the most modern of all Greek poets.*

Thebes was Dionysus' own city, where he was born, the son of Zeus and the Theban princess Semele. He was the only god whose parents were not both divine.

> At Thebes alone do mortal women bear
> Immortal gods.

Semele was the most unfortunate woman of all those Zeus fell in love with, and in her case too the reason was Hera. Zeus was madly in love with her and told her that anything she asked of him he would do; he swore it by the river Styx, the oath which not even he himself could break. She told him that what she wanted above all else was to see him in his full splendor as King of Heaven and Lord of the Thunderbolt. It was Hera who had put that wish into her heart. Zeus knew that no mortal could behold him thus and live, but he could do nothing. He had sworn by the Styx. He came as she had asked, and before that awful glory of burning light she died. But Zeus snatched from her her child that was near birth, and hid it in his own side away from Hera until the time had come for it to be born. Then Hermes carried it to be cared for by the nymphs of Nysa—the loveliest of earth's valleys, but no man has ever looked upon Nysa or knows where it lies. Some say the nymphs were the Hyades, whom Zeus afterwards placed in the sky as stars, the stars which bring rain when they near the horizon.

So the God of the Vine was born of fire and nursed by rain, the hard burning heat that ripens the grapes and the water that keeps the plant alive.

Grown to manhood, Dionysus wandered far to strange places.

> The lands of Lydia rich in gold,
> Of Phrygia too; the sun-struck plains
> Of Persia; the great walls of Bactria.
> The storm-swept country of the Medes;
> And Araby the Blest.

Everywhere he taught men the culture of the vine and the mysteries of his worship and everywhere they accepted him as a god until he drew near to his own country.

One day over the sea near Greece a pirates' ship came sailing. On a great headland by the shore they saw a beautiful youth. His rich dark hair flowed down over a purple cloak that covered his strong shoulders. He looked like a son of kings, one whose parents could pay a great ransom. Exulting, the sailors sprang ashore and seized him. On board the ship they fetched rude bonds to fetter him with, but to their amazement they were unable to bind him; the ropes would not hold together; they fell apart when they touched his hands or feet. And he sat looking at them with a smile in his dark eyes.

Alone among them the helmsman understood and cried out that this must be a god and should be set free at once or deadly harm would come to them. But the captain mocked him for a silly fool and bade the crew hasten to hoist the sail. The wind filled it and the men drew taut the sheets, but the ship did not move. Then wonder upon wonder happened. Fragrant wine ran in streams down the deck; a vine with many clusters spread out over the sail; a dark green ivy-plant twined around the mast like a garland, with flowers in it and lovely fruits. Terror-stricken, the pirates ordered the helmsman to put in to land. Too late, for as they spoke their captive became a lion, roaring and glaring terribly. At that, they leaped overboard and instantly were changed into dolphins, all except the good helmsman. On him the god had mercy. He held him back and bade him take courage, for he had found favor with one who was indeed a god— Dionysus, whom Semele bore in union with Zeus.

When he passed through Thrace on his way to Greece, the god was insulted by one of the kings there, Lycurgus, who bitterly opposed this new worship. Dionysus retreated before him and even took refuge from him in the depths of the sea. But later he came back, overpowered him and punished him for his wickedness, though mildly, by

> Imprisoning him within a rocky cave
> Until his first fierce maddening rage
> Passed slowly and he learned to know
> The god whom he had mocked.

But the other gods were not mild. Zeus struck Lycurgus blind and he died soon after. None lived long who strove with gods.

Some time during his wanderings, Dionysus came upon the princess of Crete, Ariadne, when she was utterly desolate, having been abandoned on the shore of the island of Naxos by the Athenian prince, Theseus, whose life she had saved. Dionysus had compassion upon her. He rescued her, and in the end loved her. When she died Dionysus took a crown he had given her and placed it among the stars.

The mother whom he had never seen was not forgotten. He longed for her so greatly that at last he dared the terrible descent to the lower world to seek her. When he found her, he defied the power of Death to keep her from him; and Death yielded. Dionysus brought her away, but not to live on earth. He took her up to Olympus, where the gods consented to receive her as one of themselves, a mortal, indeed, but the mother of a god and therefore fit to dwell with immortals.

The God of Wine could be kind and beneficent. He could also be cruel and drive men on to frightful deeds. Often he made them mad. The MAENADS, or the BACCHANTES, as they were also called, were women frenzied with wine. They rushed through woods and over mountains uttering sharp cries, waving pine-cone-tipped wands, swept away in a fierce ecstasy. Nothing could stop them. They would tear to pieces the wild creatures they met and devour the bloody shreds of flesh. They sang,

> Oh, sweet upon the mountain
> The dancing and the singing,
> The maddening rushing flight.
> Oh, sweet to sink to earth outworn
> When the wild goat has been hunted and caught.
> Oh, the joy of the blood and the raw red flesh!

The gods of Olympus loved order and beauty in their sacrifices and their temples. The madwomen, the Maenads, had no temples. They went to the wilderness to worship, to the wildest mountains, the deepest forests, as if they kept to the customs of an ancient time before men had thought of building houses for their gods. They went out of the dusty, crowded city, back to the clean purity of the untrodden hills and woodlands. There Dionysus gave them food and drink: herbs and berries and the milk of the wild goat. Their beds were on the soft meadow grass; under the thick-leaved trees; where the pine needles fall year after year. They woke to a sense of peace and heavenly freshness; they bathed in a clear brook. There was much that was lovely, good, and freeing in this worship under the open sky and the ecstasy of joy it brought in the wild beauty of the world. And yet always present, too, was the horrible bloody feast.

The worship of Dionysus was centered in these two ideas so far apart—of freedom and ecstatic joy and of savage brutality. The God of Wine could give either to his worshipers. Throughout the story of his life he is sometimes man's blessing, sometimes his ruin. Of all the terrible deeds laid to his account the worst was done in Thebes, his mother's city.

Dionysus came to Thebes to establish his worship there. He was accompanied, as was his custom, by a train of women dancing and singing exultant songs, wearing fawn-skins over their robes, waving ivy-wreathed wands. They seemed mad with joy. They sang,

> O Bacchanals, come,
> Oh, come.
> Sing Dionysus,
> Sing to the timbrel,
> The deep-voiced timbrel.
> Joyfully praise him,
> Him who brings joy.
> Holy, all holy
> Music is calling.
> To the hills, to the hills,
> Fly, O Bacchanal
> Swift of foot.
> On, O joyful, be fleet.

Pentheus, the King of Thebes, was the son of Semele's sister, but he had no idea that the leader of this band of excited, strange-acting women was his own cousin. He did not know that when Semele died Zeus had saved her child. The wild dancing and the loud joyous singing and the generally queer behavior of these strangers seemed to him highly objectionable, and to be stopped at once. Pentheus ordered his guards to seize and imprison the visitors, especially the leader, "whose face is flushed with wine, a cheating sorcerer from Lydia." But as he said these words he heard behind him a solemn warning: "The man you reject is a new god. He is Semele's child, whom Zeus rescued. He, with divine Demeter, is greatest upon earth for men." The speaker was the old blind prophet Teiresias, the holy man of Thebes who knew as no one else the will of the gods. But as Pentheus turned to answer him he saw that he was tricked out like the wild women: a wreath of ivy on his white hair, his old shoulders covered by a fawn-skin, a queer pine-tipped stick in his trembling hand. Pentheus laughed mockingly as he looked him over and then ordered him with contempt out of his sight. Thus he brought upon himself his doom; he would not hear when the gods spoke to him.

Dionysus was led in before him by a band of his soldiers. They said he had not tried to flee or to resist, but had done all possible to make it easy for them to seize and bring him until they felt ashamed and told him they were acting under orders, not of their own free will. They declared, too, that the maidens they had imprisoned had all escaped to the mountains. The fetters would not keep fastened; the doors unbarred themselves. "This man," they said, "has come to Thebes with many wonders—"

Pentheus by now was blind to everything except his anger and his scorn. He spoke roughly to Dionysus, who answered him with entire gentleness, seeming to try to reach his real self and open his eyes to see that he was face to face with divinity. He warned him that he could not keep him in prison, "for God will set me free."

"God?" Pentheus asked jeeringly.

"Yes," Dionysus answered. "He is here and sees my suffering."

"Not where my eyes can see him," Pentheus said.

"He is where I am," answered Dionysus. "You cannot see him for you are not pure."

Pentheus angrily ordered the soldiers to bind him and take him to the prison and Dionysus went, saying, "The wrongs you do to me are wrongs done to the gods."

But the prison could not hold Dionysus. He came forth,

and going to Pentheus again he tried to persuade him to yield to what these wonders plainly showed was divine, and welcome this new worship of a new and great god. When, however, Pentheus only heaped insults and threats upon him, Dionysus left him to his doom. It was the most horrible that there could be.

Pentheus went to pursue the god's followers among the hills where the maidens had fled when they escaped from prison. Many of the Theban women had joined them; Pentheus' mother and her sisters were there. And there Dionysus showed himself in his most terrible aspect. He made them all mad. The women thought Pentheus a wild beast, a mountain lion, and they rushed to destroy him, his mother first. As they fell upon him he knew at last that he had fought against a god and must pay with his life. They tore him limb from limb, and then, only then, the god restored their senses, and his mother saw what she had done. Looking at her in her agony the maidens, all sobered now, the dancing over and the singing and the wild wand-waving, said to one another.

> In strange ways hard to know gods come to men.
> Many a thing past hope they had fulfilled,
> And what was looked for went another way.
> A path we never thought to tread God found for us.
> So has this come to pass.

* * *

The ideas about Dionysus in these various stories seem at first sight contradictory. In one he is the joy-god—

> He whose locks are bound with gold,
> Ruddy Bacchus,
> Comrade of the Maenads, whose
> Blithe torch blazes.

In another he is the heartless god, savage, brutal—

> He who with a mocking laugh
> Hunts his prey,
> Snares and drags him to his death
> With his Bacchanals.

The truth is, however, that both ideas arose quite simply and reasonably from the fact of his being the god of wine. Wine is bad as well as good. It cheers and warms men's hearts; it also makes them drunk. The Greeks were a people who saw facts very clearly. They could not shut their eyes to the ugly and degrading side of wine-drinking and see only the delightful side. Dionysus was the God of the Vine; therefore he was a power which sometimes made men commit frightful and atrocious crimes. No one could defend them no one would ever try to defend the fate Pentheus suffered. But, the Greeks said to each other, such things really do happen when people are frenzied with drink. This truth did not blind them to the other truth, that wine was "the merry-maker," lightening men's hearts, bringing careless ease and fun and gaiety.

> The wine of Dionysus,
> When the weary cares of men
> Leave every heart.
> We travel to a land that never was.
> The poor grow rich, the rich grow great of heart.
> All-conquering are the shafts made from the Vine.

The reason that Dionysus was so different at one time from another was because of this double nature of wine and so of the god of wine. He was man's benefactor and he was man's destroyer.

On his beneficent side he was not only the god that makes men merry. His cup was

> Life-giving, healing every ill.

Under his influence courage was quickened and fear banished, at any rate for the moment. He uplifted his worshipers; he made them feel that they could do what they had thought they could not. All this happy freedom and confidence passed away, of course, as they either grew sober or got drunk, but while it lasted it was like being possessed by a power greater than themselves. So people felt about Dionysus as about no other god. He was not only outside of them, he was within them, too. They could be transformed by him into being like him. The momentary sense of exultant power wine-drinking can give was only a sign to show men that they had within them more than they knew; "they could themselves become divine."

To think in this way was far removed from the old idea of worshiping the god by drinking enough to be gay or to be freed from care or to get drunk. There were followers of Dionysus who never drank wine at all. It is not known when the great change took place, lifting the god who freed men for a moment through drunkenness to the god who freed them through inspiration, but one very remarkable result of it made Dionysus for all future ages the most important of the gods of Greece.

The Eleusinian Mysteries, which were always chiefly Demeter's, had indeed great importance. For hundreds of years they helped men, as Cicero said, "to live with joy and to die with hope." But their influence did not last, very likely because nobody was allowed to teach their ideas openly or write about them. In the end only a dim memory of them was left. It was quite otherwise with Dionysus. What was done at his great festival was open to all the world and is a living influence today. No other festival in Greece could compare with it. It took place in the spring when the vine begins to put forth its branches, and it lasted for five days. They were days of perfect peace and enjoyment. All the ordinary business of life stopped. No one could be put in prison; prisoners were even released so that they could share in the general rejoicing. But the place where people gathered to do honor to the god was not a wild wilderness made horrible by savage deeds and a bloody feast; it was not even a temple precinct with ordered sacrifices and priestly ceremonies. It was a theater; and the ceremony was the performance of a play. The greatest poetry in Greece, and among the greatest in the world, was written for Dionysus. The poets who wrote the plays, the actors and singers who took part in them, were all regarded as servants of the god. The performances were sacred; the spectators, too, along with the writers and the performers, were engaged in an act of worship. Dionysus himself was supposed to be present; his priest had the seat of honor.

It is clear, therefore, that the idea of the god of holy inspiration who could fill men with his spirit to write gloriously and to act gloriously became far more important than the earlier ideas of him. The first tragic plays, which are among the best there are, never equaled except by Shakespeare, were produced in the theater of Dionysus. Comedies were produced there, too, but tragedies far outnumbered them, and there was a reason why.

This strange god, the gay reveler, the cruel hunter, the lofty inspirer, was also the sufferer. He, like Demeter, was afflicted, not because of grief for another, as she was, but because of his own pain. He was the vine, which is always pruned as nothing else that bears fruit; every branch cut away, only the bare stock left; through the winter a dead thing to look at, an old gnarled stump seeming incapable of ever putting forth leaves again. Like Persephone Dionysus died with the coming of the cold. Unlike her, his death was terrible: he was torn to pieces, in some stories by the Titans, in others by Hera's orders. He was always brought back to life; he died and rose again. It was his joyful resurrection they celebrated in his theater, but the idea of terrible deeds done to him and done by men under his influence was too closely associated with him ever to be forgotten. He was more than the suffering god. He was the tragic god. There was none other.

He had still another side. He was the assurance that death does not end all. His worshipers believed that his death and resurrection showed that the soul lives on forever after the body dies. This faith was part of the mysteries of Eleusis. At first it centered in Persephone who also rose from the dead every spring. But as queen of the black underworld she kept even in the bright world above a suggestion of something strange and awful: how could she who carried always about her the reminder of death stand for the resurrection, the conquest of death? Dionysus, on the contrary, was never thought of as a power in the kingdom of the dead. There are many stories about Persephone in the lower world; only one about Dionysus—he rescued his mother from it. In his resurrection he was the embodiment of the life that is stronger than death. He and not Persephone became the center of the belief in immortality.

Around the year 80 A.D., a great Greek writer, Plutarch, received news, when he was far from home, that a little daughter of his had died—a child of most gentle nature, he says. In his letter to his wife he writes: "About that which you have heard, dear heart, that the soul once departed from the body vanishes and feels nothing, I know that you give no belief to such assertions because of those sacred and faithful promises given in the mysteries of Bacchus which we who are of that religious brotherhood know. We hold it firmly for an undoubted truth that our soul is incorruptible and immortal. We are to think (of the dead) that they pass into a better place and a happier condition. Let us behave ourselves accordingly, outwardly ordering our lives, while within all should be purer, wiser, incorruptible."

3 How the World and Mankind Were Created

With the exception of the story of Prometheus' punishment, told by Aeschylus in the fifth century, I have taken the material of this chapter chiefly from Hesiod, who lived at least three hundred years earlier. He is the principal authority for the myths about the beginning of everything. Both the crudity of the story of Cronus and the naïveté of the story of Pandora are characteristic of him.

> First there was Chaos, the vast immeasurable abyss,
> Outrageous as a sea, dark, wasteful, wild.

These words are Milton's, but they express with precision what the Greeks thought lay back of the very first beginning of things. Long before the gods appeared, in the dim past, uncounted ages ago, there was only the formless confusion of Chaos brooded over by unbroken darkness. At last, but how no one ever tried to explain, two children were born to this shapeless nothingness. Night was the child of Chaos and so was Erebus, which is the unfathomable depth where death dwells. In the whole universe there was nothing else; all was black, empty, silent, endless.

And then a marvel of marvels came to pass. In some mysterious way, from this horror of blank boundless vacancy the best of all things came into being. A great playwright, the comic poet Aristophanes, describes its coming in words often quoted:—

> ... Black-winged Night
> Into the bosom of Erebus dark and deep
> Laid a wind-born egg, and as the seasons rolled
> Forth sprang Love, the longed-for, shining, with
> wings of gold.

From darkness and from death Love was born, and with its birth, order and beauty began to banish blind confusion. Love created Light with its companion, radiant Day.

What took place next was the creation of the earth, but this, too, no one ever tried to explain. It just happened. With the coming of love and light it seemed natural that the earth also should appear. The poet Hesiod, the first Greek who tried to explain how things began, wrote,

> Earth, the beautiful, rose up,
> Broad-bosomed, she that is the steadfast base
> Of all things. And fair Earth first bore
> The starry Heaven, equal to herself,
> To cover her on all sides and to be
> A home forever for the blessed gods.

In all this thought about the past no distinction had as yet been made between places and persons. Earth was the solid ground, yet vaguely a personality, too. Heaven was the blue vault on high, but it acted in some ways as a human being would. To the people who told these stories all the universe was alive with the same kind of life they knew in themselves. They were individual persons, so they personified everything which had the obvious marks of life, everything which moved and changed: earth in winter and summer; the sky with its shifting stars; the restless sea, and so on. It was only a dim personification: something vague and immense which with its motion brought about change and therefore was alive.

But when they told of the coming of love and light the early storytellers were setting the scene for the appearance of mankind, and they began to personify more precisely. They gave natural forces distinct shapes. They thought of them as the precursors of men and they defined them far more clearly as individuals than they had earth and heaven. They showed them acting in every way as human beings did; walking, for instance, and eating, as Earth and Heaven obviously did not. These two were set apart. If they were alive, it was in a way peculiar to them alone.

The first creatures who had the appearance of life were the children of Mother Earth and Father Heaven (Gaea and Ouranos). They were monsters. Just as we believe that the earth was once inhabited by strange gigantic creatures, so did the Greeks. They did not, however, think of them as huge lizards and mammoths, but as somewhat like men and yet unhuman. They had the shattering, overwhelming strength of earthquake and hurricane and volcano. In the tales about them they do not seem really alive, but rather to belong to a world where as yet there was no life, only tremendous movements of irresistible forces lifting up the mountains and scooping out the seas. The Greeks apparently had some such feeling because in their stories, although they represent these creatures as living beings, they make them unlike any form of life known to man.

Three of them, monstrously huge and strong, had each a hundred hands and fifty heads. To three others was given the name of *Cyclops* (the Wheel-eyed), because each had only one enormous eye, as round and as big as a wheel, in the middle of the forehead. The Cyclopes, too, were gigantic, towering up like mighty mountain crags and devastating in their power. Last came the Titans. There were a number of these and they were in no way inferior to the others in size and strength, but they were not purely destructive. Several of them were even beneficent. One, indeed, after men had been created, saved them from destruction.

It was natural to think of these fearful creations as the children of Mother Earth, brought forth from her dark depths when the world was young. But it is extremely odd that they were also the children of Heaven. However, that was what the Greeks said, and they made Heaven out to be a very poor father. He hated the things with a hundred hands and fifty heads, even though they were his sons, and as each was born he imprisoned it in a secret place within the earth. The Cyclopes and the Titans he left at large; and Earth, enraged at the maltreatment of her other children, appealed to them to help her. Only one was bold enough, the Titan Cronus. He lay in wait for his father and wounded him terribly. The Giants, the fourth race of monsters, sprang up from his blood. From this same blood, too, the Erinyes (the Furies) were born. Their office was to pursue and punish sinners. They were called "those who walk in darkness," and they were terrible of aspect, with writhing snakes for hair and eyes that wept tears of blood. The other monsters were finally driven from the earth, but not the Erinyes. As long as there was sin in the world they could not be banished.

From that time on for untold ages, Cronus, he whom as we have seen the Romans called Saturn, was lord of the universe, with his sister-queen, Rhea (Ops in Latin). Finally one of their sons, the future ruler of heaven and earth, whose name in Greek is Zeus and in Latin Jupiter, rebelled against him. He had good cause to do so, for Cronus had learned that one of his children was destined some day to dethrone him and he thought to go against fate by swallowing them as soon as they were born. But when Rhea bore Zeus, her sixth child, she succeeded in having him secretly carried off to Crete, while she gave her husband a great stone wrapped in swaddling clothes which he supposed was the baby and swallowed down accordingly. Later, when Zeus was grown, he forced his father with the help of his grandmother, the Earth, to disgorge it along with the five earlier children, and it was set up at Delphi where eons later a great traveler, Pausanias by name, reports that he saw it about 180 A.D.: "A stone of no great size which the priests of Delphi anoint every day with oil."

There followed a terrible war between Cronus, helped by his brother Titans, against Zeus with his five brothers and sisters—a war that almost wrecked the universe.

> A dreadful sound troubled the boundless sea.
> The whole earth uttered a great cry.
> Wide heaven, shaken, groaned.
> From its foundation far Olympus reeled
> Beneath the onrush of the deathless gods,
> And trembling seized upon black Tartarus.

The Titans were conquered, partly because Zeus released from their prison the hundred-handed monsters who fought for him with their irresistible weapons—thunder, lightning, and earthquake—and also because one of the sons of the Titan Iapetus, whose name was Prometheus and who was very wise, took sides with Zeus.

Zeus punished his conquered enemies terribly. They were

> Bound in bitter chains beneath the wide-wayed earth,
> As far below the earth as over earth
> Is heaven, for even so far down lies Tartarus.
> Nine days and nights would a bronze anvil fall
> And on the tenth reach earth from heaven.
> And then again falling nine days and nights,
> Would come to Tartarus, the brazen-fenced.

Prometheus' brother Atlas suffered a still worse fate. He was condemned

> To bear on his back forever
> The cruel strength of the crushing world
> And the vault of the sky.
> Upon his shoulders the great pillar
> That holds apart the earth and heaven,
> A load not easy to be borne.

Bearing this burden he stands forever before the place that is wrapped in clouds and darkness, where Night and Day draw near and greet one another. The house within never holds both Night and Day, but always one, departing, visits the earth, and the other in the house awaits the hour for her journeying hence, one with far-seeing light for those on earth, the other holding in her hands Sleep, the brother of Death.

Even after the Titans were conquered and crushed, Zeus was not completely victorious. Earth gave birth to her last and most frightful offspring, a creature more terrible than any that had gone before. His name was Typhon.

> A flaming monster with a hundred heads,
> Who rose up against all the gods.
> Death whistled from his fearful jaws,
> His eyes flashed glaring fire.

But Zeus had now got the thunder and lightning under his own control. They had become his weapons, used by no one else. He struck Typhon down with

> The bolt that never sleeps,
> Thunder with breath of flame.
> Into his very heart the fire burned.
> His strength was turned to ashes.
> And now he lies a useless thing
> By Aetna, whence sometimes there burst
> Rivers red-hot, consuming with fierce jaws
> The level fields of Sicily,
> Lovely with fruits.
> And that is Typhon's anger boiling up,
> His fire-breathing darts.

Still later, one more attempt was made to unseat Zeus: the Giants rebelled. But by this time the gods were very strong and they were helped, too, by mighty Hercules, a son of Zeus. The Giants were defeated and hurled down to Tartarus; and the victory of the radiant powers of Heaven over the brutal forces of Earth was complete. From then on, Zeus and his brothers and sisters ruled, undisputed lords of all.

As yet there were no human beings; but the world, now cleared of the monsters, was ready for mankind. It was a place where people could live in some comfort and security, without having to fear the sudden appearance of a Titan or a Giant. The earth was believed to be a round disk, divided into two equal parts by the Sea, as the Greeks called it,—which we know as the Mediterranean,—and by what we call the Black Sea. (The Greeks called this first the Axine, which means the Unfriendly Sea, and then, perhaps as people became familiar with it, the Euxine, the Friendly Sea. It is sometimes suggested that they gave it this pleasant name to make it feel pleasantly disposed toward them.) Around the earth flowed the great river, Ocean, never troubled by wind or storm. On the farther bank of Ocean were mysterious people, whom few on earth ever found their way to. The Cimmerians lived there, but whether east, west, north or south, no one knew. It was a land cloud-wrapped and misty, where the light of day was never seen; upon which the shining sun never looked with his splendor, not when he climbed through the starry sky at dawn, nor when at evening he turned toward the earth from the sky. Endless night was spread over its melancholy people.

Except in this one country, all those who lived across Ocean were exceedingly fortunate. In the remotest North, so far away it was at the back of the North Wind, was a blissful land where the Hyperboreans lived. Only a few strangers, great heroes, had ever visited it. Not by ship nor yet on foot might one find the road to the marvelous meeting place of the Hyperboreans. But the Muses lived not far from them, such were their ways. For everywhere the dance of maidens swayed and the clear call of the lyre sounded and the ringing notes of flutes. With golden laurel they bound their hair and they feasted merrily. In that holy race, sickness and deathly old age had no part. Far to the south was the country of the Ethiopians, of whom we know only that the gods held them in such favor they would sit at joyful banquets with them in their halls.

On Ocean's bank, too, was the abode of the blessed dead. In that land, there was no snowfall nor much winter nor any storm of rain; but from Ocean the West Wind sang soft and thrillingly to refresh the souls of men. Here those who kept themselves pure from all wrong came when they left the earth.

> Their boon is life forever freed from toil.
> No more to trouble earth or the sea waters
> With their strong hands,
> Laboring for the food that does not satisfy.
> But with the honored of the gods they live
> A life where there are no more tears.
> Around those blessed isles soft sea winds breathe,
> And flowers of gold are blazing on the trees,
> Upon the waters, too.

By now all was ready for the appearance of mankind. Even the places the good and bad should go to after death had been arranged. It was time for men to be created. There is more than one account of how that came to pass. Some say it was delegated by the gods to Prometheus, the Titan who had sided with Zeus in the war with the Titans, and to his brother, Epimetheus. Prometheus, whose name means forethought, was very wise, wiser even than the gods, but Epimetheus, which means afterthought, was a scatterbrained person who invariably followed his first impulse and then changed his mind. So he did in this case. Before making men he gave all the best gifts to the animals, strength and swiftness and courage and shrewd cunning, fur and feathers and wings and shells and the like—until no good was left for men, no protective covering and no quality to make them a match for the beasts. Too late, as always, he was sorry and asked his brother's help. Prometheus, then, took over the task of creation and thought out a way to make mankind superior. He fashioned them in a nobler shape than the animals, upright like the gods; and then he went to heaven, to the sun, where he lit a torch and brought down fire, a protection to men far better than anything else, whether fur or feathers or strength or swiftness.

> And now, though feeble and short-lived,
> Mankind has flaming fire and therefrom
> Learns many crafts.

According to another story, the gods themselves created men. They made first a golden race. These, although mortal, lived like gods without sorrow of heart, far from toil and pain. The cornland of itself bore fruit abundantly. They were rich also in flocks and beloved of the gods. When the grave covered them they became pure spirits, beneficent, the guardians of mankind.

In this account of the creation the gods seemed bent on experimenting with the various metals, and, oddly enough, proceeding downward from the excellent to the good to the worse and so on. When they had tried gold they went to silver. This second race of silver was very inferior to the first. They had so little intelligence that they could not keep from injuring each other. They too passed away, but, unlike the gold race, their spirits did not live on after them. The next race was of brass. They were terrible men, immensely strong, and such lovers of war and violence that they were completely destroyed by their own hands. This, however, was all to the good, for they were followed by a splendid race of godlike heroes who fought glorious wars and went on great adventures which men have talked and sung of through all the ages since. They departed finally to the isles of the blessed, where they lived in perfect bliss forever.

The fifth race is that which is now upon the earth: the iron race. They live in evil times and their nature too has much of evil, so that they never have rest from toil and sorrow. As the generations pass, they grow worse; sons are always inferior to their fathers. A time will come when they have grown so wicked that they will worship power; might will be right to them, and reverence for the good will cease to be. At last when no man is angry any more at wrongdoing or feels shame in the presence of the miserable, Zeus will destroy them too. And yet even then something might be done, if only the common people would arise and put down rulers that oppress them.

● ● ●

These two stories of the creation,—the story of the five ages, and the story of Prometheus and Epimetheus,—different as they are, agree in one point. For a long time, certainly throughout the happy Golden Age, only men were upon the earth; there were no women. Zeus created these later, in his anger at Prometheus for caring so much for men. Prometheus had not only stolen fire for men; he had also arranged that they should get the best part of any animal sacrificed and the gods the worst. He cut up a great ox and wrapped the good eatable parts in the hide, disguising them further by piling entrails on top. Beside this heap he put another of all the bones, dressed up with cunning and covered with shining fat, and bade Zeus choose between them. Zeus took up the white fat and was angry when he saw the bones craftily tricked out. But he had made his choice and he had to abide by it. Thereafter only fat and bones were burned to the gods upon their altars. Men kept the good meat for themselves.

But the Father of Men and of Gods was not one to put up with this sort of treatment. He swore to be revenged, on mankind first and then on mankind's friend. He made a great evil for men, a sweet and lovely thing to look upon, in the likeness of a shy maiden, and all the gods gave her gifts, silvery raiment and a broidered veil, a wonder to behold, and bright garlands of blooming flowers and a crown of gold—great beauty shone out from it. Because of what they gave her they called her *Pandora*, which means "the gift of all." When this beautiful disaster had been made, Zeus brought her out and wonder took hold of gods and men when they beheld her. From her, the first woman, comes the race of women, who are an evil to men, with a nature to do evil.

Another story about Pandora is that the source of all misfortune was not her wicked nature, but only her curiosity. The gods presented her with a box into which each had put something harmful, and forbade her ever to open it. Then they sent her to Epimetheus, who took her gladly although Prometheus had warned him never to accept anything from Zeus. He took her, and afterward when that dangerous thing, a woman, was his, he understood how good his brother's advice had been. For Pandora, like all women, was possessed of a lively curiosity. She *had* to know what was in the box. One day she lifted the lid—and out flew plagues innumerable, sorrow and mis-

Pandora lifted the lid and out flew plagues
and sorrows for mankind

chief for mankind. In terror Pandora clapped the lid down, but too late. One good thing, however, was there—Hope. It was the only good the casket had held among the many evils, and it remains to this day mankind's sole comfort in misfortune. So mortals learned that it is not possible to get the better of Zeus or ever deceive him. The wise and compassionate Prometheus, too, found that out.

When Zeus had punished men by giving them women he turned his attention to the arch-sinner himself. The new ruler of the gods owed Prometheus much for helping him conquer the other Titans, but he forgot his debt. Zeus had his servants, Force and Violence, seize him and take him to the Caucasus, where they bound him

> To a high-piercing, headlong rock
> In adamantine chains that none can break,

and they told him,

> Forever shall the intolerable present grind you down.
> And he who will release you is not born.
> Such fruit you reap for your man-loving ways.
> A god yourself, you did not dread God's anger,
> But gave to mortals honor not their due.
> And therefore you must guard this joyless rock—
> No rest, no sleep, no moment's respite.
> Groans shall your speech be, lamentation your only words.

The reason for inflicting this torture was not only to punish Prometheus, but also to force him to disclose a secret very important to the lord of Olympus. Zeus knew that fate, which brings all things to pass, had decreed that a son should some day be born to him who would dethrone him and drive the gods from their home in heaven, but only Prometheus knew who would be the mother of this son. As he lay bound upon the rock in agony, Zeus sent his messenger, Hermes, to bid him disclose the secret. Prometheus told him:—

> Go and persuade the sea wave not to break.
> You will persuade me no more easily.

Hermes warned him that if he persisted in his stubborn silence, he should suffer still more terrible things.

> An eagle red with blood
> Shall come, a guest unbidden to your banquet.
> All day long he will tear to rags your body,
> Feasting in fury on the blackened liver.

But nothing, no threat, nor torture, could break Prometheus. His body was bound but his spirit was free. He refused to submit to cruelty and tyranny. He knew that he had served Zeus well and that he had done right to pity mortals in their helplessness. His suffering was utterly unjust, and he would not give in to brutal power no matter at what cost. He told Hermes:—

> There is no force which can compel my speech.
> So let Zeus hurl his blazing bolts,
> And with the white wings of the snow,
> With thunder and with earthquake,
> Confound the reeling world.
> None of all this will bend my will.

Hermes, crying out,

> Why, these are ravings you may hear from madmen,

left him to suffer what he must. Generations later we know he was released, but why and how is not told clearly anywhere. There is a strange story that the Centaur, Chiron, though immortal, was willing to die for him and that he was allowed to do so. When Hermes was urging Prometheus to give in to Zeus he spoke of this, but in such a way as to make it seem an incredible sacrifice:—

> Look for no ending to this agony
> Until a god will freely suffer for you,
> Will take on him your pain, and in your stead
> Descend to where the sun is turned to darkness,
> The black depths of death.

But Chiron did do this and Zeus seems to have accepted him as a substitute. We are told, too, that Hercules slew the eagle and delivered Prometheus from his bonds, and that Zeus was willing to have this done. But why Zeus changed his mind and whether Prometheus revealed the secret when he was freed, we do not know. One thing, however, is certain: in whatever way the two were reconciled, it was not Prometheus who yielded. His name has stood through all the centuries, from Greek days to our own, as that of the great rebel against injustice and the authority of power.

•   • •

There is still another account of the creation of mankind. In the story of the five ages men are descended from the iron race. In the story of Prometheus, it is uncertain whether the men he saved from destruction belonged to that race or the bronze race. Fire would have been as necessary to the one as to the other. In the third story, men are descended from a race of stone. This story begins with the Deluge.

All over the earth men grew so wicked that finally Zeus determined to destroy them. He decided

> To mingle storm and tempest over boundless earth
> And make an utter end of mortal man.

He sent the flood. He called upon his brother, the God of the Sea, to help him, and together, with torrents of rain from heaven and rivers loosed upon the earth, the two drowned the land.

> The might of water overwhelmed dark earth,

over the summits of the highest mountains. Only towering Parnassus was not quite covered, and the bit of dry land on its very topmost peak was the means by which mankind escaped destruction. After it had rained through nine days and nine nights, there came drifting to that spot what looked to be a great wooden chest, but safe within it were two living human beings, a man and a woman. They were Deucalion and Pyrrha—he Prometheus' son, and she his niece, the daughter of Epimetheus and Pandora. The wisest person in all the universe, Prometheus had well been able to protect his own family. He knew the flood would come, and he had bidden his son build the chest, store it with provisions, and embark in it with his wife.

Fortunately Zeus was not offended, because the two were pious, faithful worshipers of the gods. When the chest came to land and they got out, to see no sign of life anywhere, only a wild waste of waters, Zeus pitied them and drained off the flood. Slowly like the ebbing tide the sea and the rivers drew back and the earth was dry again. Pyrrha and Deucalion came down from Parnassus, the only living creatures in a dead world. They found a temple all slimy and moss-grown, but not quite in ruins, and there they gave thanks for their escape and prayed for help in their dreadful loneliness. They heard a voice. "Veil your heads and cast behind you the bones of your mother." The command struck them with horror. Pyrrha said, "We dare not do such a thing." Deucalion was forced to agree that she was right, but he tried to think out what might lie behind the words and suddenly he saw their meaning. "Earth is the mother of all," he told his wife. "Her bones are the stones. These we may cast behind us without doing wrong." So they did, and as the stones fell they took human shape. They were called the Stone People, and they were a hard, enduring race, as was to be expected and, indeed, as they had need to be, to rescue the earth from the desolation left by the flood.

4 The Earliest Heroes

PROMETHEUS AND IO

The materials for this story are taken from two poets, the Greek Aeschylus and the Roman Ovid, separated from each other by four hundred and fifty years and still more by their gifts and temperaments. They are the best sources for the tale. It is easy to distinguish the parts told by each, Aeschylus grave and direct, Ovid light and amusing. The touch about lovers' lies is characteristic of Ovid, as also the little story about Syrinx.

In those days when Prometheus had just given fire to men and when he was first bound to the rocky peak on Caucasus, he had a strange visitor. A distracted fleeing creature came clambering awkwardly up over the cliffs and crags to where he lay. It looked like a heifer, but talked like a girl who seemed mad with misery. The sight of Prometheus stopped her short. She cried,

> This that I see—
> A form storm-beaten,
> Bound to the rock.
> Did you do wrong?
> Is this your punishment?
> Where am I?
> Speak to a wretched wanderer.
> Enough—I have been tried enough—
> My wandering—long wandering.
> Yet I have found nowhere
> To leave my misery.
> I am a girl who speak to you,
> But horns are on my head.

Prometheus recognized her. He knew her story and he spoke her name.

> I know you, girl, Inachus' daughter, Io.
> You made the god's heart hot with love
> And Hera hates you. She it is
> Who drives you on this flight that never ends.

Wonder checked Io's frenzy. She stood still, all amazed. Her name—spoken by this strange being in this strange, lonely place! She begged,

> Who are you, sufferer, that speak the truth
> To one who suffers?

And he answered,

> You see Prometheus who gave mortals fire.

She knew him, then, and his story.

> You—he who succored the whole race of men?
> You, that Prometheus, the daring, the enduring?

They talked freely to each other. He told her how Zeus had treated him, and she told him that Zeus was the reason why she, once a princess and a happy girl, had been changed into

> A beast, a starving beast,
> That frenzied runs with clumsy leaps and bounds.
> Oh, shame . . .

Zeus's jealous wife, Hera, was the direct cause of her misfortunes, but back of them all was Zeus himself. He fell in love with her, and sent

> Ever to my maiden chamber
> Visions of the night
> Persuading me with gentle words:
> "O happy, happy girl,
> Why are you all too long a maid?
> The arrow of desire has pierced Zeus.
> For you he is on fire.
> With you it is his will to capture love."
> Always, each night, such dreams possessed me.

But still greater than Zeus's love was his fear of Hera's jealousy. He acted, however, with very little wisdom for the Father of Gods and Men when he tried to hide Io and himself by wrapping the earth in a cloud so thick and dark that a sudden night seemed to drive the clear daylight away. Hera knew perfectly well that there was a reason for this odd occurrence, and instantly suspected her husband. When she could not find him anywhere in heaven she glided swiftly down to the earth and ordered the cloud off. But Zeus too had been quick. As she caught sight of him he was standing beside a most lovely white heifer—Io, of course. He swore that he had never seen her until just now when she had sprung forth, newborn, from the earth. And this, Ovid says, shows that the lies lovers tell do not anger the gods. However, it also shows that they are not very useful, for Hera did not believe a word of it. She said the heifer was very pretty and would Zeus please make her a present of it. Sorry as he was, he saw at once that to refuse would give the whole thing away. What excuse could he make? An insignificant little cow . . . He turned Io reluctantly over to his wife and Hera knew very well how to keep her away from him.

She gave her into the charge of Argus, an excellent arrangement for Hera's purpose, since Argus had a hundred eyes. Before such a watchman, who could sleep with some of the eyes and keep on guard with the rest, Zeus seemed helpless. He watched Io's misery, turned into a beast, driven from her home; he dared not come to her help. At last, however, he went to his son Hermes, the messenger of the gods, and told him he must find a way to kill Argus. There was no god cleverer than Hermes. As soon as he had sprung to earth from heaven he laid aside everything that marked him as a god and approached Argus like a country fellow, playing very sweetly upon a pipe of reeds. Argus was pleased at the sound and called to the musician to come nearer. "You might as well sit by me on this rock," he said, "you see it's shady—just right for shepherds." Nothing could have been better for Hermes' plan, and yet nothing happened. He played and then he talked on and on, as drowsily and monotonously as he could; some of the hundred eyes would go to sleep, but some were always awake. At last, however, one story was successful—about the god Pan, how he loved a nymph named Syrinx who fled from him and just as he was about to seize her was turned into a tuft of reeds by her sister nymphs. Pan said, "Still you shall be mine," and he made from what she had become

> A shepherd's pipe
> Of reeds with beeswax joined.

The little story does not seem especially tiresome, as such stories go, but Argus found it so. All of his eyes went to sleep. Hermes killed him at once, of course, but Hera took the eyes and set them in the tail of the peacock, her favorite bird.

It seemed then that Io was free, but no; Hera at once

turned on her again. She sent a gad-fly to plague her, which stung her to madness. Io told Prometheus,

> He drives me all along the long sea strand.
> I may not stop for food or drink.
> He will not let me sleep.

Prometheus tried to comfort her, but he could point her only to the distant future. What lay immediately before her was still more wandering and in fearsome lands. To be sure, the part of the sea she first ran along in her frenzy would be called Ionian after her, and the Bosphorus, which means the Ford of the Cow, would preserve the memory of when she went through it, but her real consolation must be that at long last she would reach the Nile, where Zeus would restore her to her human form. She would bear him a son named Epaphus, and live forever after happy and honored. And

> Know this, that from your race will spring
> One glorious with the bow, bold-hearted,
> And he shall set me free.

Io's descendant would be Hercules, greatest of heroes, than whom hardly the gods were greater, and to whom Prometheus would owe his freedom.

EUROPA

This story, so like the Renaissance idea of the classical— fantastic, delicately decorated, bright-colored—is taken entirely from a poem of the third-century Alexandrian poet Moschus, by far the best account of it.

Io was not the only girl who gained geographical fame because Zeus fell in love with her. There was another, known far more widely—Europa, the daughter of the King of Sidon. But whereas the wretched Io had to pay dearly for the distinction, Europa was exceedingly fortunate. Except for a few moments of terror when she found herself crossing the deep sea on the back of a bull she did not suffer at all. The story does not say what Hera was about at the time, but it is clear that she was off guard and her husband free to do as he pleased.

Up in heaven one spring morning as he idly watched the earth, Zeus suddenly saw a charming spectacle. Europa had waked early, troubled just as Io had been by a dream, only this time not of a god who loved her but of two Continents who each in the shape of a woman tried to possess her, Asia saying that she had given her birth and therefore owned her, and the other, as yet nameless, declaring that Zeus would give the maiden to her.

Once awake from this strange vision which had come at dawn, the time when true dreams oftenest visit mortals, Europa decided not to try to go to sleep again, but to summon her companions, girls born in the same year as herself and all of noble birth, to go out with her to the lovely blooming meadows near the sea. Here was their favorite meeting place, whether they wanted to dance or bathe their fair bodies at the river mouth or gather flowers.

This time all had brought baskets, knowing that the flowers were now at their perfection. Europa's was of gold, exquisitely chased with figures which showed, oddly enough, the story of Io, her journeys in the shape of a cow, the death of Argus, and Zeus lightly touching her with his divine hand and changing her back into a woman. It was, as may be perceived, a marvel worth gazing upon, and had been made by no less a personage than Hephaestus, the celestial workman of Olympus.

Lovely as the basket was, there were flowers as lovely to fill it with, sweet-smelling narcissus and hyacinths and violets and yellow crocus, and most radiant of all, the crimson splendor of the wild rose. The girls gathered them delightedly, wandering here and there over the meadow, each one a maiden fairest among the fair; yet even so, Europa shone out among them as the Goddess of Love outshines the sister Graces. And it was that very Goddess of Love who brought about what next happened. As Zeus in heaven watched the pretty scene, she who alone can conquer Zeus—along with her son, the mischievous boy Cupid—shot one of her shafts into his heart, and that very instant he fell madly in love with Europa. Even though Hera was away, he thought it well to be cautious, and before appearing to Europa he changed himself into a bull. Not such a one as you might see in a stall or grazing in a field, but one beautiful beyond all bulls that ever were, bright chestnut in color, with a silver circle on his brow and horns like the crescent of the young moon. He seemed so gentle as well as so lovely that the girls were not frightened at his coming, but gathered around to caress him and to breathe the heavenly fragrance that came from him, sweeter even than that of the flowery meadow. It was Europa he drew toward, and as she gently touched him, he lowed so musically, no flute could give forth a more melodious sound.

Then he lay down before her feet and seemed to show her his broad back, and she cried to the others to come with her and mount him.

The rape of Europa

> For surely he will bear us on his back,
> He is so mild and dear and gentle to behold.
> He is not like a bull, but like a good, true man,
> Except he cannot speak.

Smiling she sat down on his back, but the others, quick though they were to follow her, had no chance. The bull leaped up and at full speed rushed to the seashore and then not into, but over, the wide water. As he went the waves grew smooth before him and a whole procession rose up from the deep and accompanied him—the strange sea-gods, Nereids riding upon dolphins, and Tritons blowing their horns, and the mighty Master of the Sea himself, Zeus's own brother.

Europa, frightened equally by the wondrous creatures she saw and the moving waters all around, clung with one hand to the bull's great horn and with the other caught up her purple dress to keep it dry, and the winds

> Swelled out the deep folds even as a sail
> Swells on a ship, and ever gently thus
> They wafted her.

No bull could this be, thought Europa, but most certainly a god; and she spoke pleadingly to him, begging him to pity her and not leave her in some strange place all alone. He spoke to her in answer and showed her she had guessed rightly what he was. She had no cause to fear, he told her. He was Zeus, greatest of gods, and all he was doing was from love of her. He was taking her to Crete, his own island, where his mother had hidden him from Cronus when he was born, and there she would bear him

> Glorious sons whose sceptres shall hold sway
> Over all men on earth.

Everything happened, of course, as Zeus had said. Crete came into sight; they landed, and the Seasons, the gatekeepers of Olympus, arrayed her for her bridal. Her sons were famous men, not only in this world but in the next—where two of them, Minos and Rhadamanthus, were rewarded for their justice upon the earth by being made the judges of the dead. But her own name remains the best known of all.

THE CYCLOPS POLYPHEMUS

The first part of this story goes back to the Odyssey; *the second part is told only by the third-century Alexandrian poet Theocritus; the last part could have been written by no one except the satirist Lucian, in the second century*

A.D. *At least a thousand years separate the beginning from the end. Homer's vigor and power of storytelling, the pretty fancies of Theocritus, the smart cynicism of Lucian, illustrate in their degree the course of Greek literature.*

All the monstrous forms of life which were first created, the hundred-handed creatures, the Giants, and so on, were permanently banished from the earth when they had been conquered, with the single exception of the Cyclopes. They were allowed to come back, and they became finally great favorites of Zeus. They were wonderful workmen and they forged his thunderbolts. At first there had been only three, but later there were many. Zeus gave them a home in a fortunate country where the vineyards and cornlands, unplowed and unsown, bore fruits plenteously. They had great flocks of sheep and goats as well, and they lived at their ease. Their fierceness and savage temper, however, did not grow less; they had no laws or courts of justice, but each one did as he pleased. It was not a good country for strangers.

Ages after Prometheus was punished, when the descendants of the men he helped had grown civilized and had learned to build far-sailing ships, a Greek prince beached his boat on the shore of this dangerous land. His name was Odysseus (Ulysses in Latin) and he was on his way home after the destruction of Troy. In the hardest battle he had fought with the Trojans, he had never come as near to death as he did then.

Not far from the spot where his crew had made the vessel fast was a cave, open toward the sea and very lofty. It looked inhabited; there was a strong fence before the entrance. Odysseus started off to explore it with twelve of his men. They were in need of food and he took with him a goatskin full of very potent and mellow wine to give whoever lived there in return for hospitality. The gate in the fence was not closed and they made their way into the cave. No one was there, but it was clearly the dwelling of some very prosperous person. Along the sides of the cave were many crowded pens of lambs and kids. Also there were racks full of cheeses and pails brimming with milk, delightful to the sea-worn travelers who ate and drank as they waited for the master.

At last he came, hideous and huge, tall as a great mountain crag. Driving his flock before him he entered and closed the cave's mouth with a ponderous slab of stone. Then looking around he caught sight of the strangers, and cried out in a dreadful booming voice, "Who are you who enter unbidden the house of Polyphemus? Traders or thieving pirates?" They were terror-stricken at the sight and sound of him, but Odysseus made swift to answer, and firmly, too: "Shipwrecked warriors from Troy are we, and your suppliants, under the protection of Zeus, the suppliants' god." But Polyphemus roared out that he cared not for Zeus. He was bigger than any god and feared none of them. With that, he stretched out his mighty arms and in each great hand he seized one of the men and dashed his brains out on the ground. Slowly he feasted off them to the last shred, and then, satisfied, stretched himself out across the cavern and slept. He was safe from attack. No one but he could roll back the huge stone before the door, and if the horrified men had been able to summon courage and strength enough to kill him they would have been imprisoned there forever.

During that long terrible night Odysseus faced the awful thing that had happened and would happen to every one of them if he could not think out some way of escape. But by the time day had dawned and the flock gathering at the entrance woke the Cyclops up, no idea at all had come to him. He had to watch two more of his company die, for Polyphemus breakfasted as he had supped. Then he drove out his flock, moving back the big block at the door and pushing it into place again as easily as a man opens and shuts the lid to his quiver. Throughout the day, shut in the cave, Odysseus thought and thought. Four of his men had perished hideously. Must they all go the same dreadful way? At last a plan shaped itself in his mind. An enormous timber lay near the pens, as long and as thick as the mast of a twenty-oared ship. From this he cut off a good piece, and then he and his men sharpened it and hardened the point by turning it round and round in the fire. They had finished and hidden it by the time the Cyclops came back. There followed the same horrible feast as before. When it was over Odysseus filled a cup with his own wine that he had brought with him and offered it to the Cyclops. He emptied it with delight and demanded more, and Odysseus poured for him until finally a drunken sleep overcame him. Then Odysseus and his men drew out the great stake from its hiding-place and heated the point in the fire until it almost burst into flame. Some power from on high breathed a mad courage into them and they drove the red-hot spike right into the Cyclops' eye. With an awful scream he sprang up and wrenched the point out. This way and that he flung around the cavern searching for his tormentors, but, blind as he was, they were able to slip away from him.

At last he pushed aside the stone at the entrance and sat down there, stretching his arms across, thinking thus to catch them when they tried to get away. But Odysseus had made a plan for this, too. He bade each man choose out three thick-fleeced rams and bind them together with strong, pliant strips of bark; then to wait for day, when the flock would be sent out to pasture. At last the dawn came and as the beasts crowding through the entrance passed out Polyphemus felt them over to be sure no one carried a man on his back. He never thought to feel underneath, but that was where the men were, each tucked under the middle ram, holding on to the great fleece. Once out of that fearful place they dropped to the ground and, hurrying to the ship, in no time launched it and were aboard. But Odysseus was too angry to leave in prudent silence. He sent a great shout over the water to the blind giant at the cave's mouth. "So, Cyclops, you were not quite strong enough to eat all of the puny men? You are rightly punished for what you did to those who were guests in your house."

The words stung Polyphemus to the heart. Up he sprang and tore a great crag from the mountain and flung it at the ship. It came within a hair's breadth of crushing the prow, and with the backwash the boat was borne landward. The crew put all their strength into their oars and just succeeded in pulling out to sea. When Odysseus saw that they were safely away, he cried again tauntingly, "Cyclops, Odysseus, wrecker of cities, put out your eye, and do you so tell anyone who asks." But they were too far off by then; the giant could do nothing. He sat blinded on the shore.

This was the only story told about Polyphemus for many years. Centuries passed and he was still the same, a frightful monster, shapeless, huge, his eye put out. But finally he changed, as what is ugly and evil is apt to change and grow milder with time. Perhaps some storyteller saw the helpless, suffering creature Odysseus left behind as a thing to be pitied. At all events, the next story about him shows him in a very pleasing light, not terrifying at all, but a most poor credulous monster, a most ridiculous monster, quite aware of how hideous and uncouth and repulsive he was, and therefore wretched, because he was madly in love with the charming, mocking sea nymph, Galatea. By this time the place where he lived was Sicily and he had somehow got his eye back, perhaps by some miracle of his father who in this story is Poseidon, the great God of the Sea. The lovelorn giant knew Galatea would never have him; his case was hopeless. And yet, whenever his pain made him harden his heart against her and bid himself, "Milk the ewe you have; why pursue what shuns you?", the minx would come softly stealing near him; then suddenly a shower of apples would pelt his flock and her voice would ring in his ears calling him a laggard in love. But no sooner was he up and after her than she would be off, laughing at his slow clumsiness as he tried to follow her. All he could do was again to sit wretched and helpless on the shore, but this time not trying in fury to kill people, only singing mournful love songs to soften the sea nymph's heart.

In a much later story, Galatea turned kind, not because the exquisite, delicate, milk-white maid, as Polyphemus called her in his songs, fell in love with the hideous one-eyed creature (in this tale, too, he has got back his eye), but because she prudently reflected that he was the favored son of the Lord of the Sea and by no means to be despised. So she told her sister nymph, Doris, who had rather hoped to attract the Cyclops herself, and who began the talk by saying scornfully, "A fine lover you've got—that Sicilian shepherd. Everybody's talking about it."

GALATEA: None of your airs, please. He's the son of Poseidon. There!

DORIS: Zeus's, for all I care. One thing's certain—he's an ugly, ill-mannered brute.

GALATEA: Just let me tell you, Doris, there's something very manly about him. Of course it's true he's got only one eye, but he sees as well with it as if he had two.

DORIS: It sounds as if you were in love yourself.

GALATEA: I in love—with Polyphemus! Not I—but of course I can guess why you're talking like this. You know perfectly well he has never noticed you—only me.

DORIS: A shepherd with only one eye thinks you handsome! That's something to be proud of. Anyway, you won't have to cook for him. He can make a very good meal off a traveler, I understand.

But Polyphemus never won Galatea. She fell in love with a beautiful young prince named Acis, whom Polyphemus, furiously jealous, killed. However, Acis was changed into a river-god, so that story ended well. But we are not told that Polyphemus ever loved any maiden except Galatea, or that any maiden ever loved Polyphemus.

FLOWER-MYTHS: NARCISSUS, HYACINTH, ADONIS

The first story about the creation of the narcissus is told only in an early Homeric Hymn of the seventh or eighth century, the second I have taken from Ovid. There is an immense difference between the two poets, who are separated from each other not only by six or seven hundred years, but also by the fundamental difference between the Greek and the Roman. The Hymn is written objectively, simply, without a touch of affectation. The poet is thinking of his subject. Ovid is as always thinking of his audience. But he tells this story well. The bit about the ghost trying to look at itself in the river of death is a subtle touch which is quite characteristic of him and quite unlike any Greek writer. Euripides gives the best account of the festival of Hyacinthus; Apollodorus and Ovid both tell his story. Whenever there is any vividness in my narrative it may be ascribed securely to Ovid. Apollodorus never deviates into anything like that. Adonis I have taken from two third-century poets, Theocritus and Bion. The tale is typical of the Alexandrian poets, tender, a little soft, but always in exquisite taste.

In Greece there are most lovely wild flowers. They would be beautiful anywhere, but Greece is not a rich and fertile country of wide meadows and fruitful fields where flowers seem at home. It is a land of rocky ways and stony hills and rugged mountains, and in such places the exquisite vivid bloom of the wild flowers,

> A profusion of delight,
> Gay, bewilderingly bright,

comes as a startling surprise. Bleak heights are carpeted in radiant colors; every crack and crevice of a frowning crag blossoms. The contrast of this laughing, luxuriant beauty with the clear-cut, austere grandeur all around arrests the attention sharply. Elsewhere wild flowers may be little noticed—but never in Greece.

That was as true in the days of old as it is now. In the faraway ages when the tales of Greek mythology were taking shape men found the brilliant blossoms of the Greek spring a wonder and a delight. Those people separated from us by thousands of years, and almost completely unknown to us, felt as we do before that miracle of loveliness, each flower so delicate, yet all together covering the land like a rainbow mantle flung over the hills. The first storytellers in Greece told story after story about them, how they had been created and why they were so beautiful.

It was the most natural thing possible to connect them with the gods. All things in heaven and earth were mysteriously linked with the divine powers, but beautiful things most of all. Often an especially exquisite flower was held to be the direct creation of a god for his own purpose. That was true of the narcissus, which was not like ours of that name, but a lovely bloom of glowing purple and silver. Zeus called it into being to help his brother, the lord of the dark underworld, when he wanted to carry away the maiden he had fallen in love with, Demeter's daughter, Persephone. She was gathering flowers with her companions in the vale of Enna, in a meadow of soft grass and roses and crocus and lovely violets and iris and hyacinths. Suddenly she caught sight of something quite new to her, a bloom more beautiful by far than any she had ever seen, a strange glory of a flower, a marvel to all, immortal gods and mortal men. A hundred blossoms grew up from the roots, and the fragrance was very sweet. The broad sky above and the whole earth laughed to see it, and the salt wave of the sea.

Only Persephone among the maidens had spied it. The rest were at the other end of the meadow. She stole toward it, half fearful at being alone, but unable to resist the desire to fill her basket with it, exactly as Zeus had supposed she would feel. Wondering she stretched out her hands to take the lovely plaything, but before she touched it a chasm opened in the earth and out of it coal-black horses sprang, drawing a chariot and driven by one who had a look of dark splendor, majestic and beautiful and terrible. He caught her to him and held her close. The next moment she was being borne away from the radiance of earth in springtime to the world of the dead by the king who rules it.

This was not the only story about the narcissus. There was another, as magical, but quite different. The hero of it was a beautiful lad, whose name was Narcissus. His beauty was so great, all the girls who saw him longed to be his, but he would have none of them. He would pass the loveliest carelessly by, no matter how much she tried to make him look at her. Heartbroken maidens were nothing to him. Even the sad case of the fairest of the nymphs, Echo, did not move him. She was a favorite of Artemis, the goddess of woods and wild creatures, but she came under the displeasure of a still mightier goddess, Hera herself, who was at her usual occupation of trying to discover what Zeus was about. She suspected that he was in love with one of the nymphs and she went to look them over to try to discover which. However, she was immediately diverted from her investigation by Echo's gay chatter. As she listened amused, the others silently stole away and Hera could come to no conclusion as to where Zeus's wandering fancy had alighted. With her usual injustice she turned against Echo. That nymph became another unhappy girl whom Hera punished. The goddess condemned her never to use her tongue again except to repeat what was said to her. "You will always have the last word," Hera said, "but no power to speak first."

This was very hard, but hardest of all when Echo, too, with all the other lovelorn maidens, loved Narcissus. She could follow him, but she could not speak to him. How then could

she make a youth who never looked at a girl pay attention
to her? One day, however, it seemed her chance had come.
He was calling to his companions. "Is anyone here?" and she
called back in rapture, "Here—Here." She was still hidden by
the trees so that he did not see her, and he shouted, "Come!"
—just what she longed to say to him. She answered joyfully,
"Come!" and stepped forth from the woods with her arms
outstretched. But he turned away in angry disgust. "Not so,"
he said; "I will die before I give you power over me." All
she could say was, humbly, entreatingly, "I give you power
over me," but he was gone. She hid her blushes and her shame
in a lonely cave, and never could be comforted. Still she
lives in places like that, and they say she has so wasted
away with longing that only her voice now is left to her.

So Narcissus went on his cruel way, a scorner of love. But
at last one of those he wounded prayed a prayer and it was
answered by the gods: "May he who loves not others love
himself." The great goddess Nemesis, which means righteous
anger, undertook to bring this about. As Narcissus bent over
a clear pool for a drink and saw there his own reflection, on
the moment he fell in love with it. "Now I know," he cried,
"what others have suffered from me, for I burn with love of
my own self—and yet how can I reach that loveliness I see
mirrored in the water? But I cannot leave it. Only death can
set me free." And so it happened. He pined away, leaning
perpetually over the pool, fixed in one long gaze. Echo was
near him, but she could do nothing; only when, dying, he
called to his image, "Farewell—farewell," she could repeat
the words as a last good-by to him.

They say that when his spirit crossed the river that encircles the world of the dead, it leaned over the boat to
catch a final glimpse of itself in the water.

The nymphs he had scorned were kind to him in death
and sought his body to give it burial, but they could not find
it. Where it had lain there was blooming a new and lovely
flower, and they called it by his name, Narcissus.

Another flower that came into being through the death of
a beautiful youth was the hyacinth, again not like the flower
we call by that name, but lily-shaped and of a deep purple,
or, some say, a splendid crimson. That was a tragic death,
and each year it was commemorated by

> The festival of Hyacinthus
> That lasts throughout the tranquil night.
> In a contest with Apollo
> He was slain.

Discus throwing they competed,
And the god's swift cast
Sped beyond the goal he aimed at

and struck Hyacinthus full in the forehead a terrible wound.
He had been Apollo's dearest companion. There was no rival-
ry between them when they tried which could throw the discus farthest; they were only playing a game. The god was hor-
ror-struck to see the blood gush forth and the lad, deathly pale,
fall to the ground. He turned as pale himself as he caught
him up in his arms and tried to staunch the wound. But it
was too late. While he held him the boy's head fell back as a
flower does when its stem is broken. He was dead and Apollo
kneeling beside him wept for him, dying so young, so beautiful. He had killed him, although through no fault of his, and
he cried, "Oh, if I could give my life for yours, or die with you."
Even as he spoke, the bloodstained grass turned green again and
there bloomed forth the wondrous flower that was to make the
lad's name known forever. Apollo himself inscribed the petals
—some say with Hyacinth's initial, and others with the two
letters of the Greek word that means "Alas"; either way, a memorial of the god's great sorrow.

There is a story, too, that Zephyr, the West Wind, not
Apollo, was the direct cause of the death, that he also loved
this fairest of youths and in his jealous anger at seeing the
god preferred to him he blew upon the discus and made it
strike Hyacinth.

* * *

Such charming tales of lovely young people who, dying in
the springtime of life, were fittingly changed into spring flowers, have probably a dark background. They give a hint of
black deeds that were done in the far-distant past. Long before there were any stories told in Greece or any poems sung
which have come down to us, perhaps even before there were
storytellers and poets, it might happen, if the fields around a
village were not fruitful, if the corn did not spring up as it
should, that one of the villagers would be killed and his—or
her—blood sprinkled over the barren land. There was no idea
as yet of the radiant gods of Olympus who would have loathed
the hateful sacrifice. Mankind had only a dim feeling that
as their own life depended utterly on seedtime and harvest,
there must be a deep connection between themselves and the
earth and that their blood, which was nourished by the corn,
could in turn nourish it at need. What more natural then, if a
beautiful boy had thus been killed, than to think when later
the ground bloomed with narcissus or hyacinths that the flow-

ers were his very self, changed and yet living again? So they would tell each other it had happened, a lovely miracle which made the cruel death seem less cruel. Then as the ages passed and people no longer believed that the earth needed blood to be fruitful, all that was cruel in the story would be dropped and in the end forgotten. No one would remember that terrible things had once been done. Hyacinthus, they would say, died not slaughtered by his kinsfolk to get food for them, but only because of a sorrowful mistake.

• • •

Of these deaths and flowery resurrections the most famous was that of Adonis. Every year the Greek girls mourned for him and every year they rejoiced when his flower, the blood-red anemone, the windflower, was seen blooming again. Aphrodite loved him; the Goddess of Love, who pierces with her shafts the hearts of gods and men alike, was fated herself to suffer that same piercing pain.

She saw him when he was born and even then loved him and decided he should be hers. She carried him to Persephone to take charge of him for her, but Persephone loved him too and would not give him back to Aphrodite, not even when the goddess went down to the underworld to get him. Neither goddess would yield, and finally Zeus himself had to judge between them. He decided that Adonis should spend half the year with each, the autumn and winter with the Queen of the Dead; the spring and summer with the Goddess of Love and Beauty.

All the time he was with Aphrodite she sought only to please him. He was keen for the chase, and often she would leave her swan-drawn car, in which she was used to glide at her ease through the air, and follow him along rough woodland ways dressed like a huntress. But one sad day she happened not to be with him and he tracked down a mighty boar. With his hunting dogs he brought the beast to bay. He hurled his spear at it, but he only wounded it, and before he could spring away, the boar mad with pain rushed at him and gored him with its great tusks. Aphrodite in her winged car high over the earth heard her lover's groan and flew to him.

He was softly breathing his life away, the dark blood flowing down his skin of snow and his eyes growing heavy and dim. She kissed him, but Adonis knew not that she kissed him as he died. Cruel as his wound was, the wound in her heart was deeper. She spoke to him, although she knew he could not hear her:—

"You die, O thrice desired,
And my desire has flown like a dream.
Gone with you is the girdle of my beauty,

But I myself must live who am a goddess
And may not follow you.
Kiss me yet once again, the last, long kiss,
Until I draw your soul within my lips
And drink down all your love."

The mountains all were calling and the oak trees answering,
Oh, woe, woe for Adonis. He is dead.
And Echo cried in answer, Oh, woe, woe for Adonis.
And all the Loves wept for him and all the Muses too.

But down in the black underworld Adonis could not hear
them, nor see the crimson flower that sprang up where each
drop of his blood had stained the earth.

PART TWO

Stories of Love and Adventure

5 Cupid and Psyche

*This story is told only by Apuleius, a Latin writer of
the second century A.D. The Latin names of the gods
are therefore used. It is a prettily told tale, after the
manner of Ovid. The writer is entertained by what he
writes; he believes none of it.*

There was once a king who had three daughters, all lovely
maidens, but the youngest, Psyche, excelled her sisters so greatly that beside them she seemed a very goddess consorting with
mere mortals. The fame of her surpassing beauty spread over
the earth, and everywhere men journeyed to gaze upon her
with wonder and adoration and to do her homage as though
she were in truth one of the immortals. They would even say
that Venus herself could not equal this mortal. As they
thronged in ever-growing numbers to worship her loveliness
no one any more gave a thought to Venus herself. Her temples
were neglected; her altars foul with cold ashes; her favorite
towns deserted and falling in ruins. All the honors once hers
were now given to a mere girl destined some day to die.

It may well be believed that the goddess would not put up
with this treatment. As always when she was in trouble she
turned for help to her son, that beautiful winged youth whom
some call Cupid and others Love, against whose arrows there
is no defense, neither in heaven nor on the earth. She told
him her wrongs and as always he was ready to do her bidding. "Use your power," she said, "and make the hussy fall
madly in love with the vilest and most despicable creature
there is in the whole world." And so no doubt he would have
done, if Venus had not first shown him Psyche, never think-

ing in her jealous rage what such beauty might do even to the God of Love himself. As he looked upon her it was as if he had shot one of his arrows into his own heart. He said nothing to his mother, indeed he had no power to utter a word, and Venus left him with the happy confidence that he would swiftly bring about Psyche's ruin.

What happened, however, was not what she had counted on. Psyche did not fall in love with a horrible wretch, she did not fall in love at all. Still more strange, no one fell in love with her. Men were content to look and wonder and worship —and then pass on to marry someone else. Both her sisters, inexpressibly inferior to her, were splendidly married, each to a king. Psyche, the all-beautiful, sat sad and solitary, only admired, never loved. It seemed that no man wanted her.

This was, of course, most disturbing to her parents. Her father finally traveled to an oracle of Apollo to ask his advice on how to get her a good husband. The god answered him, but his words were terrible. Cupid had told him the whole story and had begged for his help. Accordingly Apollo said that Psyche, dressed in deepest mourning, must be set on the summit of a rocky hill and left alone, and that there her destined husband, a fearful winged serpent, stronger than the gods themselves, would come to her and make her his wife.

The misery of all when Psyche's father brought back this lamentable news can be imagined. They dressed the maiden as though for her death and carried her to the hill with greater sorrowing than if it had been to her tomb. But Psyche herself kept her courage. "You should have wept for me before," she told them, "because of the beauty that has drawn down upon me the jealousy of Heaven. Now go, knowing that I am glad the end has come." They went in despairing grief, leaving the lovely helpless creature to meet her doom alone, and they shut themselves in their palace to mourn all their days for her.

On the high hilltop in the darkness Psyche sat, waiting for she knew not what terror. There, as she wept and trembled, a soft breath of air came through the stillness to her, the gentle breathing of Zephyr, sweetest and mildest of winds. She felt it lift her up. She was floating away from the rocky hill and down until she lay upon a grassy meadow soft as a bed and fragrant with flowers. It was so peaceful there, all her trouble left her and she slept. She woke beside a bright river; and on its bank was a mansion stately and beautiful as though built for a god, with pillars of gold and walls of silver and floors inlaid with precious stones. No sound was to be heard; the place seemed deserted and Psyche drew near, awestruck at the sight of such splendor. As she hesitated on the threshold, voices sounded in her ear. She could see no one, but the words they spoke came clearly to her. The house was for her, they told her. She must enter without fear and bathe and refresh herself. Then a banquet table would be spread for her. "We are your servants," the voices said, "ready to do whatever you desire."

The bath was the most delightful, the food the most delicious, she had ever enjoyed. While she dined, sweet music breathed around her: a great choir seemed to sing to a harp, but she could only hear, not see, them. Throughout the day, except for the strange companionship of the voices, she was alone, but in some inexplicable way she felt sure that with the coming of the night her husband would be with her. And so it happened. When she felt him beside her and heard his voice softly murmuring in her ear, all her fears left her. She knew without seeing him that here was no monster or shape of terror, but the lover and husband she had longed and waited for.

This half-and-half companionship could not fully content her; still she was happy and the time passed swiftly. One night, however, her dear though unseen husband spoke gravely to her and warned her that danger in the shape of her two sisters was approaching. "They are coming to the hill where you disappeared, to weep for you," he said; "but you must not let them see you or you will bring great sorrow upon me and ruin to yourself." She promised him she would not, but all the next day she passed in weeping, thinking of her sisters and herself unable to comfort them. She was still in tears when her husband came and even his caresses could not check them. At last he yielded sorrowfully to her great desire. "Do what you will," he said, "but you are seeking your own destruction." Then he warned her solemnly not to be persuaded by anyone to try to see him, on pain of being separated from him forever. Psyche cried out that she would never do so. She would die a hundred times over rather than live without him. "But give me this joy," she said: "to see my sisters." Sadly he promised her that it should be so.

The next morning the two came, brought down from the mountain by Zephyr. Happy and excited, Psyche was waiting for them. It was long before the three could speak to each other; their joy was too great to be expressed except by tears and embraces. But when at last they entered the palace and the elder sisters saw its surpassing treasures; when they sat at the rich banquet and heard the marvelous music, bitter envy took possession of them and a devouring curiosity as to who was the lord of all this magnificence and their sister's husband. But Psyche kept faith; she told them only that he was a young man, away now on a hunting expedition. Then filling their hands with gold and jewels, she had Zephyr bear them back to the hill. They went willingly enough, but their hearts were on fire with jealousy. All their own wealth and good fortune seemed to them as nothing compared with Psyche's, and their envious anger so worked in them that they came finally to plotting how to ruin her.

That very night Psyche's husband warned her once more. She would not listen when he begged her not to let them come again. She never could see him, she reminded him. Was she also to be forbidden to see all others, even her sisters so dear to her? He yielded as before, and very soon the two wicked women arrived, with their plot carefully worked out.

Already, because of Psyche's stumbling and contradictory answers when they asked her what her husband looked like, they had become convinced that she had never set eyes on him and did not really know what he was. They did not tell her this, but they reproached her for hiding her terrible state from them, her own sisters. They had learned, they said, and knew for a fact, that her husband was not a man, but the fearful serpent Apollo's oracle had declared he would be. He was kind now, no doubt, but he would certainly turn upon her some night and devour her.

Psyche, aghast, felt terror flooding her heart instead of love. She had wondered so often why he would never let her see him. There must be some dreadful reason. What did she really know about him? If he was not horrible to look at, then he was cruel to forbid her ever to behold him. In extreme misery, faltering and stammering, she gave her sisters to understand that she could not deny what they said, because she had been with him only in the dark. "There must be something very wrong," she sobbed, "for him so to shun the light of day." And she begged them to advise her.

They had their advice all prepared beforehand. That night she must hide a sharp knife and a lamp near her bed. When her husband was fast asleep she must leave the bed, light the lamp, and get the knife. She must steel herself to plunge it swiftly into the body of the frightful being the light would certainly show her. "We will be near," they said, "and carry you away with us when he is dead."

Then they left her torn by doubt and distracted what to do. She loved him; he was her dear husband. No; he was a horrible serpent and she loathed him. She would kill him— She would not. She must have certainty—She did not want certainty. So all day long her thoughts fought with each other. When evening came, however, she had given the struggle up.

One thing she was determined to do: she would see him.

When at last he lay sleeping quietly, she summoned all her courage and lit the lamp. She tiptoed to the bed and holding the light high above her she gazed at what lay there. Oh, the relief and the rapture that filled her heart. No monster was revealed, but the sweetest and fairest of all creatures, at whose sight the very lamp seemed to shine brighter. In her first shame at her folly and lack of faith, Psyche fell on her knees and would have plunged the knife into her own breast if it had not fallen from her trembling hands. But those same unsteady hands that saved her betrayed her, too, for as she hung over him, ravished at the sight of him and unable to deny herself the bliss of filling her eyes with his beauty, some hot oil fell from the lamp upon his shoulder. He started awake: he saw the light and knew her faithlessness, and without a word he fled from her.

She rushed out after him into the night. She could not see him, but she heard his voice speaking to her. He told her who he was, and sadly bade her farewell. "Love cannot live where there is no trust," he said, and flew away. "The God of Love!" she thought. "He was my husband, and I, wretch that I am, could not keep faith with him. Is he gone from me forever? . . . At any rate," she told herself with rising courage, "I can spend the rest of my life searching for him. If he has no more love left for me, at least I can show him how much I love him." And she started on her journey. She had no idea where to go; she knew only that she would never give up looking for him.

He meanwhile had gone to his mother's chamber to have his wound cared for, but when Venus heard his story and learned that it was Psyche whom he had chosen, she left him angrily alone in his pain, and went forth to find the girl of whom he had made her still more jealous. Venus was determined to show Psyche what it meant to draw down the displeasure of a goddess.

Poor Psyche in her despairing wanderings was trying to win the gods over to her side. She offered ardent prayers to them perpetually, but not one of them would do anything to make Venus their enemy. At last she perceived that there was no hope for her, either in heaven or on earth, and she took a desperate resolve. She would go straight to Venus; she would offer herself humbly to her as her servant, and try to soften her anger. "And who knows," she thought, "if he himself is not there in his mother's house." So she set forth to find the goddess who was looking everywhere for her.

When she came into Venus' presence the goddess laughed aloud and asked her scornfully if she was seeking a husband

Psyche gazed at the sleeping Cupid

since the one she had had would have nothing to do with her because he had almost died of the burning wound she had given him. "But really," she said, "you are so plain and ill-favored a girl that you will never be able to get you a lover except by the most diligent and painful service. I will therefore show my good will to you by training you in such ways." With that she took a great quantity of the smallest of the seeds, wheat and poppy and millet and so on, and mixed them all together in a heap. "By nightfall these must all be sorted," she said. "See to it for your own sake." And with that she departed.

Psyche, left alone, sat still and stared at the heap. Her mind was all in a maze because of the cruelty of the command; and, indeed, it was of no use to start a task so manifestly impossible. But at this direful moment she who had awakened no compassion in mortals or immortals was pitied by the tiniest creatures of the field, the little ants, the swift-runners. They cried to each other, "Come, have mercy on this poor maid and help her diligently." At once they came, waves of them, one after another, and they labored separating and dividing, until what had been a confused mass lay all ordered, every seed with its kind. This was what Venus found when she came back, and very angry she was to see it. "Your work is by no means over," she said. Then she gave Psyche a crust of bread and bade her sleep on the ground while she herself went off to her soft, fragrant couch. Surely if she could keep the girl at hard labor and half starve her, too, that hateful beauty of hers would soon be lost. Until then she must see that her son was securely guarded in his chamber where he was still suffering from his wound. Venus was pleased at the way matters were shaping.

The next morning she devised another task for Psyche, this time a dangerous one. "Down there near the riverbank," she said, "where the bushes grow thick, are sheep with fleeces of gold. Go fetch me some of their shining wool." When the worn girl reached the gently flowing stream, a great longing seized her to throw herself into it and end all her pain and despair. But as she was bending over the water she heard a little voice from near her feet, and looking down saw that it came from a green reed. She must not drown herself, it said. Things were not as bad as that. The sheep were indeed very fierce, but if Psyche would wait until they came out of the bushes toward evening to rest beside the river, she could go into the thicket and find plenty of the golden wool hanging on the sharp briars.

So spoke the kind and gentle reed, and Psyche, following the directions, was able to carry back to her cruel mistress a quantity of the shining fleece. Venus received it with an evil smile. "Someone helped you," she said sharply. "Never did you do this by yourself. However, I will give you an opportunity to prove that you really have the stout heart and the singular prudence you make such a show of. Do you see that black water which falls from the hill yonder? It is the source of the terrible river which is called hateful, the river Styx. You are to fill this flask from it." That was the worst task yet, as Psyche saw when she approached the waterfall. Only a winged creature could reach it, so steep and slimy were the rocks on all sides, and so fearful the onrush of the descending waters. But by this time it must be evident to all the readers of this story (as, perhaps, deep in her heart it had become evident to Psyche herself) that although each of her trials seemed impossibly hard, an excellent way out would always be provided for her. This time her savior was an eagle, who poised on his great wings beside her, seized the flask from her with his beak and brought it back to her full of the black water.

But Venus kept on. One cannot but accuse her of some stupidity. The only effect of all that had happened was to make her try again. She gave Psyche a box which she was to carry to the underworld and ask Proserpine to fill with some of her beauty. She was to tell her that Venus really needed it, she was so worn-out from nursing her sick son. Obediently as always Psyche went forth to look for the road to Hades. She found her guide in a tower she passed. It gave her careful directions how to get to Proserpine's palace, first through a great hole in the earth, then down to the river of death, where she must give the ferryman, Charon, a penny to take her across. From there the road led straight to the palace. Cerberus, the three-headed dog, guarded the doors, but if she gave him a cake he would be friendly and let her pass.

All happened, of course, as the tower had foretold. Proserpine was willing to do Venus a service, and Psyche, greatly encouraged, bore back the box, returning far more quickly than she had gone down.

Her next trial she brought upon herself through her curiosity and, still more, her vanity. She felt that she must see what that beauty-charm in the box was; and, perhaps, use a little of it herself. She knew quite as well as Venus did that her looks were not improved by what she had gone through, and always in her mind was the thought that she might suddenly meet Cupid. If only she could make herself more lovely for him! She was unable to resist the temptation; she opened the box. To her sharp disappointment she saw nothing there; it seemed empty. Immediately, however, a deadly languor took possession of her and she fell into a heavy sleep.

At this juncture the God of Love himself stepped forward.

Cupid was healed of his wound by now and longing for Psyche. It is a difficult matter to keep Love imprisoned. Venus had locked the door, but there were the windows. All Cupid had to do was to fly out and start looking for his wife. She was lying almost beside the palace, and he found her at once. In a moment he had wiped the sleep from her eyes and put it back into the box. Then waking her with just a prick from one of his arrows, and scolding her a little for her curiosity, he bade her take Proserpine's box to his mother and he assured her that all thereafter would be well.

While the joyful Psyche hastened on her errand, the god flew up to Olympus. He wanted to make certain that Venus would give them no more trouble, so he went straight to Jupiter himself. The Father of Gods and Men consented at once to all that Cupid asked—"Even though," he said, "you have done me great harm in the past—seriously injured my good name and my dignity by making me change myself into a bull and a swan and so on. . . . However, I cannot refuse you."

Then he called a full assembly of the gods, and announced to all, including Venus, that Cupid and Psyche were formally married, and that he proposed to bestow immortality upon the bride. Mercury brought Psyche into the palace of the gods, and Jupiter himself gave her the ambrosia to taste which made her immortal. This, of course, completely changed the situation. Venus could not object to a goddess for her daughter-in-law; the alliance had become eminently suitable. No doubt she reflected also that Psyche, living up in heaven with a husband and children to care for, could not be much on the earth to turn men's heads and interfere with her own worship.

So all came to a most happy end. Love and the Soul (for that is what Psyche means) had sought and, after sore trials, found each other; and that union could never be broken.

6 Eight Brief Tales of Lovers

PYRAMUS AND THISBE

This story is found only in Ovid. It is quite charac-teristic of him at his best: well-told; several rhetorical monologues; a little essay on Love by the way.

Once upon a time the deep red berries of the mulberry tree were white as snow. The change in color came about strangely and sadly. The death of two young lovers was the cause.

Pyramus and Thisbe, he the most beautiful youth and she the loveliest maiden of all the East, lived in Babylon, the city of Queen Semiramis, in houses so close together that one wall was common to both. Growing up thus side by side they learned to love each other. They longed to marry, but their parents forbade. Love, however, cannot be forbidden. The more that flame is covered up, the hotter it burns. Also love can always find a way. It was impossible that these two whose hearts were on fire should be kept apart.

In the wall both houses shared there was a little chink. No one before had noticed it, but there is nothing a lover does not notice. Our two young people discovered it and through it they were able to whisper sweetly back and forth. Thisbe on one side, Pyramus on the other. The hateful wall that separated them had become their means of reaching each other. "But for you we could touch, kiss," they would say. "But at least you let us speak together. You give a passage for loving words to reach loving ears. We are not ungrateful." So they would talk, and as night came on and they must part, each would press on the wall kisses that could not go through to the lips on the other side.

Every morning when the dawn had put out the stars, and the sun's rays had dried the hoarfrost on the grass, they would

steal to the crack and, standing there, now utter words of burning love and now lament their hard fate, but always in softest
whispers. Finally a day came when they could endure no
longer. They decided that that very night they would try to
slip away and steal out through the city into the open country
where at last they could be together in freedom. They agreed
to meet at a well-known place, the Tomb of Ninus, under a
tree there, a tall mulberry full of snow-white berries, near
which a cool spring bubbled up. The plan pleased them and it
seemed to them the day would never end.

At last the sun sank into the sea and night arose. In the
darkness Thisbe crept out and made her way in all secrecy to
the tomb. Pyramus had not come; still she waited for him,
her love making her bold. But of a sudden she saw by the
light of the moon a lioness. The fierce beast had made a kill;
her jaws were bloody and she was coming to slake her thirst
in the spring. She was still far enough away for Thisbe to
escape, but as she fled she dropped her cloak. The lioness came
upon it on her way back to her lair and she mouthed it and
tore it before disappearing into the woods. That is what Pyramus saw when he appeared a few minutes later. Before him
lay the bloodstained shreds of the cloak and clear in the dust
were the tracks of the lioness. The conclusion was inevitable.
He never doubted that he knew all. Thisbe was dead. He had
let his love, a tender maiden, come alone to a place full of
danger, and not been there first to protect her. "It is I who
killed you," he said. He lifted up from the trampled dust what
was left of the cloak and kissing it again and again carried
it to the mulberry tree. "Now," he said, "you shall drink my
blood too." He drew his sword and plunged it into his side.
The blood spurted up over the berries and dyed them a dark
red.

Thisbe, although terrified of the lioness, was still more
afraid to fail her lover. She ventured to go back to the tree of
the tryst, the mulberry with the shining white fruit. She could
not find it. A tree was there, but not one gleam of white was
on the branches. As she stared at it, something moved on the
ground beneath. She started back shuddering. But in a moment, peering through the shadows, she saw what was there.
It was Pyramus, bathed in blood and dying. She flew to him
and threw her arms around him. She kissed his cold lips and
begged him to look at her, to speak to her. "It is I, your Thisbe,
your dearest," she cried to him. At the sound of her name he
opened his heavy eyes for one look. Then death closed
them.

She saw his sword fallen from his hand and beside it her
cloak stained and torn. She understood all. "Your own hand

killed you," she said, "and your love for me. I too can be brave. I too can love. Only death would have had the power to separate us. It shall not have that power now." She plunged into her heart the sword that was still wet with his life's blood.

The gods were pitiful at the end, and the lovers' parents too. The deep red fruit of the mulberry is the everlasting memorial of these true lovers, and one urn holds the ashes of the two whom not even death could part.

ORPHEUS AND EURYDICE

The account of Orpheus with the Argonauts is told only by Apollonius of Rhodes, a third-century Greek poet. The rest of the story is told best by two Roman poets, Virgil and Ovid, in very much the same style. The Latin names of the gods are therefore used here. Apollonius influenced Virgil a good deal. Indeed, any one of the three might have written the entire story as it stands.

The very earliest musicians were the gods. Athena was not distinguished in that line, but she invented the flute although she never played upon it. Hermes made the lyre and gave it to Apollo who drew from it sounds so melodious that when he played in Olympus the gods forgot all else. Hermes also made the shepherd-pipe for himself and drew enchanting music from it. Pan made the pipe of reeds which can sing as sweetly as the nightingale in spring. The Muses had no instrument peculiar to them, but their voices were lovely beyond compare.

Next in order came a few mortals so excellent in their art that they almost equaled the divine performers. Of these by far the greatest was Orpheus. On his mother's side he was more than mortal. He was the son of one of the Muses and a Thracian prince. His mother gave him the gift of music and Thrace where he grew up fostered it. The Thracians were the most musical of the peoples of Greece. But Orpheus had no rival there or anywhere except the gods alone. There was no limit to his power when he played and sang. No one and nothing could resist him.

> In the deep still woods upon the Thracian mountains
> Orpheus with his singing lyre led the trees,
> Led the wild beasts of the wilderness.

Everything animate and inanimate followed him. He moved the rocks on the hillside and turned the courses of the rivers.

Little is told about his life before his ill-fated marriage, for which he is even better known than for his music, but he went on one famous expedition and proved himself a most useful member of it. He sailed with Jason on the *Argo*, and when the heroes were weary or the rowing was especially difficult he would strike his lyre and they would be aroused to fresh zeal and their oars would smite the sea together in time to the melody. Or if a quarrel threatened he would play so tenderly and soothingly that the fiercest spirits would grow calm and forget their anger. He saved the heroes, too, from the Sirens. When they heard far over the sea singing so enchantingly sweet that it drove out all other thoughts except a desperate longing to hear more, and they turned the ship to the shore where the Sirens sat, Orpheus snatched up his lyre and played a tune so clear and ringing that it drowned the sound of those lovely fatal voices. The ship was put back on her course and the winds sped her away from the dangerous place. If Orpheus had not been there the Argonauts, too, would have left their bones on the Sirens' island.

Where he first met and how he wooed the maiden he loved, Eurydice, we are not told, but it is clear that no maiden he wanted could have resisted the power of his song. They were married, but their joy was brief. Directly after the wedding, as the bride walked in a meadow with her bridesmaids, a viper stung her and she died. Orpheus' grief was overwhelming. He could not endure it. He determined to go down to the world of death and try to bring Eurydice back. He said to himself,

> With my song
> I will charm Demeter's daughter,
> I will charm the Lord of the Dead,
> Moving their hearts with my melody.
> I will bear her away from Hades.

He dared more than any other man ever dared for his love. He took the fearsome journey to the underworld. There he struck his lyre, and at the sound all that vast multitude were charmed to stillness. The dog Cerberus relaxed his guard; the wheel of Ixion stood motionless; Sisiphus sat at rest upon his stone; Tantalus forgot his thirst; for the first time the faces of the dread goddesses, the Furies, were wet with tears. The ruler of Hades drew near to listen with his queen. Orpheus sang,

> O Gods who rule the dark and silent world,
> To you all born of a woman needs must come.
> All lovely things at last go down to you.
> You are the debtor who is always paid.
> A little while we tarry up on earth.
> Then we are yours forever and forever.
> But I seek one who came to you too soon.

The bud was plucked before the flower bloomed.
I tried to bear my loss. I could not bear it.
Love was too strong a god. O King, you know
If that old tale men tell is true, how once
The flowers saw the rape of Proserpine.
Then weave again for sweet Eurydice
Life's pattern that was taken from the loom
Too quickly. See, I ask a little thing,
Only that you will lend, not give, her to me.
She shall be yours when her years' span is full.

No one under the spell of his voice could refuse him anything. He

> Drew iron tears down Pluto's cheek,
> And made Hell grant what Love did seek.

They summoned Eurydice and gave her to him, but upon one condition: that he would not look back at her as she followed him, until they had reached the upper world. So the two passed through the great doors of Hades to the path which would take them out of the darkness, climbing up and up. He knew that she must be just behind him, but he longed unutterably to give one glance to make sure. But now they were almost there, the blackness was turning gray; now he had stepped out joyfully into the daylight. Then he turned to her. It was too soon; she was still in the cavern. He saw her in the dim light, and he held out his arms to clasp her; but on the instant she was gone. She had slipped back into the darkness. All he heard was one faint word, "Farewell."

Desperately he tried to rush after her and follow her down, but he was not allowed. The gods would not consent to his entering the world of the dead a second time, while he was still alive. He was forced to return to the earth alone, in utter desolation. Then he forsook the company of men. He wandered through the wild solitudes of Thrace, comfortless except for his lyre, playing, always playing, and the rocks and the rivers and the trees heard him gladly, his only companions. But at last a band of Maenads came upon him. They were as frenzied as those who killed Pentheus so horribly. They slew the gentle musician, tearing him limb from limb, and flung the severed head into the swift river Hebrus. It was borne along past the river's mouth on to the Lesbian shore, nor had it suffered any change from the sea when the Muses found it and buried it in the sanctuary of the island. His limbs they gathered and placed in a tomb at the foot of Mount Olympus, and there to this day the nightingales sing more sweetly than anywhere else.

CEYX AND ALCYONE

Ovid is the best source for this story. The exaggeration of the storm is typically Roman. Sleep's abode with its charming details shows Ovid's power of description. The names of the gods, of course, are Latin.

Ceyx, a king in Thessaly, was the son of Lucifer, the light-bearer, the star that brings in the day, and all his father's bright gladness was in his face. His wife Alcyone was also of high descent; she was the daughter of Aeolus, King of the Winds. The two loved each other devotedly and were never willingly apart. Nevertheless, a time came when he decided he must leave her and make a long journey across the sea. Various matters had happened to disturb him and he wished to consult the oracle, men's refuge in trouble. When Alcyone learned what he was planning she was overwhelmed with grief and terror. She told him with streaming tears and in a voice broken with sobs, that she knew as few others could the power of the winds upon the sea. In her father's palace she had watched them from her childhood, their stormy meetings, the black clouds they summoned and the wild red lightning. "And many a time upon the beach," she said, "I have seen the broken planks of ships tossed up. Oh, do not go. But if I cannot persuade you, at least take me with you. I can endure whatever comes to us together."

Ceyx was deeply moved, for he loved him no better than he loved her, but his purpose held fast. He felt that he must get counsel from the oracle and he would not hear of her sharing the perils of the voyage. She had to yield and let him go alone. Her heart was so heavy when she bade him farewell it was as if she foresaw what was to come. She waited on the shore watching the ship until it sailed out of sight.

That very night a fierce storm broke over the sea. The winds all met in a mad hurricane, and the waves rose up mountain-high. Rain fell in such sheets that the whole heaven seemed falling into the sea and the sea seemed leaping up into the sky. The men on the quivering, battered boat were mad with terror, all except one who thought only of Alcyone and re-joiced that she was in safety. Her name was on his lips when the ship sank and the waters closed over him.

Alcyone was counting off the days. She kept herself busy, weaving a robe for him against his return and another for herself to be lovely in when he first saw her. And many times each day she prayed to the gods for him, to Juno most of all. The goddess was touched by those prayers for one who had long been dead. She summoned her messenger Iris and ordered her to go to the house of Somnus, God of Sleep, and bid him send a dream to Alcyone to tell her the truth about Ceyx.

The abode of Sleep is near the black country of the Cimmerians, in a deep valley where the sun never shines and dusky twilight wraps all things in shadows. No cock crows there; no watchdog breaks the silence; no branches rustle in the breeze; no clamor of tongues disturbs the peace. The only sound comes from the gently flowing stream of Lethe, the river of forgetfulness, where the waters murmuring entice to sleep. Before the door poppies bloom, and other drowsy herbs. Within, the God of Slumber lies upon a couch downy-soft and black of hue. There came Iris in her cloak of many colors, trailing across the sky in a rainbow curve, and the dark house was lit up with the shining of her garments. Even so, it was hard for her to make the god open his heavy eyes and understand what he was required to do. As soon as she was sure he was really awake and her errand done, Iris sped away, fearful that she too might sink forever into slumber.

The old God of Sleep aroused his son, Morpheus, skilled in assuming the form of any and every human being, and he gave him Juno's orders. On noiseless wings Morpheus flew through the darkness and stood by Alcyone's bed. He had taken on the face and form of Ceyx drowned. Naked and dripping wet he bent over her couch. "Poor wife," he said, "look, your husband is here. Do you know me or is my face changed in death? I am dead, Alcyone. Your name was on my lips when the waters overwhelmed me. There is no hope for me any more. But give me your tears. Let me not go down to the shadowy land unwept." In her sleep Alcyone moaned and stretched her arms out to clasp him. She cried aloud, "Wait for me. I will go with you," and her cry awakened her. She woke to the conviction that her husband was dead, that what she had seen was no dream, but himself. "I saw him, on that very spot," she told herself. "So piteous he looked. He is dead and soon I shall die. Could I stay here when his dear body is tossed about in the waves? I will not leave you, my husband; I will not try to live."

With the first daylight she went to the shore, to the headland where she had stood to watch him sail away. As she gazed seaward, far off on the water she saw something floating. The tide was setting in and the thing came nearer and nearer until she knew it was a dead body. She watched it with pity and horror in her heart as it drifted slowly toward her. And now it was close to the headland, almost beside her. It was he, Ceyx, her husband. She ran and leaped into the water, crying, "Husband, dearest!"—and then oh, wonder, instead of sinking

into the waves she was flying over them. She had wings; her
body was covered with feathers. She had been changed into
a bird. The gods were kind. They did the same to Ceyx. As
she flew to the body it was gone, and he, changed into a
bird like herself, joined her. But their love was unchanged.
They are always seen together, flying or riding the
waves.

Every year there are seven days on end when the sea lies
still and calm; no breath of wind stirs the waters. These are
the days when Alcyone broods over her nest floating on the
sea. After the young birds are hatched the charm is broken;
but each winter these days of perfect peace come, and they
are called after her, Alcyon, or, more commonly, Halcyon
days.

> While birds of calm sit brooding on the charmed wave.

PYGMALION AND GALATEA

> *This story is told only by Ovid and the Goddess of Love
> is therefore Venus. It is an excellent example of Ovid's
> way of dressing up a myth, for which see the Introduc-
> tion.*

A gifted young sculptor of Cyprus, named Pygmalion, was
a woman-hater.

> Detesting the faults beyond measure which nature
> has given to women,

he resolved never to marry. His art, he told himself, was
enough for him. Nevertheless, the statue he made and devoted
all his genius to was that of a woman. Either he could not
dismiss what he so disapproved of from his mind as easily as
from his life, or else he was bent on forming a perfect woman
and showing men the deficiencies of the kind they had to put
up with.

However that was, he labored long and devotedly on the
statue and produced a most exquisite work of art. But lovely
as it was he could not rest content. He kept on working at it
and daily under his skillful fingers it grew more beautiful. No
woman ever born, no statue ever made, could approach it.
When nothing could be added to its perfections, a strange fate
had befallen its creator: he had fallen in love, deeply, passionately in love, with the thing he had made. It must be said
in explanation that the statue did not look like a statue; no
one would have thought it was ivory or stone, but warm

Pygmalion and Galatea

human flesh, motionless for a moment only. Such was the wondrous power of this disdainful young man. The supreme achievement of art was his, the art of concealing art.

But from that time on, the sex he scorned had their revenge. No hopeless lover of a living maiden was ever so desperately unhappy as Pygmalion. He kissed those enticing lips—they could not kiss him back; he caressed her hands, her face—they were unresponsive; he took her in his arms—she remained a cold and passive form. For a time he tried to pretend, as children do with their toys. He would dress her in rich robes, trying the effect of one delicate or glowing color after another, and imagine she was pleased. He would bring her the gifts real maidens love, little birds and gay flowers and the shining tears of amber Phaëthon's sisters weep, and then dream that she thanked him with eager affection. He put her to bed at night, and tucked her in all soft and warm, as little girls do their dolls. But he was not a child; he could not keep on pretending. In the end he gave up. He loved a lifeless thing and he was utterly and hopelessly wretched.

This singular passion did not long remain concealed from the Goddess of Passionate Love. Venus was interested in something that seldom came her way, a new kind of lover, and she determined to help a young man who could be enamored and yet original.

The feast day of Venus was, of course, especially honored in Cyprus, the island which first received the goddess after she rose from the foam. Snow-white heifers whose horns had been gilded were offered in numbers to her; the heavenly odor of incense was spread through the island from her many altars; crowds thronged her temples; not an unhappy lover but was there with his gift, praying that his love might turn kind. There too, of course, was Pygmalion. He dared to ask the goddess only that he might find a maiden like his statue, but Venus knew what he really wanted and as a sign that she favored his prayer the flame on the altar he stood before leaped up three times, blazing into the air.

Very thoughtful at this good omen Pygmalion sought his house and his love, the thing he had created and given his heart to. There she stood on her pedestal, entrancingly beautiful. He caressed her and then he started back. Was it self-deception or did she really feel warm to his touch? He kissed her lips, a long lingering kiss, and felt them grow soft beneath his. He touched her arms, her shoulders; their hardness vanished. It was like watching wax soften in the sun. He clasped her wrist; blood was pulsing there. Venus, he thought. This is the goddess's doing. And with unutterable gratitude and joy he put his arms around his love and saw her smile into his eyes and blush.

Venus herself graced their marriage with her presence, but what happened after that we do not know, except that Pygmalion named the maiden Galatea, and that their son, Paphos, gave his name to Venus' favorite city.

BAUCIS AND PHILEMON

Ovid is the only source for this story. It shows especially well his love of details and the skillful way he uses them to make a fairy tale seem realistic. The Latin names of the gods are used.

In the Phrygian hill-country there were once two trees which all the peasants near and far pointed out as a great marvel, and no wonder, for one was an oak and the other a linden, yet they grew from a single trunk. The story of how this came about is a proof of the immeasurable power of the gods, and also of the way they reward the humble and the pious.

Sometimes when Jupiter was tired of eating ambrosia and drinking nectar up in Olympus and even a little weary of listening to Apollo's lyre and watching the Graces dance, he would come down to the earth, disguise himself as a mortal and go looking for adventures. His favorite companion on these tours was Mercury, the most entertaining of all the gods, the shrewdest and the most resourceful. On this particular trip Jupiter had determined to find out how hospitable the people of Phrygia were. Hospitality was, of course, very important to him, since all guests, all who seek shelter in a strange land, were under his especial protection.

The two gods, accordingly, took on the appearance of poor wayfarers and wandered through the land, knocking at each lowly hut or great house they came to and asking for food and a place to rest in. Not one would admit them; every time they were dismissed insolently and the door barred against them. They made trial of hundreds; all treated them in the same way. At last they came upon a little hovel of the humblest sort, poorer than any they had yet found, with a roof made only of reeds. But here, when they knocked, the door was opened wide and a cheerful voice bade them enter. They had to stoop to pass through the low entrance, but once inside they found themselves in a snug and very clean room, where a kindly-faced old man and woman welcomed them in the friendliest fashion and bustled about to make them comfortable.

The old man set a bench near the fire and told them to stretch out on it and rest their tired limbs, and the old woman threw a soft covering over it. Her name was Baucis, she told the strangers, and her husband was called Philemon. They had lived in that cottage all their married life and had always been happy. "We are poor folk," she said, "but poverty isn't so bad when you're willing to own up to it, and a contented spirit is a great help, too." All the while she was talking, she was busy doing things for them. The coals under the ashes on the dark hearth she fanned to life until a cheerful fire was burning. Over this she hung a little kettle full of water and just as it began to boil her husband came in with a fine cabbage he had got from the garden. Into the kettle it went, with a piece of the pork which was hanging from one of the beams. While this cooked Baucis set the table with her trembling old hands. One table-leg was too short, but she propped it up with a bit of broken dish. On the board she placed olives and radishes and several eggs which she had roasted in the ashes. By this time the cabbage and bacon were done, and the old man pushed two rickety couches up to the table and bade his guests recline and eat.

Presently he brought them cups of beechwood and an earthenware mixing bowl which held some wine very like vinegar, plentifully diluted with water. Philemon, however, was clearly proud and happy at being able to add such cheer to the supper and he kept on the watch to refill each cup as soon as it was emptied. The two old folks were so pleased and excited by the success of their hospitality that only very slowly a strange thing dawned upon them. The mixing bowl kept full. No matter how many cups were poured out from it, the level of the wine stayed the same, up to the brim. As they saw this wonder each looked in terror at the other, and dropping their eyes they prayed silently. Then in quavering voices and trembling all over they begged their guests to pardon the poor refreshments they had offered. "We have a goose," the old man said, "which we ought to have given your lordships. But if you will only wait, it shall be done at once." To catch the goose, however, proved beyond their powers. They tried in vain until they were worn out, while Jupiter and Mercury watched them greatly entertained.

But when both Philemon and Baucis had had to give up the chase panting and exhausted, the gods felt that the time had come for them to take action. They were really very kind. "You have been hosts to gods," they said, "and you shall have your reward. This wicked country which despises the poor stranger will be bitterly punished, but not you." They then escorted the two out of the hut and told them to look around them. To their amazement all they saw was water. The whole countryside had disappeared. A great lake surrounded them. Their neighbors had not been good to the old couple; nevertheless standing there they wept for them. But of a sudden their tears were dried by an overwhelming wonder. Before their eyes the tiny, lowly hut which had been their home for so long was turned into a stately pillared temple of whitest marble with a golden roof.

"Good people," Jupiter said, "ask whatever you want and you shall have your wish." The old people exchanged a hurried whisper, then Philemon spoke. "Let us be your priests, guarding this temple for you—and oh, since we have lived so long together, let neither of us ever have to live alone. Grant that we may die together."

The gods assented, well pleased with the two. A long time they served in that grand building, and the story does not say whether they ever missed their little cozy room with its cheerful hearth. But one day standing before the marble and golden magnificence they fell to talking about the former life, which had been so hard and yet so happy. By now both were in extreme old age. Suddenly as they exchanged memories each saw the other putting forth leaves. Then bark was growing around them. They had time only to cry, "Farewell, dear companion." As the words passed their lips they became trees, but still they were together. The linden and the oak grew from one trunk.

From far and wide people came to admire the wonder, and always wreaths of flowers hung on the branches in honor of the pious and faithful pair.

ENDYMION

I have taken this story from the third-century poet Theocritus. He tells it in the true Greek manner, simply and with restraint.

This youth, whose name is so famous, has a very short history. Some of the poets say he was a king, some a hunter, but most of them say he was a shepherd. All agree that he was a youth of surpassing beauty and that this was the cause of his singular fate.

> Endymion the shepherd,
> As his flock he guarded,
> She, the Moon, Selene,
> Saw him, loved him, sought him,

> Coming down from heaven
> To the glade on Latmus,
> Kissed him, lay beside him.
> Blessed is his fortune.
> Evermore he slumbers,
> Tossing not nor turning,
> Endymion the shepherd.

He never woke to see the shining silvery form bending over him. In all the stories about him he sleeps forever, immortal, but never conscious. Wondrously beautiful he lies on the mountainside, motionless and remote as if in death, but warm and living, and night after night the Moon visits him and covers him with her kisses. It is said that this magic slumber was her doing. She lulled him to sleep so that she might always find him and caress him as she pleased. But it is said, too, that her passion brings her only a burden of pain, fraught with many sighs.

DAPHNE

> *Ovid alone tells this story. Only a Roman could have written it. A Greek poet would never have thought of an elegant dress and coiffure for the wood nymph.*

Daphne was another of those independent, love-and-marriage-hating young huntresses who are met with so often in the mythological stories. She is said to have been Apollo's first love. It is not strange that she fled from him. One unfortunate maiden after another beloved of the gods had had to kill her child secretly or be killed herself. The best such a one could expect was exile, and many women thought that worse than death. The ocean nymphs who visited Prometheus on the crag in the Caucasus spoke only the most ordinary common sense when they said to him:—

> May you never, oh, never behold me
> Sharing the couch of a god.
> May none of the dwellers in heaven
> Draw near to me ever.
> Such love as the high gods know,
> From whose eyes none can hide,
> May that never be mine.
> To war with a god-lover is not war,
> It is despair.

Daphne would have agreed completely. But indeed she did not want any mortal lovers either. Her father, the river-god Peneus, was greatly tried because she refused all the handsome and eligible young men who wooed her. He would scold her gently and lament, "Am I never to have a grandson?" But when she threw her arms around him and coaxed him, "Father, dearest, let me be like Diana," he would yield and she would be off to the deep woods, blissful in her freedom.

But at last Apollo saw her, and everything ended for her. She was hunting, her dress short to the knee, her arms bare, her hair in wild disarray. Nevertheless she was enchantingly beautiful. Apollo thought, "What would she not look like properly dressed and with her hair nicely arranged?" The idea made the fire that was devouring his heart blaze up even more fiercely and he started off in pursuit. Daphne fled, and she was an excellent runner. Even Apollo for a few minutes was hard put to it to overtake her; still, of course, he soon gained. As he ran he sent his voice ahead of him, entreating her, persuading her, reassuring her. "Do not fear," he called. "Stop and find out who I am, no rude rustic or shepherd. I am the Lord of Delphi, and I love you."

But Daphne flew on, even more frightened than before. If Apollo was indeed following her, the case was hopeless, but she was determined to struggle to the very end. It had all but come; she felt his breath upon her neck, but there in front of her the trees opened and she saw her father's river. She screamed to him, "Help me! Father, help me!" At the words a dragging numbness came upon her, her feet seemed rooted in the earth she had been so swiftly speeding over. Bark was enclosing her; leaves were sprouting forth. She had been changed into a tree, a laurel.

Apollo watched the transformation with dismay and grief. "O fairest of maidens, you are lost to me," he mourned. "But at least you shall be my tree. With your leaves my victors shall wreathe their brows. You shall have your part in all my triumphs. Apollo and his laurel shall be joined together wherever songs are sung and stories told."

The beautiful shining-leaved tree seemed to nod its waving head as if in happy consent.

ALPHEUS AND ARETHUSA

This story is told in full only by Ovid. There is nothing noteworthy in his treatment of it. The verse at the end is taken from the Alexandrian poet Moschus.

In Ortygia, an island which formed part of Syracuse, the greatest city of Sicily, there is a sacred spring called Arethusa. Once, however, Arethusa was not water or even a water nymph, but a fair young huntress and a follower of Artemis. Like her mistress she would have nothing to do with men; like her she loved hunting and the freedom of the forest.

One day, tired and hot from the chase, she came upon a crystal-clear river deeply shaded by silvery willows. No more delightful place for a bath could be imagined. Arethusa undressed and slipped into the cool delicious water. For a while she swam idly to and fro in utter peace; then she seemed to feel something stir in the depths beneath her. Frightened, she sprang to the bank—and as she did so she heard a voice: "Why such haste, fairest maiden?" Without looking back she fled away from the stream to the woods and ran with all the speed her fear gave her. She was hotly pursued and by one stronger if not swifter than she. The unknown called to her to stop. He told her he was the god of the river, Alpheus, and that he was following her only because he loved her. But she wanted none of him; she had but one thought, to escape. It was a long race, but the issue was never in doubt; he could keep on running longer than she. Worn out at last, Arethusa called to her goddess, and not in vain. Artemis changed her into a spring of water, and cleft the earth so that a tunnel was made under the sea from Greece to Sicily. Arethusa plunged down and emerged in Ortygia, where the place in which her spring bubbles up is holy ground, sacred to Artemis.

But it is said that even so she was not free of Alpheus. The story is that the god, changing back into a river, followed her through the tunnel and that now his water mingles with hers in the fountain. They say that often Greek flowers are seen coming up from the bottom, and that if a wooden cup is thrown into the Alpheus in Greece, it will reappear in Arethusa's well in Sicily.

Alpheus makes his way far under the deep with his waters,
Travels to Arethusa with bridal gifts, fair leaves and flowers.
Teacher of strange ways is Love, that knavish boy, maker of mischief.
With his magical spell he taught a river to dive.

7 The Quest of the Golden Fleece

This is the title of a long poem, very popular in classical days, by the third-century poet Apollonius of Rhodes. He tells the whole story of the Quest except the part about Jason and Pelias which I have taken from Pindar. It is the subject of one of his most famous odes, written in the first half of the fifth century. Apollonius ends his poem with the return of the heroes to Greece. I have added the account of what Jason and Medea did there, taking it from the fifth-century tragic poet Euripides, who made it the subject of one of his best plays.

These three writers are very unlike each other. No prose paraphrase can give any idea of Pindar, except, perhaps, something of his singular power for vivid and minutely detailed description. Readers of the Aeneid will be reminded of Virgil by Apollonius. The difference between Euripides' Medea and Apollonius' heroine and also Virgil's Dido is in its degree a measure of what Greek tragedy was.

The first hero in Europe who undertook a great journey was the leader of the Quest of the Golden Fleece. He was supposed to have lived a generation earlier than the most famous Greek traveler, the hero of the *Odyssey*. It was of course a journey by water. Rivers, lakes, and seas, were the only highways; there were no roads. All the same, a voyager had to face perils not only on the deep, but on the land as well. Ships did not sail by night, and any place where sailors put in might harbor a monster or a magician who could work more deadly harm than storm and shipwreck. High courage was necessary to travel, especially outside of Greece.

No story proved this fact better than the account of what the heroes suffered who sailed in the ship *Argo* to find the Golden Fleece. It may be doubted, indeed, if there ever was a voyage on which sailors had to face so many and such varied dangers. However, they were all heroes of renown, some of them the greatest in Greece, and they were quite equal to their adventures.

The tale of the Golden Fleece begins with a Greek king named Athamas, who got tired of his wife, put her away, and married another, the Princess Ino. Nephele, the first wife, was afraid for her two children, especially the boy, Phrixus. She thought the second wife would try to kill him so that her own son could inherit the kingdom, and she was right. This second wife came from a great family. Her father was Cadmus, the excellent King of Thebes; her mother and her three sisters were women of blameless lives. But she herself, Ino, determined to bring about the little boy's death, and she made an elaborate plan how this was to be done. Somehow she got possession of all the seed-corn and parched it before the men went out for the sowing, so that, of course, there was no harvest at all. When the King sent a man to ask the oracle what he should do in this fearful distress, she persuaded or, more probably, bribed the messenger to say that the oracle had declared the corn would not grow again unless they offered up the young Prince as a sacrifice.

The people, threatened with starvation, forced the King to yield and permit the boy's death. To the later Greeks the idea of such a sacrifice was as horrible as it is to us, and when it played a part in a story they almost always changed it into something less shocking. As this tale has come down to us, when the boy had been taken to the altar a wondrous ram, with a fleece of pure gold, snatched him and his sister up and bore them away through the air. Hermes had sent him in answer to their mother's prayer.

While they were crossing the strait which separates Europe and Asia, the girl, whose name was Helle, slipped and fell into the water. She was drowned; and the strait was named for her: the Sea of Helle, the Hellespont. The boy came safely to land, to the country of Colchis on the Unfriendly Sea (the Black Sea, which had not yet become friendly). The Colchians were a fierce people. Nevertheless, they were kind to Phrixus; and their King, Æetes, let him marry one of his daughters. It seems odd that Phrixus sacrificed to Zeus the ram that had saved him, in gratitude for having been saved; but he did so, and he gave the precious Golden Fleece to King Æetes.

Phrixus had an uncle who was by rights a king in Greece, but had had his kingdom taken away from him by his nephew, a man named Pelias. The King's young son, Jason, the rightful heir to the kingdom, had been sent secretly away to a place of safety, and when he was grown he came boldly back to claim the kingdom from his wicked cousin.

The usurper Pelias had been told by an oracle that he would die at the hands of kinsmen, and that he should beware of anyone whom he saw shod with only a single sandal. In due time such a man came to the town. One foot was bare, although in all other ways he was well-clad—a garment fitting close to his splendid limbs, and around his shoulders a leopard's skin to turn the showers. He had not shorn the bright locks of his hair; they ran rippling down his back. He went straight into the town and entered the marketplace fearlessly, at the time when the multitude filled it.

None knew him, but one and another wondered at him and said, "Can he be Apollo? Or Aphrodite's lord? Not one of Poseidon's bold sons, for they are dead." So they questioned each other. But Pelias came in hot haste at the tidings and when he saw the single sandal he was afraid. He hid his terror in his heart, however, and addressed the stranger: "What country is your fatherland? No hateful and defiling lies, I beg you. Tell me the truth." With gentle words the other answered: "I have come to my home to recover the ancient honor of my house, this land no longer ruled aright, which Zeus gave to my father. I am your cousin, and they call me by the name of Jason. You and I must rule ourselves by the law of right—not appeal to brazen swords or spears. Keep all the wealth you have taken, the flocks and the tawny herds of cattle and the fields, but the sovereign scepter and the throne release to me, so that no evil quarrel will arise from them."

Pelias gave him a soft answer. "So shall it be. But one thing must first be done. The dead Phrixus bids us bring back the Golden Fleece and thus bring back his spirit to his home. The oracle has spoken. But for me, already old age is my companion, while the flower of your youth is only now coming into full bloom. Do you go upon this quest, and I swear with Zeus as witness that I will give up the kingdom and the sovereign rule to you." So he spoke, believing in his heart that no one could make the attempt and come back alive.

The idea of the great adventure was delightful to Jason. He agreed, and let it be known everywhere that this would be a voyage indeed. The young men of Greece joyfully met the challenge. They came, all the best and noblest, to join the company. Hercules, the greatest of all heroes, was there; Orpheus, the master musician; Castor with his brother Pollux; Achilles' father, Peleus; and many another. Hera was helping Jason, and it was she who kindled in each one the desire not to be left behind nursing a life without peril by his mother's side, but even at the price of death to drink with his comrades the peerless elixir of valor. They set sail in the ship *Argo*. Jason took in his hands a golden goblet and, pouring a libation of wine into the sea, called upon Zeus whose lance is the lightning to speed them on their way.

Great perils lay before them, and some of them paid with their lives for drinking that peerless elixir. They put in first at Lemnos, a strange island where only women lived. They had risen up against the men and had killed them all, except one, the old king. His daughter, Hypsipyle, a leader among the women, had spared her father and set him afloat on the sea in a hollow chest, which finally carried him to safety. These fierce creatures, however, welcomed the Argonauts, and helped them with good gifts of food and wine and garments before they sailed away.

Soon after they left Lemnos the Argonauts lost Hercules from the company. A lad named Hylas, his armor-bearer, very dear to him, was drawn under the water as he dipped his pitcher in a spring, by a water nymph who saw the rosy flush of his beauty and wished to kiss him. She threw her arms around his neck and drew him down into the depths and he was seen no more. Hercules sought him madly everywhere, shouting his name and plunging deeper and deeper into the forest away from the sea. He had forgotten the Fleece and the *Argo* and his comrades: everything except Hylas. He did not come back, and finally the ship had to sail without him.

Their next adventure was with the Harpies, frightful flying creatures with hooked beaks and claws who always left behind them a loathsome stench, sickening to all living creatures. Where the Argonauts had beached their boat for the night lived a lonely and wretched old man, to whom Apollo, the truth-teller, had given the gift of prophecy. He foretold unerringly what would happen, and this had displeased Zeus, who always liked to wrap in mystery what he would do—and very sensibly, too, in the opinion of all who knew Hera. So he inflicted a terrible punishment upon the old man. Whenever he was about to dine, the Harpies who were called "the hounds of Zeus" swooped down and defiled the food, leaving it so foul that no one could bear to be near it, much less eat it. When the Argonauts saw the poor old creature—his name was Phineus—he was like a lifeless dream, creeping on withered feet, trembling for weakness, and only the skin on his body held his bones together. He welcomed them gladly and begged them to help him. He knew through his gift of prophecy that he could be defended from the Harpies by two men alone, who were among the company on the *Argo*—the sons of Boreas, the great North Wind. All listened to him with pity and the two gave him eagerly their promise to help.

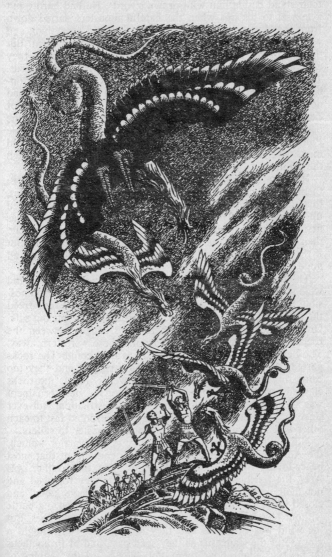

The Harpies and the Argonauts

While the others set forth food for him, Boreas' sons took their stand beside him with drawn swords. He had hardly put a morsel to his lips when the hateful monsters darted down from the sky and in a moment had devoured everything and were flying off, leaving the intolerable odor behind them. But the wind-swift sons of the North Wind followed them; they caught up with them and struck at them with their swords. They would assuredly have cut them to pieces if Iris, the rainbow messenger of the gods, gliding down from heaven, had not checked them. They must forbear to kill the hounds of Zeus, she said, but she swore by the waters of the Styx, the oath that none can break, that they would never again trouble Phineus. So the two returned gladly and comforted the old man, who in his joy sat feasting with the heroes all through the night.

He gave them wise advice, too, about the dangers before them, in especial about the Clashing Rocks, the Symplegades, that rolled perpetually against one another while the sea boiled up around them. The way to pass between them, he said, was first to make trial with a dove. If she passed through safely, then the chances were that they too would get through. But if the dove were crushed, they must turn back and give up all hope of the Golden Fleece.

The next morning they started, with a dove, of course, and were soon in sight of the great rolling rocks. It seemed impossible that there could be a way between them, but they freed the dove and watched her. She flew through and came out safe. Only the tips of her tail-feathers were caught between the rocks as they rolled back together; and those were torn away. The heroes went after her as swiftly as they could. The rocks parted, the rowers put forth all their strength, and they too came through safely. Just in time, however, for as the rocks clashed together again the extreme end of the stern ornament was shorn off. By so little they escaped destruction. But ever since they passed them the rocks have been rooted fast to each other and have never any more brought disaster to sailors.

Not far from there was the country of the warrior women, the Amazons—the daughters, strangely enough, of that most peace-loving nymph, sweet Harmony. But their father was Ares, the terrible god of war, whose ways they followed and not their mother's. The heroes would gladly have halted and closed in battle with them, and it would not have been a battle without bloodshed, for the Amazons were not gentle foes. But the wind was favorable and they hurried on. They caught a glimpse of the Caucasus as they sped past, and of Prometheus on his rock high above them, and they heard the fanning of the eagle's huge wings as it darted down to its bloody feast.

They stopped for nothing, and that same day at sunset they reached Colchis, the country of the Golden Fleece.

They spent the night facing they knew not what and feeling that there was no help for them anywhere except in their own valor. Up in Olympus, however, a consultation was being held about them. Hera, troubled at the danger they were in, went to ask Aphrodite's help. The Goddess of Love was surprised at the visit, for Hera was no friend of hers. Still, when the great Queen of Olympus begged for her aid, she was awed and promised to do all she could. Together they planned that Aphrodite's son Cupid should make the daughter of the Colchian King fall in love with Jason. That was an excellent plan —for Jason. The maiden, who was named Medea, knew how to work very powerful magic, and could undoubtedly save the Argonauts if she would use her dark knowledge for them. So Aphrodite went to Cupid and told him she would give him a lovely plaything, a ball of shining gold and deep blue enamel, if he would do what she wanted. He was delighted, seized his bow and quiver, and swept down from Olympus through the vast expanse of air to Colchis.

Meantime the heroes had started for the city to ask the King for the Golden Fleece. They were safe from any trouble on the way, for Hera wrapped them in a thick mist, so that they reached the palace unseen. It dissolved when they approached the entrance, and the warders, quick to notice the band of splendid young strangers, led them courteously within and sent word to the King of their arrival.

He came at once and bade them welcome. His servants hastened to make all ready, build fires and heat water for the baths and prepare food. Into this busy scene stole the Princess Medea, curious to see the visitors. As her eyes fell upon Jason, Cupid swiftly drew his bow and shot a shaft deep into the maiden's heart. It burned there like a flame and her soul melted with sweet pain, and her face went now white, now red. Amazed and abashed she stole back to her chamber.

Only after the heroes had bathed and refreshed themselves with meat and drink could King Æetes ask them who they were and why they had come. It was accounted great discourtesy to put any question to a guest before his wants had been satisfied. Jason answered that they were all men of noblest birth, sons or grandsons of the gods, who had sailed from Greece in the hope that he would give them the Golden Fleece in return for whatever service he would ask of them. They would conquer his enemies for him, or do anything he wished.

A great anger filled King Æetes' heart as he listened. He did not like foreigners, any more than the Greeks did; he wanted them to keep away from his country, and he said to himself.

"If these strangers had not eaten at my table I would kill them." In silence he pondered what he should do, and a plan came to him.

He told Jason that he bore no grudge against brave men and that if they proved themselves such he would give the Fleece to them. "And the trial of your courage," he said, "shall be only what I myself have done." This was to yoke two bulls he had, whose feet were of bronze and whose breath was flaming fire, and with them to plow a field. Then the teeth of a dragon must be cast into the furrows, like seed-corn—which would spring up at once into a crop of armed men. These must be cut down as they advanced to the attack—a fearful harvesting. "I have done all this myself," he said; "and I will give the Fleece to no man less brave than I." For a time Jason sat speechless. The contest seemed impossible, beyond the strength of anyone. Finally he answered, "I will make the trial, monstrous though it is, even if it is my doom to die." With that he rose up and led his comrades back to the ship for the night, but Medea's thoughts followed after him. All through the long night when he had left the palace she seemed to see him, his beauty and his grace, and to hear the words he had uttered. Her heart was tormented with fear for him. She guessed what her father was planning.

Returned to the ship, the heroes held a council and one and another urged Jason to let him take the trial upon himself; but in vain, Jason would yield to none of them. As they talked there came to them one of the King's grandsons whose life Jason once had saved, and he told them of Medea's magic power. There was nothing she could not do, he said, check the stars, even, and the moon. If she were persuaded to help, she could make Jason able to conquer the bulls and the dragon-teeth men. It seemed the only plan that offered any hope and they urged the prince to go back and try to win Medea over, not knowing that the God of Love had already done that.

She sat alone in her room, weeping and telling herself she was shamed forever because she cared so much for a stranger that she wanted to yield to a mad passion and go against her father. "Far better die," she said. She took in her hand a casket which held herbs for killing, but as she sat there with it, she thought of life and the delightful things that are in the world; and the sun seemed sweeter than ever before. She put the casket away; and no longer wavering she determined to use her power for the man she loved. She had a magic ointment which would make him who rubbed it on his body safe for that day; he could not be harmed by anything. The plant it was made from sprang up first when Prometheus' blood dripped down upon the earth. She put it in her bosom and went to find her nephew, the prince whom Jason had helped. She met him as he was looking for her to beg her to do just what she had already decided on. She agreed at once to all he said and sent him to the ship to tell Jason to meet her without delay in a certain place. As soon as he heard the message Jason started, and as he went Hera shed radiant grace upon him, so that all who saw him marveled at him. When he reached Medea it seemed to her as if her heart left her to go to him; a dark mist clouded her eyes and she had no strength to move. The two stood face to face without a word, as lofty pine trees when the wind is still. Then again when the wind stirs they murmur; so these two also, stirred by the breath of love, were fated to tell out all their tale to each other.

He spoke first and implored her to be kind to him. He could not but have hope, he said, because her loveliness must surely mean that she excelled in gentle courtesy. She did not know how to speak to him; she wanted to pour out all she felt at once. Silently she drew the box of ointment from her bosom and gave it to him. She would have given her soul to him if he had asked her. And now both were fixing their eyes on the ground abashed, and again were throwing glances at each other, smiling with love's desire.

At last Medea spoke and told him how to use the charm and that when it was sprinkled on his weapons it would make them as well as himself invincible for a day. If too many of the dragon-teeth men rushed to attack him, he must throw a stone into their midst, which would make them turn against each other and fight until all were killed. "I must go back to the palace now," she said. "But when you are once more safe at home remember Medea, as I will remember you forever." He answered passionately, "Never by night and never by day will I forget you. If you will come to Greece, you shall be worshiped for what you have done for us, and nothing except death will come between us."

They parted, she to the palace to weep over her treachery to her father, he to the ship to send two of his comrades for the dragon's teeth. Meantime he made trial of the ointment and at the touch of it a terrible, irresistible power entered into him and the heroes all exulted. Yet, even so, when they reached the field where the King and the Colchians were waiting, and the bulls rushed out from their lair breathing forth flames of fire, terror overcame them. But Jason withstood the fearful creatures as a great rock in the sea withstands the waves. He forced first one and then the other down on its knees and fastened the yoke upon them, while all wondered at his mighty prowess. Over the field he drove them, pressing the plow down firmly and casting the dragon's teeth into the furrows. By the time the plowing was done the crop was springing up, men bristling with arms who came rushing to attack him. Jason remembered Medea's words and flung a huge stone into their midst. With that, the warriors turned upon each other and fell beneath their own spears while the furrows ran with blood. So Jason's contest was ended in victory, bitter to King Æetes.

The King went back to the palace planning treachery against the heroes and vowing they should never have the Golden Fleece. But Hera was working for them. She made Medea, all bewildered with love and misery, determine to fly with Jason. That night she stole out of the house and sped along the dark path to the ship, where they were rejoicing in their good fortune with no thought of evil. She fell on her knees before them and begged them to take her with them. They must get the Fleece at once, she told them, and then make all haste away or they would be killed. A terrible serpent guarded the Fleece, but she would lull it to sleep so that it would do them no harm. She spoke in anguish, but Jason rejoiced and raised her gently and embraced her, and promised her she would be his own wedded wife when once they were back in Greece. Then taking her on board they went where she directed and reached the sacred grove where the Fleece hung. The guardian serpent was very terrible, but Medea approached it fearlessly and singing a sweet magical song she charmed it to sleep. Swiftly Jason lifted the golden wonder from the tree it hung on, and hurrying back they reached the ship as dawn was breaking. The strongest were put at the oars and they rowed with all their might down the river to the sea.

By now what had happened was known to the King, and he sent his son in pursuit—Medea's brother, Apsyrtus. He led an army so great that it seemed impossible for the little band of heroes either to conquer it or to escape, but Medea saved them again, this time by a horrible deed. She killed her brother. Some say she sent him word that she was longing to go back to her home and that she had the Fleece for him if he would meet her that night at a certain spot. He came all unsuspecting and Jason struck him down and his dark blood dyed his sister's silvery robe as she shrank away. With its leader dead, the army scattered in disorder and the way to the sea lay open to the heroes.

Others say that Apsyrtus set sail on the *Argo* with Medea, although why he did so is not explained, and that it was the King who pursued them. As his ship gained on them, Medea herself struck her brother down and cutting him limb from limb cast the pieces into the sea. The King stopped to gather them, and the *Argo* was saved.

By then the adventures of the Argonauts were almost over.

One terrible trial they had while passing between the smooth, sheer rock of Scylla and the whirlpool of Charybdis, where the sea forever spouted and roared and the furious waves mounting up touched the very sky. But Hera had seen to it that sea nymphs should be at hand to guide them and send the ship on to safety.

Next came Crete—where they would have landed but for Medea. She told them that Talus lived there, the last man left of the ancient bronze race, a creature made all of bronze except one ankle where alone he was vulnerable. Even as she spoke, he appeared, terrible to behold, and threatened to crush the ship with rocks if they drew nearer. They rested on their oars, and Medea kneeling prayed to the hounds of Hades to come and destroy him. The dread powers of evil heard her. As the bronze man lifted a pointed crag to hurl it at the *Argo* he grazed his ankle and the blood gushed forth until he sank and died. Then the heroes could land and refresh themselves for the voyage still before them.

Upon reaching Greece they disbanded, each hero going to his home, and Jason with Medea took the Golden Fleece to Pelias. But they found that terrible deeds had been done there. Pelias had forced Jason's father to kill himself and his mother had died of grief. Jason, bent upon punishing this wickedness, turned to Medea for the help which had never failed him. She brought about the death of Pelias by a cunning trick. To his daughters she said that she knew a secret, how to make the old young again; and to prove her words she cut up before them a ram worn out with many years, and put the pieces into a pot of boiling water. Then she uttered a charm and in a moment out from the water sprang a lamb and ran frisking away. The maidens were convinced. Medea gave Pelias a potent sleeping-draught and called upon his daughters to cut him into bits. With all their longing to make him young again they could hardly force themselves to do so, but at last the dreadful task was done, the pieces in the water, and they looked to Medea to speak the magic words that would bring him back to them and to his youth. But she was gone—gone from the palace and from the city, and horrified they realized that they were their father's murderers. Jason was revenged, indeed.

There is a story, too, that Medea restored Jason's father to life and made him young again, and that she gave to Jason the secret of perpetual youth. All that she did of evil and of good was done for him alone, and in the end, all the reward she got was that he turned traitor to her.

They came to Corinth after Pelias' death. Two sons were born to them and all seemed well, even to Medea in her exile, lonely as exile must always be. But her great love for Jason made the loss of her family and her country seem to her a little thing. And then Jason showed the meanness that was in him, brilliant hero though he had seemed to be: he engaged himself to marry the daughter of the King of Corinth. It was a splendid marriage and he thought of ambition only, never of love or of gratitude. In the first amazement at his treachery and in the passion of her anguish, Medea let fall words which made the King of Corinth fear she would do harm to his daughter, —he must have been a singularly unsuspicious man not to have thought of that before,—and he sent her word that she and her sons must leave the country at once. That was a doom almost as bad as death. A woman in exile with little helpless children had no protection for herself or them.

As she sat brooding over what she should do and thinking of her wrongs and her wretchedness,—wishing for death to end the life she could no longer bear; sometimes remembering with tears her father and her home; sometimes shuddering at the stain nothing could wash out of her brother's blood, of Pelias', too; conscious above all of the wild passionate devotion that had brought her to this evil and this misery,—as she sat thus, Jason appeared before her. She looked at him; she did not speak. He was there beside her, yet she was far away from him, alone with her outraged love and her ruined life. His feelings had nothing in them to make him silent. He told her coldly that he had always known how uncontrolled her spirit was. If it had not been for her foolish, mischievous talk about his bride she might have stayed on comfortably in Corinth. However, he had done his best for her. It was entirely through his efforts that she was only to be exiled, not killed. He had had a very hard time indeed to persuade the King, but he had spared no pains. He had come to her now because he was not a man to fail a friend, and he would see that she had plenty of gold and everything necessary for her journey.

This was too much. The torrent of Medea's wrongs burst forth. "You come to me?" she said—

To me, of all the race of men?
Yet it is well you came.
For I shall ease the burden of my heart
If I can make your baseness manifest.
I saved you. Every man in Greece knows that.
The bulls, the dragon-men, the serpent warder of the Fleece,
I conquered them. I made you victor.
I held the light that saved you.
Father and home—I left them
For a strange country.
I overthrew your foes,
Contrived for Pelias the worst of deaths.

Now you forsake me.
Where shall I go? Back to my father's house?
To Pelias' daughters? I have become for you
The enemy of all.
Myself, I had no quarrel with them.
Oh, I have had in you
A loyal husband, to be admired of men.
An exile now, O God, O God.
No one to help. I am alone.

His answer was that he had been saved not by her, but by Aphrodite, who had made her fall in love with him, and that she owed him a great deal for bringing her to Greece, a civilized country. Also that he had done very well for her in letting it be known how she had helped the Argonauts, so that people praised her. If only she could have had some common sense, she would have been glad of his marriage, as such a connection would have been profitable for her and the children, too. Her exile was her own fault only.

Whatever else she lacked Medea had plenty of intelligence. She wasted no more words upon him except to refuse his gold. She would take nothing, no help from him. Jason flung away angrily from her. "Your stubborn pride," he told her—

It drives away all those who would be kind.
But you will grieve the more for it.

From that moment Medea set herself to be revenged, as well she knew how.

By death, oh, by death, shall the conflict of life be decided,
Life's little day ended.

She determined to kill Jason's bride, and then—then? But she would not think of what else she saw before her. "Her death first," she said.

She took from a chest a most lovely robe. This she anointed with deadly drugs and placing it in a casket she sent her sons with it to the new bride. They must ask her, she told them, to show that she accepted the gift by wearing it at once. The Princess received them graciously, and agreed. But no sooner had she put it on than a fearful, devouring fire enveloped her. She dropped dead; her very flesh had melted away.

When Medea knew the deed was done she turned her mind to one still more dreadful. There was no protection for her children, no help for them anywhere. A slave's life might be theirs, nothing more. "I will not let them live for strangers to ill-use," she thought—

To die by other hands more merciless than mine.
No; I who gave them life will give them death.
Oh, now no cowardice, no thought how young they are,
How dear they are, how when they first were born—
Not that—I will forget they are my sons
One moment, one short moment—then forever sorrow.

When Jason came full of fury for what she had done to his bride and determined to kill her, the two boys were dead, and Medea on the roof of the house was stepping into a chariot drawn by dragons. They carried her away through the air out of his sight as he cursed her, never himself, for what had come to pass.

8 Four Great Adventures

PHAËTHON

This is one of Ovid's best stories, vividly told, details used not for mere decoration, but to heighten the effect.

The palace of the Sun was a radiant place. It shone with gold and gleamed with ivory and sparkled with jewels. Everything without and within flashed and glowed and glittered. It was always high noon there. Shadowy twilight never dimmed the brightness. Darkness and night were unknown. Few among mortals could have long endured that unchanging brilliancy of light, but few had ever found their way thither.

Nevertheless, one day a youth, mortal on his mother's side, dared to approach. Often he had to pause and clear his dazzled eyes, but the errand which had brought him was so urgent that his purpose held fast and he pressed on, up to the palace, through the burnished doors, and into the throne-room where surrounded by a blinding, blazing splendor the Sun-god sat. There the lad was forced to halt. He could bear no more.

Nothing escapes the eyes of the Sun. He saw the boy instantly and he looked at him very kindly. "What brought you here?" he asked. "I have come," the other answered boldly, "to find out if you are my father or not. My mother said you were, but the boys at school laugh when I tell them I am your son. They will not believe me. I told my mother and she said I had better go and ask you." Smiling, the Sun took off his crown of burning light so that the lad could look at him without distress. "Come here, Phaëthon," he said. "You are my son. Clymene told you the truth. I expect you will not doubt my word too? But I will give you a proof. Ask anything you want of me and you shall have it. I call the Styx to be witness to my promise, the river of the oath of the gods."

No doubt Phaëthon had often watched the Sun riding through the heavens and had told himself with a feeling, half awe, half excitement, "It is my father up there." And then he would wonder what it would be like to be in that chariot, guiding the steeds along that dizzy course, giving light to the world. Now at his father's words this wild dream had become possible. Instantly he cried, "I choose to take your place, Father. That is the only thing I want. Just for a day, a single day, let me have your car to drive."

The Sun realized his own folly. Why had he taken that fatal oath and bound himself to give in to anything that happened to enter a boy's rash young head? "Dear lad," he said, "this is the only thing I would have refused you. I know I cannot refuse. I have sworn by the Styx. I must yield if you persist. But I do not believe you will. Listen while I tell you what this is you want. You are Clymene's son as well as mine. You are mortal and no mortal could drive my chariot. Indeed, no god except myself can do that. The ruler of the gods cannot. Consider the road. It rises up from the sea so steeply that the horses can hardly climb it, fresh though they are in the early morning. In midheaven it is so high that even I do not like to look down. Worst of all is the descent, so precipitous that the Sea-gods waiting to receive me wonder how I can avoid falling headlong. To guide the horses, too, is a perpetual struggle. Their fiery spirits grow hotter as they climb and they scarcely suffer my control. What would they do with you?

"Are you fancying that there are all sorts of wonders up there, cities of the gods full of beautiful things? Nothing of the kind. You will have to pass beasts, fierce beasts of prey, and they are all that you will see. The Bull, the Lion, the Scorpion, the great Crab, each will try to harm you. Be persuaded. Look around you. See all the goods the rich world holds. Choose from them your heart's desire and it shall be yours. If what you want is to be proved my son, my fears for you are proof enough that I am your father."

But none of all this wise talk meant anything to the boy. A glorious prospect opened before him. He saw himself proudly standing in that wondrous car, his hands triumphantly guiding those steeds which Jove himself could not master. He did not give a thought to the dangers his father detailed. He felt not a quiver of fear, not a doubt of his own powers. At last the Sun gave up trying to dissuade him. It was hopeless, as he saw. Besides, there was no time. The moment for starting was at hand.

Already the gates of the east glowed purple, and Dawn had opened her courts full of rosy light. The stars were leaving the sky; even the lingering morning star was dim.

There was need for haste, but all was ready. The seasons, the gatekeepers of Olympus, stood waiting to fling the doors wide. The horses had been bridled and yoked to the car. Proudly and joyously Phaëthon mounted it and they were off. He had made his choice. Whatever came of it he could not change now. Not that he wanted to in that first exhilarating rush through the air, so swift that the East Wind was outstripped and left far behind. The horses' flying feet went through the low-banked clouds near the ocean as through a thin sea mist and then up and up in the clear air, climbing the height of heaven. For a few ecstatic moments Phaëthon felt himself the Lord of the Sky. But suddenly there was a change. The chariot was swinging wildly to and fro; the pace was faster; he had lost control. Not he, but the horses were directing the course. That light weight in the car, those feeble hands clutching the reins, had told them their own driver was not there. They were the masters then. No one else could command them. They left the road and rushed where they chose, up, down, to the right, to the left. They nearly wrecked the chariot against the Scorpion; they brought up short and almost ran into the Crab. By this time the poor charioteer was half fainting with terror, and he let the reins fall.

That was the signal for still more mad and reckless running. The horses soared up to the very top of the sky and then, plunging headlong down, they set the world on fire. The highest mountains were the first to burn, Ida and Helicon, where the Muses dwell, Parnassus, and heaven-piercing Olympus. Down their slopes the flame ran to the low-lying valleys and the dark forest lands, until all things everywhere were ablaze. The springs turned into steam; the rivers shrank. It is said that it was then the Nile fled and hid his head, which still is hidden.

In the car Phaëthon, hardly keeping his place there, was wrapped in thick smoke and heat as if from a fiery furnace. He wanted nothing except to have this torment and terror ended. He would have welcomed death. Mother Earth, too, could bear no more. She uttered a great cry which reached up to the gods. Looking down from Olympus they saw that they must act quickly if the world was to be saved. Jove seized his thunderbolt and hurled it at the rash, repentant driver. It struck him dead, shattered the chariot, and made the maddened horses rush down into the sea.

Phaëthon all on fire fell from the car through the air to the earth. The mysterious river Eridanus, which no mortal eyes have ever seen, received him and put out the flames and cooled the body. The naiads, in pity for him, so bold and so young to die, buried him and carved upon the tomb:—

> Here Phaëthon lies who drove the Sun-god's car.
> Greatly he failed, but he had greatly dared.

His sisters, the Heliades, the daughters of Helios, the Sun, came to his grave to mourn for him. There they were turned into poplar trees, on the bank of the Eridanus,

> Where sorrowing they weep into the stream forever.
> And each tear as it falls shines in the water
> A glistening drop of amber.

PEGASUS AND BELLEROPHON

Two of the episodes in this story are taken from the earliest poets. Hesiod in the eighth or ninth century tells about the Chimaera, and Anteia's love and the sad end of Bellerophon are in the Iliad. The rest of the story is told first and best by Pindar in the first half of the fifth century.

In Ephyre, the city later called Corinth, Glaucus was King. He was the son of Sisyphus who in Hades must forever try to roll a stone uphill because he once betrayed a secret of Zeus. Glaucus, too, drew down on himself the displeasure of heaven. He was a great horseman and he fed his horses human flesh to make them fierce in battle. Such monstrous deeds always angered the gods and they served him as he had served others. He was thrown from his chariot and his horses tore him to pieces and devoured him.

In the city a bold and beautiful young man named Bellerophon was generally held to be his son. It was rumored, however, that Bellerophon had a mightier father, Poseidon himself, the Ruler of the Sea, and the youth's surpassing gifts of spirit and body made this account of his birth seem likely. Moreover his mother, Eurynome, although a mortal, had been taught by Athena until in wit and wisdom she was the peer of the gods. It was only to be expected on all scores that Bellerophon should seem less mortal than divine. Great adventures would call to such a one as he and no peril would ever hold him back. And yet the deed for which he is best known needed no courage at all, no effort, even. Indeed, it proved that

> What man would swear cannot be done,—
> Must not be hoped for,—the great Power on high
> Can give into his hand, in easy mastery.

More than anything on earth Bellerophon wanted Pegasus, a marvelous horse which had sprung from the Gorgon's blood when Perseus killed her.* He was

> A winged steed, unwearying of flight,
> Sweeping through air swift as a gale of wind.

Wonders attended him. The spring beloved of poets, Hippocrene, on Helicon, the Muses' mountain, had sprung up where his hoof had struck the earth. Who could catch and tame such a creature? Bellerophon suffered from hopeless longing.

The wise seer of Ephyre (Corinth), Polyidus, to whom he told his desperate desire, advised him to go to Athena's temple and sleep there. The gods often spoke to men in their dreams. So Bellerophon went to the holy place and when he was lying deep in slumber beside the altar he seemed to see the goddess standing before him with some golden thing in her hand. She said to him, "Asleep? Nay, wake. Here is what will charm the steed you covet." He sprang to his feet. No goddess was there, but a marvelous object lay in front of him, a bridle all of gold, such as never had been seen before. Hopeful at last with it in his hand, he hurried out to the fields to find Pegasus. He caught sight of him, drinking from the far-famed spring of Corinth, Pirene; and he drew gently near. The horse looked at him tranquilly, neither startled nor afraid, and suffered himself to be bridled without the least trouble. Athena's charm had worked. Bellerophon was master of the glorious creature.

In his full suit of bronze armor he leaped upon his back and put him through his paces, the horse seeming to delight in the sport as much as he himself. Now he was lord of the air, flying wherever he would, envied of all. As matters turned out, Pegasus was not only a joy, but a help in time of need as well, for hard trials lay before Bellerophon.

In some way, we are not told how except that it was purely through accident, he killed his brother; and he went to Argos where the King, Proetus, purified him. There his trials began and his great deeds as well. Anteia, the wife of Proetus, fell in love with him, and when he turned from her and would have nothing to do with her, in her bitter anger she told her husband that his guest had wronged her and must die. Enraged though he was, Proetus would not kill him. Bellerophon had eaten at his table; he could not bring himself to use violence against him. However, he made a plan which seemed certain to have the same result. He asked the youth to take a letter to the King of Lycia in Asia and Bellerophon easily agreed. Long journeys meant nothing to him on Pegasus' back. The Lycian king

* See Part Three, Chapter 9.

Bellerophon on Pegasus killing the Chimaera

received him with antique hospitality and entertained him splendidly for nine days before he asked to see the letter. Then he read that Proetus wanted the young man killed.

He did not care to do so, for the same reason that had made Proetus unwilling: Zeus's well-known hostility to those who broke the bond between host and guest. There could be no objection, however, to sending the stranger on an adventure, him and his winged horse. So he asked him to go and slay the Chimaera, feeling quite assured that he would never come back. The Chimaera was held to be unconquerable. She was a most singular portent, a lion in front, a serpent behind, a goat in between—

> A fearful creature, great and swift of foot and strong,
> Whose breath was flame unquenchable.

But for Bellerophon riding Pegasus there was no need to come anywhere near the flaming monster. He soared up over her and shot her with his arrows at no risk to himself.

When he went back to Proetus, the latter had to think out other ways of disposing of him. He got him to go on an expedition, against the Solymi, mighty warriors; and then when Bellerophon had succeeded in conquering these, on another against the Amazons, where he did equally well. Finally Proetus was won over by his courage and his good fortune, too; he became friends with him and gave him his daughter to marry.

He lived happily thus for a long time; then he made the gods angry. His eager ambition along with his great success led him to think "thoughts too great for man," the thing of all others the gods objected to. He tried to ride Pegasus up to Olympus. He believed he could take his place there with the immortals. The horse was wiser. He would not try the flight, and he threw his rider. Thereafter Bellerophon, hated of the gods, wandered alone, devouring his own soul and avoiding the paths of men until he died.

Pegasus found shelter in the heavenly stalls of Olympus where the steeds of Zeus were cared for. Of them all he was foremost, as was proved by the extraordinary fact the poets report, that when Zeus wished to use his thunderbolt, it was Pegasus who brought the thunder and lightning to him.

OTUS AND EPHIALTES

> *This story is alluded to in the* Odyssey *and the* Aeneid, *but only Apollodorus tells it in full. He wrote, probably, in the first or second century* A.D. *A dull writer, but less dull than usual in this tale.*

These twin brothers were Giants, but they did not look like the monsters of old. They were straight of form and noble of face. Homer says they were

Tallest of all that the life-giving earth with her bread ever nourished,
Handsomest too, after peerless Orion alone.

Virgil speaks chiefly of their mad ambition. He says they were

Twins, huge-bodied, who strove with their hands to destroy the high heavens,
Strove to push Jupiter down from his kingdom supernal.

They were the sons of Iphimedia, some say; others, of Canace. At all events, whoever their mother was, their father was certainly Poseidon, although they went generally by the name of the Aloadae, the sons of Aloeus, their mother's husband.

They were still very young when they set about proving that they were the gods' superiors. They imprisoned Ares, bound him with chains of brass and shut him up. The Olympians were reluctant to try to free him by force. They sent the cunning Hermes to his assistance, who contrived stealthily by night to get him out of his prison. Then the two arrogant youths dared still more. They threatened that they would pile Mount Pelion on Mount Ossa and scale the heights of heaven, as the Giants of old had piled Ossa on Pelion. This passed the endurance of the immortals, and Zeus got ready his thunderbolt to strike them. But before he hurled it Poseidon came begging him to spare them and promising to keep them in order. Zeus agreed and Poseidon was as good as his word. The twins stopped warring against heaven and Poseidon felt pleased with himself, but the fact was that the two had turned to other plans which interested them more.

Otus thought it would be an excellent adventure to carry Hera off, and Ephialtes was in love with Artemis, or thought he was. In truth the two brothers cared only for each other. Theirs was a great devotion. They drew lots to decide which should first seize his lady, and fortune favored Ephialtes. They sought Artemis everywhere over the hills and in the woods, but when at last they caught sight of her she was on the seashore, making directly for the sea. She knew their evil purpose and she knew too how she would punish them. They sprang after her, but she kept straight on over the sea. All of Poseidon's sons had the same power: they could run dry-shod on the sea as on the land, so the two followed her with no trouble. She led them to the wooded island of Naxos, and there, when they had all but caught up with her, she disappeared. They saw instead a most lovely milk-white hind springing into the forest. At the sight they forgot the goddess and turned in pursuit of the beautiful creature. They lost her in the thick woods and they separated in order to double the chance of finding her. At the same moment each suddenly saw her standing with ears pricked in an open glade, but neither saw that back in the trees just beyond her was his brother. They threw their javelins and the hind vanished. The weapons sped on across the empty glade into the wood and there found their mark. The towering forms of the young hunters crashed to the ground, each pierced by the spear of the other, each slaying and being slain by the only creature he loved.

Such was the vengeance of Artemis.

DAEDALUS

> Both Ovid and Apollodorus tell this story. Apollodorus lived probably more than a hundred years after Ovid. He is a very pedestrian writer and Ovid is far from that. But in this case I have followed Apollodorus. Ovid's account shows him at his worst, sentimental and exclamatory.

Daedalus was the architect who had contrived the Labyrinth for the Minotaur in Crete, and who showed Ariadne how Theseus could escape from it.* When King Minos learned that the Athenians had found their way out, he was convinced that they could have done so only if Daedalus had helped them. Accordingly he imprisoned him and his son Icarus in the Labyrinth, certainly a proof that it was excellently devised since not even the maker of it could discover the exit without a clue. But the great inventor was not at a loss. He told his son,

Escape may be checked by water and land, but the air and the sky are free,

and he made two pairs of wings for them. They put them on and just before they took flight Daedalus warned Icarus to keep a middle course over the sea. If he flew too high the sun might melt the glue and the wings drop off. However, as stories so often show, what elders say youth disregards. As the two flew lightly and without effort away from Crete the delight of

* See Part Three. Chapter 10.

this new and wonderful power went to the boy's head. He soared exultingly up and up, paying no heed to his father's anguished commands. Then he fell. The wings had come off. He dropped into the sea and the waters closed over him. The afflicted father flew safely to Sicily, where he was received kindly by the King.

Minos was enraged at his escape and determined to find him. He made a cunning plan. He had it proclaimed everywhere that a great reward would be given to whoever could pass a thread through an intricately spiraled shell. Daedalus told the Sicilian king that he could do it. He bored a small hole in the closed end of the shell, fastened a thread to an ant, introduced the ant into the hole, and then closed it. When the ant finally came out at the other end, the thread, of course, was running clear through all the twists and turns. "Only Daedalus would think of that," Minos said, and he came to Sicily to seize him. But the King refused to surrender him, and in the contest Minos was slain.

PART THREE

The Great Heroes before the Trojan War

9 Perseus

This story is on the level of the fairy story. Hermes and Athena act like the fairy godmother in Cinderella. The magical wallet and cap belong to the properties fairy tales abound in everywhere. It is the only myth in which magic plays a decisive part, and it seems to have been a great favorite in Greece. Many poets allude to it. The description of Danaë in the wooden chest was the most famous passage of a famous poem by Simonides of Ceos, a great lyric poet who lived in the sixth century. The entire story is told by both Ovid and Apollodorus. The latter, probably a hundred years later than Ovid, is here the superior of the two. His account is simple and straightforward; Ovid's extremely verbose—for instance, he takes a hundred lines to kill the sea serpent. I have followed Apollodorus, but I have added the fragment from Simonides, and short quotations from other poets, notably Hesiod and Pindar.

King Acrisius of Argos had only one child, a daughter, Danaë. She was beautiful above all the other women of the land, but this was small comfort to the King for not having a son. He journeyed to Delphi to ask the god if there was any hope that some day he would be the father of a boy. The priestess told him no, and added what was far worse: that his daughter would have a son who would kill him.

The only sure way to escape that fate was for the King to have Danaë instantly put to death—taking no chances, but seeing to it himself. This Acrisius would not do. His fatherly affection was not strong, as events proved, but his fear of the gods was. They visited with terrible punishment those who shed the blood of kindred. Acrisius did not dare slay his daughter. Instead, he had a house built all of bronze and sunk underground, but with part of the roof open to the sky so that light and air could come through. Here he shut her up and guarded her.

> So Danaë endured, the beautiful,
> To change the glad daylight for brass-bound walls,
> And in that chamber secret as the grave
> She lived a prisoner. Yet to her came
> Zeus in the golden rain.

As she sat there through the long days and hours with nothing to do, nothing to see except the clouds moving by overhead, a mysterious thing happened, a shower of gold fell from the sky and filled her chamber. How it was revealed to her that it was Zeus who had visited her in this shape we are not told, but she knew that the child she bore was his son.

For a time she kept his birth secret from her father, but it became increasingly difficult to do so in the narrow limits of that bronze house and finally one day the little boy—his name was Perseus—was discovered by his grandfather. "Your child!" Acrisius cried in great anger. "Who is his father?" But when Danaë answered proudly, "Zeus," he would not believe her. One thing only he was sure of, that the boy's life was a terrible danger to his own. He was afraid to kill him for the same reason that had kept him from killing her, fear of Zeus and the Furies who pursue such murderers. But if he could not kill them outright, he could put them in the way of tolerably certain death. He had a great chest made, and the two placed in it. Then it was taken out to sea and cast into the water.

In that strange boat Danaë sat with her little son. The daylight faded and she was alone on the sea.

> When in the carven chest the winds and waves
> Struck fear into her heart she put her arms,
> Not without tears, round Perseus tenderly
> She said, "O son, what grief is mine.
> But you sleep softly, little child,
> Sunk deep in rest within your cheerless home,
> Only a box, brass-bound. The night, this darkness visible,
> The scudding waves so near to your soft curls,
> The shrill voice of the wind, you do not heed,
> Nestled in your red cloak, fair little face."

Through the night in the tossing chest she listened to the waters that seemed always about to wash over them. The dawn came, but with no comfort to her for she could not see it. Neither could she see that around them there were islands rising high above the sea, many islands. All she knew was that presently a wave seemed to lift them and carry them swiftly on and then, retreating, leave them on something solid and motionless. They had made land; they were safe from the sea, but they were still in the chest with no way to get out.

Fate willed it—or perhaps Zeus, who up to now had done little for his love and his child—that they should be discovered by a good man, a fisherman named Dictys. He came upon the great box and broke it open and took the pitiful cargo home to his wife who was as kind as he. They had no children and they cared for Danaë and Perseus as if they were their own. The two lived there many years, Danaë content to let her son follow the fisherman's humble trade, out of harm's way. But in the end more trouble came. Polydectes, the ruler of the little island, was the brother of Dictys, but he was a cruel and ruthless man. He seems to have taken no notice of the mother and son for a long time, but at last Danaë attracted his attention. She was still radiantly beautiful even though Perseus by now was full grown, and Polydectes fell in love with her. He wanted her, but he did not want her son, and he set himself to think out a way of getting rid of him.

There were some fearsome monsters called Gorgons who lived on an island and were known far and wide because of their deadly power. Polydectes evidently talked to Perseus about them; he probably told him that he would rather have the head of one of them than anything else in the world. This seems practically certain from the plan he devised for killing Perseus. He announced that he was about to be married and he called his friends together for a celebration, including Perseus in the invitation. Each guest, as was customary, brought a gift for the bride-to-be, except Perseus alone. He had nothing he could give. He was young and proud and keenly mortified. He stood up before them all and did exactly what the King had hoped he would do, declared that he would give him a present better than any there. He would go off and kill Medusa and bring back her head as his gift. Nothing could have suited the King better. No one in his senses would have made such a proposal. Medusa was one of the Gorgons,

> And they are three, the Gorgons, each with wings
> And snaky hair, most horrible to mortals.
> Whom no man shall behold and draw again
> The breath of life,

for the reason that whoever looked at them was turned instantly into stone. It seemed that Perseus had been led by his angry pride into making an empty boast. No man unaided could kill Medusa.

But Perseus was saved from his folly. Two great gods were watching over him. He took ship as soon as he left the King's hall, not daring to see his mother first and tell her what he intended, and he sailed to Greece to learn where the three monsters were to be found. He went to Delphi, but all the priestess would say was to bid him seek the land where men eat not Demeter's golden grain, but only acorns. So he went to Dodona, in the land of oak trees, where the talking oaks were which declared Zeus's will and where the Selli lived who made their bread from acorns. They could tell him, however, no more than this, that he was under the protection of the gods. They did not know where the Gorgons lived.

When and how Hermes and Athena came to his help is not told in any story, but he must have known despair before they did so. At last, however, as he wandered on, he met a strange and beautiful person. We know what he looked like from many a poem, a young man with the first down upon his cheek when youth is loveliest, carrying, as no other young man ever did, a wand of gold with wings at one end, wearing a winged hat, too, and winged sandals. At sight of him hope must have entered Perseus' heart, for he would know that this could be none other than Hermes, the guide and the giver of good.

This radiant personage told him that before he attacked Medusa he must first be properly equipped, and that what he needed was in the possession of the nymphs of the North. To find the nymphs' abode, they must go to the Gray Women who alone could tell them the way. These women dwelt in a land where all was dim and shrouded in twilight. No ray of sun looked ever on that country, nor the moon by night. In that gray place the three women lived, all gray themselves and withered as in extreme old age. They were strange creatures, indeed, most of all because they had but one eye for the three, which it was their custom to take turns with, each removing it from her forehead when she had had it for a time and handing it to another.

All this Hermes told Perseus and then he unfolded his plan. He would himself guide Perseus to them. Once there Perseus must keep hidden until he saw one of them take the eye out of her forehead to pass it on. At that moment, when none of the three could see, he must rush forward and seize the eye and refuse to give it back until they told him how to reach the nymphs of the North.

He himself, Hermes said, would give him a sword to attack Medusa with—which could not be bent or broken by the Gorgon's scales, no matter how hard they were. This was a wonderful gift, no doubt, and yet of what use was a sword when the creature to be struck by it could turn the swordsman into stone before he was within striking distance? But another great deity was at hand to help. Pallas Athena stood beside Perseus. She took off the shield of polished bronze which covered her breast and held it out to him. "Look into this when you attack the Gorgon," she said. "You will be able to see her in it as in a mirror, and so avoid her deadly power."

Now, indeed, Perseus had good reason to hope. The journey to the twilight land was long, over the stream of Ocean and on to the very border of the black country where the Cimmerians dwell, but Hermes was his guide and he could not go astray. They found the Gray Women at last, looking in the wavering light like gray birds, for they had the shape of swans. But their heads were human and beneath their wings they had arms and hands. Perseus did just as Hermes had said, he held back until he saw one of them take the eye out of her forehead. Then before she could give it to her sister, he snatched it out of her hand. It was a moment or two before the three realized they had lost it. Each thought one of the others had it. But Perseus spoke out and told them he had taken it and that it would be theirs again only when they showed him how to find the nymphs of the North. They gave him full directions at once; they would have done anything to get their eye back. He returned it to them and went on the way they had pointed out to him. He was bound, although he did not know it, to the blessed country of the Hyperboreans, at the back of the North Wind, of which it is said: "Neither by ship nor yet by land shall one find the wondrous road to the gathering place of the Hyperboreans." But Perseus had Hermes with him, so that the road lay open to him, and he reached that host of happy people who are always banqueting and holding joyful revelry. They showed him great kindness: they welcomed him to their feast, and the maidens dancing to the sound of flute and lyre paused to get for him the gifts he sought. These were three: winged sandals, a magic wallet which would always become the right size for whatever was to be carried in it, and, most important of all, a cap which made the wearer invisible. With these and Athena's shield and Hermes' sword Perseus was ready for the Gorgons. Hermes knew where they lived, and leaving the happy land the two flew back across Ocean and over the sea to the Terrible Sisters' island.

By great good fortune they were all asleep when Perseus found them. In the mirror of the bright shield he could see them clearly, creatures with great wings and bodies covered with golden scales and hair a mass of twisting snakes. Athena was beside him now as well as Hermes. They told him which one was Medusa and that was important, for she alone of the three could be killed; the other two were immortal. Perseus on his winged sandals hovered above them, looking, however, only at the shield. Then he aimed a stroke down at Medusa's throat and Athena guided his hand. With a single sweep of his sword he cut through her neck and, his eyes still fixed on the shield with never a glance at her, he swooped low enough to seize the head. He dropped it into the wallet which closed around it. He had nothing to fear from it now. But the two other Gorgons had awakened and, horrified at the sight of their sister slain, tried to pursue the slayer. Perseus was safe; he had on the cap of darkness and they could not find him.

> So over the sea rich-haired Danaë's son,
> Perseus, on his winged sandals sped,
> Flying swift as thought.
> In a wallet of silver,
> A wonder to behold,
> He bore the head of the monster,
> While Hermes, the son of Maia,
> The messenger of Zeus,
> Kept ever at his side.

On his way back he came to Ethiopia and alighted there. By this time Hermes had left him. Perseus found, as Hercules was later to find, that a lovely maiden had been given up to be devoured by a horrible sea serpent. Her name was Andromeda and she was the daughter of a silly vain woman,

> That starred Ethiop queen who strove
> To set her beauty's praise above
> The sea-nymphs, and their power offended.

She had boasted that she was more beautiful than the daughters of Nereus, the Sea-god. An absolutely certain way in those days to draw down on one a wretched fate was to claim superiority in anything over any deity; nevertheless people were perpetually doing so. In this case the punishment for the arrogance the gods detested fell not on Queen Cassiopeia, Andromeda's mother, but on her daughter. The Ethiopians were being devoured in numbers by the serpent; and, learning from the oracle that they could be freed from the pest only if Andromeda were offered up to it, they forced Cepheus, her father, to consent. When Perseus arrived the maiden was on a rocky ledge by the sea, chained there to wait for the coming

Perseus holding Medusa's head

of the monster. Perseus saw her and on the instant loved her. He waited beside her until the great snake came for its prey; then he cut its head off just as he had the Gorgon's. The headless body dropped back into the water; Perseus took Andromeda to her parents and asked for her hand, which they gladly gave him.

With her he sailed back to the island and his mother, but in the house where he had lived so long he found no one. The fisherman Dictys' wife was long since dead, and the two others, Danaë and the man who had been like a father to Perseus, had had to fly and hide themselves from Polydectes, who was furious at Danaë's refusal to marry him. They had taken refuge in a temple, Perseus was told. He learned also that the King was holding a banquet in the palace and all the men who favored him were gathered there. Perseus instantly saw his opportunity. He went straight to the palace and entered the hall. As he stood at the entrance, Athena's shining buckler on his breast, the silver wallet at his side, he drew the eyes of every man there. Then before any could look away he held up the Gorgon's head; and at the sight one and all, the cruel King and his servile courtiers, were turned into stone. There they sat, a row of statues, each, as it were, frozen stiff in the attitude he had struck when he first saw Perseus.

When the islanders knew themselves freed from the tyrant it was easy for Perseus to find Danaë and Dictys. He made Dictys king of the island, but he and his mother decided that they would go back with Andromeda to Greece and try to be reconciled to Acrisius, to see if the many years that had passed since he had put them in the chest had not softened him so that he would be glad to receive his daughter and grandson. When they reached Argos, however, they found that Acrisius had been driven away from the city, and where he was no one could say. It happened that soon after their arrival Perseus heard that the King of Larissa, in the North, was holding a great athletic contest, and he journeyed there to take part. In the discus-throwing when his turn came and he hurled the heavy missile, it swerved and fell among the spectators. Acrisius was there on a visit to the King, and the discus struck him. The blow was fatal and he died at once.

So Apollo's oracle was again proved true. If Perseus felt any grief, at least he knew that his grandfather had done his best to kill him and his mother. With his death their troubles came to an end. Perseus and Andromeda lived happily ever after. Their son, Electryon, was the grandfather of Hercules.

Medusa's head was given to Athena, who bore it always upon the aegis, Zeus's shield, which she carried for him.

10 Theseus

This dearest of heroes to the Athenians engaged the attention of many writers. Ovid, who lived in the Augustan Age, tells his life in detail and so does Apollodorus, in the first or second century A.D. Plutarch, too, toward the end of the first century A.D. He is a prominent character in three of Euripides' plays and in one of Sophocles. There are many allusions to him in prose writers as well as poets. I have followed Apollodorus on the whole, but I have added from Euripides the stories of the appeal of Adrastus, the madness of Hercules, and the fate of Hippolytus; from Sophocles his kindness to Oedipus; from Plutarch the story of his death, to which Apollodorus gives only a sentence.

The great Athenian hero was Theseus. He had so many adventures and took part in so many great enterprises that there grew up a saying in Athens, "Nothing without Theseus."

He was the son of the Athenian King, Aegeus. He spent his youth, however, in his mother's home, a city in southern Greece. Aegeus went back to Athens before the child was born, but first he placed in a hollow a sword and a pair of shoes and covered them with a great stone. He did this with the knowledge of his wife and told her that whenever the boy—if it was a boy—grew strong enough to roll away the stone and get the things beneath it, she could send him to Athens to claim him as his father. The child was a boy and he grew up strong far beyond others, so that when his mother finally took him to the stone he lifted it with no trouble at all. She told him then that the time had come for him to seek his father, and a ship was placed at his disposal by his grandfather. But Theseus refused to go by water, because the voyage was safe and easy. His idea was to become a great hero as quickly as possible, and easy safety was certainly not the way to do that. Hercules,* who was the most magnificent of all the heroes of Greece, was always in his mind, and the determination to be just as magnificent himself. This was quite natural since the two were cousins.

He steadfastly refused, therefore, the ship his mother and grandfather urged on him, telling them that to sail on it would be a contemptible flight from danger, and he set forth to go to Athens by land. The journey was long and very hazardous because of the bandits that beset the road. He killed them all, however; he left not one alive to trouble future travelers. His idea of dealing justice was simple, but effective: what each had done to others, Theseus did to him. Sciron, for instance, who had made those he captured kneel to wash his feet and then kicked them down into the sea, Theseus hurled over a precipice. Sinis, who killed people by fastening them to two pine trees bent down to the ground and letting the trees go, died in that way himself. Procrustes was placed upon the iron bed which he used for his victims, tying them to it and then making them the right length for it by stretching those who were too short and cutting off as much as was necessary from those who were too long. The story does not say which of the two methods was used in his case, but there was not much to choose between them and in one way or the other Procrustes' career ended.

It can be imagined how Greece rang with the praises of the young man who had cleared the land of these banes to travelers. When he reached Athens he was an acknowledged hero and he was invited to a banquet by the King, who of course was unaware that Theseus was his son. In fact he was afraid of the young man's great popularity, thinking that he might win the people over to make him king, and he invited him with the idea of poisoning him. The plan was not his, but Medea's, the heroine of the Quest of the Golden Fleece who knew through her sorcery who Theseus was. She had fled to Athens when she left Corinth in her winged car, and she had acquired great influence over Aegeus, which she did not want disturbed by the appearance of a son. But as she handed him the poisoned cup Theseus, wishing to make himself known at once to his father, drew his sword. The King instantly recognized it and dashed the cup to the ground. Medea escaped as she always did and got safely away to Asia.

Aegeus then proclaimed to the country that Theseus was his son and heir. The new heir apparent soon had an opportunity to endear himself to the Athenians.

Years before his arrival in Athens, a terrible misfortune

* See next chapter.

had happened to the city. Minos, the powerful ruler of Crete, had lost his only son, Androgeus, while the young man was visiting the Athenian King. King Aegeus had done what no host should do, he had sent his guest on an expedition full of peril—to kill a dangerous bull. Instead, the bull had killed the youth. Minos invaded the country, captured Athens and declared that he would raze it to the ground unless every nine years the people sent him a tribute of seven maidens and seven youths. A horrible fate awaited these young creatures. When they reached Crete they were given to the Minotaur to devour.

The Minotaur was a monster, half bull, half human, the off-spring of Minos' wife Pasiphaë and a wonderfully beautiful bull. Poseidon had given this bull to Minos in order that he should sacrifice it to him, but Minos could not bear to slay it and had kept it for himself. To punish him, Poseidon had made Pasiphaë fall madly in love with it.

When the Minotaur was born Minos did not kill him. He had Daedalus, a great architect and inventor, construct a place of confinement for him from which escape was impossible. Daedalus built the Labyrinth, famous throughout the world. Once inside, one would go endlessly along its twisting paths without ever finding the exit. To this place the young Athenians were each time taken and left to the Minotaur. There was no possible way to escape. In whatever direction they ran they might be running straight to the monster; if they stood still he might at any moment emerge from the maze. Such was the doom which awaited fourteen youths and maidens a few days after Theseus reached Athens. The time had come for the next installment of the tribute.

At once Theseus came forward and offered to be one of the victims. All loved him for his goodness and admired him for his nobility, but they had no idea that he intended to try to kill the Minotaur. He told his father, however, and promised him that if he succeeded, he would have the black sail which the ship with its cargo of misery always carried changed to a white one, so that Aegeus could know long before it came to land that his son was safe.

When the young victims arrived in Crete they were paraded before the inhabitants on their way to the Labyrinth. Minos' daughter Ariadne was among the spectators and she fell in love with Theseus at first sight as he marched past her. She sent for Daedalus and told him he must show her a way to get out of the Labyrinth, and she sent for Theseus and told him she would bring about his escape if he would promise to take her back to Athens and marry her. As may be imagined, he made no difficulty about that, and she gave him the clue she had got from Daedalus, a ball of thread which he was to fasten at one end to the inside of the door and unwind as he went on. This he did and, certain that he could retrace his steps whenever he chose, he walked boldly into the maze looking for the Minotaur. He came upon him asleep and fell upon him, pinning him to the ground; and with his fists—he had no other weapon—he battered the monster to death.

> As an oak tree falls on the hillside
> Crushing all that lies beneath,
> So Theseus. He presses out the life,
> The brute's savage life, and now it lies dead.
> Only the head sways slowly, but the horns are useless now.

When Theseus lifted himself up from that terrific struggle, the ball of thread lay where he had dropped it. With it in his hands, the way out was clear. The others followed and taking Ariadne with them they fled to the ship and over the sea toward Athens.

On the way there they put in at the island of Naxos and what happened then is differently reported. One story says that Theseus deserted Ariadne. She was asleep and he sailed away without her, but Dionysus found her and comforted her. The other story is much more favorable to Theseus. She was extremely seasick, and he set her ashore to recover while he returned to the ship to do some necessary work. A violent wind carried him out to sea and kept him there a long time. On his return he found that Ariadne had died, and he was deeply afflicted.

Both stories agree that when they drew near to Athens he forgot to hoist the white sail. Either his joy at the success of his voyage put every other thought out of his head, or his grief for Ariadne. The black sail was seen by his father, King Aegeus, from the Acropolis, where for days he had watched the sea with straining eyes. It was to him the sign of his son's death and he threw himself down from a rocky height into the sea, and was killed. The sea into which he fell was called the Aegean ever after.

So Theseus became King of Athens, a most wise and disinterested king. He declared to the people that he did not wish to rule over them; he wanted a people's government where all would be equal. He resigned his royal power and organized a commonwealth, building a council hall where the citizens should gather and vote. The only office he kept for himself was that of Commander in Chief. Thus Athens became, of all earth's cities, the happiest and most prosperous, the only true home of liberty, the one place in the world where the

The Minotaur in the Labyrinth

people governed themselves. It was for this reason that in the great War of the Seven against Thebes,* when the victorious Thebans refused burial to those of the enemy who had died, the vanquished turned to Theseus and Athens for help, believing that free men under such a leader would never consent to having the helpless dead wronged. They did not turn in vain. Theseus led his army against Thebes, conquered her and forced her to allow them to be buried. But when he was victor he did not return evil to the Thebans for the evil they had done. He showed himself the perfect knight. He refused to let his army enter and loot the city. He had come not to harm Thebes, but to bury the Argive dead, and that duty done he led his soldiers back to Athens.

In many other stories he shows the same qualities. He received the aged Oedipus whom everyone else had cast out.* He was with him when he died, sustaining and comforting him. He protected his two helpless daughters and sent them safely home after their father's death. When Hercules ** in his madness killed his wife and children and upon his return to sanity determined to kill himself, Theseus alone stood by him. Hercules' other friends fled, fearing to be polluted by the presence of one who had done so horrible a deed, but Theseus gave him his hand, roused his courage, told him to die would be a coward's act, and took him to Athens.

All the cares of state, however, and all the deeds of knight-errantry to defend the wronged and helpless, could not restrain Theseus' love of danger for the sake of danger. He went to the country of the Amazons, the women warriors, some say with Hercules, some say alone, and brought away one of them, whose name is given sometimes as Antiope, sometimes as Hippolyta. It is certain that the son she bore Theseus was named Hippolytus, and also that after his birth the Amazons came to rescue her and invaded Attica, the country around Athens, even making their way into the city. They were finally defeated and no other enemy entered Attica as long as Theseus lived.

But he had many other adventures. He was one of the men who sailed on the *Argo* to find the Golden Fleece. He took part in the great Calydonian Hunt, when the King of Calydon called upon the noblest in Greece to help him kill the terrible boar which was laying waste his country. During the hunt Theseus saved the life of his rash friend Pirithoüs, as he did, indeed, a number of times. Pirithoüs was quite as adventurous as Theseus, but by no means as successful, so that he was perpetually in trouble. Theseus was devoted to him and al-

* See Part Five, Chapter 18.
** See Part Three, Chapter 11.

ways helped him out. The friendship between them came about through an especially rash act on Pirithoüs' part. It occured to him that he would like to see for himself if Theseus was as great a hero as he was said to be, and he forthwith went into Attica and stole some of Theseus' cattle. When he heard that Theseus was pursuing him, instead of hurrying away he turned around and went to meet him, with the intention, of course, of deciding then and there which was the better man. But as the two faced each other Pirithoüs, impulsive as always, suddenly forgot everything in his admiration of the other. He held out his hand to him and cried, "I will submit to any penalty you impose. You be the judge." Theseus, delighted at this warm-hearted action, answered, "All I want is for you to be my friend and brother-in-arms." And they took a solemn oath of friendship.

When Pirithoüs, who was King of the Lapithae, married, Theseus was, of course, one of the guests, and was exceedingly useful there. The marriage feast was perhaps the most unfortunate that ever took place. The Centaurs, creatures who each had the body of a horse and the chest and face of a man, were related to the bride and came to the wedding. They proceeded to get drunk and to seize the women. Theseus leaped to the defense of the bride and struck down the Centaur who was trying to carry her off. A terrible battle followed, but the Lapithae conquered and finally drove the whole race of Centaurs out of the country, Theseus helping them to the end.

But in the last adventure the two undertook he could not save his friend. Quite characteristically, Pirithoüs, after the bride of the disastrous wedding feast was dead, decided that for his second wife he would try to get the most carefully guarded lady in all the universe, none other than Persephone herself. Theseus agreed, of course, to help him, but, stimulated probably by the idea of this magnificently dangerous undertaking, declared that first he would himself carry off Helen, the future heroine of Troy,* then a child, and when she was grown marry her. This, though less hazardous than the rape of Persephone, was perilous enough to satisfy the most ambitious. Helen's brothers were Castor and Pollux, more than a match for any mortal hero. Theseus succeeded in kidnaping the little girl, just how we are not told, but the two brothers marched against the town she had been taken to, and got her back. Luckily for him they did not find Theseus there. He was on his way to the underworld with Pirithoüs.

The details of their journey and arrival there are not known

* See Part Four, Chapters 13 and 14.

beyond the fact that the Lord of Hades was perfectly aware of their intention and amused himself by frustrating it in a novel way. He did not kill them, of course, as they were already in the realm of death, but he invited them as a friendly gesture to sit in his presence. They did so on the seat he pointed them to—and there they stayed. They could not arise from it. It was called the Chair of Forgetfulness. Whoever sat on it forgot everything. His mind became a blank and he did not move. There Pirithoüs sits forever, but Theseus was freed by his cousin. When Hercules came to the underworld he lifted Theseus from the seat and brought him back to earth. He tried to do the same for Pirithoüs, but could not. The King of the Dead knew that it was he who had planned to carry off Persephone, and he held him fast.

In the later years of his life Theseus married Ariadne's sister Phaedra, and thereby drew down terrible misfortunes on her and on himself and on his son Hippolytus, the son the Amazon had borne him. He had sent Hippolytus away while still a young child to be brought up in the southern city where Theseus had spent his own youth. The boy grew to splendid manhood, a great athlete and hunter, despising those who lived in luxurious ease and still more those who were soft enough and silly enough to fall in love. He scorned Aphrodite, he worshiped only Artemis, the huntress chaste and fair. So matters stood when Theseus came to his old home bringing Phaedra with him. A strong affection grew up at once between father and son. They delighted in each other's company. As for Phaedra, her stepson Hippolytus took no notice of her; he never noticed women. But it was far otherwise with her. She fell in love with him, madly and miserably, overwhelmed with shame at such a love, but utterly unable to conquer it. Aphrodite was back of this wretched and ominous state of affairs. She was angry at Hippolytus and determined to punish him to the utmost.

Phaedra, in her anguish, desperate, seeing no help for her anywhere, resolved to die and let no one know why. Theseus at the time was away from home, but her old nurse—completely devoted to her and unable to think anything bad that Phaedra wanted—discovered all, her secret passion, her despair, and her determination to kill herself. With only one thought in her mind, to save her mistress, she went straight to Hippolytus.

"She is dying for love of you," she said. "Give her life. Give her love for love."

Hippolytus drew away from her with loathing. The love of any woman would have disgusted him, but this guilty love sickened and horrified him. He rushed out into the courtyard, she following him and beseeching him. Phaedra was sitting there, but he never saw her. He turned in furious indignation on the old woman.

"You pitiable wretch," he said, "trying to make me betray my father. I feel polluted by merely hearing such words. Oh, women, vile women—every one of them vile. I will never enter this house again except when my father is in it."

He flung away and the nurse, turning, faced Phaedra. She had risen and there was a look on her face which frightened the old woman.

"I'll help you still," she stammered.

"Hush," Phaedra said. "I will settle my own affairs." With that she entered the house and the nurse trembling crept after her.

A few minutes later the voices of men were heard greeting the master of the house on his return and Theseus entered the courtyard. Weeping women met him there. They told him that Phaedra was dead. She had killed herself. They had just found her, quite dead, but in her hand a letter to her husband.

"O dearest and best," Theseus said. "Are your last desires written here? This is your seal—yours who will never more smile up at me."

He opened and read it and read it again. Then he turned to the servants filling the courtyard.

"This letter cries aloud," he said. "The words speak—they have a tongue. Know all of you that my son laid violent hands upon my wife. O Poseidon, God, hear me while I curse him, and fulfill my curse."

The silence that followed was broken by hurrying footsteps. Hippolytus entered.

"What happened?" he cried. "How did she die? Father, tell me yourself. Do not hide your grief from me."

"There ought to be a true yardstick to measure affection by," said Theseus, "some means to know who is to be trusted and who is not. You here, look at my son—proved base by the hand of her who is dead. He offered her violence. Her letter outweighs any words he could speak. Go. You are an exile from this land. Go to your ruin and at once."

"Father," Hippolytus answered, "I have no skill in speaking and there is no witness to my innocence. The only one is dead. All I can do is to swear by Zeus above that I never touched your wife, never desired to, never gave her a thought. May I die in wretchedness if I am guilty."

"Dead she proves her truth," Theseus said. "Go. You are banished from the land."

Hippolytus went, but not into exile; death was waiting close at hand for him too. As he drove along the sea-road away from the home he was leaving forever, his father's curse was fulfilled. A monster came up from the water and his horses, terrified beyond even his firm control, ran away. The chariot was shattered and he was mortally hurt.

Theseus was not spared. Artemis appeared to him and told him the truth.

> I do not come to bring you help, but only pain,
> To show you that your son was honorable.
> Your wife was guilty, mad with love for him,
> And yet she fought her passion and she died.
> But what she wrote was false.

As Theseus listened, overwhelmed by this sum of terrible events, Hippolytus still breathing was carried in.

He gasped out, "I was innocent. Artemis, you? My goddess, your huntsman is dying."

"And no other can take your place, dearest of men to me," she told him.

Hippolytus turned his eyes from her radiance to Theseus brokenhearted.

"Father, dear Father," he said. "It was not your fault."

"If only I could die for you," Theseus cried.

The calm sweet voice of the goddess broke in on their anguish. "Take your son in your arms, Theseus," she said. "It was not you that killed him. It was Aphrodite. Know this, that he will never be forgotten. In song and story men will remember him."

She vanished from sight, but Hippolytus, too, was gone. He had started on the road that leads down to the realm of death.

Theseus' death, also, was wretched. He was at the court of a friend, King Lycomedes, where a few years later Achilles was to hide disguised as a girl. Some say that Theseus had gone there because Athens had banished him. At all events, the King, his friend and his host, killed him, we are not told why.

Even if the Athenians did banish him, very soon after his death they honored him as no other mortal. They built a great tomb for him and decreed that it should be forever a sanctuary for slaves and for all poor and helpless people, in memory of one who through his life had been the protector of the defenseless.

11 Hercules

Ovid gives an account of Hercules' life, but very briefly, quite unlike his usual extremely detailed method. He never cares to dwell on heroic exploits; he loves best a pathetic story. At first sight it seems odd that he passes over Hercules' slaying of his wife and children, but that tale had been told by a master, the fifth-century poet Euripides, and Ovid's reticence was probably due to his intelligence. He has very little to say about any of the myths the Greek tragedians write of. He passes over also one of the most famous tales about Hercules, how he freed Alcestis from death, which was the subject of another of Euripides' plays. Sophocles, Euripides' contemporary, describes how the hero died. His adventure with the snakes when he was a baby is told by Pindar in the fifth century and by Theocritus in the third. In my account I have followed the stories given by the two tragic poets and by Theocritus, rather than Pindar, one of the most difficult of poets to translate or even to paraphrase. For the rest I have followed Apollodorus, a prose writer of the first or second century A.D. who is the only writer except Ovid to tell Hercules' life in full. I have preferred his treatment to Ovid's because, in this instance only, it is more detailed.

The greatest hero of Greece was Hercules. He was a personage of quite another order from the great hero of Athens, Theseus. He was what all Greece except Athens most admired. The Athenians were different from the other Greeks and their hero therefore was different. Theseus was, of course, bravest of the brave as all heroes are, but unlike other heroes he was as compassionate as he was brave and a man of great intellect as well as great bodily strength. It was natural that the Athenians should have such a hero because they valued thought and ideas as no other part of the country did. In Theseus their ideal was embodied. But Hercules embodied what the rest of Greece most valued. His qualities were those the Greeks in general honored and admired. Except for unflinching courage, they were not those that distinguished Theseus.

Hercules was the strongest man on earth and he had the supreme self-confidence magnificent physical strength gives. He considered himself on an equality with the gods—and with some reason. They needed his help to conquer the Giants. In the final victory of the Olympians over the brutish sons of Earth, Hercules' arrows played an important part. He treated the gods accordingly. Once when the priestess at Delphi gave no response to the question he asked, he seized the tripod she sat on and declared that he would carry it off and have an oracle of his own. Apollo, of course, would not put up with this, but Hercules was perfectly willing to fight him and Zeus had to intervene. The quarrel was easily settled, however. Hercules was quite good-natured about it. He did not want to quarrel with Apollo, he only wanted an answer from his oracle. If Apollo would give it the matter was settled as far as he was concerned. Apollo on his side, facing this undaunted person, felt an admiration for his boldness and made his priestess deliver the response.

Throughout his life Hercules had this perfect confidence that no matter who was against him he could never be defeated, and facts bore him out. Whenever he fought with anyone the issue was certain beforehand. He could be overcome only by a supernatural force. Hera used hers against him with terrible effect and in the end he was killed by magic, but nothing that lived in the air, sea, or on land ever defeated him.

Intelligence did not figure largely in anything he did and was often conspicuously absent. Once when he was too hot he pointed an arrow at the sun and threatened to shoot him. Another time when the boat he was in was tossed about by the waves he told the waters that he would punish them if they did not grow calm. His intellect was not strong. His emotions were. They were quickly aroused and apt to get out of control, as when he deserted the *Argo* and forgot all about his comrades and the Quest of the Golden Fleece in his despairing grief at losing his young armor-bearer, Hylas. This power of deep feeling in a man of his tremendous strength was oddly endearing, but it worked immense harm, too. He had sudden outbursts of furious anger which were always fatal to the often innocent objects. When the rage had passed and he had come to himself he would show a most disarming penitence and agree humbly to any punishment it was proposed to inflict on him. Without his consent he could not have been punished by anyone—yet nobody ever endured so many punishments. He spent a large part of his life expiating one unfortunate deed after another and never rebelling against the almost impossible demands made upon him. Sometimes he punished himself when others were inclined to exonerate him.

It would have been ludicrous to put him in command of a kingdom as Theseus was put; he had more than enough to do to command himself. He could never have thought out any new or great idea as the Athenian hero was held to have done. His thinking was limited to devising a way to kill a monster which was threatening to kill him. Nevertheless he had true greatness. Not because he had complete courage based upon overwhelming strength, which is merely a matter of course, but because, by his sorrow for wrongdoing and his willingness to do anything to expiate it, he showed greatness of soul. If only he had had some greatness of mind as well, at least enough to lead him along the ways of reason, he would have been the perfect hero.

He was born in Thebes and for a long time was held to be the son of Amphitryon, a distinguished general. In those earlier years he was called Alcides, or descendant of Alcaeus who was Amphitryon's father. But in reality he was the son of Zeus, who had visited Amphitryon's wife Alcmena in the shape of her husband when the general was away fighting. She bore two children, Hercules to Zeus and Iphicles to Amphitryon. The difference in the boys' descent was clearly shown in the way each acted in face of a great danger which came to them before they were a year old. Hera, as always, was furiously jealous and she determined to kill Hercules.

One evening Alcmena gave both the children their baths and their fill of milk and laid them in their crib, caressing them and saying, "Sleep, my little ones, soul of my soul. Happy be your slumber and happy your awakening." She rocked the cradle and in a moment the babies were asleep. But at darkest midnight when all was silent in the house two great snakes came crawling into the nursery. There was a light in the room and as the two reared up above the crib, with weaving heads and flickering tongues, the children woke. Iphicles screamed and tried to get out of bed, but Hercules sat up and grasped the deadly creatures by the throat. They turned and twisted and wound their coils around his body, but he held them fast. The mother heard Iphicles' screams and, calling to her husband, rushed to the nursery. There sat Hercules laughing, in each hand a long limp snake. He gave them gleefully to Amphitryon. They were dead. All knew then that the child was destined to great things. Teiresias, the blind prophet of Thebes, told Alcmena: "I swear that many a Greek

woman as she cards the wool at eventide shall sing of this
your son and you who bore him. He shall be the hero of all
mankind."

Great care was taken with his education, but teaching him
what he did not wish to learn was a dangerous business. He
seems not to have liked music, which was a most important
part of a Greek boy's training, or else he disliked his music
master. He flew into a rage with him and brained him with his
lute. This was the first time he dealt a fatal blow without
intending it. He did not mean to kill the poor musician; he
just struck out on the impulse of the moment without thinking, hardly aware of his strength. He was sorry, very sorry,
but that did not keep him from doing the same thing again
and again. The other subjects he was taught, fencing, wrestling,
and driving, he took to more kindly, and his teachers in these
branches all survived. By the time he was eighteen he was
full-grown and he killed, alone by himself, a great lion which
lived in the woods of Cithaeron, the Thespian lion. Ever
after he wore its skin as a cloak with the head forming a kind
of hood over his own head.

His next exploit was to fight and conquer the Minyans,
who had been exacting a burdensome tribute from the Thebans. The grateful citizens gave him as a reward the hand
of the Princess Megara. He was devoted to her and to their
children and yet this marriage brought upon him the greatest sorrow of his life as well as trials and dangers such as no
one ever went through, before or after. When Megara had
borne him three sons he went mad. Hera who never forgot a
wrong sent the madness upon him. He killed his children and
Megara, too, as she tried to protect the youngest. Then his
sanity returned. He found himself in his bloodstained hall,
the dead bodies of his sons and his wife beside him. He had
no idea what had happened, how they had been killed. Only
a moment since, as it seemed to him, they had all been talking
together. As he stood there in utter bewilderment the terrified
people who were watching him from a distance saw that the
mad fit was over, and Amphitryon dared to approach him.
There was no keeping the truth from Hercules. He had to know
how this horror had come to pass and Amphitryon told him.
Hercules heard him out; then he said, "And I myself am the
murderer of my dearest."

"Yes," Amphitryon answered trembling. "But you were out
of your mind."

Hercules paid no attention to the implied excuse.

"Shall I spare my own life then?" he said. "I will avenge
upon myself these deaths."

But before he could rush out and kill himself, even as he

started to do so, his desperate purpose was changed and his life was spared. This miracle—it was nothing less—of recalling Hercules, from frenzied feeling and violent action to sober reason and sorrowful acceptance, was not wrought by a god descending from the sky. It was a miracle caused by human friendship. His friend Theseus stood before him and stretched out his hands to clasp those bloodstained hands. Thus according to the common Greek idea he would himself become defiled and have a part in Hercules' guilt.

"Do not start back," he told Hercules. "Do not keep me from sharing all with you. Evil I share with you is not evil to me. And hear me. Men great of soul can bear the blows of heaven and not flinch."

Hercules said, "Do you know what I have done?"

"I know this," Theseus answered. "Your sorrows reach from earth to heaven."

"So I will die," said Hercules.

"No hero spoke those words," Theseus said.

"What can I do but die?" Hercules cried. "Live? A branded man, for all to say, 'Look. There is he who killed his wife and sons!' Everywhere my jailers, the sharp scorpions of the tongue!"

"Even so, suffer and be strong," Theseus answered. "You shall come to Athens with me, share my home and all things with me. And you will give to me and to the city a great return, the glory of having helped you."

A long silence followed. At last Hercules spoke, slow, heavy words. "So let it be," he said, "I will be strong and wait for death."

The two went to Athens, but Hercules did not stay there long. Theseus, the thinker, rejected the idea that a man could be guilty of murder when he had not known what he was doing and that those who helped such a one could be reckoned defiled. The Athenians agreed and welcomed the poor hero. But he himself could not understand such ideas. He could not think the thing out at all; he could only feel. He had killed his family. Therefore he was defiled and a defiler of others. He deserved that all should turn from him with loathing. At Delphi where he went to consult the oracle, the priestess looked at the matter just as he did. He needed to be purified, she told him, and only a terrible penance could do that. She bade him go to his cousin Eurystheus, King of Mycenae (of Tiryns in some stories) and submit to whatever he demanded of him. He went willingly, ready to do anything that could make him clean again. It is plain from the rest of the story that the priestess knew what Eurystheus was like and that he would beyond question purge Hercules thoroughly.

Eurystheus was by no means stupid, but of a very ingenious turn of mind, and when the strongest man on earth came to him humbly prepared to be his slave, he devised a series of penances which from the point of view of difficulty and danger could not have been improved upon. It must be said, however, that he was helped and urged on by Hera. To the end of Hercules' life she never forgave him for being Zeus's son. The tasks Eurystheus gave him to do are called "the Labors of Hercules." There were twelve of them and each one was all but impossible.

The first was to kill the lion of Nemea, a beast no weapons could wound. That difficulty Hercules solved by choking the life out of him. Then he heaved the huge carcass up on his back and carried it into Mycenae. After that, Eurystheus, a cautious man, would not let him inside the city. He gave him his orders from afar.

The second labor was to go to Lerna and kill a creature with nine heads called the Hydra which lived in a swamp there. This was exceedingly hard to do, because one of the heads was immortal and the others almost as bad, inasmuch as when Hercules chopped off one, two grew up instead. However, he was helped by his nephew Iolaus who brought him a burning brand with which he seared the neck as he cut each head off so that it could not sprout again. When all had been chopped off he disposed of the one that was immortal by burying it securely under a great rock.

The third labor was to bring back alive a stag with horns of gold, sacred to Artemis, which lived in the forests of Cerynitia. He could have killed it easily, but to take it alive was another matter and he hunted it a whole year before he succeeded.

The fourth labor was to capture a great boar which had its lair on Mount Erymanthus. He chased the beast from one place to another until it was exhausted; then he drove it into deep snow and trapped it.

The fifth labor was to clean the Augean stables in a single day. Augeas had thousands of cattle and their stalls had not been cleared out for years. Hercules diverted the courses of two rivers and made them flow through the stables in a great flood that washed out the filth in no time at all.

The sixth labor was to drive away the Stymphalian birds, which were a plague to the people of Stymphalus because of their enormous numbers. He was helped by Athena to drive them out of their coverts, and as they flew up he shot them.

The seventh labor was to go to Crete and fetch from there the beautiful savage bull that Poseidon had given Minos. Hercules mastered him, put him in a boat and brought him to Eurystheus.

The eighth labor was to get the man-eating mares of King Diomedes of Thrace. Hercules slew Diomedes first and then drove off the mares unopposed.

The ninth labor was to bring back the girdle of Hippolyta, the Queen of the Amazons. When Hercules arrived she met him kindly and told him she would give him the girdle, but Hera stirred up trouble. She made the Amazons think that Hercules was going to carry off their queen, and they charged down on his ship. Hercules, without a thought of how kind Hippolyta had been, without any thought at all, instantly killed her, taking it for granted that she was responsible for the attack. He was able to fight off the others and get away with the girdle.

The tenth labor was to bring back the cattle of Geryon, who was a monster with three bodies living on Erythia, a western island. On his way there Hercules reached the land at the end of the Mediterranean and he set up as a memorial of his journey two great rocks, called the pillars of Hercules (now Gibraltar and Ceuta). Then he got the oxen and took them to Mycenae.

The eleventh labor was the most difficult of all so far. It was to bring back the Golden Apples of the Hesperides, and he did not know where they were to be found. Atlas, who bore the vault of heaven upon his shoulders, was the father of the Hesperides, so Hercules went to him and asked him to get the apples for him. He offered to take upon himself the burden of the sky while Atlas was away. Atlas, seeing a chance of being relieved forever from his heavy task, gladly agreed. He came back with the apples, but he did not give them to Hercules. He told Hercules he could keep on holding up the sky, for Atlas himself would take the apples to Eurystheus. On this occasion Hercules had only his wits to trust to; he had to give all his strength to supporting that mighty load. He was successful, but because of Atlas' stupidity rather than his own cleverness. He agreed to Atlas' plan, but asked him to take the sky back for just a moment so that Hercules could put a pad on his shoulders to ease the pressure. Atlas did so, and Hercules picked up the apples and went off.

The twelfth labor was the worst of all. It took him down to the lower world, and it was then that he freed Theseus from the Chair of Forgetfulness. His task was to bring Cerberus, the three-headed dog, up from Hades. Pluto gave him permission provided Hercules used no weapons to overcome him. He could use his hands only. Even so, he forced the terrible mon-

Hercules carrying Cerberus

ster to submit to him. He lifted him and carried him all the way up to the earth and on to Mycenae. Eurystheus very sensibly did not want to keep him and made Hercules carry him back. This was his last labor.

When all were completed and full expiation made for the death of his wife and children, he would seem to have earned ease and tranquillity for the rest of his life. But it was not so. He was never tranquil and at ease. An exploit quite as difficult as most of the labors was the conquest of Antaeus, a Giant and a mighty wrestler who forced strangers to wrestle with him on condition that if he was victor he should kill them. He was roofing a temple with the skulls of his victims. As long as he could touch the earth he was invincible. If thrown to the ground he sprang up with renewed strength from the contact. Hercules lifted him up and holding him in the air strangled him.

Story after story is told of his adventures. He fought the river-god Achelous because Achelous was in love with the girl Hercules now wanted to marry. Like everyone else by this time, Achelous had no desire to fight him and he tried to reason with him. But that never worked with Hercules. It only made him more angry. He said, "My hand is better than my tongue. Let me win fighting and you may win talking." Achelous took the form of a bull and attacked him fiercely, but Hercules was used to subduing bulls. He conquered him and broke off one of his horns. The cause of the contest, a young princess named Deianira, became his wife.

He traveled to many lands and did many other great deeds. At Troy he rescued a maiden who was in the same plight as Andromeda, waiting on the shore to be devoured by a sea monster which could be appeased in no other way. She was the daughter of King Laomedon, who had cheated Apollo and Poseidon of their wages after at Zeus's command they had built for the King the walls of Troy. In return Apollo sent a pestilence, and Poseidon the sea serpent. Hercules agreed to rescue the girl if her father would give him the horses Zeus had given his grandfather. Laomedon promised, but when Hercules had slain the monster the King refused to pay. Hercules captured the city, killed the King, and gave the maiden to his friend, Telamon of Salamis, who had helped him.

On his way to Atlas to ask him about the Golden Apples, Hercules came to the Caucasus, where he freed Prometheus, slaying the eagle that preyed on him.

Along with these glorious deeds there were others not glorious. He killed with a careless thrust of his arm a lad who was serving him by pouring water on his hands before a feast. It was an accident and the boy's father forgave Hercules, but Her-

cules could not forgive himself and he went into exile for a
time. Far worse was his deliberately slaying a good friend in
order to avenge an insult offered him by the young man's father,
King Eurytus. For this base action Zeus himself punished him:
he sent him to Lydia to be a slave to the Queen, Omphale,
some say for a year, some for three years. She amused herself with him, making him at times dress up as a woman and
do woman's work, weave or spin. He submitted patiently, as
always, but he felt himself degraded by this servitude and with
complete unreason blamed Eurytus for it and swore he would
punish him to the utmost when he was freed.

All the stories told about him are characteristic, but the one
which gives the clearest picture of him is the account of a
visit he made when he was on his way to get the man-eating
mares of Diomedes, one of the twelve labors. The house he had
planned to spend a night in, that of his friend Admetus, a king
in Thessaly, was a place of deep mourning when he came to
it although he did not know. Admetus had just lost his wife
in a very strange way.

The cause of her death went back into the past, to the time
when Apollo in anger at Zeus for killing his son Aesculapius
killed Zeus's workmen, the Cyclopes. He was punished by being forced to serve on earth as a slave for a year and Admetus was the master he chose or Zeus chose for him. During his
servitude Apollo made friends with the household, especially
with the head of it and his wife Alcestis. When he had an
opportunity to prove how strong his friendship was he took it.
He learned that the three Fates had spun all of Admetus' thread
of life, and were on the point of cutting it. He obtained from
them a respite. If someone would die in Admetus' stead, he
could live. This news he took to Admetus, who at once set
about finding a substitute for himself. He went first quite con-
fidently to his father and mother. They were old and they were
devoted to him. Certainly one or the other would consent to
take his place in the world of the dead. But to his astonishment
he found they would not. They told him, "God's daylight is
sweet even to the old. We do not ask you to die for us. We will
not die for you." And they were completely unmoved by his
angry contempt: "You, standing palsied at the gate of death
and yet afraid to die!"

He would not give up, however. He went to his friends begging one after another of them to die and let him live. He
evidently thought his life was so valuable that someone would
surely save it even at the cost of the supreme sacrifice. But he
met with an invariable refusal. At last in despair he went back
to his house and there he found a substitute. His wife Alcestis
offered to die for him. No one who has read so far will need to

be told that he accepted the offer. He felt exceedingly sorry for her and still more for himself in having to lose so good a wife, and he stood weeping beside her as she died. When she was gone he was overwhelmed with grief and decreed that she should have the most magnificent of funerals.

It was at this point that Hercules arrived, to rest and enjoy himself under a friend's roof on his journey north to Diomedes. The way Admetus treated him shows more plainly than any other story we have how high the standards of hospitality were, how much was expected from a host to a guest.

As soon as Admetus was told of Hercules' arrival, he came to meet him with no appearance of mourning except in his dress. His manner was that of one gladly welcoming a friend. To Hercules' question who was dead he answered quietly that a woman of his household, but no relative of his, was to be buried that day. Hercules instantly declared that he would not trouble him with his presence at such a time, but Admetus steadily refused to let him go elsewhere. "I will not have you sleep under another's roof," he told him. To his servants he said that the guest was to be taken to a distant room where he could hear no sounds of grief, and given dinner and lodging there. No one must let him know what had happened.

Hercules dined alone, but he understood that Admetus must as a matter of form attend the funeral and the fact did not stand in the way of his enjoying himself. The servants left at home to attend to him were kept busy satisfying his enormous appetite and, still more, refilling his wine-jug. Hercules became very happy and very drunk and very noisy. He roared out songs at the top of his voice, some of them highly objectionable songs, and behaved himself in a way that was nothing less than indecent at the time of a funeral. When the servants looked their disapproval he shouted at them not to be so solemn. Couldn't they give him a smile now and then like good fellows? Their gloomy faces took away his appetite. "Have a drink with me," he cried, "many drinks."

One of them answered timidly that it was not a time for laughter and drinking.

"Why not?" thundered Hercules. "Because a stranger woman is dead?"

"A stranger—" faltered the servant.

"Well, that's what Admetus told me," Hercules said angrily. "I suppose you won't say he lied to me."

"Oh, no," the servant answered. "Only—he's too hospitable. But please have some more wine. Our trouble is only our own."

He turned to fill the winecup but Hercules seized him—and no one ever disregarded that grasp.

"There's something strange here," he said to the frightened man. "What is wrong?"

"You see for yourself we are in mourning," the other answered.

"But why, man, why?" Hercules cried. "Has my host made a fool of me? Who is dead?"

"Alcestis," the servant whispered. "Our Queen."

There was a long silence. Then Hercules threw down his cup. "I might have known," he said. "I saw he had been weeping. His eyes were red. But he swore it was a stranger. He made me come in. Oh, good friend and good host. And I—got drunk, made merry, in this house of sorrow. Oh, he should have told me."

Then he did as always, he heaped blame upon himself. He had been a fool, a drunken fool, when the man he cared for was crushed with grief. As always, too, his thoughts turned quickly to find some way of atoning. What could he do to make amends? There was nothing he could not do. He was perfectly sure of that, but what was there which would help his friend? Then light dawned on him. "Of course," he said to himself. "That is the way. I must bring Alcestis back from the dead. Of course. Nothing could be clearer. I'll find that old fellow, Death. He is sure to be near her tomb and I'll wrestle with him. I will crack his body between my arms until he gives her to me. If he is not by the grave I will go down to Hades after him. Oh, I will return good to my friend who has been so good to me." He hurried out exceedingly pleased with himself and enjoying the prospect of what promised to be a very good wrestling match.

When Admetus returned to his empty and desolate house Hercules was there to greet him, and by his side was a woman. "Look at her, Admetus," he said. "Is she like anyone you know?" And when Admetus cried out, "A ghost! Is it a trick—some mockery of the gods?" Hercules answered, "It is your wife. I fought Death for her and I made him give her back."

There is no other story about Hercules which shows so clearly his character as the Greeks saw it: his simplicity and blundering stupidity; his inability not to get roaring drunk in a house where someone was dead; his quick penitence and desire to make amends at no matter what cost; his perfect confidence that not even Death was his match. That is the portrait of Hercules. To be sure, it would have been still more accurate if it had shown him in a fit of rage killing one of the servants who were annoying him with their gloomy faces, but the poet Euripides from whom we get the story kept it clear of everything that did not bear directly on Alcestis' death and return to life. Another death or two, however natural when Hercules was present, would have blurred the picture he wanted to paint.

As Hercules had sworn to do while he was Omphale's slave, no sooner was he free than he started to punish King Eurytus because he himself had been punished by Zeus for killing Eurytus' son. He collected an army, captured the King's city and put him to death. But Eurytus, too, was avenged, for indirectly this victory was the cause of Hercules' own death.

Before he had quite completed the destruction of the city, he sent home—where Deianira, his devoted wife, was waiting for him to come back from Omphale in Lydia—a band of captive maidens, one of them especially beautiful, Iole, the King's daughter. The man who brought them to Deianira told her that Hercules was madly in love with this Princess. This news was not so hard for Deianira as might be expected, because she believed she had a powerful love-charm which she had kept for years against just such an evil, a woman in her own house preferred before her. Directly after her marriage, when Hercules was taking her home, they had reached a river where the Centaur Nessus acted as ferryman, carrying travelers over the water. He took Deianira on his back and in midstream insulted her. She shrieked and Hercules shot the beast as he reached the other bank. Before he died he told Deianira to take some of his blood and use it as a charm for Hercules if ever he loved another woman more than her. When she heard about Iole, it seemed to her the time had come, and she anointed a splendid robe with the blood and sent it to Hercules by the messenger.

As the hero put it on, the effect was the same as that of the robe Medea had sent her rival whom Jason was about to marry. A fearful pain seized him, as though he were in a burning fire. In his first agony he turned on Deianira's messenger, who was, of course, completely innocent, seized him and hurled him down into the sea. He could still slay others, but it seemed that he himself could not die. The anguish he felt hardly weakened him. What had instantly killed the young Princess of Corinth could not kill Hercules. He was in torture, but he lived and they brought him home. Long before, Deianira had heard what her gift had done to him and had killed herself. In the end he did the same. Since death would not come to him, he would go to death. He ordered those around him to build a great pyre on Mount Oeta and carry him to it. When at last he reached it he knew that now he could die and he was glad. "This is rest," he said. "This is the end." And as they lifted him to the pyre he lay down on it as one who at a banquet table lies down upon his couch.

He asked his youthful follower, Philoctetes, to hold the torch to set the wood on fire; and he gave him his bow and arrows, which were to be far-famed in the young man's hands, too, at Troy. Then the flames rushed up and Hercules was seen no more on earth. He was taken to heaven, where he was reconciled to Hera and married her daughter Hebe, and where

> After his mighty labors he has rest.
> His choicest prize eternal peace
> Within the homes of blessedness.

But it is not easy to imagine him contentedly enjoying rest and peace, or allowing the blessed gods to do so, either.

12 Atalanta

*Her story is told in full only by the late writers Ovid
and Apollodorus, but it is an old tale. One of the
poems ascribed to Hesiod, but probably of a somewhat later date, say, the early seventh century, describes the race and the golden apples, and the* Iliad
*gives an account of the Calydonian boar hunt. I have
followed in my account Apollodorus, who probably
wrote in the first or second century A.D. Ovid's tale is
good only occasionally. He gives a charming picture
of Atalanta among the hunters which I have put into
my account, but often, as in the description of the
boar, he is so exaggerated, he verges on the ridiculous.
Apollodorus is not picturesque, but he is never absurd.*

Sometimes there are said to have been two heroines of that
name. Certainly two men, Iasus and Schoenius, are each called
the father of Atalanta, but then it often happens in old stories
that different names are given to unimportant persons. If there
were two Atalantas it is certainly remarkable that both wanted
to sail on the *Argo*, both took part in the Calydonian boar hunt,
both married a man who beat them in a foot race, and both
were ultimately changed into lionesses. Since the story of each
is practically the same as that of the other it is simpler to take
it for granted that there was only one. Indeed it would seem
passing the bounds of the probable even in mythological stories
to suppose that there were two maidens living at the same time
who loved adventure as much as the most dauntless hero, and
who could outshoot and outrun and outwrestle, too, the men
of one of the two great ages of heroism.

Atalanta's father, whatever his name was, when a daughter
and not a son was born to him, was, of course, bitterly disap-
pointed. He decided that she was not worth bringing up and
had the tiny creature left on a wild mountainside to die of cold
and hunger. But, as so often happens in stories, animals proved

kinder than humans. A she-bear took charge of her, nursed her and kept her warm, and the baby grew up thus into an active, daring little girl. Kind hunters then found her and took her to live with them. She became in the end more than their equal in all the arduous feats of a hunter's life. Once two Centaurs, swifter and stronger by far than any mortal, caught sight of her when she was alone and pursued her. She did not run from them; that would have been folly. She stood still and fitted an arrow to her bow and shot. A second arrow followed. Both Centaurs fell, mortally wounded.

Then came the famous hunt of the Calydonian boar. This was a terrible creature sent to ravage the country of Calydon by Artemis in order to punish the King, Oeneus, because he forgot her when he was sacrificing the first fruits to the gods at the harvest-time. The brute devastated the land, destroyed the cattle, killed the men who tried to kill it. Finally Oeneus called for help upon the bravest men of Greece, and a splendid band of young heroes assembled, many of whom sailed later on the *Argo*. With them came as a matter of course Atalanta, "The pride of the woods of Arcady." We have a description of how she looked when she walked in on that masculine gathering: "A shining buckle clasped her robe at the neck; her hair was simply dressed, caught up in a knot behind. An ivory quiver hung upon her left shoulder and in her hand was a bow. Thus was she attired. As for her face, it seemed too maidenly to be that of a boy, and too boyish to be that of a maiden." To one man there, however, she looked lovelier and more desirable than any maiden he had ever seen. Oeneus' son, Meleager, fell in love with her at first sight. But, we may be sure, Atalanta treated him as a good comrade, not as a possible lover. She had no liking for men except as companions in the hunt and she was determined never to marry.

Some of the heroes resented her presence and felt it beneath them to go hunting with a woman, but Meleager insisted and they finally gave in to him. It proved well for them that they did, because when they surrounded the boar, the brute rushed upon them so swiftly that it killed two men before the others could come to their help, and, what was equally ominous, a third man fell pierced by a misdirected javelin. In this confusion of dying men and wildly flying weapons Atalanta kept her head and wounded the boar. Her arrow was the first to strike it. Meleager then rushed on the wounded creature and stabbed it to the heart. Technically speaking it was he who killed it, but the honors of the hunt went to Atalanta and Meleager insisted that they should give her the skin.

Strangely enough this was the cause of his own death. When he was just a week old the Fates had appeared to his mother,

Althea, and thrown a log of wood into the fire burning in her chamber. Then spinning as they ever did, twirling the distaff and twisting the thread of destiny, they sang,

> To you, O new-born child, we grant a gift,
> To live until this wood turns into ash.

Althea snatched the brand from the fire, quenched the flame, and hid it in a chest. Her brothers were among those who went to hunt the boar. They felt themselves insulted and were furiously angry at having the prize go to a girl—as, no doubt, was the case with others, but they were Meleager's uncles and did not need to stand on any ceremony with him. They declared that Atalanta should not have the skin and told Meleager he had no more right to give it away than anyone else had. Whereupon Meleager killed them both, taking them completely off their guard.

This news was brought to Althea. Her beloved brothers had been slain by her son because he had made a fool of himself over a shameless hussy who went hunting with men. A passion of rage took possession of her. She rushed to the chest for the brand and threw it into the fire. As it blazed up, Meleager fell to the ground dying, and by the time it was consumed his spirit had slipped away from his body. It is said that Althea, horror-stricken at what she had done, hanged herself. So the Calydonian boar hunt ended in tragedy.

To Atalanta, however, it was only the beginning of her adventures. Some say that she sailed with the Argonauts; others that Jason persuaded her not to do so. She is never mentioned in the story of their exploits and she was certainly not one to hold back when deeds of daring were to be done, so that it seems probable that she did not go. The next time we hear of her is after the Argonauts returned, when Medea had killed Jason's uncle Pelias under the pretext of restoring him to youth. At the funeral games held in his honor Atalanta appeared among the contestants, and in the wrestling match conquered the young man who was to be the father of Achilles, the great hero Peleus.

It was after this achievement that she discovered who her parents were and went to live with them, her father apparently being reconciled to having a daughter who really seemed almost if not quite as good as a son. It seems odd that a number of men wanted to marry her because she could hunt and shoot and wrestle, but it was so; she had a great many suitors. As a way of disposing of them easily and agreeably she declared that she would marry whoever could beat her in a foot race, knowing well that there was no such man alive. She had a delightful

Atalanta and the golden apples

me. Fleet-footed young men were always arriving to race with
er and she always outran them.

But at last one came who used his head as well as his heels.
He knew he was not as good a runner as she, but he had a plan.
By the favor of Aphrodite, always on the lookout to subdue
wild young maidens who despised love, this ingenious young
man, whose name was either Melanion (Milanion) or Hippomenes, got possession of three wondrous apples, all of pure gold,
beautiful as those that grew in the garden of the Hesperides.
No one alive could see them and not want them.

On the race course as Atalanta—poised for the starting signal, and a hundredfold more lovely disrobed than with her
garments on—looked fiercely around her, wonder at her beauty
took hold of all who saw her, but most of all the man who was
waiting to run against her. He kept his head, however, and held
fast to his golden apples. They started, she flying swift as an
arrow, her hair tossed back over her white shoulders, a rosy
flush tinging her fair body. She was outstripping him when he
rolled one of the apples directly in front of her. It needed but
a moment for her to stoop and pick the lovely thing up, but
that brief pause brought him abreast of her. A moment more
and he threw the second, this time a little to the side. She had
to swerve to reach it and he got ahead of her. Almost at once,
however, she had caught up with him and the goal was now
very near. But then the third golden sphere flashed across her
path and rolled far into the grass beside the course. She saw
the gleam through the green, she could not resist it. As she
picked the apple up, her lover panting and almost winded
touched the goal. She was his. Her free days alone in the forest
and her athletic victories were over.

The two are said to have been turned into lions because of
some affront offered either to Zeus or to Aphrodite. But before
that Atalanta had borne a son, Parthenopaeus, who was one of
the Seven against Thebes.

PART FOUR

The Heroes of the Trojan War

13 The Trojan War

> *This story, of course, is taken almost entirely from*
> *Homer. The Iliad, however, begins after the Greeks*
> *have reached Troy, when Apollo sends the pestilence*
> *upon them. It does not mention the sacrifice of Iphi-*
> *genia, and makes only a dubious allusion to the Judg-*
> *ment of Paris. I have taken Iphigenia's story from*
> *a play by the fifth-century tragic poet Aeschylus,*
> *the* Agamemnon, *and the Judgment of Paris from*
> *the* Trojan Woman, *a play by his contemporary,*
> *Euripides, adding a few details, such as the tale of*
> *Oenone, from the prose-writer Apollodorus, who*
> *wrote probably in the first or second century A.D. He*
> *is usually very uninteresting, but in treating the events*
> *leading up to the Iliad he was apparently inspired by*
> *touching so great a subject and he is less dull than in*
> *almost any other part of his book.*

More than a thousand years before Christ, near the eastern end
of the Mediterranean was a great city very rich and powerful,
second to none on earth. The name of it was Troy and even today no city is more famous. The cause of this long-lasting fame
was a war told of in one of the world's greatest poems, the
Iliad, and the cause of the war went back to a dispute between
three jealous goddesses.

Prologue: THE JUDGMENT OF PARIS

The evil goddess of Discord, Eris, was naturally not popular in Olympus, and when the gods gave a banquet they were apt to leave her out. Resenting this deeply, she determined to make trouble—and she succeeded very well indeed. At an important marriage, that of King Peleus and the sea nymph Thetis, to which she alone of all the divinities was not invited, she threw into the banqueting hall a golden apple marked *For the Fairest*. Of course all the goddesses wanted it, but in the end the choice was narrowed down to three: Aphrodite, Hera and Pallas Athena. They asked Zeus to judge between them, but very wisely he refused to have anything to do with the matter. He told them to go to Mount Ida, near Troy, where the young prince Paris, also called Alexander, was keeping his father's sheep. He was an excellent judge of beauty, Zeus told them. Paris, though a royal prince, was doing shepherd's work because his father Priam, the King of Troy, had been warned that this prince would some day be the ruin of his country, and so had sent him away. At the moment Paris was living with a lovely nymph named Oenone.

His amazement can be imagined when there appeared before him the wondrous forms of the three great goddesses. He was not asked, however, to gaze at the radiant divinities and choose which of them seemed to him the fairest, but only to consider the bribes each offered and choose which seemed to him best worth taking. Nevertheless, the choice was not easy. What men care for most was set before him. Hera promised to make him Lord of Europe and Asia; Athena, that he would lead the Trojans to victory against the Greeks and lay Greece in ruins; Aphrodite, that the fairest woman in all the world should be his. Paris, a weakling and something of a coward, too, as later events showed, chose the last. He gave Aphrodite the golden apple.

That was the Judgment of Paris, famed everywhere as the real reason why the Trojan War was fought.

THE TROJAN WAR

The fairest woman in the world was Helen, the daughter of Zeus and Leda and the sister of Castor and Pollux. Such was the report of her beauty that not a young prince in Greece but wanted to marry her. When her suitors assembled in her home to make a formal proposal for her hand they were so many and from such powerful families that her reputed father, King

The judgment of Paris

Tyndareus, her mother's husband, was afraid to select one among them, fearing that the others would unite against him. He therefore exacted first a solemn oath from all that they would champion the cause of Helen's husband, whoever he might be, if any wrong was done to him through his marriage. It was, after all, to each man's advantage to take the oath, since each was hoping he would be the person chosen, so they all bound themselves to punish to the uttermost anyone who carried or tried to carry Helen away. Then Tyndareus chose Menelaus, the brother of Agamemnon, and made him King of Sparta as well.

So matters stood when Paris gave the golden apple to Aphrodite. The Goddess of Love and Beauty knew very well where the most beautiful woman on earth was to be found. She led the young shepherd, with never a thought of Oenone left forlorn, straight to Sparta, where Menelaus and Helen received him graciously as their guest. The ties between guest and host were strong. Each was bound to help and never harm the other. But Paris broke that sacred bond. Menelaus trusting completely to it left Paris in his home and went off to Crete. Then,

> Paris who coming
> Entered a friend's kind dwelling,
> Shamed the hand there that gave him food,
> Stealing away a woman.

Menelaus got back to find Helen gone, and he called upon all Greece to help him. The chieftains responded, as they were bound to do. They were eager for the great enterprise, to cross the sea and lay mighty Troy in ashes. Two, however, of the first rank, were missing: Odysseus, King of the Island of Ithaca, and Achilles, the son of Peleus and the sea nymph Thetis. Odysseus, who was one of the shrewdest and most sensible men in Greece, did not want to leave his house and family to embark on a romantic adventure overseas for the sake of a faithless woman. He pretended, therefore, that he had gone mad, and when a messenger from the Greek Army arrived, the King was plowing a field and sowing it with salt instead of seed. But the messenger was shrewd too. He seized Odysseus' little son and put him directly in the way of the plow. Instantly the father turned the plow aside, thus proving that he had all his wits about him. However reluctant, he had to join the Army.

Achilles was kept back by his mother. The sea nymph knew that if he went to Troy he was fated to die there. She sent him to the court of Lycomedes, the king who had treacherously killed Theseus, and made him wear women's clothes and hide among the maidens. Odysseus was dispatched by the chieftains to find him out. Disguised as a pedlar he went to the court where the lad was said to be, with gay ornaments in his pack such as women love, and also some fine weapons. While the girls flocked around the trinkets, Achilles fingered the swords and daggers. Odysseus knew him then, and he had no trouble at all in making him disregard what his mother had said and go to the Greek camp with him.

So the great fleet made ready. A thousand ships carried the Greek host. They met at Aulis, a place of strong winds and dangerous tides, impossible to sail from as long as the north wind blew. And it kept on blowing, day after day.

> It broke men's heart,
> Spared not ship nor cable.
> The time dragged,
> Doubling itself in passing.

The Army was desperate. At last the soothsayer, Calchas, declared that the gods had spoken to him: Artemis was angry. One of her beloved wild creatures, a hare, had been slain by the Greeks, together with her young, and the only way to calm the wind and ensure a safe voyage to Troy was to appease her by sacrificing to her a royal maiden, Iphigenia, the eldest daughter of the Commander in Chief, Agamemnon. This was terrible to all, but to her father hardly bearable.

> If I must slay
> The joy of my house, my daughter.
> A father's hands
> Stained with dark streams flowing
> From blood of a girl
> Slaughtered before the altar.

Nevertheless he yielded. His reputation with the Army was at stake, and his ambition to conquer Troy and exalt Greece.

> He dared the deed,
> Slaying his child to help a war.

He sent home for her, writing his wife that he had arranged a great marriage for her, to Achilles, who had already shown himself the best and greatest of all the chieftains. But when she came to her wedding she was carried to the altar to be killed.

> And all her prayers—cries of Father, Father,
> Her maiden life,
> These they held as nothing,
> The savage warriors, battle-mad.

She died and the north wind ceased to blow and the Greek ships sailed out over a quiet sea, but the evil price they had paid was bound some day to bring evil down upon them.

When they reached the mouth of the Simois, one of the rivers of Troy, the first man to leap ashore was Protesilaus. It was a brave deed, for the oracle had said that he who landed first would be the first to die. Therefore when he had fallen by a Trojan spear the Greeks paid him honors as though he were divine and the gods, too, greatly distinguished him. They had Hermes bring him up from the dead to see once again his deeply mourning wife, Laodamia. She would not give him up a second time, however. When he went back to the underworld she went with him; she killed herself.

The thousand ships carried a great host of fighting men and the Greek Army was very strong, but the Trojan City was strong, too. Priam, the King, and his Queen, Hecuba, had many brave sons to lead the attack and to defend the walls, one above all, Hector, than whom no man anywhere was nobler or more brave, and only one a greater warrior, the champion of the Greeks, Achilles. Each knew that he would die before Troy was taken. Achilles had been told by his mother: "Very brief is your lot. Would that you could be free now from tears and troubles, for you shall not long endure, my child, short-lived beyond all men and to be pitied." No divinity had told Hector, but he was equally sure. "I know well in my heart and in my soul," he said to his wife Andromache, "the day shall come when holy Troy will be laid low and Priam and Priam's people." Both heroes fought under the shadow of certain death.

For nine years victory wavered, now to this side, now to that. Neither was ever able to gain any decided advantage. Then a quarrel flared up between two Greeks, Achilles and Agamemnon, and for a time it turned the tide in favor of the Trojans. Again a woman was the reason, Chryseis, daughter of Apollo's priest, whom the Greeks had carried off and given to Agamemnon. Her father came to beg for her release, but Agamemnon would not let her go. Then the priest prayed to the mighty god he served and Phoebus Apollo heard him. From his sun-chariot he shot fiery arrows down upon the Greek Army, and men sickened and died so that the funeral pyres were burning continually.

At last Achilles called an assembly of the chieftains. He told them that they could not hold out against both the pestilence and the Trojans, and that they must either find a way to appease Apollo or else sail home. Then the prophet Calchas stood up and said he knew why the god was angry, but that he was afraid to speak unless Achilles would guarantee his safety. "I do so," Achilles answered, "even if you accuse Agamemnon himself." Every man there understood what that meant; they knew how Apollo's priest had been treated. When Calchas declared that Chryseis must be given back to her father, he had all the chiefs behind him and Agamemnon, greatly angered, was obliged to agree. "But if I lose her who was my prize of honor," he told Achilles, "I will have another in her stead."

Therefore when Chryseis had been returned to her father, Agamemnon sent two of his squires to Achilles' tent to take his prize of honor away from him, the maiden Briseis. Most unwillingly they went and stood before the hero in heavy silence. But he knowing their errand told them it was not they who were wronging him. Let them take the girl without fear for themselves, but hear him first while he swore before gods and men that Agamemnon would pay dearly for the deed.

That night Achilles' mother, silver-footed Thetis the sea nymph, came to him. She was as angry as he. She told him to have nothing more to do with the Greeks, and with that she went up to heaven and asked Zeus to give success to the Trojans. Zeus was very reluctant. The war by now had reached Olympus—the gods were ranged against each other. Aphrodite, of course, was on the side of Paris. Equally, of course, Hera and Athena were against him. Ares, God of War, always took sides with Aphrodite; while Poseidon, Lord of the Sea, favored the Greeks, a sea people, always great sailors. Apollo cared for Hector and for his sake helped the Trojans, and Artemis, as his sister, did so too. Zeus liked the Trojans best, on the whole, but he wanted to be neutral because Hera was so disagreeable whenever he opposed her openly. However, he could not resist Thetis. He had a hard time with Hera, who guessed, as she usually did, what he was about. He was driven finally into telling her that he would lay hands upon her if she did not stop talking. Hera kept silence then, but her thoughts were busy as to how she might help the Greeks and circumvent Zeus.

The plan Zeus made was simple. He knew that the Greeks without Achilles were inferior to the Trojans, and he sent a lying dream to Agamemnon promising him victory if he attacked. While Achilles stayed in his tent a fierce battle followed, the hardest yet fought. Up on the wall of Troy the old King Priam and the other old men, wise in the ways of war, sat watching the contest. To them came Helen, the cause of all that agony and death, yet as they looked at her, they could not feel any blame. "Men must fight for such as she," they said to each other. "For her face was like to that of an immortal spirit." She stayed by them, telling them the names of this and that Greek hero, until to their astonishment the battle ceased. The armies drew back on either side and in the space between, Paris and Menelaus faced each other. It was evident that the sensible decision had been reached to let the two most concerned fight it out alone.

Paris struck first, but Menelaus caught the swift spear on his shield, then hurled his own. It rent Paris' tunic, but did not wound him. Menelaus drew his sword, his only weapon now, but as he did so it fell from his hand broken. Undaunted though unarmed he leaped upon Paris and seizing him by his helmet's crest swung him off his feet. He would have dragged him to the Greeks victoriously if it had not been for Aphrodite. She tore away the strap that kept the helmet on so that it came away in Menelaus' hand. Paris himself, who had not fought at all except to throw his spear, she caught up in a cloud and took back to Troy.

Furiously Menelaus went through the Trojan ranks seeking Paris, and not a man there but would have helped him for they all hated Paris, but he was gone, no one knew how or where. So Agamemnon spoke to both armies, declaring that Menelaus was victor and bidding the Trojans give Helen back. This was just, and the Trojans would have agreed if Athena, at Hera's prompting, had not interfered. Hera was determined that the war should not end until Troy was ruined. Athena, sweeping down to the battlefield, persuaded the foolish heart of Pandarus, a Trojan, to break the truce and shoot an arrow at Menelaus. He did so and wounded him, only slightly, but the Greeks in rage at the treachery turned upon the Trojans and the battle was on again. Terror and Destruction and Strife, whose fury never slackens, all friends of the murderous War-god, were there to urge men on to slaughter each other. Then the voice of groaning was heard and the voice of triumph from slayer and from slain and the earth streamed with blood.

On the Greek side, with Achilles gone, the two greatest champions were Ajax and Diomedes. They fought gloriously that day and many a Trojan lay on his face in the dust before them. The best and bravest next to Hector, the Prince Aeneas, came near to death at Diomedes' hands. He was of more than royal blood; his mother was Aphrodite herself, and when Diomedes wounded him she hastened down to the battlefield to save him. She lifted him in her soft arms, but Diomedes, knowing she was a coward goddess, not one of those who like Athena are masters where warriors fight, leaped toward her and wounded her hand. Crying out she let Aeneas fall, and weeping for pain made her way to Olympus, where Zeus smiling to see the laughter-loving goddess in tears bade her stay away from battle and remember hers were the works of love and not of war. But although his mother failed him Aeneas was not killed. Apollo enveloped him in a cloud and carried him to sacred Pergamos, the holy place of Troy, where Artemis healed him of his wound.

But Diomedes raged on, working havoc in the Trojan ranks until he came face to face with Hector. There to his dismay

he saw Ares too. The bloodstained murderous god of war was
fighting for Hector. At the sight Diomedes shuddered and cried
to the Greeks to fall back, slowly, however, and with their faces
toward the Trojans. Then Hera was angry. She urged her
horses to Olympus and asked Zeus if she might drive that bane
of men, Ares, from the battlefield. Zeus who loved him no
more than Hera did even though he was their son, willingly
gave her leave. She hastened down to stand beside Diomedes and
urge him to smite the terrible god and have no fear. At that,
joy filled the hero's heart. He rushed at Ares and hurled his
spear at him. Athena drove it home, and it entered Ares' body.
The War-god bellowed as loud as ten thousand cry in battle,
and at the awful sound trembling seized the whole host,
Greeks and Trojans alike.

Ares, really a bully at heart and unable to bear what he
brought upon unnumbered multitudes of men, fled up to Zeus
in Olympus and complained bitterly of Athena's violence. But
Zeus looked at him sternly and told him he was as intolerable as his mother, and bade him cease his whining. With Ares
gone, however, the Trojans were forced to fall back. At this
crisis a brother of Hector's, wise in discerning the will of the
gods, urged Hector to go with all speed to the city and tell
the Queen, his mother, to offer to Athena the most beautiful
robe she owned and pray her to have mercy. Hector felt the
wisdom of the advice and sped through the gates to the palace,
where his mother did all as he said. She took a robe so precious
that it shone like a star, and laying it on the goddess's knees
she besought her: "Lady Athena, spare the city and the wives of
the Trojans and the little children." But Pallas Athena denied
the prayer.

As Hector went back to the battle he turned aside to see
once more, perhaps for the last time, the wife he tenderly
loved, Andromache, and his son Astyanax. He met her on the
wall where she had gone in terror to watch the fighting when
she heard the Trojans were in retreat. With her was a hand-
maid carrying the little boy. Hector smiled and looked at them
silently, but Andromache took his hand in hers and wept. "My
dear lord," she said, "you who are father and mother and
brother unto me as well as husband, stay here with us. Do not
make me a widow and your child an orphan." He refused her
gently. He could not be a coward, he said. It was for him to
fight always in the forefront of the battle. Yet she could know
that he never forgot what her anguish would be when he died.
That was the thought that troubled him above all else, more
than his many other cares. He turned to leave her, but first he
held out his arms to his son. Terrified the little boy shrank
back, afraid of the helmet and its fierce nodding crest. Hector

laughed and took the shining helmet from his head. Then holding the child in his arms he caressed him and prayed, "O Zeus, in after years may men say of this my son when he returns from battle, 'Far greater is he than his father was.'"

So he laid the boy in his wife's arms and she took him, smiling, yet with tears. And Hector pitied her and touched her tenderly with his hand and spoke to her: "Dear one, be not so sorrowful. That which is fated must come to pass, but against my fate no man can kill me." Then taking up his helmet he left her and she went to her house, often looking back at him and weeping bitterly.

Once again on the battlefield he was eager for the fight, and better fortune for a time lay before him. Zeus had by now remembered his promise to Thetis to avenge Achilles' wrong. He ordered all the other immortals to stay in Olympus; he himself went down to earth to help the Trojans. Then it went hard with the Greeks. Their great champion was far away. Achilles sat alone in his tent, brooding over his wrongs. The great Trojan champion had never before shown himself so brilliant and so brave. Hector seemed irresistible. Tamer of horses, the Trojans always called him, and he drove his car through the Greek ranks as if the same spirit animated steeds and driver. His glancing helm was everywhere and one gallant warrior after another fell beneath his terrible bronze spear. When evening ended the battle, the Trojans had driven the Greeks back almost to their ships.

There was rejoicing in Troy that night, but grief and despair in the Greek camp. Agamemnon himself was all for giving up and sailing back to Greece. Nestor, however, who was the oldest among the chieftains and therefore the wisest, wiser even than the shrewd Odysseus, spoke out boldly and told Agamemnon that if he had not angered Achilles they would not have been defeated. "Try to find some way of appeasing him," he said, "instead of going home disgraced." All applauded the advice and Agamemnon confessed that he had acted like a fool. He would send Briseis back, he promised them, and with her many other splendid gifts, and he begged Odysseus to take his offer to Achilles.

Odysseus and the two chieftains chosen to accompany him found the hero with his friend Patroclus, who of all men on earth was dearest to him. Achilles welcomed them courteously and set food and drink before them, but when they told him why they had come and all the rich gifts that would be his if he would yield, and begged him to have pity on his hard-pressed countrymen, they received an absolute refusal. Not all the treasures of Egypt could buy him, he told them. He was sailing home and they would be wise to do the same.

But all rejected that counsel when Odysseus brought back the answer. The next day they went into battle with the desperate courage of brave men cornered. Again they were driven back, until they stood fighting on the beach where their ships were drawn up. But help was at hand. Hera had laid her plans. She saw Zeus sitting on Mount Ida watching the Trojans conquer, and she thought how she detested him. But she knew well that she could get the better of him only in one way. She must go to him looking so lovely that he could not resist her. When he took her in his arms she would pour sweet sleep upon him and he would forget the Trojans. So she did. She went to her chamber and used every art she knew to make herself beautiful beyond compare. Last of all she borrowed Aphrodite's girdle wherein were all her enchantments, and with this added charm she appeared before Zeus. As he saw her, love overcame his heart so that he thought no more of his promise to Thetis.

At once the battle turned in favor of the Greeks. Ajax hurled Hector to the ground, although before he could wound him Aeneas lifted him and bore him away. With Hector gone, the Greeks were able to drive the Trojans far back from the ships and Troy might have been sacked that very day if Zeus had not awakened. He leaped up and saw the Trojans in flight and Hector lying gasping on the plain. All was clear to him and he turned fiercely to Hera. This was her doing, he said, her crafty, crooked ways. He was half-minded to give her then and there a beating. When it came to that kind of fighting Hera knew she was helpless. She promptly denied that she had had anything to do with the Trojans' defeat. It was all Poseidon, she said, and indeed the Sea-god had been helping the Greeks contrary to Zeus's orders, but only because she had begged him. However, Zeus was glad enough of an excuse not to lay hands on her. He sent her back to Olympus and summoned Iris, the rainbow messenger, to carry his command to Poseidon to withdraw from the field. Sullenly the Sea-god obeyed and once more the tide of battle turned against the Greeks.

Apollo had revived the fainting Hector and breathed into him surpassing power. Before the two, the god and the hero, the Greeks were like a flock of frightened sheep driven by mountain lions. They fled in confusion to the ships, and the wall they had built to defend them went down like a sand wall children heap up on the shore and then scatter in their play. The Trojans were almost near enough to set the ships on fire. The Greeks, hopeless, thought only of dying bravely.

Patroclus, Achilles' beloved friend, saw the rout with horror. Not even for Achilles' sake could he stay longer away from the battle. "You can keep your wrath while your countrymen go down in ruin," he cried to Achilles. "I cannot. Give me your armor. If they think I am you, the Trojans may pause and the worn-out Greeks have a breathing space. You and I are fresh. We might yet drive back the enemy. But if you will sit nursing your anger, at least let me have the armor." As he spoke one of the Greek ships burst into flame. "That way they can cut off the Army's retreat," Achilles said. "Go. Take my armor, my men too, and defend the ships. I cannot go. I am a man dishonored. For my own ships, if the battle comes near them, I will fight. I will not fight for men who have disgraced me."

So Patroclus put on the splendid armor all the Trojans knew and feared, and led the Myrmidons, Achilles' men, to the battle. At the first onset of this new band of warriors the Trojans wavered; they thought Achilles led them on. And indeed for a time Patroclus fought as gloriously as that great hero himself could have done. But at last he met Hector face to face and his doom was sealed as surely as a boar is doomed when he faces a lion. Hector's spear gave him a mortal wound and his soul fled from his body down to the house of Hades. Then Hector stripped his armor from him and casting his own aside, put it on. It seemed as though he had taken on, too, Achilles' strength, and no man of the Greeks could stand before him.

Evening came that puts an end to battle. Achilles sat by his tent waiting for Patroclus to return. But instead he saw old Nestor's son running toward him, fleet-footed Antilochus. He was weeping hot tears as he ran. "Bitter tidings," he cried out. "Patroclus is fallen and Hector has his armor." Grief took hold of Achilles, so black that those around him feared for his life. Down in the sea caves his mother knew his sorrow and came up to try to comfort him. "I will no longer live among men," he told her, "if I do not make Hector pay with his death for Patroclus dead." Then Thetis weeping bade him remember that he himself was fated to die straightway after Hector. "So may I do," Achilles answered, "I who did not help my comrade in his sore need. I will kill the destroyer of him I loved; then I will accept death when it comes."

Thetis did not attempt to hold him back. "Only wait until morning," she said, "and you will not go unarmed to battle. I will bring you arms fashioned by the divine armorer, the god Hephaestus himself."

Marvelous arms they were when Thetis brought them, worthy of their maker, such as no man on earth had ever borne. The Myrmidons gazed at them with awe and a flame of fierce joy blazed in Achilles' eyes as he put them on. Then at last he left the tent in which he had sat so long, and went down to where the Greeks were gathered, a wretched company, Diomedes grievously wounded, Odysseus, Agamemnon, and many another. He felt shame before them and he told them he saw his own exceeding folly in allowing the loss of a mere girl to make him forget everything else. But that was over; he was ready to lead them as before. Let them prepare at once for the battle. The chieftains applauded joyfully, but Odysseus spoke for all when he said they must first take their fill of food and wine, for fasting men made poor fighters. "Our comrades lie dead on the field and you call to food," Achilles answered scornfully. "Down my throat shall go neither bite nor sup until my dear comrade is avenged." And to himself he said, "O dearest of friends, for want of you I cannot eat, I cannot drink."

When the others had satisfied their hunger he led the attack. This was the last fight between the two great champions, as all the immortals knew. They also knew how it would turn out. Father Zeus hung his golden balances and set in one the lot of Hector's death and in the other that of Achilles. Hector's lot sank down. It was appointed that he should die.

Nevertheless, the victory was long in doubt. The Trojans under Hector fought as brave men fight before the walls of their home. Even the great river of Troy, which the gods call Xanthus and men Scamander, took part and strove to drown Achilles as he crossed its waters. In vain, for nothing could check him as he rushed on slaughtering all in his path and seeking everywhere for Hector. The gods by now were fighting, too, as hotly as the men, and Zeus sitting apart in Olympus laughed pleasantly to himself when he saw god matched against god: Athena felling Ares to the ground; Hera seizing the bow of Artemis from her shoulders and boxing her ears with it this way and that; Poseidon provoking Apollo with taunting words to strike him first. The Sun-god refused the challenge. He knew it was of no use now to fight for Hector.

By this time the gates, the great Scaean gates of Troy, had been flung wide, for the Trojans at last were in full flight and were crowding into the town. Only Hector stood immovable before the wall. From the gates old Priam, his father, and his mother Hecuba cried to him to come within and save himself, but he did not heed. He was thinking, "I led the Trojans. Their defeat is my fault. Then am I to spare myself? And yet—what if I were to lay down shield and spear and go tell Achilles that we will give Helen back and half of Troy's treasures with her? Useless. He would but kill me unarmed as if I were a woman. Better to join battle with him now even if I die."

On came Achilles, glorious as the sun when he rises. Beside him was Athena, but Hector was alone. Apollo had left him to his fate. As the pair drew near he turned and fled. Three times around the wall of Troy pursued and pursuer ran with flying feet. It was Athena who made Hector halt. She appeared beside him in the shape of his brother, Deiphobus, and with this ally as he thought, Hector faced Achilles. He cried out to him, "If I kill you I will give back your body to your friends and do you do the same to me." But Achilles answered, "Madman. There are no covenants between sheep and wolves, nor between you and me." So saying he hurled his spear. It missed its aim, but Athena brought it back. Then Hector struck with a true aim; the spear hit the center of Achilles' shield. But to what good? That armor was magical and could not be pierced. He turned quickly to Deiphobus to get his spear, but he was not there. Then Hector knew the truth. Athena had tricked him and there was no way of escape. "The gods have summoned me to death," he thought. "At least I will not die without a struggle, but in some great deed of arms which men yet to be born will tell each other." He drew his sword, his only weapon now, and rushed upon his enemy. But Achilles had a spear, the one Athena had recovered for him. Before Hector could approach, he who knew well that armor taken by Hector from the dead Patroclus aimed at an opening in it near the throat, and drove the spearpoint in. Hector fell, dying at last. With his last breath he prayed, "Give back my body to my father and my mother." "No prayers from you to me, you dog," Achilles answered. "I would that I could make myself devour raw your flesh for the evil you have brought upon me." Then Hector's soul flew forth from his body and was gone to Hades, bewailing his fate, leaving vigor and youth behind.

Achilles stripped the bloody armor from the corpse while the Greeks ran up to wonder how tall he was as he lay there and how noble to look upon. But Achilles' mind was on other matters. He pierced the feet of the dead man and fastened them with thongs to the back of his chariot, letting the head trail. Then he lashed his horses and round and round the walls of Troy he dragged all that was left of glorious Hector.

At last when his fierce soul was satisfied with vengeance he stood beside the body of Patroclus and said, "Hear me even in the house of Hades. I have dragged Hector behind my chariot and I will give him to the dogs to devour beside your funeral pyre."

Up in Olympus there was dissension. This abuse of the dead displeased all the immortals except Hera and Athena and Poseidon. Especially it displeased Zeus. He sent Iris to Priam, to order him to go without fear to Achilles to redeem Hector's body, bearing a rich ransom. She was to tell him that violent as Achilles was, he was not really evil, but one who would treat properly a suppliant.

Then the aged King heaped a car with splendid treasures, the best in Troy, and went over the plain to the Greek camp. Hermes met him, looking like a Greek youth and offering himself as a guide to Achilles' tent. So accompanied the old man passed the guards and came into the presence of the man who had killed and maltreated his son. He clasped his knees and kissed his hands and as he did so Achilles felt awe and so did all the others there, looking strangely upon one another. "Remember, Achilles," Priam said, "your own father, of like years with me and like me wretched for want of a son. Yet I am by far more to be pitied who have braved what no man on earth ever did before, to stretch out my hand to the slayer of my son."

Grief stirred within Achilles' heart as he listened. Gently he raised the old man. "Sit by me here," he said, "and let our sorrow lie quiet in our hearts. Evil is all men's lot, but yet we must keep courage." Then he bade his servants wash and anoint Hector's body and cover it with a soft robe, so that Priam should not see it, frightfully mangled as it was, and be unable to keep back his wrath. He feared for his own self-control if Priam vexed him. "How many days do you desire to make his funeral?" he asked. "For so long I will keep the Greeks back from battle." Then Priam brought Hector home, mourned in Troy as never another. Even Helen wept. "The other Trojans upbraid me," she said, "but always I had comfort from you through the gentleness of your spirit and your gentle words. You only were my friend."

Nine days they lamented him; then they laid him on a lofty pyre and set fire to it. When all was burned they quenched the flame with wine and gathered the bones into a golden urn, shrouding them in soft purple. They set the urn in a hollow grave and piled great stones over it.

This was the funeral of Hector, tamer of horses.

And with it the *Iliad* ends.

14 The Fall of Troy

The greater part of this story comes from Virgil. The capture of Troy is the subject of the second book of the Aeneid, *and it is one of the best, if not the best, story Virgil ever told—concise, pointed, vivid. The beginning and the end of my account are not in Virgil. I have taken the story of Philoctetes and the death of Ajax from two plays of the fifth-century tragic poet Sophocles. The end, the tale of what happened to the Trojan women when Troy fell, comes from a play by Sophocles' fellow playwright, Euripides. It is a curious contrast to the martial spirit of the* Aeneid. *To Virgil as to all Roman poets, war was the noblest and most glorious of human activities. Four hundred years before Virgil a Greek poet looked at it differently. What was the end of that far-famed war? Euripides seems to ask. Just this, a ruined town, a dead baby, a few wretched women.*

With Hector dead, Achilles knew, as his mother had told him, that his own death was near. One more great feat of arms he did before his fighting ended forever. Prince Memnon of Ethiopia, the son of the Goddess of the Dawn, came to the assistance of Troy with a large army and for a time, even though Hector was gone, the Greeks were hard-pressed and lost many a gallant warrior, including swift-footed Antilochus, old Nestor's son. Finally, Achilles killed Memnon in a glorious combat, the Greek hero's last battle. Then he himself fell beside the Scaean gates. He had driven the Trojans before him up to the wall of Troy. There Paris shot an arrow at him and Apollo guided it so that it struck his foot in the one spot where he could be wounded, his heel. His mother Thetis when he was born had intended to make him invulnerable by dipping him into the

River Styx, but she was careless and did not see to it that the water covered the part of the foot by which she was holding him. He died, and Ajax carried his body out of the battle while Odysseus held the Trojans back. It is said that after he had been burned on the funeral pyre his bones were placed in the same urn that held those of his friend Patroclus.

His arms, those marvelous arms Thetis had brought him from Hephaestus, caused the death of Ajax. It was decided in full assembly that the heroes who best deserved them were Ajax and Odysseus. A secret vote was then taken between the two, and Odysseus got the arms. Such a decision was a very serious matter in those days. It was not only that the man who won was honored; the man who was defeated was held to be dishonored. Ajax saw himself disgraced and in a fit of furious anger he determined to kill Agamemnon and Menelaus. He believed and with reason that they had turned the vote against him. At nightfall he went to find them and he had reached their quarters when Athena struck him with madness. He thought the flocks and herds of the Greeks were the Army, and rushed to kill them, believing that he was slaying now this chieftain, now that. Finally he dragged to his tent a huge ram which to his distracted mind was Odysseus, bound him to the tent-pole and beat him savagely. Then his frenzy left him. He regained his reason and saw that his disgrace in not winning the arms had been but a shadow as compared with the shame his own deeds had drawn down upon him. His rage, his folly, his madness, would be apparent to everyone. The slaughtered animals were lying all over the field. "The poor cattle," he said to himself, "killed to no purpose by my hand! And I stand here alone, hateful to men and to gods. In such a state only a coward clings to life. A man if he cannot live nobly can die nobly." He drew his sword and killed himself. The Greeks would not burn his body; they buried him. They held that a suicide should not be honored with a funeral pyre and urn-burial.

His death following so soon upon Achilles' dismayed the Greeks. Victory seemed as far off as ever. Their prophet Calchas told them that he had no message from the gods for them, but that there was a man among the Trojans who knew the future, the prophet Helenus. If they captured him they could learn from him what they should do. Odysseus succeeded in making him a prisoner, and he told the Greeks Troy would not fall until some one fought against the Trojans with the bow and arrows of Hercules. These had been given when Hercules died to the Prince Philoctetes, the man who had fired his funeral pyre and who later had joined the Greek host when they sailed to Troy. On the voyage the Greeks stopped at an island to offer a sacrifice and Philoctetes was bitten by a serpent, a most frightful wound. It would not heal; it was impossible to carry him to Troy as he was; the Army could not wait. They left him finally at Lemnos, then an uninhabited island although once the heroes of the Quest of the Golden Fleece had found plenty of women there.

It was cruel to desert the helpless sufferer, but they were desperate to get on to Troy, and with his bow and arrows he would at least never lack for food. When Helenus spoke, however, the Greeks knew well that it would be hard to persuade him whom they had so wronged, to give his precious weapons to them. So they sent Odysseus, the master of crafty cunning, to get them by trickery. Some say that Diomedes went with him and others Neoptolemus, also called Pyrrhus, the young son of Achilles. They succeeded in stealing the bow and arrows, but when it came to leaving the poor wretch alone there deprived of them, they could not do it. In the end they persuaded him to go with them. Back at Troy the wise physician of the Greeks healed him, and when at last he went joyfully once again into battle the first man he wounded with his arrows was Paris. As he fell Paris begged to be carried to Oenone, the nymph he had lived with on Mount Ida before the three goddesses came to him. She had told him that she knew a magic drug to cure any ailment. They took him to her and he asked her for his life, but she refused. His desertion of her, his long forgetfulness, could not be forgiven in a moment because of his need. She watched him die; then she went away and killed herself.

Troy did not fall because Paris was dead. He was, indeed, no great loss. At last the Greeks learned that there was a most sacred image of Pallas Athena in the city, called the Palladium, and that as long as the Trojans had it Troy could not be taken. Accordingly, the two greatest of the chieftains left alive by then, Odysseus and Diomedes, determined to try to steal it. Diomedes was the one who bore the image off. In a dark night he climbed the wall with Odysseus' help, found the Palladium and took it to the camp. With this great encouragement the Greeks determined to wait no longer, but devise some way to put an end to the endless war.

They saw clearly by now that unless they could get their Army into the city and take the Trojans by surprise, they would never conquer. Almost ten years had passed since they had first laid siege to the town, and it seemed as strong as ever. The walls stood uninjured. They had never suffered a real attack. The fighting had taken place, for the most part, at a distance from them. The Greeks must find a secret way of entering the city, or accept defeat. The result of this new determination and new vision was the stratagem of the wooden horse. It was, as anyone would guess, the creation of Odysseus' wily mind.

He had a skillful worker in wood make a huge wooden horse which was hollow and so big that it could hold a number of men. Then he persuaded—and had a great deal of difficulty in doing so—certain of the chieftains to hide inside it, along with himself, of course. They were all terror-stricken except Achilles' son Neoptolemus, and indeed what they faced was no slight danger. The idea was that all the other Greeks should strike camp, and apparently put out to sea, but they would really hide beyond the nearest island where they could not be seen by the Trojans. Whatever happened they would be safe; they could sail home if anything went wrong. But in that case the men inside the wooden horse would surely die.

Odysseus, as can be readily believed, had not overlooked this fact. His plan was to leave a single Greek behind in the deserted camp, primed with a tale calculated to make the Trojans draw the horse into the city—and without investigating it. Then, when night was darkest, the Greeks inside were to leave their wooden prison and open the city gates to the Army, which by that time would have sailed back, and be waiting before the wall.

A night came when the plan was carried out. Then the last day of Troy dawned. On the wall the Trojan watchers saw with astonishment two sights, each as startling as the other. In front of the Scaean gates stood an enormous figure of a horse, such a thing as no one had ever seen, an apparition so strange that it was vaguely terrifying, even though there was no sound or movement coming from it. No sound or movement anywhere, indeed. The noisy Greek camp was hushed; nothing was stirring there. And the ships were gone. Only one conclusion seemed possible: The Greeks had given up. They had sailed for Greece; they had accepted defeat. All Troy exulted. Her long warfare was over; her sufferings lay behind her.

The people flocked to the abandoned Greek camp to see the sights: here Achilles had sulked so long; there Agamemnon's tent had stood; this was the quarters of the trickster, Odysseus. What rapture to see the places empty, nothing in them now to fear. At last they drifted back to where that monstrosity, the wooden horse, stood, and they gathered around it, puzzled what to do with it. Then the Greek who had been left behind in the camp discovered himself to them. His name was Sinon, and he was a most plausible speaker. He was seized and dragged to Priam, weeping and protesting that he no longer wished to be a Greek. The story he told was one of Odysseus' master-

The wooden horse

pieces. Pallas Athena had been exceedingly angry, Sinon said, at the theft of the Palladium, and the Greeks in terror had sent to the oracle to ask how they could appease her. The oracle answered: "With blood and with a maiden slain you calmed the winds when first you came to Troy. With blood must your return be sought. With a Greek life make expiation." He himself, Sinon told Priam, was the wretched victim chosen to be sacrificed. All was ready for the awful rite, which was to be carried out just before the Greeks' departure, but in the night he had managed to escape and hidden in a swamp had watched the ships sail away.

It was a good tale and the Trojans never questioned it. They pitied Sinon and assured him that he should henceforth live as one of themselves. So it befell that by false cunning and pretended tears those were conquered whom great Diomedes had never overcome, nor savage Achilles, nor ten years of warfare, nor a thousand ships. For Sinon did not forget the second part of his story. The wooden horse had been made, he said, as a votive offering to Athena, and the reason for its immense size was to discourage the Trojans from taking it into the city. What the Greeks hoped for was that the Trojans would destroy it and so draw down upon them Athena's anger. Placed in the city, it would turn her favor to them and away from the Greeks. The story was clever enough to have had by itself, in all probability, the desired effect; but Poseidon, the most bitter of all the gods against Troy, contrived an addition which made the issue certain. The priest Laocoön, when the horse was first discovered, had been urgent with the Trojans to destroy it. "I fear the Greeks even when they bear gifts," he said. Cassandra, Priam's daughter, had echoed his warning, but no one ever listened to her and she had gone back to the palace before Sinon appeared. Laocoön and his two sons heard his story with suspicion, the only doubters there. As Sinon finished, suddenly over the sea came two fearful serpents swimming to the land. Once there, they glided straight to Laocoön. They wrapped their huge coils around him and the two lads and they crushed the life out of them. Then they disappeared within Athena's temple.

There could be no further hesitation. To the horrified spectators Laocoön had been punished for opposing the entry of the horse which most certainly no one else would now do. All the people cried,

"Bring the carven image in.
Bear it to Athena,
Fit gift for the child of Zeus."

Who of the young but hurried forth?
Who of the old would stay at home?
With song and rejoicing they brought death in,
Treachery and destruction.

They dragged the horse through the gate and up to the temple of Athena. Then, rejoicing in their good fortune, believing the war ended and Athena's favor restored to them, they went to their houses in peace as they had not for ten years.

In the middle of the night the door in the horse opened. One by one the chieftains let themselves down. They stole to the gates and threw them wide, and into the sleeping town marched the Greek Army. What they had first to do could be carried out silently. Fires were started in buildings throughout the city. By the time the Trojans were awake, before they realized what had happened, while they were struggling into their armor, Troy was burning. They rushed out to the street one by one in confusion. Bands of soldiers were waiting there to strike each man down before he could join himself to others. It was not fighting, it was butchery. Very many died without ever a chance of dealing a blow in return. In the more distant parts of the town the Trojans were able to gather together here and there and then it was the Greeks who suffered. They were borne down by desperate men who wanted only to kill before they were killed. They knew that the one safety for the conquered was to hope for no safety. This spirit often turned the victors into the vanquished. The quickest-witted Trojans tore off their own armor and put on that of the dead Greeks, and many and many a Greek thinking he was joining friends discovered too late that they were enemies and paid for his error with his life.

On top of the houses they tore up the roofs and hurled the beams down upon the Greeks. An entire tower standing on the roof of Priam's palace was lifted from its foundations and toppled over. Exulting the defenders saw it fall and annihilate a great band who were forcing the palace doors. But the success brought only a short respite. Others rushed up carrying a huge beam. Over the debris of the tower and the crushed bodies they battered the doors with it. It crashed through and the Greeks were in the palace before the Trojans could leave the roof. In the inner courtyard around the altar were the women and children and one man, the old King. Achilles had spared Priam, but Achilles' son struck him down before the eyes of his wife and daughters.

By now the end was near. The contest from the first had been unequal. Too many Trojans had been slaughtered in the first surprise. The Greeks could not be beaten back anywhere. Slowly the defense ceased. Before morning all the leaders were dead, except one. Aphrodite's son Aeneas alone among the Trojan chiefs escaped. He fought the Greeks as long as he could find a living Trojan to stand with him, but as the slaughter spread and death came near he thought of his home, the helpless people he had left there. He could do nothing more for Troy, but perhaps something could be done for them. He hurried to them, his old father, his little son, his wife, and as he went his mother Aphrodite appeared to him, urging him on and keeping him safe from the flames and from the Greeks. Even with the goddess's help he could not save his wife. When they left the house she got separated from him and was killed. But the other two he brought away, through the enemy, past the city gates, out into the country, his father on his shoulders, his son clinging to his hand. No one but a divinity could have saved them, and Aphrodite was the only one of the gods that day who helped a Trojan.

She helped Helen too. She got her out of the city and took her to Menelaus. He received her gladly, and as he sailed for Greece she was with him.

When morning came what had been the proudest city in Asia was a fiery ruin. All that was left of Troy was a band of helpless captive women, whose husbands were dead, whose children had been taken from them. They were waiting for their masters to carry them overseas to slavery.

Chief among the captives was the old Queen, Hecuba, and her daughter-in-law, Hector's wife Andromache. For Hecuba all was ended. Crouched on the ground, she saw the Greek ships getting ready and she watched the city burn. Troy is no longer, she told herself, and I—who am I? A slave men drive like cattle. An old gray woman that has no home.

> What sorrow is there that is not mine?
> Country lost and husband and children.
> Glory of all my house brought low.

And the women around her answered:—

> We stand at the same point of pain.
> We too are slaves.
> Our children are crying, call to us with tears,
> "Mother, I am all alone.
> To the dark ships now they drive me,
> And I cannot see you, Mother."

One woman still had her child. Andromache held in her arms her son Astyanax, the little boy who had once shrunk back from his father's high-crested helmet. "He is so young," she thought. "They will let me take him with me." But from the Greek camp a herald came to her and spoke faltering words. He told her that she must not hate him for the news he brought to her against his will. Her son . . . She broke in,

> Not that he does not go with me?

He answered,

> The boy must die—be thrown
> Down from the towering wall of Troy.
> Now—now—let it be done. Endure
> Like a brave woman. Think. You are alone.
> One woman and a slave and no help anywhere.

She knew what he said was true. There was no help. She said good-by to her child.

> Weeping, my little one? There, there.
> You cannot know what waits for you.
> —How will it be? Falling down—down—all broken—
> And none to pity.
> Kiss me. Never again. Come closer, closer.
> Your mother who bore you—put your arms around my neck.
> Now kiss me, lips to lips.

The soldiers carried him away. Just before they threw him from the wall they had killed on Achilles' grave a young girl, Hecuba's daughter Polyxena. With the death of Hector's son, Troy's last sacrifice was accomplished. The women waiting for the ships watched the end.

> Troy has perished, the great city.
> Only the red flame now lives there.

> The dust is rising, spreading out like a great wing of smoke,
>   And all is hidden.
> We now are gone, one here, one there.
>   And Troy is gone forever.

> Farewell, dear city.
>   Farewell, my country, where my children lived.
> There below, the Greek ships wait.

15 The Adventures of Odysseus

The only authority for this story is the Odyssey, *except for the account of Athena's agreement with Poseidon to destroy the Greek Fleet, which is not in the* Odyssey *and which I have taken from Euripides'* Trojan Women. *Part of the interest of the* Odyssey, *as distinguished from the* Iliad, *lies in the details, such as are given in the story of Nausicaä and the visit of Telemachus to Menelaus. They are used with admirable skill to enliven the story and make it seem real, never to hold it up or divert the reader's attention from the main issue.*

When the victorious Greek Fleet put out to sea after the fall of Troy, many a captain, all unknowing, faced troubles as black as those he had brought down on the Trojans. Athena and Poseidon had been the Greeks' greatest allies among the gods, but when Troy fell all that had changed. They became their bitterest enemies. The Greeks went mad with victory the night they entered the city; they forgot what was due to the gods; and on their voyage home they were terribly punished.

Cassandra, one of Priam's daughters, was a prophetess. Apollo had loved her and given her the power to foretell the future. Later he turned against her because she refused his love, and although he could not take back his gift—divine favors once bestowed might not be revoked—he made it of no account: no one ever believed her. She told the Trojans each time what would happen; they would never listen to her. She declared that Greeks were hidden in the wooden horse; no one gave her words a thought. It was her fate always to know the disaster that was coming and be unable to avert it. When the Greeks sacked the city she was in Athena's temple clinging to her image, under the goddess's protection. The Greeks found her there and they dared to lay violent hands on her. Ajax—not the great Ajax, of course, who was dead, but a lesser chieftain of the same name—tore her from the altar and dragged her out of the sanctuary. Not one Greek protested against the sacrilege. Athena's wrath was deep. She went to Poseidon and laid her wrongs before him. "Help me to vengeance," she said. "Give the Greeks a bitter homecoming. Stir up your waters with wild whirlwinds when they sail. Let dead men choke the bays and line the shores and reefs."

Poseidon agreed. Troy was a heap of ashes by now. He could afford to lay aside his anger against the Trojans. In the fearful tempest which struck the Greeks after they left for Greece, Agamemnon came near to losing all his ships; Menelaus was blown to Egypt; and the arch-sinner, sacrilegious Ajax, was drowned. At the height of the storm his boat was shattered and sank, but he succeeded in swimming to shore. He would have been saved if in his mad folly he had not cried out that he was one that the sea could not drown. Such arrogance always aroused the anger of the gods. Poseidon broke off the jagged bit of rock to which he was clinging. Ajax fell and the waves swept him away to his death.

Odysseus did not lose his life, but if he did not suffer as much as some of the Greeks, he suffered longer than them all. He wandered for ten years before he saw his home. When he reached it, the little son he had left there was grown to manhood. Twenty years had passed since Odysseus sailed for Troy.

On Ithaca, the island where his home was, things had gone from bad to worse. Everyone by now took it for granted that he was dead, except Penelope, his wife, and his son Telemachus. They almost despaired, but not quite. All the people assumed that Penelope was a widow and could and should marry again. From the islands round about and, of course, from Ithaca, men came swarming to Odysseus' house to woo his wife. She would have none of them; the hope that her husband would return was faint, but it never died. Moreover she detested every one of them and so did Telemachus, and with good reason. They were rude, greedy, overbearing men, who spent their days sitting in the great hall of the house devouring Odysseus' store of provisions, slaughtering his cattle, his sheep, his swine, drinking his wine, burning his wood, giving orders to his servants. They would never leave, they declared, until Penelope consented to marry one of them. Telemachus they treated with amused contempt as if he were a mere boy and quite beneath their notice. It was an intolerable state of things to both mother and son, and yet they were helpless, only two and one of them a woman against a great company.

Penelope had at first hoped to tire them out. She told them that she could not marry until she had woven a very fine and exquisitely wrought shroud for Odysseus' father, the aged Laertes, against the day of his death. They had to give in to so pious a purpose, and they agreed to wait until the work was finished. But it never was, inasmuch as Penelope unwove each night what she had woven during the day. But finally the trick failed. One of her handmaidens told the suitors and they discovered her in the very act. Of course after that they were more insistent and unmanageable than ever. So matters stood when the tenth year of Odysseus' wanderings neared its close.

Because of the wicked way they had treated Cassandra, Athena had been angry at all the Greeks indiscriminately, but before that, during the Trojan War, she had especially favored Odysseus. She delighted in his wily mind, his shrewdness and his cunning; she was always forward to help him. After Troy fell she included him with the others in her wrathful displeasure and he too was caught by the storm when he set sail and driven so completely off his course that he never found it again. Year after year he voyaged, hurried from one perilous adventure to another.

Ten years, however, is a long time for anger to last. The gods had by now grown sorry for Odysseus, with the single exception of Poseidon, and Athena was sorriest of all. Her old feeling for him had returned; she was determined to put an end to his sufferings and bring him home. With these thoughts in her mind, she was delighted to find one day that Poseidon was absent from the gathering in Olympus. He had gone to visit the Ethiopians, who lived on the farther bank of Ocean, to the south, and it was certain he would stay there some time, feasting merrily with them. Instantly she brought the sad case of Odysseus before the others. He was at the moment, she told them, a virtual prisoner on an island ruled over by the nymph Calypso, who loved him and planned never to let him go. In every other way except in giving him his freedom she overwhelmed him with kindness; all that she had was at his disposal. But Odysseus was utterly wretched. He longed for his home, his wife, his son. He spent his days on the seashore, searching the horizon for a sail that never came, sick with longing to see even the smoke curling up from his house.

The Olympians were moved by her words. They felt that Odysseus had deserved better at their hands and Zeus spoke for them all when he said they must put their heads together and contrive a way for him to return. If they were agreed Poseidon could not stand alone against them. For his part,

Zeus said, he would send Hermes to Calypso to tell her that she must start Odysseus on his voyage back. Athena well-pleased left Olympus and glided down to Ithaca. She had already made her plans.

She was exceedingly fond of Telemachus, not only because he was her dear Odysseus' son, but because he was a sober, discreet young man, steady and prudent and dependable. She thought it would do him good to take a journey while Odysseus was sailing home, instead of perpetually watching in silent fury the outrageous behavior of the suitors. Also it would advance him in the opinion of men everywhere if the object of his journey was to seek for some news of his father. They would think him, as indeed, he was, a pious youth with the most admirable filial sentiments. Accordingly, she disguised herself to look like a seafaring man and went to the house. Telemachus saw her waiting by the threshold and was vexed to the heart that a guest should not find instant welcome. He hastened to greet the stranger, take his spear, and seat him on a chair of honor. The attendants also hurried to show the hospitality of the great house, setting food and wine before him and stinting him in nothing. Then the two talked together. Athena began by asking gently was this some sort of drinking-bout she had happened upon? She did not wish to offend, but a well-mannered man might be excused for showing disgust at the way the people around them were acting. Then Telemachus told her all, the fear that Odysseus must surely by now be dead; how every man from far and near had come wooing his mother who could not reject their offers out-and-out, but would not accept any of them, and how the suitors were ruining them, eating up their substance and making havoc of the house. Athena showed great indignation. It was a shameful tale, she said. If once Odysseus got home those evil men would have a short shrift and a bitter end. Then she advised him strongly to try to find out something about his father's fate. The men most likely to be able to give the news, she said, were Nestor and Menelaus. With that she departed, leaving the young man full of ardor and decision, all his former uncertainty and hesitation gone. He felt the change with amazement and the belief took hold of him that his visitor had been divine.

The next day he summoned the assembly and told them what he purposed to do and asked them for a well-built ship and twenty rowers to man her, but he got no answer except jeers and taunts. Let him sit at home and get his news there, the suitors bade him. They would see to it that he went on no voyage. With mocking laughter they swaggered off to Odysseus' palace. Telemachus in despair went far away along the seashore and as he walked he prayed to Athena. She heard him and came. She had put on the appearance of Mentor, whom of all the Ithacans Odysseus had most trusted, and she spoke good words of comfort and courage to him. She promised him that a fast ship should be made ready for him, and that she herself would sail with him. Telemachus of course had no idea except that it was Mentor himself speaking to him, but with this help he was ready to defy the suitors and he hurried home to get all ready for the voyage. He waited prudently until night to leave. Then, when all in the house were asleep, he went down to the ship where Mentor (Athena) was waiting, embarked and put out to sea toward Pylos, old Nestor's home.

They found him and his sons on the shore offering a sacrifice to Poseidon. Nestor made them heartily welcome, but about the object of their coming he could give them little help. He knew nothing of Odysseus; they had not left Troy together and no word of him had reached Nestor since. In his opinion the man most likely to have news would be Menelaus, who had voyaged all the way to Egypt before coming home. If Telemachus wished he would send him to Sparta in a chariot with one of his sons who knew the way, which would be much quicker than by sea. Telemachus accepted gratefully and leaving Mentor in charge of the ship he started the next day for Menelaus' palace with Nestor's son.

They drew rein in Sparta before the lordly dwelling, a house far more splendid than either young man had ever seen. A princely welcome awaited them. The house-maidens led them to the bath place where they bathed them in silver bathtubs and rubbed them with sweet-smelling oil. Then they wrapped them in warm purple mantles over fine tunics, and conducted them to the banquet hall. There a servant hastened to them with water in a golden ewer which she poured over their fingers into a silver bowl. A shining table was set beside them and covered with rich food in profusion, and a golden goblet full of wine was placed for each. Menelaus gave them a courteous greeting and bade them eat their fill. The young men were happy, but a little abashed by all the magnificence. Telemachus whispered to his friend, very softly for fear someone might hear, "Zeus's hall in Olympus must be like this. It takes my breath away." But a moment later he had forgotten his shyness, for Menelaus began to speak of Odysseus—of his greatness and his long sorrows. As the young man listened tears gathered in his eyes and he held his cloak before his face to hide his agitation. But Menelaus had remarked it and he guessed who he must be.

Just then, however, came an interruption which distracted the thoughts of every man there. Helen the beautiful came down from her fragrant chamber attended by her women, one carrying her chair, another a soft carpet for her feet, and a third her silver work-basket filled with violet wool. She recognized Telemachus instantly from his likeness to his father and she called him by name. Nestor's son answered and said that she was right. His friend was Odysseus' son and he had come to them for help and advice. Then Telemachus spoke and told them of the wretchedness at home from which only his father's return could deliver them, and asked Menelaus if he could give him any news about him, whether good or bad.

"It is a long story," answered Menelaus, "but I did learn something about him and in a very strange way. It was in Egypt. I was weather-bound for many days on an island there called Pharos. Our provisions were giving out and I was in despair when a sea-goddess had pity on me. She let me know that her father, the sea-god Proteus, could tell me how to leave the hateful island and get safely home if only I could make him do so. For that I must manage to catch him and hold him until I learned from him what I wanted. The plan she made was an excellent one. Each day Proteus came up from the sea with a number of seals and lay down with them on the sand, always in the same place. There I dug four holes in which I and three of my men hid, each under a sealskin the goddess gave us. When the old god lay down not far from me it was no task at all for us to spring up out of our holes and seize him. But to hold him—that was another matter. He had the power of changing his shape at will, and there in our hands he became a lion and a dragon and many other animals, and finally even a high-branched tree. But we held him firmly throughout, and at last he gave in and told me all I wished to know. Of your father he said that he was on an island, pining away from homesickness, kept there by a nymph, Calypso. Except for that, I know nothing of him since we left Troy, ten years ago." When he finished speaking, silence fell upon the company. They all thought of Troy and what had happened since, and they wept—Telemachus for his father; Nestor's son for his brother, swift-footed Antilochus, dead before the walls of Troy; Menelaus for many a brave comrade fallen on the Trojan plain, and Helen—but who could say for whom Helen's tears fell? Was she thinking of Paris as she sat in her husband's splendid hall?

That night the young men spent in Sparta. Helen ordered her house-maidens to arrange beds for them in the entry porch, soft and warm with thick purple blankets covered by smoothly woven rugs and on top of all woolen cloaks. A servant, torch in hand, showed them out and they slept there in comfort until the dawn appeared.

Meantime Hermes had gone to carry Zeus's command to Calypso. He laced to his feet the sandals of imperishable gold which bore him swift as a breath of air over sea and earth. He took his wand with which he could charm men's eyes to slumber, and springing into the air he flew down to sea-level. Skimming the wave-crests he reached at last the lovely island which had become for Odysseus a hateful prison. He found the divine nymph alone; Odysseus as usual was on the sandy shore letting his salt tears flow while he gazed at the empty sea. Calypso took Zeus's orders in very ill part. She had saved the man's life, she said, when his ship was wrecked near the island, and cared for him ever since. Of course everyone must give in to Zeus, but it was very unfair. And how was she to manage the voyage back? She had no ships and crews at command. But Hermes felt this was not his affair. "Just take care not to make Zeus angry," he said and went gaily off.

Calypso gloomily set about the necessary preparations. She told Odysseus, who was at first inclined to think it all a trick on her part to do something detestable to him,—drown him, very likely,—but she finally convinced him. She would help him build a splendidly strong raft, she promised him, and send him away on it equipped with everything necessary. Never did any man do work more joyfully than Odysseus made his raft. Twenty great trees furnished the wood, all very dry so that they would float high. On the raft Calypso put food and drink in abundance, even a sack of the dainties Odysseus specially liked. The fifth morning after Hermes' visit found Odysseus putting out to sea before a fair wind over quiet waters.

Seventeen days he journeyed without change of weather, always steering, never letting sleep close his eyes. On the eighteenth day a cloudy mountain top arose up across the sea. He believed that he was saved.

At that very moment, however, Poseidon, on his way back from Ethiopia, caught sight of him. He knew at once what the gods had done. "But," he muttered to himself, "I think I can give him even yet a long journey into sorrow before he reaches land." With that he summoned all the violent winds and let them loose, blinding sea and land with storm-clouds. The East Wind fought with the South, and the ill-blowing West with the North, and the waves rose up mightily. Odysseus saw death before him. "Oh, happy the men who fell gloriously on the plain of Troy!" he thought. "For me to die thus ignobly!" It seemed indeed that he could not escape. The raft was tossed as a dried thistle goes rolling over a field in autumn days.

But a kindly goddess was at hand, Ino of the slim ankles, who had once been a Theban princess. She pitied him and rising lightly from the water like a sea-gull she told him his one chance was to abandon the raft and swim to shore. She gave him her veil, which would keep him from harm as long as he was in the sea. Then she disappeared beneath the billows.

Odysseus had no choice but to follow her advice. Poseidon sent a wave of waves to him, a terror of the sea. It tore the logs of the raft apart as a great wind scatters a heap of dried chaff; it flung Odysseus into the wild waters. But, if he had only known it, bad as things seemed the worst was over. Poseidon felt satisfied and went off contentedly to plan some other storm somewhere, and Athena, left free to act, calmed the waves. Even so, Odysseus had to swim for two days and nights before he reached land and could find a safe landing-place. He came out of the surf exhausted and starving and naked. It was evening; not a house, not a living creature, was to be seen. But Odysseus was not only a hero, he was a man of great resourcefulness. He found a place where a few trees grew so thick and close to the ground, no moisture could penetrate them. Beneath were heaps of dry leaves, enough to cover many men. He scooped out a hollow and lying down piled the leaves over him like a thick coverlet. Then, warm and still at last, with the sweet land odors blowing to him, he slept in peace.

He had of course no idea where he was, but Athena had arranged matters well for him. The country belonged to the Phaeacians, a kind people and splendid sailors. Their king, Alcinoüs, was a good, sensible man who knew that his wife Arete was a great deal wiser than he and always let her decide anything important for him. They had a fair daughter as yet unmarried.

Nausicaä, for so the girl was called, never imagined the next morning that she was to play the part of rescuer to a hero. When she woke up she thought only about doing the family washing. She was a princess, indeed, but in those days high-born ladies were expected to be useful, and the household linen was in Nausicaä's charge. Washing clothes was then a very agreeable occupation. She had the servants make ready an easy-running mule-cart and pack it with the soiled clothes. Her mother filled a box for her with all sorts of good things to eat and drink; she gave her too a golden flask of limpid olive oil to use if she and her maids went bathing. Then they started, Nausicaä driving. They were bound for the very place where Odysseus had landed. A lovely river flowed into the sea there which had excellent washing pools with an abundance of clear bubbling water. What the girls did was to lay the clothes in the water and dance on them until all the dirt was worked out. The pools were cool and shadowy; it was very pleasant work. Afterwards they stretched the linen smooth to dry on the shore where the sea had washed it clean.

Then they could take their ease. They bathed and anointed themselves with the sleek oil, and had their lunch, and amused themselves with a ball which they threw to one another, dancing all the while. But at last the setting sun warned them the delightful day was over. They gathered up the linen, yoked in the mules, and were about to start home when they saw a wild-looking naked man suddenly step out of the bushes. Odysseus had been awakened by the girls' voices. In terror they ran away, all except Nausicaä. She faced him fearlessly and he spoke to her as persuasively as his eloquent tongue could. "I am a suppliant at your knees, O Queen," he said. "But whether you are mortal or divine I cannot tell. Never anywhere have I set eyes on such a one. I wonder as I look at you. Be gracious to your suppliant, a shipwrecked man, friendless and helpless, without a rag to cover him."

Nausicaä answered him kindly. She told him where he was and that the people of the country were kind to luckless wanderers. The King, her father, would receive him with all courteous hospitality. She summoned the frightened maids and bade them give the stranger the oil so that he could cleanse himself and find for him a mantle and a tunic. They waited while he bathed and dressed, then all set forth for the city. Before they reached Nausicaä's home, however, that discreet maiden directed Odysseus to fall back and let her and the girls go on alone. "People's tongues are so ill-natured," she said. "If they saw a handsome man like you with me, they would be hinting at all sorts of things. And you can easily find my father's house, it is so much the most splendid. Enter boldly and go straight to my mother, who will be spinning at the hearth. What my mother says my father will do."

Odysseus agreed at once. He admired her good sense, and he followed her directions exactly. Entering the house he strode through the hall to the hearth and sank down before the Queen, clasping her knees and praying her for help. The King quickly raised him and bade him sit at table and take his fill of food and drink without fear. Whoever he was and wherever his home, he could rest assured that they would arrange to send him there in one of their ships. It was now the time for sleep, but in the morning he could tell them his name and how he had made his way to them. So they slept through the night,

Odysseus blissfully, on a couch soft and warm as he had not known since he left Calypso's isle.

The next day in the presence of all the Phaeacian chiefs he told the story of his ten years' wandering. He began with the departure from Troy and the storm that struck the Fleet. He and his ships were driven across the sea for nine days. On the tenth they made the land of the Lotus-eaters and put in there. But weary though they were and in need of refreshment they were forced to leave quickly. The inhabitants met them with kindness and gave them their flower-food to eat, but those who tasted it, only a few fortunately, lost their longing for home. They wanted only to dwell in the Lotus Land, and let the memory of all that had been fade from their minds. Odysseus had to drag them on shipboard and chain them there. They wept, so great was their desire to stay, tasting forever the honey-sweet flowers.

Their next adventure was with the Cyclops Polyphemus, a full account of which is given in Part One, Chapter 4. They lost a number of their comrades at his hands, and what was even worse, made Poseidon, who was Polyphemus' father, so angry that he swore Odysseus should reach his own country again only after long misery and when he had lost all his men. For these ten years his anger had followed him over the sea.

From the Cyclops' island they came to the country of the Winds, ruled over by King Aeolus. Zeus had made him keeper of the Winds, to still them or arouse them at his will. Aeolus received them hospitably and when they left gave Odysseus as a parting gift a leather sack, into which he had put all the Storm Winds. It was so tightly fastened that not the very least puff of any Wind that spells danger for a ship could leak out. In this excellent situation for sailors Odysseus' crew managed to bring them all near to death. They thought the carefully stored bag was probably full of gold; at any rate, they wanted to see what was in it. They opened it, with the result, of course, that all the Winds rushed out at once and swept them away in a terrific tempest. Finally, after days of danger, they saw land, but they had better have stayed on the stormy sea for it was the country of the Laestrygons, a people of gigantic size and cannibals too. These horrible folk destroyed all Odysseus' ships except the one he himself was in—which had not yet entered the harbor when the attack was made.

This was by far the worst disaster yet, and it was with despairing hearts that they put in at the next island they reached. Never would they have landed if they had known what lay before them. They had come to Aeaea, the realm of Circe, a most beautiful and most dangerous witch. Every man who ap-

proached her she turned into a beast. Only his reason remained
as before: he knew what had happened to him. She enticed
into her house the party Odysseus dispatched to spy out the
land, and there she changed them into swine. She penned them
in a sty and gave them acorns to eat. They ate them; they were
swine. Yet inside they were men, aware of their vile state, but
completely in her power.

Luckily for Odysseus, one of the party had been too cautious to enter the house. He watched what happened and fled
in horror back to the ship. The news drove any thought of
caution out of Odysseus. He started off, all alone—not one of
the crew would go with him—to try to do something, bring
some help to his men. On his way Hermes met him. He seemed
a young man, of that age when youth looks its loveliest. He
told Odysseus he knew a herb which could save him from
Circe's deadly art. With it he could taste anything she gave
him and suffer no harm. When he had drunk the cup she offered him, Hermes said, he must threaten to run her through
with his sword unless she freed his followers. Odysseus took
the herb and went thankfully on his way. All turned out even
better than Hermes had predicted. When Circe had used on
Odysseus the magic which had always hitherto been successful
and to her amazement saw him stand unchanged before her,
she so marveled at the man who could resist her enchantment
that she loved him. She was ready to do whatever he asked
and she turned his companions at once back into men again.
She treated them all with such kindness, feasting them sump-
tuously in her house, that for a whole year they stayed happily
with her.

When at last they felt that the time had come to depart she
used her magical knowledge for them. She found out what
they must do next in order to reach home safely. It was a
fearful undertaking she put before them. They must cross the
river Ocean and beach the ship on Persephone's shore where
there was an entrance to the dark realm of Hades. Odysseus
then must go down and find the spirit of the prophet Teiresias
who had been the holy man of Thebes. He would tell Odysseus how to get back home. There was only one way to induce his ghost to come to him, by killing sheep and filling a
pit with their blood. All ghosts had an irresistible craving to
drink blood. Every one of them would come rushing to the
pit, but Odysseus must draw his sword and keep them away
until Teiresias spoke to him.

This was bad news, indeed, and all were weeping when they
left Circe's isle and turned their prow toward Erebus where
Hades rules with awesome Persephone. It was terrible indeed
when the trench was dug and filled with blood and the spirits

Odysseus and Circe

of the dead flocked to it. But Odysseus kept his courage. He held them off with his sharp weapon until he saw the ghost of Teiresias. He let him approach and drink of the black blood, then put his question to him. The seer was ready with his answer. The chief danger that threatened them, he said, was that they might do some injury to the oxen of the Sun when they reached the island where they lived. The doom of all who harmed them was certain. They were the most beautiful oxen in the world and very much prized by the Sun. But in any event Odysseus himself would reach home and although he would find trouble waiting for him, in the end he would prevail.

After the prophet ceased speaking, a long procession of the dead came up to drink the blood and speak to Odysseus and pass on, great heroes and fair women of old; warriors, too, who had fallen at Troy. Achilles came and Ajax, still wrathful because of the armor of Achilles which the Greek captains had given to Odysseus and not to him. Many others came, all eager to speak to him. Too many, in the end. Terror at the thronging numbers took hold of Odysseus. He hastened back to the ship and bade his crew set sail.

From Circe he had learned that they must pass the island of the Sirens. These were marvelous singers whose voices would make a man forget all else, and at last their song would steal his life away. Moldering skeletons of those they had lured to their death lay banked high up around them where they sat singing on the shore. Odysseus told his men about them and that the only way to pass them safely was for each man to stop his ears with wax. He himself, however, was determined to hear them, and he proposed that the crew should tie him to the mast so strongly that he could not get away however much he tried. This they did and drew near the island, all except Odysseus deaf to the enchanting song. He heard it and the words were even more enticing than the melody, at least to a Greek. They would give knowledge to each man who came to them, they said, ripe wisdom and a quickening of the spirit. "We know all things which shall be hereafter upon the earth." So rang their song in lovely cadences, and Odysseus' heart ached with longing.

But the ropes held him and that danger was safely passed. A sea peril next awaited them—the passage between Scylla and Charybdis. The Argonauts had got through it; Aeneas, who just about that time had sailed for Italy, had been able to avoid it because of a prophet's warning; of course Odysseus with Athena looking after him succeeded in passing it. But it was a frightful ordeal and six of the crew lost their lives there. However, they would not in any case have lived much longer, for at their next stopping place, the Island of the Sun, the men cted with incredible folly. They were hungry and they killed the sacred oxen. Odysseus was away. He had gone into the island alone by himself to pray. He was in despair when he returned, but the beasts had been roasted and eaten and nothing could be done. The vengeance of the Sun was swift. As soon as the men left the island a thunderbolt shattered the ship. All were drowned except Odysseus. He clung to the keel and was able to ride out the storm. Then he drifted for days, until finally he was cast ashore on Calypso's island, where he had to stay for many years. At last he started home, but a tempest shipwrecked him and only after many and great dangers had he succeeded in reaching the Phaeacian land, a helpless, destitute man.

The long story was ended, but the audience sat silent, entranced by the tale. At last the King spoke. His troubles were over, he assured Odysseus. They would send him home that very day and every man present would give him a parting gift to enrich him. All agreed. The ship was made ready, the presents were stowed within, and Odysseus embarked after taking a grateful leave of his kind hosts. He stretched himself on the deck and a sweet sleep closed his eyes. When he woke he was on dry land, lying on a beach. The sailors had set him ashore just as he was, ranged his belongings beside him, and departed. He started up and stood staring around him. He did not recognize his own country. A young man approached him, seemingly a shepherd lad, but fine and well-mannered like the sons of kings when they tend sheep. So he seemed to Odysseus, but really it was Athena in his semblance. She answered his eager question and told him he was in Ithaca. Even in his joy at the news Odysseus kept his caution. He spun her a long tale about who he was and why he had come, with not a word of truth in it, at the end of which the goddess smiled and patted him. Then she appeared in her own form, divinely tall and beautiful. "You crooked, shifty rogue!" she laughed. "Anyone who would keep pace with your craftiness must be a canny dealer." Odysseus greeted her with rapture, but she bade him remember how much there was to do and the two settled down to work out a plan. Athena told him how things were in his house and promised she would help him clear it of the suitors. For the present she would change him into an old beggar so that he could go everywhere unrecognized. That night he must spend with his swineherd, Eumaeus, a man faithful and trustworthy beyond praise. When they had hidden the treasures in a near-by cave they separated, she to summon Telemachus home, he, whom her art had turned into a shambling ragged old man, to seek the swineherd. Eumaeus welcomed the poor stranger, fed him well and lodged him for the night, giving him his own thick mantle to cover him.

Meanwhile, at Pallas Athena's prompting, Telemachus took leave of Helen and Menelaus, and as soon as he reached his ship embarked, eager to get home with all speed. He planned—and again Athena had put the thought in his mind—not to go directly to the house on landing, but first to the swineherd to learn if anything had happened in his absence. Odysseus was helping prepare breakfast when the young man appeared at the door. Eumaeus greeted him with tears of joy and begged him to sit and eat. Before he would do so, however, he dispatched the swineherd to inform Penelope of his return. Then father and son were alone together. At that moment Odysseus perceived Athena just beyond the door beckoning to him. He went out to her and in a flash she turned him back into his own form and bade him tell Telemachus who he was. That young man had noticed nothing until instead of the old beggar a majestic-looking person returned to him. He started up amazed, believing he saw a god. "I am your father," Odysseus said, and the two embraced each other and wept. But the time was short and there was much to plan. An anxious talk followed. Odysseus was determined to drive the suitors away by force, but how could two men take on a whole company? At last it was decided that the next morning they should go to the house, Odysseus disguised, of course, and that Telemachus should hide all the weapons of war, leaving only enough for the two of them where they could easily get at them. Athena was quick to aid. When Eumaeus came back he found the old beggar he had left.

Next day Telemachus went on alone, leaving the other two to follow. They reached the town, they came to the palace, and at last after twenty years Odysseus entered his dear dwelling. As he did so an old dog lying there lifted his head and pricked his ears. It was Argos, whom Odysseus had bred before he went to Troy. Yet the moment his master appeared he knew him and wagged his tail, but he had no strength to drag himself even a little toward him. Odysseus knew him too and brushed away a tear. He dared not go to him for fear of arousing suspicion in the swineherd, and as he turned away that moment the old dog died.

Within the hall the suitors, idly loafing after their meal, were in a mood to make fun of the miserable old beggar who entered, and Odysseus listened to all their mocking words with submissive patience. At last one of them, an evil-tempered man, became irritated and gave him a blow. He dared to strike a stranger who was asking for hospitality. Penelope heard of the outrage and declared that she would herself speak with the ill-treated man, but she decided first to pay a visit to the banqueting hall. She wanted to see Telemachus and also it seemed wise to her to show herself to the suitors. She was as prudent as her son. If Odysseus was dead, it would certainly be well for her to marry the richest of these men and the most liberal. She must not discourage them too much. Besides, she had an idea which seemed to promise very well. So she went down from her room into the hall, attended by two maids and holding a veil before her face, looking so lovely her courtiers trembled to see her. One and another arose to compliment her, but the discreet lady answered she knew very well that she had lost all her looks by now, what with her grieving and her many cares. Her purpose in coming to speak to them was a serious one. No doubt her husband would never come back. Why then did they not court her in the proper way for a lady of family and fortune by giving her costly gifts? The suggestion was acted upon at once. All had their pages bring and present her with most lovely things, robes and jewels and golden chains. Her maids carried them upstairs and demure Penelope retired with great contentment in her heart.

Then she sent for the stranger who had been ill-used. She spoke graciously to him and Odysseus told her a tale of meeting her husband on his way to Troy which made her weep until he pitied her. Still he did not reveal himself, but kept his face hard as iron. By and by Penelope remembered her duties as hostess. She summoned an old nurse, Eurycleia, who had cared for Odysseus from babyhood, and bade her wash the stranger's feet. Odysseus was frightened, for on one foot was a scar made in boyhood days by a wild boar he had hunted, and he thought she would recognize it. She did, and she let the foot fall so that the tub was upset. Odysseus caught her hand and muttered, "Dear nurse, you know. But not a word to another soul." She whispered her promise, and Odysseus took his leave. He found a bed in the entrance hall, but he could not sleep for wondering how he could overcome so many shameless fellows. At last he reminded himself that his state in the Cyclops' cave had been still worse and that with Athena's help he could hope here too to be successful, and then he slept.

Morning brought the suitors back, more insolent even than before. Carelessly and at ease they sat down to the rich feast spread for them, not knowing that the goddess and the much-enduring Odysseus were preparing a ghastly banquet for them.

Penelope all unknowing forwarded their plan. During the night she had made one of her own. When morning came she went to her store-chamber where among many treasures was a great bow and a quiver full of arrows. They belonged to Odysseus and no hand but his had ever strung the bow or used it.

Carrying them herself she descended to where the suitors were gathered. "Hear me, my lords," she said. "I set before you the bow of godlike Odysseus. He who strings the bow and shoots an arrow straight through twelve rings in a line, I will take as my husband." Telemachus instantly saw how this could be turned to their advantage and he was quick to play up to her. "Come on, suitors all," he cried. "No holding back or excuses. But stay. I will try first and see if I am man enough to bear my father's arms." With this he set the rings in order, placing them exactly in line. Then he took the bow and did his utmost to string it. Perhaps he might in the end have succeeded if Odysseus had not signed to him to give up. After him the others, one by one, took their turn, but the bow was too stiff; the strongest could not bend it even a little.

Certain that no one would be successful Odysseus left the contest and stepped out into the courtyard where the swineherd was talking to the keeper of the cattle, a fellow as trustworthy as himself. He needed their help and he told them who he was. As proof he showed them the scar on his foot which in other years they had both seen many a time. They recognized it and burst out weeping for joy. But Odysseus hushed them quickly. "None of that now," he said. "Listen to what I want of you. Do you, Eumaeus, find some way to put the bow and arrows into my hands; then see that the women's quarters are closed so that no one can enter. And you, O herder of cattle, must shut and bar the gates of the court here." He turned back to the hall, the two following him. When they entered the last suitor to make the trial had just failed. Odysseus said, "Pass me the bow and let me see if the strength I once had is still mine." An angry clamor broke out at the words. A beggarly foreigner should never touch the bow, they cried. But Telemachus spoke sternly to them. It was for him, not them, to say who should handle the bow, and he bade Eumaeus give it to Odysseus.

All watched intently as he took it and examined it. Then, with effortless ease, as a skilled musician fits a bit of catgut to his lyre, he bent the bow and strung it. He notched an arrow to the string and drew, and not moving from his seat he sent it straight through the twelve rings. The next instant with one leap he was at the door and Telemachus was beside him. "At last, at last," he cried in a great voice and he shot an arrow. It found its mark; one of the suitors fell dying to the floor. The others sprang up in horror. Their weapons—where were they? None were to be seen. And Odysseus was shooting steadily. As each arrow whistled through the hall a man fell dead. Telemachus on guard with his long spear kept the crowd back so that they could not rush out through the door either to escape or to attack Odysseus from the rear. They made an easy target, gathered there together, and as long as the supply of arrows held out they were slaughtered without a chance to defend themselves. Even with the arrows gone they fared little better, for Athena had now come to take a part in the great deeds being done and she made each attempt to reach Odysseus miscarry. But his flashing spear never missed its stroke and the dreadful sound of cracking skulls was heard and the floor flowed with blood.

At last only two of that roistering, impudent band were left, the priest of the suitors and their bard. Both of them cried for mercy, but the priest, clasping Odysseus' knees in his agony of supplication, met with none. The hero's sword ran him through and he died in the midst of his prayer. The bard was fortunate. Odysseus shrank from killing such a man, taught by the gods to sing divinely, and he spared him for further song.

The battle—slaughter, rather—was ended. The old nurse Eurycleia and her maids were summoned to cleanse the place and restore all to order. They surrounded Odysseus, weeping and laughing and welcoming him home until they stirred within his own heart the desire to weep. At last they set to work, but Eurycleia climbed the stairs to her mistress's chamber. She stood by her bed. "Awake, my dear," she said, "for Odysseus has come home and all the suitors are dead." "O crazy old woman," Penelope complained. "And I was sleeping so sweetly. Off with you and be glad you are not smartly slapped as anyone else would have been who waked me." But Eurycleia persisted, "Indeed, indeed Odysseus is here. He showed me the scar. It is his very self." Still Penelope could not believe her. She hurried down to the hall to see with her own eyes.

A man tall and princely-looking was sitting by the hearth where the firelight fell full on him. She sat down opposite him and looked at him in silence. She was bewildered. At one moment she seemed to recognize him, the next, he was a stranger to her. Telemachus cried out at her: "Mother, Mother, oh, cruel! What other woman would hold herself aloof when her man came home after twenty years?" "My son," she answered, "I have no strength to move. If this is in truth Odysseus, then we two have ways of knowing each other." At this Odysseus smiled and bade Telemachus leave her alone. "We will find each other out presently," he said.

Then the well-ordered hall was filled with rejoicing. The minstrel drew sweet sounds from his lyre and waked in all the longing for the dance. Gaily they trod a measure, men and fair-robed women, till the great house around them rang with their footfalls. For Odysseus at last after long wandering had come home and every heart was glad.

16 The Adventures of Aeneas

The Aeneid, *the greatest of Latin poems, is the chief authority for this story. It was written when Augustus had taken over the bankrupt Roman world after the chaos that followed Caesar's assassination. His strong hand ended the furious civil wars and brought about the Pax Augusta, which lasted for nearly half a century. Virgil and all his generation were fired with enthusiasm for the new order, and the Aeneid was written to exalt the Empire, to provide a great national hero and a founder for "the race destined to hold the world beneath its rule." Virgil's patriotic purpose is probably responsible for the change from the human Aeneas of the first books to the unhuman prodigy of the last. The poet was finally carried away into the purely fantastic by his determination to create a hero for Rome that would make all other heroes seem insignificant. A tendency to exaggeration was a Roman trait. The Latin names of the gods are, of course, used; and the Latin forms in the case of any personage who has a Latin as well as a Greek name. Ulysses, for instance, is Latin for Odysseus.*

Part One: FROM TROY TO ITALY

Aeneas, the son of Venus, was among the most famous of the heroes who fought the Trojan War. On the Trojan side he was second only to Hector. When the Greeks captured Troy, he was able with his mother's help to escape from the city with his father and his little son, and to sail away to a new home.

After long wanderings and many trials on land and sea he reached Italy, where he defeated those who opposed his entering the country, married the daughter of a powerful king and founded a city. He was always held to be the real founder of Rome because Romulus and Remus, the actual founders, were born in the city his son built, in Alba Longa.

When he set sail from Troy many Trojans had joined him. All were eager to find somewhere to settle, but no one had any clear idea where that should be. Several times they started to build a city, but they were always driven away by misfortunes or bad omens. At last Aeneas was told in a dream that the place destined for them was a country far away to the west, Italy— in those days called Hesperia, the Western Country. They were then on the island of Crete, and although the promised land was distant by a long voyage over unknown seas they were thankful for the assurance that they would some day have their own home and they started at once on the journey. Before they reached their desired haven, however, a long time passed, and much happened which if they had known beforehand might have checked their eagerness.

Although the Argonauts had sailed east from Greece and Aeneas' company were westward bound from Crete, the Trojans came upon the Harpies just as Jason and his men had done. The Greek heroes had been bolder, however, or else better swordsmen. They were on the point of killing the horrid creatures when Iris intervened, but the Trojans were driven away by them, and forced to put out to sea to escape them.

At their next landing place they met to their amazement Hector's wife Andromache. When Troy fell she had been given to Neoptolemus, sometimes called Pyrrhus, Achilles' son, the man who had killed old Priam at the altar. He soon abandoned her for Hermione, Helen's daughter, but he did not long survive this marriage and after his death Andromache married the Trojan prophet Helenus. They were now ruling the country and of course were rejoiced to welcome Aeneas and his men. They entertained them with the utmost hospitality and before they bade them farewell Helenus gave them useful advice about their journey. They must not land on the nearest coast of Italy, the east coast, he told them, because it was full of Greeks. Their destined home was on the west coast, somewhat to the north, but they must by no means take the shortest way and go up between Sicily and Italy. In those waters was that most perilous strait guarded by Scylla and Charybdis, which the Argonauts had succeeded in passing only because Thetis helped them and where Ulysses had lost six of his men. It is not clear how the Argonauts on their way from Asia to Greece got to the west coast of Italy, nor for that matter how Ulysses did, either, but at any rate there was no doubt in Helenus' mind exactly where the strait was and he gave Aeneas careful directions how to avoid those pests to mariners—by making a long circuit southward around Sicily, and reaching Italy far to the north of the whirlpool of implacable Charybdis and the black cavern into which Scylla sucked whole ships.

When the Trojans had taken leave of their kind hosts and had successfully rounded the eastern tip of Italy, they kept on sailing southwestward around Sicily with all confidence in their prophetic guide. Apparently, however, for all his mysterious powers Helenus was not aware that Sicily, at least the southern part, was now occupied by the Cyclopes, for he did not warn the Trojans against landing there. They reached the island after sunset and made camp on the shore with no hesitation at all. Probably they would all have been captured and eaten if very early the next morning, before any of the monsters were astir, a poor wretch of a man had not come running to where Aeneas was lying. He threw himself upon his knees, but indeed his obvious misery was enough of an appeal, his pallor like that of one half dead from starvation, his clothes held together only by thorns, his face squalid in the extreme with a thick growth of hair. He was one of Ulysses' sailors, he told them, who had been left behind unintentionally in Polyphemus' cave and had ever since lived in the woods on whatever he could find there, terrified perpetually lest one of the Cyclopes should come upon him. There were a hundred of them, he said, all as big and as frightful as Polyphemus. "Fly," he urged them. "Up and away with all speed. Break the ropes that hold the boats to the shore." They did as he said, cutting the cables, making breathless haste, all as silently as possible. But they had only launched the ships when the blind giant was seen slowly making his way down to the shore to wash the cavity where his eye had been, which still flowed with blood. He heard the splashing of the oars and he rushed toward the sound out into the sea. The Trojans, however, had got enough of a start. Before he could reach them the water had deepened too much even for his towering height.

They escaped that peril, but only to meet another as great. While rounding Sicily they were struck by a storm such as there never was before or since: the waves were so high that their crests licked the stars, and the gulfs between them so deep that the floor of the ocean was disclosed. It was clearly something more than a mere mortal storm and in point of fact Juno was back of it.

She hated all Trojans, of course; she never forgot the judgment of Paris and she had been Troy's bitterest enemy during the war, but she felt an especial hatred for Aeneas. She knew that Rome, which was to be founded by men of Trojan blood, although generations after Aeneas, was destined by the Fates to conquer Carthage some day, and Carthage was her pet city, beloved by her beyond all other places on earth. It is not known whether she really thought she could go against the decrees of the Fates, which Jupiter himself could not do, but certainly she did her best to drown Aeneas. She went to Aeolus, the King of the Winds, who had tried to help Ulysses, and asked him to sink the Trojan ships, promising him in return her loveliest nymph for his wife. The stupendous storm was the result. It would undoubtedly have done all that Juno wished if it had not been for Neptune. As Juno's brother he was quite aware of her way of doing things and it did not suit him to have her interfere with his sea. He was as cautious, however, in dealing with her as Jupiter always was. He said not a word to her, but contented himself with sending a stern reprimand to Aeolus. Then he calmed the sea, and made it possible for the Trojans to get to land. The north coast of Africa was where they finally beached their ships. They had been blown all the way down there from Sicily. As it happened, the place they came ashore was quite near to Carthage and Juno began at once to consider how she could turn this arrival to their disadvantage and the advantage of the Carthaginians.

Carthage had been founded by a woman, Dido, who was still its ruler and under whom it was growing into a great and splendid city. She was beautiful and a widow; Aeneas had lost his wife on the night he left Troy. Juno's plan was to have the two fall in love with each other and so divert Aeneas from Italy and induce him to settle down with Dido. It would have been a good plan if it had not been for Venus. She suspected what was in Juno's mind, and was determined to block it. She had her own plan. She was quite willing to have Dido fall in love with Aeneas, so that no harm could come to him in Carthage; but she intended to see to it that his feeling for Dido should be no more than an entire willingness to take anything she wanted to give; by no means such as to interfere in the least with his sailing away to Italy whenever that seemed best. At this juncture she went up to Olympus to talk to Jupiter. She reproached him and her lovely eyes filled with tears. Her dear son Aeneas was all but ruined, she said. And he, the King of Gods and Men, had sworn to her that Aeneas should be the ancestor of a race who would some day rule the world. Jupiter laughed and kissed away her tears. He told her that what he had promised would surely come to pass. Aeneas' descendants would be the Romans, to whom the Fates had decreed a boundless and endless empire.

Venus took her leave greatly comforted, but to make matters still more sure she turned for help to her son Cupid. Dido, she thought, could be trusted to make unaided the necessary impression upon Aeneas, but she was not at all certain that Aeneas by himself could get Dido to fall in love with him. She was known to be not susceptible. All the kings of the country round about had tried to persuade her to marry them with no success. So Venus summoned Cupid, who promised that he would set Dido's heart on fire with love as soon as she laid eyes on Aeneas. It was a simple matter for Venus to bring about a meeting between the two.

The morning after they landed, Aeneas with his friend, the faithful Achates, left his wretched shipwrecked followers to try to find out what part of the world they were in. He spoke cheering words to them before he started.

Comrades, you and I have had long acquaintance with sorrow.
Evils still worse we have known. These also will end. Call back
     courage.
Send away gloomy fear. Perhaps some day to remember
This trouble too will bring pleasure. . . .

As the two heroes explored the strange country, Venus disguised as a huntress appeared to them. She told them where they were and advised them to go straight to Carthage whose Queen would surely help them. Greatly reassured they took the path Venus pointed out, protected, although they did not know it, by a thick mist she wrapped around them. So they reached the city without interference and walked unnoticed through the busy streets. Before a great temple they paused wondering how they could get to the Queen, and there new hope came to them. As they gazed at the splendid building they saw marvelously carved upon the walls the battles around Troy in which they themselves had taken part. They saw the likenesses of their foes and their friends: the sons of Atreus, old Priam stretching out his hand to Achilles, the dead Hector. "I take courage," Aeneas said. "Here too there are tears for things, and hearts are touched by the fate of all that is mortal."

At that moment Dido, lovely as Diana herself, approached with a great train of attendants. Forthwith the mist around Aeneas dissolved and he stood forth beautiful as Apollo. When he told her who he was the Queen received him with the utmost graciousness and welcomed him and his company to her city. She knew how these desolate homeless men felt, for she herself had come to Africa with a few friends fleeing from her brother who wanted to murder her. "Not ignorant of suffering, I have learned how to help the unfortunate," she said.

She gave a splendid banquet for the strangers that night at which Aeneas told their story, the fall of Troy first and then their long journeying. He spoke admirably and eloquently, and perhaps Dido would have succumbed to such heroism and such beautiful language even if there had been no god in the case, but as it was, Cupid was there and she had no choice.

For a time she was happy. Aeneas seemed devoted to her, and she for her part lavished everything she had on him. She gave him to understand that her city was his as well as she herself. He, a poor shipwrecked man, had equal honor with her. She made the Carthaginians treat him as if he too were their ruler. His companions as well were distinguished by her favor. She could not do enough for them. In all this she wanted only to give; she asked nothing for herself except Aeneas' love. On his side he received what her generosity bestowed with great contentment. He lived at his ease with a beautiful woman and a powerful Queen to love him and provide everything for him and arrange hunting parties for his amusement and not only permit him, but beg him, to tell over and over again the tale of his adventures.

It is small wonder that the idea of setting sail for an unknown land grew less and less attractive to him. Juno was very well satisfied with the way things were going, but even so Venus was quite undisturbed. She understood Jupiter better than his wife did. She was sure that he would make Aeneas in the end go to Italy and that this little interlude with Dido would not be in the least to her son's discredit. She was quite right. Jupiter was very effective when he once roused himself. He dispatched Mercury to Carthage with a stinging message for Aeneas. The god found the hero walking about dressed to admiration, with a superb sword at his side studded with jasper and over his shoulders a beautiful cloak of purple inwrought with thread of gold, both Dido's presents, of course, the latter, indeed, the work of her own hands. Suddenly this elegant gentleman was startled out of his state of indolent contentment. Stern words sounded in his ear. "How long are you going to waste time here in idle luxury?" a severe voice asked. He turned and Mercury, visibly the god, stood before him. "The ruler of heaven himself has sent me to you," he said. "He bids you depart and seek the kingdom which is your destiny." With that he vanished as a wreath of mist dissolves into the air, leaving Aeneas awed and excited, indeed, and determined to obey, but chiefly wretchedly conscious how very difficult it was going to be with Dido.

He called his men together and ordered them to fit out a fleet and prepare for immediate departure, but to do all secretly. Nevertheless Dido learned and she sent for him. She was very gentle with him at first. She could not believe that he really meant to leave her. "Is it from me you would fly?" she asked. "Let these tears plead for me, this hand I gave to you. If I have in any way deserved well of you, if anything of mine was ever sweet to you—"

He answered that he was not the man to deny that she had done well by him and that he would never forget her. But she on her side must remember that he had not married her and was free to leave her whenever he chose. Jupiter had ordered him to go and he must obey. "Cease these complaints," he begged her, "which only trouble us both."

Then she told him what she thought. How he had come to her cast away, starving, in need of everything, and how she had given herself and her kingdom to him. But before his complete impassivity her passion was helpless. In the midst of her burning words her voice broke. She fled from him and hid herself where no one could see her.

The Trojans sailed that same night, very wisely. One word from the Queen and their departure would have been forever impossible. On shipboard looking back at the walls of Carthage Aeneas saw them illumined by a great fire. He watched the flames leap up and slowly die down and he wondered what was the cause. All unknowing he was looking at the glow of Dido's funeral pyre. When she saw that he was gone she killed herself.

Part Two: THE DESCENT INTO THE LOWER WORLD

The journey from Carthage to the west coast of Italy was easy as compared with what had gone before. A great loss, however, was the death of the trusty pilot Palinurus who was drowned as they neared the end of their perils by sea.

Aeneas had been told by the prophet Helenus as soon as he reached the Italian land to seek the cave of the Sibyl of Cumae, a woman of deep wisdom, who could foretell the future and would advise him what to do. He found her and she told him she would guide him to the underworld where he would learn all he needed to know from his father Anchises, who had died just before the great storm. She warned him, however, that it was no light undertaking:—

Trojan, Anchises' son, the descent of Avernus is easy.
All night long, all day, the doors of dark Hades stand open.
But to retrace the path, to come up to the sweet air of heaven,
That is labor indeed.

Nevertheless, if he was determined she would go with him. First he must find in the forest a golden bough growing on a tree, which he must break off and take with him. Only with this in his hand would he be admitted to Hades. He started at once to look for it, accompanied by the ever-faithful Achates.

They went almost hopelessly into the great wilderness of trees where it seemed impossible to find anything. But suddenly they caught sight of two doves, the birds of Venus. The men followed as they flew slowly on until they were close to Lake Avernus, a dark foul-smelling sheet of water where the Sibyl had told Aeneas was the cavern from which the road led down to the underworld. Here the doves soared up to a tree through whose foliage came a bright yellow gleam. It was the golden bough. Aeneas plucked it joyfully and took it to the Sibyl. Then, together, prophetess and hero started on their journey.

Other heroes had taken it before Aeneas and not found it especially terrifying. The crowding ghosts had, to be sure, finally frightened Ulysses, but Theseus, Hercules, Orpheus, Pollux, had apparently encountered no great difficulty on the way. Indeed, the timid Psyche had gone there all alone to get the beauty charm for Venus from Proserpine and had seen nothing worse than the three-headed dog Cerberus, who had been easily mollified by a bit of cake. But the Roman hero found horrors piled upon horrors. The way the Sibyl thought it necessary to start was calculated to frighten any but the boldest. At dead of night in front of the dark cavern on the bank of the somber lake she slaughtered four coal-black bullocks to Hecate, the dread Goddess of Night. As she placed the sacrificial parts upon a blazing altar, the earth rumbled and quaked beneath their feet and from afar dogs howled through the darkness. With a cry to Aeneas, "Now will you need all your courage," she rushed into the cave, and undaunted he followed her. They found themselves soon on a road wrapped in shadows which yet permitted them to see frightful forms on either side, pale Disease and avenging Care, and Hunger that persuades to crime, and so on, a great company of terrors. Death-dealing War was there and mad Discord with snaky, bloodstained hair, and many another curse to mortals. They passed unmolested through them and finally reached a place where an old man was rowing a boat over a stretch of water. There they saw a pitiful sight, spirits on the shore innumerable as the leaves which fall in the forest at the first cold of winter, all stretching out their hands and praying the ferryman to carry them across to the farther bank. But the gloomy old man made his own choice among them; some he admitted to his skiff, others he pushed away. As Aeneas stared in wonder the Sibyl told him they had reached the junction of two great rivers of the underworld, the Cocytus, named of lamentation loud, and the Acheron. The ferryman was Charon and those he would not admit to his boat were the unfortunates who had not been duly buried. They were doomed to wander aimlessly for a hundred years, with never a place to rest in.

Charon was inclined to refuse Aeneas and his guide when they came down to the boat. He bade them halt and told them he did not ferry the living, only the dead. At sight of the golden bough, however, he yielded and took them across. The dog Cerberus was there on the other bank to dispute the way, but they followed Psyche's example. The Sibyl, too, had some cake for him and he gave them no trouble. As they went on they came to the solemn place in which Minos, Europa's son, the inflexible judge of the dead, was passing the final sentence on the souls before him. They hastened away from that inexorable presence and found themselves in the Fields of Mourning, where the unhappy lovers dwelt who had been driven by their misery to kill themselves. In that sorrowful but lovely spot, shaded with groves of myrtle, Aeneas caught sight of Dido. He wept as he greeted her. "Was I the cause of your death?" he asked her. "I swear I left you against my will." She neither looked at him nor answered him. A piece of marble could not have seemed less moved. He himself, however, was a good deal shaken, and he continued to shed tears for some time after he lost sight of her.

At last they reached a spot where the road divided. From the left branch came horrid sounds, groans and savage blows and the clanking of chains. Aeneas halted in terror. The Sibyl, however, bade him have no fear, but fasten boldly the golden bough on the wall that faced the crossroads. The regions to the left, she said, were ruled over by stern Rhadamanthus, also a son of Europa, who punished the wicked for their misdeeds. But the road to the right led to the Elysian Fields where Aeneas would find his father. There when they arrived everything was delightful, soft green meadows, lovely groves, a delicious life-giving air, sunlight that glowed softly purple, an abode of peace and blessedness. Here dwelt the great and good dead, heroes, poets, priests, and all who had made men remember them by helping others. Among them Aeneas soon came upon Anchises, who greeted him with incredulous joy. Father and son alike shed happy tears at this strange meeting between the dead and the living whose love had been strong enough to bring him down to the world of death.

They had much, of course, to say to each other. Anchises led Aeneas to Lethe, the river of forgetfulness, of which the souls on their way to live again in the world above must all drink. "A draught of long oblivion," Anchises said. And he showed his son those who were to be their descendants, his own and Aeneas', now waiting by the river for their time to drink and lose the memory of what in former lives they had done and suffered. A magnificent company they were—the future Romans, the masters of the world. One by one Anchises pointed

Aeneas and the Sibyl enter Charon's boat

them out, and told of the deeds they would do which men would never through all time forget. Finally, he gave his son instructions how he would best establish his home in Italy and how he could avoid or endure all the hardships that lay before him.

Then they took leave of each other, but calmly, knowing that they were parting only for a time. Aeneas and the Sibyl made their way back to the earth and Aeneas returned to his ships. Next day the Trojans sailed up the coast of Italy looking for their promised home.

Part Three: THE WAR IN ITALY

Terrible trials awaited the little band of adventurers. Juno was again the cause of the trouble. She made the most powerful peoples of the country, the Latins and the Rutulians, fiercely opposed to the Trojans settling there. If it had not been for her, matters would have gone well. The aged Latinus, a great-grandson of Saturn and King of the City of Latium, had been warned by the spirit of his father, Faunus, not to marry his daughter Lavinia, his only child, to any man of the country, but to a stranger who was soon to arrive. From that union would be born a race destined to hold the entire world under their sway. Therefore, when an embassy arrived from Aeneas asking for a narrow resting place upon the coast and the common liberty of air and water, Latinus received them with great good will. He felt convinced that Aeneas was the son-in-law Faunus had predicted, and he said as much to the envoys. They would never lack a friend while he lived, he told them. To Aeneas he sent this message, that he had a daughter forbidden by heaven to wed with any except a foreigner, and that he believed the Trojan chief was this man of destiny.

But here Juno stepped in. She summoned Alecto, one of the Furies, from Hades and bade her loose bitter war over the land. She obeyed gladly. First she inflamed the heart of Queen Amata, wife of Latinus, to oppose violently a marriage between her daughter and Aeneas. Then she flew to the King of the Rutulians, Turnus, who up to now had been the most favored among the many suitors for Lavinia's hand. Her visit to arouse him against the Trojans was hardly necessary. The idea of anyone except himself marrying Lavinia was enough to drive Turnus to frenzy. As soon as he heard of the Trojan embassy to the King he started with his army to march to Latium and prevent by force any treaty between the Latins and the strangers.

Alecto's third effort was cleverly devised. There was a pet stag belonging to a Latin farmer, a beautiful creature, so tame that it would run free by day, but at nightfall always come to the well-known door. The farmer's daughter tended it with loving care; she would comb its coat and wreathe its horns with garlands. All the farmers far and near knew it and protected it. Anyone, even of their own number, who had harmed it would have been severely punished. But for a foreigner to dare such a deed was to enrage the whole countryside. And that is what Aeneas' young son did under the guiding hand of Alecto. Ascanius was out hunting and he and his hounds were directed by the Fury to where the stag was lying in the forest. He shot at it and wounded it mortally, but it succeeded in reaching its home and its mistress before it died. Alecto took care that the news should spread quickly, and fighting started at once, the furious farmers bent upon killing Ascanius and the Trojans defending him.

This news reached Latium just after Turnus had arrived. The fact that his people were already in arms and the still more ominous fact that the Rutulian Army had encamped before his gates were too much for King Latinus. His furious Queen, too, undoubtedly played a part in his final decision. He shut himself up in his palace and let matters go as they would. If Lavinia was to be won Aeneas could not count on any help from his future father-in-law.

There was a custom in the city that when war was determined upon, the two folding-gates of the temple of the god Janus, always kept closed in time of peace, should be unbarred by the King while trumpets blared and warriors shouted. But Latinus, locked in his palace, was not available for the sacred rite. As the citizens hesitated as to what to do, Juno herself swept down from heaven, smote with her own hand the bars and flung wide the doors. Joy filled the city, joy in the battle-array, the shining armor and spirited chargers and proud standards, joy at facing a war to the death.

A formidable army, Latins and Rutulians together, were now opposed to the little band of Trojans. Their leader, Turnus, was a brave and skilled warrior; another able ally was Mezentius, an excellent soldier, but so cruel that his subjects, the great Etruscan people, had rebelled against him and he had fled to Turnus. A third ally was a woman, the maiden Camilla, who had been reared by her father in a remote wilderness, and as a baby, with a sling or a bow in her tiny hand, had learned to bring down the swift-flying crane or the wild swan, herself hardly less swift of foot than they of wing. She was mistress of all the ways of warfare, unexcelled with the javelin and the two-edged ax as well as with the bow. Marriage she disdained. She loved the chase and the battle and her freedom. A band of warriors followed her, among them a number of maidens.

In this perilous situation for the Trojans, Father Tiber, the god of the great river they were encamped near, visited Aeneas in a dream. He bade him go swiftly upstream to where Evander dwelt, a King of a poor little town which was destined to become in future ages the proudest of earth's cities, whence the towers of Rome should soar up to the skies. Here, the river-god promised, Aeneas would get the help he needed. At dawn he started with a chosen few and for the first time a boat filled with armed men floated on the Tiber. When they reached Evander's home a warm welcome was given them by the King and his young son, Pallas. As they led their guests to the rude building which served as palace they pointed out the sights: the great Tarpeian rock; near it a hill sacred to Jove, now rough with brambles, where some day the golden, glittering Capitol would rise; a meadow filled with lowing cattle, which would be the gathering place of the world, the Roman Forum. "Once fauns and nymphs lived here," the King said, "and a savage race of men. But Saturn came to the country, a homeless exile fleeing from his son Jupiter. Everything then was changed. Men forsook their rude and lawless ways. He ruled with such justice and in such peace that ever since his reign has been called 'the Golden Age.' But in later times other customs prevailed; peace and justice fled before the greed for gold and the frenzy for war. Tyrants ruled the land until fate brought me here, an exile from Greece, from my dear home in Arcady."

As the old man ended his story they reached the simple hut where he lived and there Aeneas spent the night on a couch of leaves with a bear's skin to cover him. Next morning, awakened by the dawn and the call of birds, they all arose. The King went forth with two great dogs following him, his sole retinue and bodyguard. After they had broken their fast he gave Aeneas the advice he had come to seek. Arcady—he had called his new country after his old—was a feeble state, he said, and could do little to help the Trojans. But on the farther bank of the river lived the rich and powerful Etruscans, whose fugitive king, Mezentius, was helping Turnus. This fact alone would make the nation choose Aeneas' side in the war, so intense was the hatred felt for their former ruler. He had shown himself a monster of cruelty; he delighted in inflicting suffering. He had devised a way of killing people more horrible than any other known to man: he would link dead and living together, coupling hand with hand and face with face, and leave the slow poison of that sickening embrace to bring about a lingering death.

All Etruria had finally risen against him, but he had succeeded in escaping. They were determined, however, to get him back and punish him as he deserved. Aeneas would find them willing and powerful allies. For himself, the old king said, he would send Pallas who was his only son, to enter the service of the War-god under the Trojan hero's guidance, and with him a band of youths, the flower of the Arcadian chivalry. Also he gave each of his guests a gallant steed, to enable them to reach quickly the Etruscan Army and enlist their help.

Meantime the Trojan camp, fortified only by earthworks and deprived of its leader and its best warriors, was hard-pressed. Turnus attacked it in force. Throughout the first day the Trojans defended themselves successfully, following the strict orders which Aeneas at his departure had given them on no account to undertake an offensive. But they were greatly outnumbered; the prospect was dark unless they could get word to Aeneas what was happening. The question was whether this was possible, with the Rutulians completely surrounding the fort. However, there were two men in that little band who scorned to weigh the chances of success or failure, to whom the extreme peril of the attempt was a reason for making it. These two resolved to try to pass through the enemy under the cover of the night and reach Aeneas.

Nisus and Euryalus were their names, the first a valiant and experienced soldier, the other only a stripling, but equally brave and full of generous ardor for heroic deeds. It was their habit to fight side by side. Wherever one was, whether on guard or in the field, there the other would always be found. The idea of the great enterprise came first to Nisus as he looked over the ramparts at the enemy and observed how few and dim the lights were and how deep a silence reigned as of men fast asleep. He told his plan to his friend, but with no thought of his going too. When the lad cried out that he would never be left behind, that he scorned life in comparison with death in so glorious an attempt, Nisus felt only grief and dismay. "Let me go alone," he begged. "If by chance something goes amiss—and in such a venture as this there are a thousand chances—you will be here to ransom me or to give me the rites of burial. Remember too that you are young; life is all before you." "Idle words," Euryalus answered. "Let us start and with no delay." Nisus saw the impossibility of persuading him and sorrowfully yielded.

They found the Trojan leaders holding a council, and they put their plan before them. It was instantly accepted and the princes with choked voices and falling tears thanked them and promised them rich rewards. "I want only one," said Euryalus. "My mother is here in the camp. She would not stay behind with the other women. She would follow me. I am all she has. If I die—" "She will be my mother," Ascanius broke in. "She shall have the place of the mother I lost that last night in Troy.

I swear it to you. And take this with you, my own sword. It will not fail you."

Then the two started, through the trench and on to the enemy's camp. All around lay sleeping men. Nisus whispered, "I am going to clear a path for us. Do you keep watch." With that he killed man after man, so skillfully that not one uttered a sound as he died. Not a groan gave the alarm. Euryalus soon joined in the bloody work. When they reached the end of the camp they had cleared as it were a great highway through it, where only dead men were lying. But they had been wrong to delay. Daylight was dawning; a troop of horses coming from Latium caught sight of the shining helmet of Euryalus and challenged him. When he pushed on through the trees without answering they knew he was an enemy and they surrounded the wood. In their haste the two friends got separated and Euryalus took the wrong path. Nisus wild with anxiety turned back to find him. Unseen himself he saw him in the hands of the troopers. How could he rescue him? He was all alone. It was hopeless and yet he knew it was better to make the attempt and die than leave him. He fought them, one man against a whole company, and his flying spear struck down warrior after warrior. The leader, not knowing from what quarter this deadly attack was coming, turned upon Euryalus shouting, "You shall pay for this!" Before his lifted sword could strike him, Nisus rushed forward. "Kill me, me," he cried. "The deed is all mine. He only followed me." But with the words still on his lips, the sword was thrust into the lad's breast. As he fell dying, Nisus cut down the man who had killed him; then pierced with many darts he too fell dead beside his friend.

The rest of the Trojans' adventures were all on the battlefield. Aeneas came back with a large army of Etruscans in time to save the camp, and furious war raged. From then on, the story turns into little more than an account of men slaughtering each other. Battle follows battle, but they are all alike. Countless heroes are always slain, rivers of blood drench the earth, the brazen throats of trumpets blare, arrows plenteous as hail fly from sharp-springing bows, hoofs of fiery steeds spurting gory dew trample on the dead. Long before the end, the horrors have ceased to horrify. All the Trojans' enemies are killed, of course. Camilla falls after giving a very good account of herself; the wicked Mezentius meets the fate he so richly deserves, but only after his brave young son is killed defending him. Many good allies die, too, Evander's son Pallas among them.

Finally Turnus and Aeneas meet in single combat. By this time Aeneas, who in the earlier part of the story seemed as human as Hector or Achilles, has changed into something strange and portentous; he is not a human being. Once he carried tenderly his old father out of burning Troy and encouraged his little son to run beside him; when he came to Carthage he felt what it meant to meet with compassion, to reach a place where "There are tears for things"; he was very human too when he strutted about Dido's palace in his fine clothes. But on the Latin battlefields he is not a man, but a fearful prodigy. He is "vast as Mount Athos, vast as Father Apennine himself when he shakes his mighty oaks and lifts his snow-topped peak to the sky"; like "Aegaeon who had a hundred arms and a hundred hands and flashed fire through fifty mouths, thundering on fifty strong shields and drawing fifty sharp swords—even so Aeneas slakes his victorious fury the whole field over." When he faces Turnus in the last combat there is no interest in the outcome. It is as futile for Turnus to fight Aeneas as to fight the lightning or an earthquake.

Virgil's poem ends with Turnus' death. Aeneas, we are given to understand, married Lavinia and founded the Roman race —who, Virgil said, "left to other nations such things as art and science, and ever remembered that they were destined to bring under their empire the peoples of earth, to impose the rule of submissive nonresistance, to spare the humbled and to crush the proud."

PART FIVE

The Great Families of Mythology

17 The House of Atreus

The chief importance of the story of Atreus and his descendants is that the fifth-century tragic poet Aeschylus took it for the subject of his greatest drama, the Oresteia, *which is made up of three plays, the* Agamemnon, *the* Libation Bearers, *the* Eumenides. *It has no rival in Greek tragedy except the four plays of Sophocles about Oedipus and his children. Pindar in the early fifth century tells the current tale about the feast Tantalus made the gods and protests that it is not true. The punishment of Tantalus is described often, first in the* Odyssey, *from which I have taken it. Amphion's story, and Niobe's, I have taken from Ovid, who alone tells them in full. For Pelops' winning the chariot race I have preferred Apollodorus, of the first or second century* A.D., *who gives the fullest account that has come down to us. The story of Atreus' and Thyestes' crimes and all that followed them is taken from Aeschylus'* Oresteia.

The House of Atreus is one of the most famous families in mythology. Agamemnon, who led the Greeks against Troy, belonged to it. All of his immediate family, his wife Clytemnestra, his children, Iphigenia, Orestes and Electra, were as well known as he was. His brother Menelaus was the husband of Helen, for whose sake the Trojan War was fought.

It was an ill-fated house. The cause of all the misfortunes was held to be an ancestor, a King of Lydia named Tantalus, who brought upon himself a most terrible punishment by a most wicked deed. That was not the end of the matter. The evil he started went on after his death. His descendants also did wickedly and were punished. A curse seemed to hang over the family, making men sin in spite of themselves and bringing suffering and death down upon the innocent as well as the guilty.

TANTALUS AND NIOBE

Tantalus was the son of Zeus and honored by the gods beyond all the mortal children of Zeus. They allowed him to eat at their table, to taste the nectar and ambrosia which except for him alone none but the immortals could partake of. They did more; they came to a banquet in his palace; they condescended to dine with him. In return for their favor he acted so atrociously that no poet ever tried to explain his conduct. He had his only son Pelops killed, boiled in a great cauldron, and served to the gods. Apparently he was driven by a passion of hatred against them which made him willing to sacrifice his son in order to bring upon them the horror of being cannibals. It may be, too, that he wanted to show in the most startling and shocking way possible how easy it was to deceive the awful, venerated, humbly adored divinities. In his scorn of the gods and his measureless self-confidence he never dreamed that his guests would realize what manner of food he had set before them.

He was a fool. The Olympians knew. They drew back from the horrible banquet and they turned upon the criminal who had contrived it. He should be so punished, they declared, that no man to come, hearing what this man had suffered, would dare ever again to insult them. They set the arch-sinner in a pool in Hades, but whenever in his tormenting thirst he stooped to drink he could not reach the water. It disappeared, drained into the ground as he bent down. When he stood up it was there again. Over the pool fruit trees hung heavy laden with pears, pomegranates, rosy apples, sweet figs. Each time he stretched out his hand to grasp them the wind tossed them high away out of reach. Thus he stood forever, his undying throat always athirst, his hunger in the midst of plenty never satisfied.

His son Pelops was restored to life by the gods, but they had to fashion a shoulder for him out of ivory. One of the goddesses, some say Demeter, some Thetis, inadvertently had eaten of the loathsome dish and when the boy's limbs were reassembled one shoulder was wanting. This ugly story seems to have come down in its early brutal form quite unsoftened. The latter Greeks did not like it and protested against it. The poet Pindar called it

A tale decked out with glittering lies against the word of truth.
Let a man not speak of cannibal deeds among the blessed gods.

However that might be, the rest of Pelops' life was successful. He was the only one of Tantalus' descendants not marked out by misfortune. He was happy in his marriage, although he wooed a dangerous lady who had been the cause of many deaths, the Princess Hippodamia. The reason men died for her was not her own fault, but her father's. This King had a wonderful pair of horses Ares had given him—superior, of course, to all mortal horses. He did not want his daughter to marry, and whenever a suitor came for her hand the youth was told he could race with her father for her. If the suitor's horses won, she would be his; if her father's won, the suitor must pay with his life for his defeat. In this way a number of rash young men met their death. Even so, Pelops dared. He had horses he could trust, a present from Poseidon. He won the race; but there is a story that Hippodamia had more to do with the victory than Poseidon's horses. Either she fell in love with Pelops or she felt the time had come to put a stop to that sort of racing. She bribed her father's charioteer, a man named Myrtilus, to help her. He pulled out the bolts that held the wheels of the King's chariot, and the victory was Pelops' with no trouble at all. Later, Myrtilus was killed by Pelops, cursing him as he died, and some said that this was the cause of the misfortunes that afterward followed the family. But most writers said, and certainly with better reason, that it was the wickedness of Tantalus which doomed his descendants.

None of them suffered a worse doom than his daughter Niobe. And yet it seemed at first that the gods had chosen her out for good fortune as they had her brother Pelops. She was happy in her marriage. Her husband was Amphion, a son of Zeus and an incomparable musician. He and his twin brother Zethus undertook once to fortify Thebes, building a lofty wall around it. Zethus was a man of great physical strength who despised his brother's neglect of manly sports and his devotion to his art. Yet when it came to the heavy task of getting enough rocks for the wall, the gentle musician outdid the strong athlete: he drew such entrancing sounds from his lyre that the very stones were moved and followed him to Thebes.

There he and Niobe ruled in entire content until she showed that the mad arrogance of Tantalus lived on in her. She held herself raised by her great prosperity above all that ordinary mortals fear and reverence. She was rich and nobly born and powerful. Seven sons had been born to her, brave and beautiful young men, and seven daughters, the fairest of the fair. She thought herself strong enough not only to deceive the gods as her father had tried to do, but to defy them openly.

She called upon the people of Thebes to worship her. "You burn incense to Leto," she said, "and what is she as compared with me? She had but two children, Apollo and Artemis. I have seven times as many. I am a queen. She was a homeless wanderer until tiny Delos alone of all places on earth consented to receive her. I am happy, strong, great—too great for any, men or gods, to do me harm. Make your sacrifices to me in Leto's temple, mine now, not hers."

Insolent words uttered in the arrogant consciousness of power were always heard in heaven and always punished. Apollo and Artemis glided swiftly to Thebes from Olympus, the archer god and the divine huntress, and shooting with deadly aim they struck down all of Niobe's sons and daughters. She saw them die with anguish too great for expression. Beside those bodies so lately young and strong, she sank down motionless in stony grief, dumb as a stone and her heart like a stone within her. Only her tears flowed and could not stop. She was changed into a stone which forever, night and day, was wet with tears.

To Pelops two sons were born, Atreus and Thyestes. The inheritance of evil descended to them in full force. Thyestes fell in love with his brother's wife and succeeded in making her false to her marriage vows. Atreus found out and swore that Thyestes should pay as no man ever had. He killed his brother's two little children, had them cut limb from limb, boiled, and served up to their father. When he had eaten—

> Poor wretch, when he had learned the deed abhorrent,
> He cried a great cry, falling back—spewed out
> That flesh, called down upon that house a doom
> Intolerable, the banquet board sent crashing.

Atreus was King. Thyestes had no power. The atrocious crime was not avenged in Atreus' lifetime, but his children and his children's children suffered.

AGAMEMNON AND HIS CHILDREN

On Olympus the gods were met in full assembly. The father of Gods and Men began first to speak. Zeus was sorely vexed at the mean way men perpetually acted toward the gods, blaming the divine powers for what their own wickedness brought about, and that too even when the Olympians had tried to hold them back. "You all know about Aegisthus, whom Agamemnon's son Orestes has slain," Zeus said, "how he loved the wife of Agamemnon and killed him on his return from Troy. Certainly no blame attaches to us from that. We warned him by the mouth of Hermes. 'The death of the son of Atreus will be avenged by Orestes.' Those were Hermes' very words, but not even such friendly advice could restrain Aegisthus, who now pays the final penalty."

This passage in the *Iliad* is the first mention of the House of Atreus. In the *Odyssey* when Odysseus reached the land of the Phaeacians and was telling them about his descent to Hades and the ghosts he encountered, he said that, of them all, the spirit of Agamemnon had most moved him to pity. He had begged him to say how he had died and the chief told him that he was killed ingloriously as he sat at table, struck down as one butchers an ox. "It was Aegisthus," he said, "with the aid of my accursed wife. He invited me to his house and as I feasted he killed me. My men too. You have seen many die in single combat or in battle, but never one who died as we did, by the wine bowl and the loaded tables in a hall where the floor flowed with blood. Cassandra's death-shriek rang in my ears as she fell. Clytemnestra slew her over my body. I tried to lift up my hands for her, but they fell back. I was dying then."

That was the way the story was first told: Agamemnon had been killed by his wife's lover. It was a sordid tale. How long it held the stage we do not know, but the next account we have, centuries later, written by Aeschylus about 450 B.C., is very different. It is a great story now of implacable vengeance and tragic passions and inevitable doom. The motive for Agamemnon's death is no longer the guilty love of a man and a woman, but a mother's love for a daughter killed by her own father, and a wife's determination to avenge that death by killing her husband. Aegisthus fades; he is hardly in the picture. The wife of Agamemnon, Clytemnestra, has all the foreground to herself.

The two sons of Atreus, Agamemnon, the commander of the Greek forces at Troy, and Menelaus, the husband of Helen, ended their lives very differently. Menelaus, at first the less successful, was notably prosperous in his later years. He lost his wife for a time, but after the fall of Troy he got her back. His ship was driven all the way to Egypt by the storm Athena sent to the Greek Fleet, but finally he reached home safely and lived happily with Helen ever after. It was far otherwise with his brother.

When Troy fell, Agamemnon was the most fortunate of the victorious chieftains. His ship came safely through the storm which wrecked or drove to distant countries so many others. He entered his city not only safe after peril by land and sea, but triumphant, the proud conqueror of Troy. His home was expecting him. Word had been sent that he had landed, and the townspeople joined in a great welcome to him. It seemed that he was of all men the most gloriously successful, after a brilliant victory back with his own again, peace and prosperity before him.

But in the crowd that greeted him with thanksgiving for his return there were anxious faces, and words of dark foreboding passed from one man to another. "He will find evil happenings," they muttered. "Things once were right there in the palace, but no more. That house could tell a tale if it could speak."

Before the palace the elders of the city were gathered to do their king honor, but they too were in distress, with a still heavier anxiety, a darker foreboding, than that which weighed upon the doubtful crowd. As they waited they talked in low tones of the past. They were old and it was almost more real to them than the present. They recalled the sacrifice of Iphigenia, lovely, innocent young thing, trusting her father utterly, and then confronted with the altar, the cruel knives, and only pitiless faces around her. As the old men spoke, it was like a vivid memory to them, as if they themselves had been there, as if they had heard with her the father she loved telling men to lift her and hold her over the altar to slay her. He had killed her, not willingly, but driven by the Army impatient for good winds to sail to Troy. And yet the matter was not as simple as that. He yielded to the Army because the old wickedness in generation after generation of his race was bound to work out in evil for him too. The elders knew the curse that hung over the house.

> . . . The thirst for blood—
> It is in their flesh. Before the old wound
> Can be healed, there is fresh blood flowing.

Ten years had passed since Iphigenia died, but the results of her death reached through to the present. The elders were wise. They had learned that every sin causes fresh sin; every wrong brings another in its train. A menace from the dead girl hung over her father in this hour of triumph. And yet perhaps, they said to each other, perhaps it would not take actual shape for a time. So they tried to find some bit of hope, but at the bottom of their hearts they knew and dared not say aloud that vengeance was already there in the palace waiting for Agamemnon.

It had waited ever since the Queen, Clytemnestra, had come back from Aulis, where she had seen her daughter die. She did not keep faith with her husband who had killed her child and his; she took a lover and all the people knew it. They knew too that she had not sent him away when the news of Agamemnon's return reached her. He was still there with her. What was being planned behind the palace doors? As they wondered and feared, a tumult of noise reached them, chariots rolling, voices shouting. Into the courtyard swept the royal car with the King and beside him a girl, very beautiful, but very strange-looking. Attendants and townspeople were following them and as they came to a halt the doors of the great house swung open and the Queen appeared.

The King dismounted, praying aloud, "O Victory now mine, be mine forever." His wife advanced to meet him. Her face was radiant, her head high. She knew that every man there except Agamemnon was aware of her infidelity, but she faced them all and told them with smiling lips that even in their presence she must at such a moment speak out the great love she bore her husband and the agonizing grief she had suffered in his absence. Then in words of exultant joy she bade him welcome. "You are our safety," she told him, "our sure defense. The sight of you is dear as land after storm to the sailor, as a gushing stream to a thirsty wayfarer."

He answered her, but with reserve, and he turned to go into the palace. First he pointed to the girl in the chariot. She was Cassandra, Priam's daughter, he told his wife—the Army's gift to him, the flower of all the captive women. Let Clytemnestra see to her and treat her well. With that he entered the house and the doors closed behind the husband and the wife. They would never open again for both of them.

The crowd had gone. Only the old men still waited uneasily before the silent building and the blank doors. The captive princess caught their attention and they looked curiously at her. They had heard of her strange fame as a prophetess whom no one ever believed and yet whose prophecies were always proved true by the event. She turned a terrified face to them. Where had she been brought, she asked them wildly—What house was this? They answered soothingly that it was where the son of Atreus lived. She cried out, "No! It is a house God hates, where men are killed and the floor is red with blood."

The old men stole frightened glances at each other. Blood, men killed, that was what they too were thinking of, the dark past with its promise of more darkness. How could she, a stranger and a foreigner, know that past? "I hear children crying," she wailed,

> . . . Crying for wounds that bleed.
> A father feasted—and the flesh his children.

Thyestes and his sons . . . Where had she heard of that? More wild words poured from her lips. It seemed as if she had seen what had happened in that house through the years, as if she had stood by while death followed death, each a crime and all working together to produce more crime. Then from the past she turned to the future. She cried out that on that very day two more deaths would be added to the list, one her own. "I will endure to die," she said, as she turned away and moved toward the palace. They tried to hold her back from that ominous house, but she would not have it; she entered and the doors closed forever on her, too. The silence that followed when she had gone was suddenly and terribly broken. A cry rang out, the voice of a man in agony: "God! I am struck! My death blow—" and silence again. The old men, terrified, bewildered, huddled together. That was the King's voice. What should they do? "Break into the palace? Quick, be quick," they urged each other. "We must know." But there was no need now of any violence. The doors opened and on the threshold stood the Queen.

Dark red stains were on her dress, her hands, her face, yet she herself looked unshaken, strongly sure of herself. She proclaimed for all to hear what had been done. "Here lies my husband dead, struck down justly by my hand," she said. It was his blood that stained her dress and face and she was glad.

> He fell and as he gasped, his blood
> Spouted and splashed me with dark spray, a dew
> Of death, sweet to me as heaven's sweet raindrops
> When the corn-land buds.

She saw no reason to explain her act or excuse it. She was not a murderer in her own eyes, she was an executioner. She had punished a murderer, the murderer of his own child,

> Who cared no more than if a beast should die
> When flocks are plenty in the fleecy fold,
> But slew his daughter—slew her for a charm
> Against the Thracian winds.

Her lover followed her and stood beside her—Aegisthus, the youngest child of Thyestes, born after that horrible feast. He had no quarrel with Agamemnon himself, but Atreus, who had had the children slaughtered and placed on the banquet table for their father, was dead and vengeance could not reach him. Therefore his son must pay the penalty.

The two, the Queen and her lover, had reason to know that wickedness cannot be ended by wickedness. The dead body of the man they had just killed was a proof. But in their triumph they did not stop to think that this death, too, like all the others, would surely bring evil in its train. "No more blood for you and me," Clytemnestra said to Aegisthus. "We are lords here now. We two will order all things well." It was a baseless hope.

Iphigenia had been one of three children. The other two were a girl and a boy, Electra and Orestes. Aegisthus would certainly have killed the boy if Orestes had been there, but he had been sent away to a trusted friend. The girl Aegisthus disdained to kill; he only made her utterly wretched in every way possible until her whole life was concentrated in one hope, that Orestes would come back and avenge their father. That vengeance—what would it be? Over and over she asked herself this. Aegisthus, of course, must die, but to kill him alone would never satisfy justice. His crime was less black than another's. What then? Could it be justice that a son should take a mother's life to avenge a father's death? So she brooded through the bitter days of the long years that followed, while Clytemnestra and Aegisthus ruled the land.

As the boy grew to manhood he saw even more clearly than she the terrible situation. It was a son's duty to kill his father's murderers, a duty that came before all others. But a son who killed his mother was abhorrent to gods and to men. A most sacred obligation was bound up with a most atrocious crime. He who wanted only to do right was so placed that he must choose between two hideous wrongs. He must be a traitor to his father or he must be the murderer of his mother.

In this agony of doubt he journeyed to Delphi to ask the oracle to help him, and Apollo spoke to him in clear words bidding him,

> Slay the two who slew.
> Atone for death by death.
> Shed blood for old blood shed.

And Orestes knew that he must work out the curse of his house, exact vengeance and pay with his own ruin. He went to the home he had not seen since he was a little boy, and with him went his cousin and friend Pylades. The two had grown up together and were devoted in a way far beyond usual friendship. Electra, with no idea that they were actually arriving, was yet on the watch. Her life was spent in watching for the brother who would bring her the only thing life held for her.

One day at her father's tomb she made an offering to the dead and prayed, "O Father, guide Orestes to his home." Suddenly he was beside her, claiming her as his sister, showing her as proof the cloak he wore, the work of her hands, which she had wrapped him in when he went away. But she did not need a proof. She cried, "Your face is my father's face." And she poured out to him all the love no one had wanted from her through the wretched years:—

> All, all is yours,
> The love I owed my father who is dead,
> The love I might have given to my mother,
> And my poor sister cruelly doomed to die.
> All yours now, only yours.

He was too sunk in his own thought, too intent upon the thing he faced, to answer her or even to listen. He broke in upon her words to tell her what filled his mind so that nothing else could reach it: the terrible words of the oracle of Apollo. Orestes spoke with horror:—

> He told me to appease the angry dead.
> That who hears not when his dead cry to him,
> For such there is no home, no refuge anywhere.
> No altarfire burns for him, no friend greets him.
> He dies alone and vile. O God, shall I believe
> Such oracles? But yet—but yet
> The deed is to be done and I must do it.

The three made their plans. Orestes and Pylades were to go to the palace claiming to be the bearers of a message that Orestes had died. It would be joyful news to Clytemnestra and Aegisthus who had always feared what he might do, and they would certainly want to see the messengers. Once in the palace the brother and his friend could trust to their own swords and the complete surprise of their attack.

They were admitted and Electra waited. That had been her bitter part all through her life. Then the doors opened slowly and a woman came out and stood tranquilly on the steps. It was Clytemnestra. She had been there only a moment or so when a slave rushed out screaming, "Treason! Our master! Treason!" He saw Clytemnestra and gasped, "Orestes—alive—here." She knew then. Everything was clear to her, what had happened and what was still to come. Sternly she bade the slave bring her a battle-ax. She was resolved to fight for her life, but the weapon was no sooner in her hand than she changed her mind. A man came through the doors, his sword red with blood, whose blood she knew as she knew too who held the sword. Instantly she saw a surer way to defend herself than with an ax. She was the mother of the man before her. "Stop, my son," she said. "Look—my breast. Your heavy head dropped on it and you slept, oh, many a time. Your baby mouth, where never a tooth was, sucked the milk, and so you grew—" Orestes cried, "O Pylades, she is my mother. May I spare—" His friend told him solemnly: No. Apollo had commanded. The gods must be obeyed. "I will obey," Orestes said. "You—follow me." Clytemnestra knew that she had lost. She said calmly, "It seems, my son, that you will kill your mother." He motioned her into the house. She went and he followed her.

When he came out again those waiting in the courtyard did not need to be told what he had done. Asking no question they watched him, their master now, with compassion. He seemed not to see them; he was looking at a horror beyond them. Stammering words came from his lips: "The man is dead. I am not guilty there. An adulterer. He had to die. But she—Did she do it or did she not? O you, my friends. I say I killed my mother—yet not without reason—she was vile and she killed my father and God hated her."

His eyes were fixed always on that unseen horror. He screamed, "Look! Look! Women there. Black, all black, and long hair like snakes." They told him eagerly there were no women. "It is only your fancy. Oh, do not fear." "You do not see them?" he cried. "No fancy. I—I see them. My mother has sent them. They crowd around me and their eyes drip blood. Oh, let me go." He rushed away, alone except for those invisible companions.

When next he came to his country, years had passed. He had been a wanderer in many lands, always pursued by the same terrible shapes. He was worn with suffering, but in his loss of everything men prize there was a gain too. "I have been taught by misery," he said. He had learned that no crime was beyond atonement, that even he, defiled by a mother's murder, could be made clean again. He traveled to Athens, sent there by Apollo to plead his case before Athena. He had come to beg for help; nevertheless, in his heart there was confidence. Those who desire to be purified cannot be refused and the black stain of his guilt had grown fainter and fainter through his years of lonely wandering and pain. He believed that by now it had faded away. "I can speak to Athena with pure lips," he said.

Clytemnestra and Orestes

The goddess listened to his plea. Apollo was beside him. "It is I who am answerable for what he did," he said. "He killed at my command." The dread forms of his pursuers, the Erinyes, the Furies, were arrayed against him, but Orestes listened calmly to their demand for vengeance. "I, not Apollo, was guilty of my mother's murder," he said, "but I have been cleansed of my guilt." These were words never spoken before by any of the House of Atreus. The killers of that race had never suffered from their guilt and sought to be made clean. Athena accepted the plea. She persuaded the avenging goddesses also to accept it, and with this new law of mercy established they themselves were changed. From the Furies of frightful aspect they became the Benignant Ones, the Eumenides, protectors of the suppliant. They acquitted Orestes, and with the words of acquittal the spirit of evil which had haunted his house for so long was banished. Orestes went forth from Athena's tribunal a free man. Neither he nor any descendant of his would ever again be driven into evil by the irresistible power of the past. The curse of the House of Atreus was ended.

IPHIGENIA AMONG THE TAURIANS

I have taken this story entirely from two plays of Euripides, the fifth-century tragic poet. No other writer tells the story in full. The happy end brought about by a divinity, the deus ex machina, is a common device with Euripides alone of the three tragic poets. According to our ideas it is a weakness; and certainly it is unnecessary in this case, where the same end could have been secured by merely omitting the head-wind. Athena's appearance, in point of fact, harms a good plot. A possible reason for this lapse on the part of one of the greatest poets the world has known is that the Athenians, who were suffering greatly at the time from the war with Sparta, were eager for miracles and that Euripides chose to humor them.

The Greeks, as has been said, did not like stories in which human beings were offered up, whether to appease angry gods or to make Mother Earth bear a good harvest or to bring about anything whatsoever. They thought about such sacrifices as we do. They were abominable. Any deity who demanded them was thereby proved to be evil, and, as the poet Euripides said, "If gods do evil then they are not gods." It was inevitable therefore that another story should grow up about the sacrifice of Iphigenia at Aulis. According to the old account, she was killed because one of the wild animals Artemis loved had been slain by the Greeks and the guilty hunters could win back the goddess's favor only by the death of a young girl. But to the later Greeks this was to slander Artemis. Never would such a demand have been made by the lovely lady of the woodland and the forest, who was especially the protector of little helpless creatures.

> So gentle is she, Artemis the holy,
> To dewy youth, to tender nurslings,
> The young of all that roam the meadow,
> Of all who live within the forest.

So another ending was given to the story. When the Greek soldiers at Aulis came to get Iphigenia where she was waiting for the summons to death, her mother beside her, she forbade Clytemnestra to go with her to the altar. "It is better so for me as well as for you," she said. The mother was left alone. At last she saw a man approaching. He was running and she wondered why anyone should hasten to bring her the tidings he must bear. But he cried out to her, "Wonderful news!" Her daughter had not been sacrificed, he said. That was certain, but exactly what had happened to her no one knew. As the priest was about to strike her, anguish troubled every man there and all bowed their heads. But a cry came from the priest and they looked up to see a marvel hardly to be believed. The girl had vanished, but on the ground beside the altar lay a deer, its throat cut. "This is Artemis' doing," the priest proclaimed. "She will not have her altar stained with human blood. She has herself furnished the victim and she receives the sacrifice." "I tell you, O Queen," the messenger said, "I was there and the thing happened thus. Clearly your child has been borne away to the gods."

But Iphigenia had not been carried to heaven. Artemis had taken her to the land of the Taurians (today the Crimea) on the shore of the Unfriendly Sea—a fierce people whose savage custom it was to sacrifice to the goddess any Greek found in the country. Artemis took care that Iphigenia should be safe; she made her priestess of her temple. But as such it was her terrible task to conduct the sacrifices, not actually herself kill her countrymen, but consecrate them by long-established rites and deliver them over to those who would kill them.

She had been serving the goddess thus for many years when a Greek galley put in at the inhospitable shore, not under stern necessity, storm-driven, but voluntarily. And yet it was known everywhere what the Taurians did to the Greeks they captured. An overwhelmingly strong motive made the ship

anchor there. From it in the early dawn two young men came
and stealthily found their way to the temple. Both were clearly
of exalted birth; they looked like the sons of kings, but the
face of one was deeply marked with lines of pain. It was he
who whispered to his friend, "Don't you think this is the
temple, Pylades?" "Yes, Orestes," the other answered. "It must
be that bloodstained spot."

Orestes here and his faithful friend? What were they doing
in a country so perilous to Greeks? Did this happen before or
after Orestes had been absolved of the guilt of his mother's
murder? It was some time after. Although Athena had pronounced him clear of guilt, in this story all the Erinyes had
not accepted the verdict. Some of them continued to pursue
him, or else Orestes thought that they did. Even the acquittal
pronounced by Athena had not restored to him his peace of
mind. His pursuers were fewer, but they were still with him.

In his despair he went to Delphi. If he could not find help
there, in the holiest place of Greece, he could find it nowhere.
Apollo's oracle gave him hope, but only at the risk of his life.
He must go to the Taurian country, the Delphic priestess
said, and bring away the sacred image of Artemis from her
temple. When he had set it up in Athens he would at last be
healed and at peace. He would never again see terrible forms
haunting him. It was a most perilous enterprise, but everything for him depended on it. At whatever cost he was bound
to make the attempt and Pylades would not let him make it
alone.

When the two reached the temple they saw at once that
they must wait for the night before doing anything. There was
no chance by day of getting into the place unseen. They retreated to keep under cover in some dark lonely spot.

Iphigenia, sorrowful as always, was going through her
round of duties to the goddess when she was interrupted by a
messenger who told her that two young men, Greeks, had been
taken prisoners and were to be sacrificed at once. He had been
sent on to bid her make all ready for the sacred rites. The
horror which she had felt so often seized her again. She shuddered at the thought, terribly familiar though it was, of the
hideous bloodshed, of the agony of the victims. But this time
a new thought came as well. She asked herself, "Would a
goddess command such things? Would she take pleasure in
sacrificial murder? I do not believe it," she told herself. "It is
the men of this land who are bloodthirsty and they lay their
own guilt on the gods."

As she stood thus, deep in meditation, the captives were
led in. She sent the attendants into the temple to make ready
for them, and when the three were alone together she spoke

to the young men. Where was their home, she asked, the home which they would never see again? She could not keep her tears back and they wondered to see her so compassionate. Orestes told her gently not to grieve for them. When they came to the land they had faced what might befall them. But she continued questioning. Were they brothers? Yes, in love, Orestes replied, but not by birth. What were their names? "Why ask that of a man about to die?" Orestes said.

"Will you not even tell me what your city is?" she asked.

"I come from Mycenae," Orestes answered, "that city once so prosperous."

"The King of it was certainly prosperous," Iphigenia said. "His name was Agamemnon."

"I do not know about him," Orestes said abruptly. "Let us end this talk."

"No—no. Tell me of him," she begged.

"Dead," said Orestes. "His own wife killed him. Ask me no more."

"One thing more," she cried. "Is she—the wife—alive?"

"No," Orestes told her. "Her son killed her."

The three looked at each other in silence.

"It was just," Iphigenia whispered shuddering; "just—yet evil, horrible." She tried to collect herself. Then she asked, "Do they ever speak of the daughter who was sacrificed?"

"Only as one speaks of the dead," Orestes said. Iphigenia's face changed. She looked eager, alert.

"I have thought of a plan to help both you and me," she said. "Would you be willing to carry a letter to my friends in Mycenae if I can save you?"

"No, not I," Orestes said. "But my friend will. He came here only for my sake. Give him your letter and kill me."

"So be it," Iphigenia answered. "Wait while I fetch the letter." She hurried away and Pylades turned to Orestes.

"I will not leave you here to die alone," he told him. "All will call me a coward if I do so. No. I love you—and I fear what men may say."

"I gave my sister to you to protect," Orestes said. "Electra is your wife. You cannot abandon her. As for me—it is no misfortune for me to die." As they spoke to each other in hurried whispers, Iphigenia entered with a letter in her hand. "I will persuade the King. He will let my messenger go, I am sure. But first—" she turned to Pylades—"I will tell you what is in the letter so that even if through some mischance you lose your belongings, you will carry my message in your memory and bear it to my friends."

"A good plan," Pylades said. "To whom am I to bear it?"

"To Orestes," Iphigenia said. "Agamemnon's son."

She was looking away, her thoughts were in Mycenae. She did not see the startled gaze the two men fixed on her.

"You must say to him," she went on, "that she who was sacrificed at Aulis sends this message. She is not dead—"

"Can the dead return to life?" Orestes cried.

"Be still," Iphigenia said with anger. "The time is short. Say to him, 'Brother, bring me back home. Free me from this murderous priesthood, this barbarous land.' Mark well, young man, the name is Orestes."

"O God, God," Orestes groaned. "It is not credible."

"I am speaking to you, not to him," Iphigenia said to Pylades. "You will remember the name?"

"Yes," Pylades answered, "but it will not take me long to deliver your message. Orestes, here is a letter. I bring it from your sister."

"And I accept it," Orestes said, "with a happiness words cannot utter."

The next moment he held Iphigenia in his arms. But she freed herself.

"I do not know," she cried. "How can I know? What proof is there?"

"Do you remember the last bit of embroidery you did before you went to Aulis?" Orestes asked. "I will describe it to you. Do you remember your chamber in the palace? I will tell you what was there."

He convinced her and she threw herself into his arms. She sobbed out, "Dearest! You are my dearest, my darling, my dear one. A baby, a little baby, when I left you. More than marvelous is this thing that has come to me."

"Poor girl," Orestes said, "mated to sorrow, as I have been. And you might have killed your own brother."

"Oh, horrible," Iphigenia cried. "But I have brought myself to do horrible things. These hands might have slain you. And even now—how can I save you? What god, what man, will help us?" Pylades had been waiting in silence, sympathetic, but impatient. He thought the hour for action had emphatically arrived. "We can talk," he reminded the brother and sister, "when once we are out of this dreadful place."

"Suppose we kill the King," Orestes proposed eagerly, but Iphigenia rejected the idea with indignation. King Thoas had been kind to her. She would not harm him. At that moment a plan flashed into her mind, perfect, down to the last detail. Hurriedly she explained it and the young men agreed at once. All three then entered the temple.

After a few moments Iphigenia came out bearing an image in her arms. A man was just stepping across the threshold of the temple enclosure. Iphigenia cried out, "O King, halt. Stay where you are." In astonishment he asked her what was happening. She told him that the two men he had sent her for the goddess were not pure. They were tainted, vile; they had killed their mother, and Artemis was angry.

"I am taking the image to the seashore to purify it," she said. "And there too I will cleanse the men from their pollution. Only after that can the sacrifice be made. All that I do must be done in solitude. Let the captives be brought forth and proclaim to the city that no one may draw near to me."

"Do as you wish," Thoas answered, "and take all the time you need." He watched the procession move off, Iphigenia leading with the image, Orestes and Pylades following, and attendants carrying vessels for the purifying rite. Iphigenia was praying aloud: "Maiden and Queen, daughter of Zeus and Leto, you shall dwell where purity is, and we shall be happy." They passed out of sight on their way to the inlet where Orestes' ship lay. It seemed as if Iphigenia's plan could not fail.

And yet it did. She was able indeed to make the attendants leave her alone with her brother and Pylades before they reached the sea. They stood in awe of her and they did just what she bade them. Then the three made all haste and boarded the ship and the crew pushed it off. But at the mouth of the harbor where it opened out to the sea a heavy wind blowing landward struck them and they could make no headway against it. They were driven back in spite of all they could do. The vessel seemed rushing on the rocks. The men of the country by now were aroused to what was being done. Some watched to seize the ship when it was stranded; others ran with the news to King Thoas. Furious with anger, he was hurrying from the temple to capture and put to death the impious strangers and the treacherous priestess, when suddenly above him in the air a radiant form appeared—manifestly a goddess. The King started back and awe checked his steps.

"Stop, O King," the Presence said. "I am Athena. This is my word to you. Let the ship go. Even now Poseidon is calming the winds and waves to give it a safe passage. Iphigenia and the others are acting under divine guidance. Dismiss your anger."

Thoas answered submissively, "Whatever is your pleasure, Goddess, shall be done." And the watchers on the shore saw the wind shift, the waves subside, and the Greek ship leave the harbor, flying under full sail to the sea beyond.

18 The Royal House of Thebes

The story of the Theban family rivals that of the House of Atreus in fame and for the same reason. Just as the greatest plays of Aeschylus, in the fifth century, are about Atreus' descendants, so the greatest plays of his contemporary Sophocles are about Oedipus and his children.

CADMUS AND HIS CHILDREN

The tale of Cadmus and his daughters is only a prologue to the greater story. It was popular in classical days, and several writers told it in whole or part. I have preferred the account of Apollodorus, who wrote in the first or second century A.D. He tells it simply and clearly.

When Europa was carried away by the bull, her father sent her brothers to search for her, bidding them not to return until they had found her. One of them, Cadmus, instead of looking vaguely here and there, went very sensibly to Delphi to ask Apollo where she was. The god told him not to trouble further about her or his father's determination not to receive him without her, but to found a city of his own. He would come upon a heifer when he left Delphi, Apollo said; he was to follow her and build his city at the spot where she lay down to rest. In this way Thebes was founded and the country round about got the name of the heifer's land, Boeotia. First, however, Cadmus had to fight and kill a terrible dragon which guarded a spring near by and slew all his companions when they went to get water. Alone he could never have built the city, but when the dragon was dead Athena appeared to him and told him to sow the earth with the dragon's teeth. He obeyed with no idea what was to happen, and to his terror saw armed men spring up from the furrows. However, they paid no attention to him, but turned upon each other until all were killed except five whom Cadmus induced to become his helpers.

With the aid of the five Cadmus made Thebes a glorious city and ruled over it in great prosperity and with great wisdom. Herodotus says that he introduced the alphabet into Greece. His wife was Harmonia, the daughter of Ares and Aphrodite. The gods graced their marriage with their presence and Aphrodite gave Harmonia a wondrous necklace which had been made by Hephaestus, the workman of Olympus, but which for all its divine origin was to bring disaster in a later generation.

They had four daughters and one son, and they learned through their children that the wind of the gods' favor never blows steadily for long. All of their daughters were visited by great misfortunes. One of them was Semele, mother of Dionysus, who perished before the unveiled glory of Zeus. Ino was another. She was the wicked stepmother of Phrixus, the boy who was saved from death by the ram of the Golden Fleece. Her husband was struck with madness and killed their son, Melicertes. With his dead body in her arms she leaped into the sea. The gods saved them both, however. She became a sea-goddess, the one who saved Odysseus from drowning when his raft was shattered, and her son became a sea-god. In the *Odyssey* she is still called Ino, but later her name was changed to Leucothea and her son was called Palaemon. Like her sister Semele she was fortunate in the end. The two others were not. Both suffered through their sons. Agave was the most wretched of all mothers, driven mad by Dionysus so that she believed her son Pentheus was a lion and killed him with her own hands. Autonoe's son was Actaeon, a great hunter. Autonoe was less wretched than Agave, in that she did not herself kill her son, but she had to endure his dying a terrible death in the strength of his young manhood, a death, too, completely undeserved; he had done no wrong.

He was out hunting and hot and thirsty entered a grotto where a little stream widened into a pool. He wanted only to cool himself in the crystal water. But all unknowing he had chanced upon the favorite bathing place of Artemis—and at the very moment when the goddess had let fall her garments and stood in her naked beauty on the water's edge. The offended divinity gave not a thought to whether the youth had purposely insulted her or had come there in all innocence. She flung into his face drops from her wet hand and as they fell upon him he was changed into a stag. Not only outwardly. His heart became a deer's heart and he who had never known fear before was afraid and fled. His dogs saw him running and chased him. Even his agony of terror could not make him swift enough to outstrip the keen-scented pack. They fell upon him, his own faithful hounds, and killed him.

Thus great sorrows for their children and grandchildren came upon Cadmus and Harmonia in old age after great prosperity. After Pentheus died they fled from Thebes as if trying to flee also from misfortune. But misfortune followed them. When they reached far-distant Illyria the gods changed them into serpents, not as a punishment, for they had done no wrong. Their fate indeed was a proof that suffering was not a punishment for wrongdoing; the innocent suffered as often as the guilty.

Of all that unfortunate race no one was more innocent of wrongdoing than Oedipus, a great-great-grandson of Cadmus, and no one suffered so greatly.

OEDIPUS

> *I have taken this story entirely from Sophocles' play of that name except for the riddle of the Sphinx which Sophocles merely alludes to. It is given by many writers, always in substantially the same form.*

King Laius of Thebes was the third in descent from Cadmus. He married a distant cousin, Jocasta. With their reign Apollo's oracle at Delphi began to play a leading part in the family's fortunes.

Apollo was the God of Truth. Whatever the priestess at Delphi said would happen infallibly came to pass. To attempt to act in such a way that the prophecy would be made void was as futile as to set oneself against the decrees of fate. Nevertheless, when the oracle warned Laius that he would die at the hands of his son he determined that this should not be. When the child was born he bound its feet together and had it exposed on a lonely mountain where it must soon die. He felt no more fear; he was sure that on this point he could foretell the future better than the god. His folly was not brought home to him. He was killed, indeed, but he thought the man who attacked him was a stranger. He never knew that in his death he had proved Apollo's truth.

When he died he was away from home and many years had passed since the baby had been left on the mountain. It was reported that a band of robbers had slain him together with his attendants, all except one, who brought the news home. The matter was not carefully investigated because Thebes was in sore straits at the time. The country around was beset by a frightful monster, the Sphinx, a creature shaped like a winged lion, but with the breast and face of a woman. She lay in wait for the wayfarers along the roads to the city and whomever she seized she put a riddle to, telling him if he could answer it, she would let him go. No one could, and the horrible creature devoured man after man until the city was in a state of siege. The seven great gates which were the Thebans' pride remained closed, and famine drew near to the citizens.

So matters stood when there came into the stricken country a stranger, a man of great courage and great intelligence, whose name was Oedipus. He had left his home, Corinth, where he was held to be the son of the King, Polybus, and the reason for his self-exile was another Delphic oracle. Apollo had declared that he was fated to kill his father. He, too, like Laius, thought to make it impossible for the oracle to come true; he resolved never to see Polybus again. In his lonely wanderings he came into the country around Thebes and he heard what was happening there. He was a homeless, friendless man to whom life meant little and he determined to seek the Sphinx out and try to solve the riddle. "What creature," the Sphinx asked him, "goes on four feet in the morning, on two at noonday, on three in the evening?" "Man," answered Oedipus. "In childhood he creeps on hands and feet; in manhood he walks erect; in old age he helps himself with a staff." It was the right answer. The Sphinx, inexplicably, but most fortunately, killed herself; the Thebans were saved. Oedipus gained all and more than he had left. The grateful citizens made him their King and he married the dead King's wife, Jocasta. For many years they lived happily. It seemed that in this case Apollo's words had been proved to be false.

But when their two sons had grown to manhood Thebes was visited by a terrible plague. A blight fell upon everything. Not only were men dying throughout the country, the flocks and herds and the fruits of the field were blasted as well. Those who were spared death by disease faced death by famine. No one suffered more than Oedipus. He regarded himself as the father of the whole state; the people in it were his children; the misery of each one was his too. He dispatched Jocasta's brother Creon to Delphi to implore the god's help.

Creon returned with good news. Apollo had declared that the plague would be stayed upon one condition: whoever

Oedipus and the Sphinx

had murdered King Laius must be punished. Oedipus was enormously relieved. Surely the men or the man could be found even after all these years, and they would know well how to punish him. He proclaimed to the people gathered to hear the message Creon brought back:—

> ... Let no one of this land
> Give shelter to him. Bar him from your homes,
> As one defiled, companioned by pollution.
> And solemnly I pray, may he who killed
> Wear out his life in evil, being evil.

Oedipus took the matter in hand with energy. He sent for Teiresias, the old blind prophet, the most revered of Thebans. Had he any means of finding out, he asked him, who the guilty were? To his amazement and indignation the seer at first refused to answer. "For the love of God," Oedipus implored him. "If you have knowledge—" "Fools," Teiresias said. "Fools all of you. I will not answer." But when Oedipus went so far as to accuse him of keeping silence because he had himself taken part in the murder, the prophet in his turn was angered and words he had meant never to speak fell heavily from his lips: "You are yourself the murderer you seek." To Oedipus the old man's mind was wandering; what he said was sheer madness. He ordered him out of his sight and never again to appear before him.

Jocasta too treated the assertion with scorn. "Neither prophets nor oracles have any sure knowledge," she said. She told her husband how the priestess at Delphi had prophesied that Laius should die at the hand of his son and how he and she together had seen to it that this should not happen by having the child killed. "And Laius was murdered by robbers, where three roads meet on the way to Delphi," she concluded triumphantly. Oedipus gave her a strange look. "When did this happen?" he asked slowly. "Just before you came to Thebes," she said.

"How many were with him?" Oedipus asked. "They were five in all," Jocasta spoke quickly, "all killed but one." "I must see that man," he told her. "Send for him." "I will," she said. "At once. But I have a right to know what is in your mind." "You shall know all that I know," he answered. "I went to Delphi just before I came here because a man had flung it in my face that I was not the son of Polybus. I went to ask the god. He did not answer me, but he told me horrible things— that I should kill my father, marry my mother, and have children men would shudder to look upon. I never went back to Corinth. On my way from Delphi, at a place where three roads met, I came upon a man with four attendants. He tried to force me from the path; he struck me with his stick. Angered I fell upon them and I killed them. Could it be the leader was Laius?" "The one man left alive brought back a tale of robbers," Jocasta said, "Laius was killed by robbers, not by his son—the poor innocent who died upon the mountain."

As they talked a further proof seemed given them that Apollo could speak falsely. A messenger came from Corinth to announce to Oedipus the death of Polybus. "O oracle of the god," Jocasta cried, "where are you now? The man died, but not by his son's hand." The messenger smiled wisely. "Did the fear of killing your father drive you from Corinth?" he asked. "Ah, King, you were in error. You never had reason to fear—for you were not the son of Polybus. He brought you up as though you were his, but he took you from my hands." "Where did you get me?" Oedipus asked. "Who were my father and mother?" "I know nothing of them," the messenger said. "A wandering shepherd gave you to me, a servant of Laius."

Jocasta turned white; a look of horror was on her face. "Why waste a thought upon what such a fellow says?" she cried. "Nothing he says can matter." She spoke hurriedly, yet fiercely. Oedipus could not understand her. "My birth does not matter?" he asked. "For God's sake, go no further," she said. "My misery is enough." She broke away and rushed into the palace.

At that moment an old man entered. He and the messenger eyed each other curiously. "The very man, O King," the messenger cried. "The shepherd who gave you to me." "And you," Oedipus asked the other, "do you know him as he knows you?" The old man did not answer, but the messenger insisted. "You must remember. You gave me once a little child you had found—and the King here is that child." "Curse you," the other muttered. "Hold your tongue." "What!" Oedipus said angrily. "You would conspire with him to hide from me what I desire to know? There are ways, be sure, to make you speak."

The old man wailed, "Oh, do not hurt me. I did give him the child, but do not ask more, master, for the love of God." "If I have to order you a second time to tell me where you got him, you are lost," Oedipus said. "Ask your lady," the old man cried. "She can tell you best." "She gave him to you?" asked Oedipus. "Oh, yes, oh, yes," the other groaned. "I was to kill the child. There was a prophecy—" "A prophecy!" Oedipus repeated. "That he should kill his father?" "Yes," the old man whispered.

A cry of agony came from the King. At last he understood.

"All true! Now shall my light be changed to darkness. I am accursed." He had murdered his father, he had married his father's wife, his own mother. There was no help for him, for her, for their children. All were accursed.

Within the palace Oedipus wildly sought for his wife that was his mother. He found her in her chamber. She was dead. When the truth broke upon her she had killed herself. Standing beside her he too turned his hand against himself, but not to end his life. He changed his light to darkness. He put out his eyes. The black world of blindness was a refuge; better to be there than to see with strange shamed eyes the old world that had been so bright.

ANTIGONE

> *I have taken this story from the* Antigone *and the* Oedipus at Colonus, *two of Sophocles' plays, with the exception of the death of Menoeceus, which is told in a play of Euripides,* The Suppliants.

After Jocasta's death and all the evils that came with it, Oedipus lived on in Thebes while his children were growing up. He had two sons, Polyneices and Eteocles, and two daughters, Antigone and Ismene. They were very unfortunate young people, but they were far from being monsters all would shudder to look at, as the oracle had told Oedipus. The two lads were well liked by the Thebans and the two girls were as good daughters as a man could have.

Oedipus of course resigned the throne. Polyneices, the elder son, did the same. The Thebans felt that this was wise because of the terrible position of the family, and they accepted Creon, Jocasta's brother, as the regent. For many years they treated Oedipus with kindness, but at last they decided to expel him from the city. What induced them to do this is not known, but Creon urged it and Oedipus' sons consented to it. The only friends Oedipus had were his daughters. Through all his misfortunes they were faithful to him. When he was driven out of the city Antigone went with him to guide him in his blindness and care for him, and Ismene stayed in Thebes to look out for his interests and keep him informed of whatever happened that touched him.

After he had gone his two sons asserted their right to the throne, and each tried to be made king. Eteocles succeeded although he was the younger, and he expelled his brother from Thebes. Polyneices took refuge in Argos and did all he could to arouse enmity against Thebes. His intention was to collect an army to march against the city.

In the course of their desolate wanderings Oedipus and Antigone came to Colonus, a lovely spot near Athens, where the one-time Erinyes, the Furies, now the Benignant Goddesses, had a place sacred to them and therefore a refuge for suppliants. The blind old man and his daughter felt safe there, and there Oedipus died. Most unhappy in much of his life, he was happy at the end. The oracle which once had spoken terrible words to him comforted him when he was dying. Apollo promised that he, the disgraced, the homeless wanderer, would bring to the place where his grave should be a mysterious blessing from the gods. Theseus, the King of Athens, received him with all honor, and the old man died rejoicing that he was no longer hateful to men, but welcomed as a benefactor to the land that harbored him.

Ismene, who had come to tell her father the good news of this oracle, was with her sister when he died and afterward they were both sent safely home by Theseus. They arrived to find one brother marching against their city, resolved to capture it, and the other determined to defend it to the end. Polyneices, the one who attacked it, had the better right to it, but the younger, Eteocles, was fighting for Thebes, to save her from capture. It was impossible for the two sisters to take sides against either brother.

Polyneices had been joined by six chieftains, one of them the King of Argos, Adrastus, and another Adrastus' brother-in-law, Amphiaraus. This last joined the enterprise most unwillingly because he was a prophet and he knew that none of the seven would come back alive except Adrastus. However, he was under oath to let his wife Eriphyle decide whenever there was a dispute between him and her brother. He had sworn this once when he and Adrastus had quarreled and Eriphyle had reconciled them. Polyneices won her over to his side by bribing her with the wonderful necklace that had been the wedding gift of his ancestress Harmonia, and she made her husband go to the war.

There were seven champions to attack the seven gates of Thebes, and seven others within as bold to defend them. Eteocles defended the gate which Polyneices attacked, and Antigone and Ismene within the palace waited to hear which had killed the other. But before any decisive combat had taken place, a youth in Thebes not yet grown to manhood had died for his country and in his death had shown himself the noblest of all. This was Creon's younger son, Menoeceus.

Teiresias, the prophet who had brought so many distressful prophecies to the royal family, came to bring still another. He told Creon that Thebes would be saved only if Menoeceus was killed. The father utterly refused to bring this about. He would

e willing to die himself, he said—"But not even for my own
city will I slay my son." He bade the boy, who was present
when Teiresias spoke, "Up, my child, and fly with all speed
from the land before the city learns." "Where, Father?" asked
the lad. "What city seek—what friend?" "Far, far away," the
father answered. "I will find means—I will find gold." "Go get
it then," said Menoeceus, but when Creon had hurried away
he spoke other words:—

> My father—he would rob our town of hope,
> Make me a coward. Ah well—he is old
> And so to be forgiven. But I am young.
> If I betray Thebes there is no forgiveness.
> How can he think I will not save the city
> And for her sake go forth to meet my death?
> What would my life be if I fled away
> When I can free my country?

He went to join the battle and, all unskilled in warfare, he was
killed at once.

Neither the besiegers nor the besieged could gain any real
advantage and finally both sides agreed to let the matter be
decided by a combat between the brothers. If Eteocles was the
victor, the Argive Army would withdraw; if Eteocles was conquered, Polyneices should be king. Neither was victor; they
killed each other, Eteocles dying looked upon his brother and
wept; he had no strength to speak. Polyneices could murmur
a few words: "My brother, my enemy, but loved, always loved.
Bury me in my homeland—to have so much at least of my
city."

The combat had decided nothing and the battle was renewed. But Menoeceus had not died in vain; in the end the
Thebans prevailed and of the seven champions all were killed
except Adrastus only. He fled with the broken Army to Athens.
In Thebes, Creon was in control and he proclaimed that none
of those who had fought against the city should be given burial.
Eteocles should be honored with every rite that the noblest
received at death, but Polyneices should be left for beasts
and birds to tear and devour. This was to carry vengeance beyond the ordinance of the gods, beyond the law of right; it
was to punish the dead. The souls of the unburied might not
pass the river that encircles the kingdom of death, but must
wander in desolation, with no abiding-place, no rest ever for
their weariness. To bury the dead was a most sacred duty, not
only to bury one's own, but any stranger one might come upon.
But this duty, Creon's proclamation said, was changed in the
case of Polyneices to a crime. He who buried him would be
put to death.

Antigone and Ismene heard with horror what Creon had decided. To Ismene, shocking as it was, overwhelming her with anguish for the pitiful dead body and the lonely, homeless soul, it seemed, nevertheless, that nothing could be done except to acquiesce. She and Antigone were utterly alone. All Thebes was exulting that the man who had brought war upon them should be thus terribly punished. "We are women," she told her sister. "We must obey. We have no strength to defy the State." "Choose your own part," Antigone said. "I go to bury the brother I love." "You are not strong enough," Ismene cried. "Why, then when my strength fails," Antigone answered, "I will give up." She left her sister; Ismene dared not follow her.

Some hours later, Creon in the palace was startled by a shout, "Against your orders Polyneices has been buried." He hurried out to be confronted with the guards he had set on the dead body and with Antigone. "This girl buried him," they cried. "We saw her. A thick dust-storm gave her her chance. When it cleared, the body had been buried and the girl was making an offering to the dead." "You knew my edict?" Creon asked. "Yes," Antigone replied. "And you transgressed the law?" "Your law, but not the law of Justice who dwells with the gods," Antigone said. "The unwritten laws of heaven are not of today nor yesterday, but from all time."

Ismene weeping came from the palace to stand with her sister. "I helped do it," she said. But Antigone would not have that. "She had no share in it," she told Creon. And she bade her sister say no more. "Your choice was to live," she said, "mine to die."

As she was led away to death, she spoke to the bystanders:—

> . . . Behold me, what I suffer
> Because I have upheld that which is high.

Ismene disappears. There is no story, no poem, about her. The House of Oedipus, the last of the royal family of Thebes, was known no more.

THE SEVEN AGAINST THEBES

> *Two great writers told this story. It is the subject of one of Aeschylus' plays and one of Euripides'. I have chosen Euripides' version which, as so often with him, reflects remarkably our own point of view. Aeschylus tells the tale splendidly, but in his hands it is a stirring martial poem. Euripides' play,* The Suppliants, *shows his modern mind better than any of his other plays.*

Polyneices had been given burial at the price of his sister's life; his soul was free to be ferried across the river and find a home among the dead. But five of the chieftains who had marched with him to Thebes lay unburied, and according to Creon's decree would be left so forever.

Adrastus, the only one alive of the seven who had started the war, came to Theseus, King of Athens, to beseech him to induce the Thebans to allow the bodies to be buried. With him were the mothers and the sons of the dead men. "All we seek," he told Theseus, "is burial for our dead. We come to you for help, because Athens of all cities is compassionate."

"I will not be your ally," Theseus answered. "You led your people against Thebes. The war was of your doing, not hers."

But Aethra, Theseus' mother, to whom those other sorrowing mothers had first turned, was bold to interrupt the two Kings. "My son," she said, "may I speak for your honor and for Athens?"

"Yes, speak," he answered and listened intently while she told him what was in her mind.

"You are bound to defend all who are wronged," she said. "These men of violence who refuse the dead their right of burial, you are bound to compel them to obey the law. It is sacred through all Greece. What holds our states together and all states everywhere, except this, that each one honors the great laws of right?"

"Mother," Theseus cried, "these are true words. Yet of myself I cannot decide the matter. For I have made this land a free state with an equal vote for all. If the citizens consent, then I will go to Thebes."

The poor women waited, Aethra with them, while he went to summon the assembly which would decide the misery or happiness of their dead children. They prayed: "O city of Athena, help us, so that the laws of justice shall not be defiled and through all lands the helpless and oppressed shall be delivered." When Theseus returned he brought good news. The assembly had voted to tell the Thebans that Athens wished to be a good neighbor, but that she could not stand by and see a great wrong done. "Yield to our request," they would ask Thebes. "We want only what is right. But if you will not, then you choose war, for we must fight to defend those who are defenseless."

Before he finished speaking a herald entered. He asked, "Who is the master here, the lord of Athens? I bring a message to him from the master of Thebes."

"You seek one who does not exist," Theseus answered. "There is no master here. Athens is free. Her people rule."

"That is well for Thebes," the herald cried. "Our city is not governed by a mob which twists this way and that, but by one man. How can the ignorant crowd wisely direct a nation's course?"

"We in Athens," Theseus said, "write our own laws and then are ruled by them. We hold there is no worse enemy to a state than he who keeps the law in his own hands. This great advantage then is ours, that our land rejoices in all her sons who are strong and powerful by reason of their wisdom and just dealing. But to a tyrant such are hateful. He kills th.m, fearing they will shake his power.

"Go back to Thebes and tell her we know how much better peace is for men than war. Fools rush on war to make a weaker country their slave. We would not harm your state. We seek the dead only, to return to earth the body, of which no man is the owner, but only for a brief moment the guest. Dust must return to dust again."

Creon would not listen to Theseus' plea, and the Athenians marched against Thebes. They conquered. The panic-stricken people in the town thought only that they would be killed or enslaved and their city ruined. But although the way lay clear to the victorious Athenian Army, Theseus held them back. "We came not to destroy the town," he said, "but only to reclaim the dead." "And our King," said the messenger who brought the news to the anxiously waiting people of Athens, "Theseus himself, made ready for the grave those five poor bodies, washed them and covered them and set them on a bier."

Some measure of comfort came to the sorrowful mothers as their sons were laid upon the funeral pyre with all reverence and honor. Adrastus spoke the last words for each: "Capaneus lies here, a mighty man of wealth, yet humble as a poor man always and a true friend to all. He knew no guile; upon his lips were kind words only. Eteocles is next, poor in everything save honor. There he was rich indeed. When men would give him gold he would not take it. He would not be a slave to wealth. Beside him Hippomedon lies. He was a man who suffered hardship gladly, a hunter and a soldier. From boyhood he disdained an easy life. Atalanta's son is next, Parthenopaeus, of many a man, of many a woman loved, and one who never did a wrong to any man. His joy was in his country's good, his grief when it went ill with her. The last is Tydeus, a silent man. He could best reason with his sword and shield. His soul was lofty; deeds, not words, revealed how high it soared."

As the pyre was kindled, on a rocky height above it a woman appeared. It was Evadne, the wife of Capaneus. She cried,

I have found the light of your pyre, your tomb.
I will end there the grief and the anguish of life.
Oh, sweet death to die with the dear dead I love.

She leaped down to the blazing pyre and went with her husband to the world below.

Peace came to the mothers, with the knowledge that at last their children's spirits were at rest. Not so to the young sons of the dead men. They vowed as they watched the pyre burn that when they were grown they would take vengeance upon Thebes. "Our fathers sleep in the tomb, but the wrong done to them can never sleep," they said. Ten years later they marched to Thebes. They were victorious; the conquered Thebans fled and their city was leveled to the ground. Teiresias the prophet perished during the flight. All that was left of the old Thebes was Harmonia's necklace, which was taken to Delphi and for hundreds of years shown to the pilgrims there. The sons of the seven champions, although they succeeded where their fathers failed, were always called the Epigoni, "the After-Born," as if they had come into the world too late, after all great deeds had been done. But when Thebes fell, the Greek ships had not yet sailed to the Trojan land; and the son of Tydeus, Diomedes, was to be famed as one of the most glorious of the warriors who fought before the walls of Troy.

19 The Royal House of Athens

I have taken the Procne and Philomela story from Ovid. He tells it better than anyone else, but even so he is sometimes inconceivably bad. He describes in fifteen long lines (which I omit) exactly how Philomela's tongue was cut out and what it looked like as it lay "palpitating" on the earth where Tereus had flung it. The Greek poets were not given to such details, but the Latin had no manner of objection to them. I have followed Ovid, too, for the most part in the stories of Procris and Orithyia, taking a few details from Apollodorus. The tale of Creüsa and Ion is the subject of a play of Euripides, one of the many plays in which he tried to show the Athenians what the gods of the myths really were when judged by the ordinary human standards of mercy, honor, self-control. Greek mythology was full of stories such as that of the rape of Europa, in which never a suggestion was allowed that the deity in question had acted somewhat less than divinely. In his version of the story of Creüsa Euripides said to his audience, "Look at your Apollo, the sun-bright Lord of the Lyre, the pure God of Truth. This is what he did. He brutally forced a helpless young girl and then he abandoned her." The end of Greek mythology was at hand when such plays drew full houses in Athens.

This family was especially marked, even among the other remarkable mythological families, by the very peculiar happenings which visited its members. There is nothing stranger told in any story than some of the events in their lives.

CECROPS

The first King of Attica was named Cecrops. He had no human ancestor and he was himself only half human.

> Cecrops, lord and hero,
> Born of a dragon,
> Dragon-shaped below.

He was the person usually held to be responsible for Athena's becoming the protector of Athens. Poseidon, too, wanted the city, and to show how great a benefactor he could be, he struck open the rock of the Acropolis with his trident so that salt water leaped forth from the cleft and subsided into a deep well. But Athena did still better. She made an olive tree grow there, the most prized of all the trees of Greece.

> The gray-gleaming olive
> Athena showed to men,
> The glory of shining Athens,
> Her crown from on high.

In return for this good gift Cecrops, who had been made arbiter, decided that Athens was hers. Poseidon was greatly angered and punished the people by sending a disastrous flood.

In one story of this contest between the two deities, woman's suffrage plays a part. In those early days, we are told, women voted as well as men. All the women voted for the goddess, and all the men for the god. There was one more woman than there were men, so Athena won. But the men, along with Poseidon, were greatly chagrined at this female triumph; and while Poseidon proceeded to flood the land the men decided to take the vote away from the women. Nevertheless, Athena kept Athens.

Most writers say that these events happened before the Deluge, and that the Cecrops who belonged to the famous Athenian family was not the ancient half-dragon, half-human creature but an ordinary man, important only because of his relatives. He was the son of a distinguished king, a nephew of two well-known mythological heroines, and the brother of three. Above all, he was the great-grandfather of Athens' hero, Theseus.

His father, King Erechtheus of Athens, was usually said to be the king in whose reign Demeter came to Eleusis and agriculture began. He had two sisters, Procne and Philomela, noted for their misfortunes. Their story was tragic in the extreme.

PROCNE AND PHILOMELA

Procne, the elder of the two, was married to Tereus of Thrace, a son of Ares, who proved to have inherited all his father's detestable qualities. The two had a son, Itys, and when he was five years old Procne, who had all this while been living in Thrace separated from her family, begged Tereus to let her invite her sister Philomela to visit her. He agreed, and said he would go to Athens himself and escort her. But as soon as he set eyes on the girl he fell in love with her. She was beautiful as a nymph or a naiad. He easily persuaded her father to allow her to go back with him, and she herself was happy beyond words at the prospect. All went well on the voyage, but when they disembarked and started overland for the palace, Tereus told Philomela that he had received news of Procne's death and he forced her into a pretended marriage. Within a very short time, however, she learned the truth, and she was ill-advised enough to threaten him. She would surely find means to let the world know what he had done, she told him, and he would be an outcast among men. She aroused both his fury and his fear. He seized her and cut out her tongue. Then he left her in a strongly guarded place and went to Procne with a story that Philomela had died on the journey.

Philomela's case looked hopeless. She was shut up; she could not speak; in those days there was no writing. It seemed that Tereus was safe. However, although people then could not write, they could tell a story without speaking because they were marvelous craftsmen, such as have never been known since. A smith could make a shield which showed on its surface a lion-hunt, two lions devouring a bull while herdsmen urged their dogs on to attack them. Or he could depict a harvest scene, a field with reapers and sheaf-binders, and a vineyard teeming with clusters of grapes which youths and maidens gathered into baskets while one of them played on a shepherd's pipe to cheer their labors. The women were equally remarkable in their kind of work. They could weave, into the lovely stuffs they made, forms so lifelike anyone could see what tale they illustrated. Philomela accordingly turned to her loom. She had a greater motive to make clear the story she wove than any artist ever had. With infinite pains and surpassing skill she produced a wondrous tapestry on which the whole account of her wrongs was unfolded. She gave it to the old woman who attended her and signified that it was for the Queen.

Proud of bearing so beautiful a gift the aged creature carried it to Procne, who was still wearing deep mourning for her sister and whose spirit was as mournful as her garments.

She unrolled the web. There she saw Philomela, her very face and form, and Tereus equally unmistakable. With horror she read what had happened, all as plain to her as if in print. Her deep sense of outrage helped her to self-control. Here was no room for tears or for words, either. She bent her whole mind to delivering her sister and devising a fit punishment for her husband. First, she made her way to Philomela, doubtless through the old woman messenger, and when she had told her, who could not speak in return, that she knew all, she took her back to the palace. There while Philomela wept, Procne thought. "Let us weep hereafter," she told her sister. "I am prepared for any deed that will make Tereus pay for what he has done to you." At this moment her little son, Itys, ran into the room and suddenly as she looked at him it seemed to her that she hated him. "How like your father you are," she said slowly, and with the words her plan was clear to her. She killed the child with one stroke of a dagger. She cut the little dead body up, put the limbs in a kettle over the fire, and served them to Tereus that night for supper. She watched him as he ate; then she told him what he had feasted on.

In his first sickening horror he could not move, and the two sisters were able to flee. Near Daulis, however, he overtook them, and was about to kill them when suddenly the gods turned them into birds, Procne into a nightingale and Philomela into a swallow, which, because her tongue was cut out, only twitters and can never sing. Procne,

> The bird with wings of brown,
> Musical nightingale,
> Mourns forever; O Itys, child,
> Lost to me, lost.

Of all the birds her song is sweetest because it is saddest. She never forgets the son she killed.

The wretched Tereus too was changed into a bird, an ugly bird with a huge beak, said sometimes to be a hawk.

The Roman writers who told the story somehow got the sisters confused and said that the tongueless Philomela was the nightingale, which was obviously absurd. But so she is always called in English poetry.

PROCRIS AND CEPHALUS

The niece of these unfortunate women was Procris, and she was almost as unfortunate as they. She was married very happily to Cephalus, a grandson of the King of the Winds, Aeolus; but they had been married only a few weeks when Cephalus was carried off by no less a personage than Aurora herself, the Goddess of the Dawn. He was a lover of the chase and used to rise early to track the deer. So it happened that many a time as the day broke Dawn saw the young hunter, and finally she fell in love with him. But Cephalus loved Procris. Not even the radiant goddess could make him faithless. Procris alone was in his heart. Enraged at this obstinate devotion which none of her wiles could weaken, Aurora at last dismissed him and told him to go back to his wife, but to make sure that she had been as true to him during his absence as he to her.

This malicious suggestion drove Cephalus mad with jealousy. He had been so long away and Procris was so beautiful. . . . He decided that he could never rest satisfied unless he proved to himself beyond all doubt that she loved him alone and would not yield to any other lover. Accordingly, he disguised himself. Some say that Aurora helped him, but at all events, the disguise was so good that when he went back to his home no one recognized him. It was comforting to see that the whole household was longing for his return, but his purpose held firm. When he was admitted to Procris' presence, however, her manifest grief, her sad face and subdued manner, came near to making him give up the test he had planned. He did not do so, however; he could not forget Aurora's mocking words. He began at once to try to get Procris to fall in love with him, a stranger, as she supposed him to be. He made passionate love to her, always reminding her, too, that her husband had forsaken her. Nevertheless for a long time he could not move her. To all his pleas she made the same answer, "I belong to him. Wherever he is I keep my love for him."

But one day when he was pouring out petitions, persuasions, promises, she hesitated. She did not give in; she only did not firmly oppose him, but that was enough for Cephalus. He cried out, "O false and shameless woman, I am your husband. By my own witness you are a traitor." Procris looked at him. Then she turned and without a word left him and the house, too. Her love for him seemed turned into hate; she loathed the whole race of men and she went to the mountains to live alone. Cephalus, however, had quickly come to his senses and realized the poor part he had played. He searched everywhere for her until he found her. Then he humbly begged her forgiveness.

She could not give it to him at once, she had resented too deeply the deception he had practised upon her. In the end, however, he won her back and they spent some happy years together. Then one day they went hunting, as they often did. Procris had given Cephalus a javelin that never failed to strike what it was aimed at. The husband and wife, reaching the woods, separated in search of game. Cephalus looking keenly around saw something move in the thicket ahead and threw the javelin. It found the mark. Procris was there and she sank to the ground dead, pierced to the heart.

ORITHYIA AND BOREAS

One of the sisters of Procris was Orithyia. Boreas, the North Wind, fell in love with her, but her father, Erechtheus, and the people of Athens, too, were opposed to his suit. Because of Procne's and Philomela's sad fate and the fact that the wicked Tereus came from the North, they had conceived a hatred for all who lived there and they refused to give the maiden to Boreas. But they were foolish to think they could keep what the great North Wind wanted. One day when Orithyia was playing with her sisters on the bank of a river, Boreas swept down in a great gust and carried her away. The two sons she bore him, Zetes and Calais, went on the Quest of the Golden Fleece with Jason.

Once Socrates, the great Athenian teacher, who lived hundreds of years, thousands, perhaps, after the mythological stories were first told, went on a walk with a young man he was fond of named Phaedrus. They talked as they wandered idly on and Phaedrus asked, "Is not the place somewhere near here where Boreas is said to have carried off Orithyia from the banks of the Ilissus?"

"That is the story," Socrates answered.

"Do you suppose this is the exact spot?" Phaedrus wondered. "The little stream is delightfully clear and bright. I can fancy that there might be maidens playing near."

"I believe," replied Socrates, "the spot is about a quarter of a mile lower down, and there is, I think, some sort of altar to Boreas there."

"Tell me, Socrates," said Phaedrus. "Do you believe the story?"

"The wise are doubtful," Socrates returned, "and I should not be singular if I too doubted."

This conversation took place in the last part of the fifth century B.C. The old stories had begun by then to lose their hold on men's minds.

CREÜSA AND ION

Creüsa was the sister of Procris and Orithyia, and she too was an unfortunate woman. One day when she was hardly more than a child she was gathering crocuses on a cliff where there was a deep cave. Her veil, which she had used for a basket was full of the yellow blooms and she had turned to go home when she was caught up in the arms of a man who had appeared from nowhere, as if the invisible had suddenly become visible. He was divinely beautiful, but in her agony of terror she never noticed what he was like. She screamed for her mother, but there was no help for her. Her abductor was Apollo himself. He carried her off to the dark cave.

God though he was she hated him, especially when the time came for her child to be born and he showed her no sign, gave her no aid. She did not dare tell her parents. The fact that the lover was a god and could not be resisted was, as many stories show, not accepted as an excuse. A girl ran every risk of being killed if she confessed.

When Creüsa's time had come she went all alone to that same dark cave, and there her son was born. There, too, she left him to die. Later, driven by an agony of longing to know what had happened to him, she went back. The cave was empty and no bloodstains could be seen anywhere. The child had certainly not been killed by a wild animal. Also, what was very strange, the soft things she had wrapped him in, her veil and a cloak woven by her own hands, were gone. She wondered fearfully if a great eagle or vulture had entered and had carried all away in its cruel talons, the clothing with the baby. It seemed the only possible explanation.

After a time she was married. King Erechtheus, her father, rewarded with her hand a foreigner who had helped him in a war. This man, Xuthus by name, was a Greek, to be sure, but he did not belong to Athens or to Attica, and he was considered a stranger and an alien, and as such was so looked down on that when he and Creüsa had no children the Athenians did not think it a misfortune. Xuthus did, however. He more than Creüsa passionately desired a son. They went accordingly to Delphi, the Greeks' refuge in time of trouble, to ask the god if they could hope for a child.

Creüsa, leaving her husband in the town with one of the priests, went on up to the sanctuary by herself. She found in the outer court a beautiful lad in priestly attire intent on purifying the sacred place with water from a golden vessel, singing as he worked a hymn of praise to the god. He looked at the lovely stately lady with kindness and she at him, and they began to talk. He told her that he could see that she was highly born and blessed by good fortune. She answered bitterly, "Good fortune! Say, rather, sorrow that makes life insupportable." All her misery was in the words, her terror and her pain of long ago, her grief for her child, the burden of the secret she had carried through the years. But at the wonder in the boy's eyes she collected herself and asked him who he was, so young and yet seemingly so dedicated to this high service in Greece's holy of holies. He told her that his name was Ion, but that he did not know where he had come from. The Pythoness, Apollo's priestess and prophetess, had found him one morning, a little baby, lying on the temple stairway, and had brought him up as tenderly as a mother. Always he had been happy, working joyfully in the temple, proud to serve not men, but gods.

He ventured then to question her. Why, he asked her gently, was she so sad, her eyes wet with tears? That was not the way pilgrims to Delphi came, but rejoicing to approach the pure shrine of Apollo, the God of Truth.

"Apollo!" Creüsa said. "No! I do not so approach him." Then, in answer to Ion's startled reproachful look, she told him that she had come on a secret errand to Delphi. Her husband was here to ask if he might hope for a son, but her purpose was to find out what had been the fate of a child who was the son of . . . She faltered, and was silent. Then she spoke quickly, ". . . of a friend of mine, a wretched woman whom this Delphic holy god of yours wronged. And when the child was born that he forced her to bear, she abandoned it. It must be dead. Years ago it happened. But she longs to be sure, and to know how it died. So I am here to ask Apollo for her."

Ion was horrified at the accusation she brought against his lord and master. "It is not true," he said hotly. "It was some man, and she excused her shame by putting it on the god."

"No," Creüsa said positively. "It was Apollo."

Ion was silent. Then he shook his head. "Even if it were true," he said, "what you would do is folly. You must not approach the god's altar to try to prove him a villain."

Creüsa felt her purpose grow weak and ebb away while the strange boy spoke. "I will not," she said submissively. "I will do as you say."

Feelings she did not understand were stirring within her. As the two stood looking at each other Xuthus entered, triumph in his face and bearing. He held out his arms to Ion, who stepped back in cold distaste. But Xuthus managed to enfold him, to his great discomfort.

"You are my son," he cried. "Apollo has declared it."

A sense of bitter antagonism stirred in Creüsa's heart. "Your son?" she questioned clearly. "Who is his mother?"

"I don't know." Xuthus was confused. "I think he is my son, but perhaps the god gave him to me. Either way he is mine."

To this group, Ion icily remote, Xuthus bewildered but happy, Creüsa feeling that she hated men and that she would not put up with having the son of some unknown, low woman foisted on her, there entered the aged priestess, Apollo's prophetess. In her hands she carried two things that made Creüsa, in all her preoccupation, start and look sharply at them. One was a veil and the other a maiden's cloak. The holy woman told Xuthus that the priest wished to speak to him, and when he was gone she held out to Ion what she was carrying.

"Dear lad," she said, "you must take these with you when you go to Athens with your new-found father. They are the clothes you were wrapped in when I found you."

"Oh," Ion cried, "my mother must have put them around me. They are a clue to my mother. I will seek her everywhere —through Europe and through Asia."

But Creüsa had stolen up to him and, before he could draw back offended a second time, she had thrown her arms around his neck; and weeping and pressing her face to his she was calling him, "My son—my son!"

This was too much for Ion. "She must be mad," he cried.

"No, no," Creüsa said. "That veil, that cloak, they are mine. I covered you with them when I left you. See. That friend I told you of. . . . It was no friend, but my own self. Apollo is your father. Oh, do not turn away. I can prove it. Unfold these wrappings. I will tell you all the embroideries on them. I made them with these hands. And look. You will find two little serpents of gold fastened to the cloak. I put them there."

Ion found the jewels and looked from them to her. "My mother," he said wonderingly. "But then is the God of Truth false? He said I was Xuthus' son. O Mother, I am troubled."

"Apollo did not say you were Xuthus' own son. He gave you to him as a gift," Creüsa cried, but she was trembling, too.

A sudden radiance from on high fell on the two and made them look up. Then all their distress was forgotten in awe and wonder. A divine form stood above them, beautiful and majestic beyond compare.

"I am Pallas Athena," the vision said. "Apollo has sent me to you to tell you that Ion is his son and yours. He had him brought here from the cave where you left him. Take him with you to Athens, Creüsa. He is worthy to rule over my land and city."

She vanished. The mother and son looked at each other, Ion with perfect joy. But Creüsa? Did Apollo's late reparation make up to her for all that she had suffered? We can only guess; the story does not say.

Athena appears to Creüsa and Ion

ment Midas wished that whatever he touched would

PART SIX
The Less Important Myths

20 Midas—and Others

The story of Midas is told best by Ovid from whom I have taken it. Pindar is my authority for Aesculapius, whose life he tells in full. The Danaïds are the subject of one of the plays of Aeschylus. Glaucus and Scylla, Pomona and Vertumnus, Erysichthon, all come from Ovid.

Midas, whose name has become a synonym for a rich man, had very little profit from his riches. The experience of possessing them lasted for less than a day and it threatened him with speedy death. He was an example of folly being as fatal as sin, for he meant no harm; he merely did not use any intelligence. His story suggests that he had none to use.

He was King of Phrygia, the land of roses, and he had great rose gardens near his palace. Into them once strayed old Silenus, who, intoxicated as always, had wandered off from Bacchus' train where he belonged and lost his way. The fat old drunkard was found asleep in a bower of roses by some of the servants of the palace. They bound him with rosy garlands, set a flowering wreath on his head, woke him up, and bore him in this ridiculous guise to Midas as a great joke. Midas welcomed him and entertained him for ten days. Then he led him to Bacchus, who, delighted to get him back, told Midas whatever wish he made would come true. Without giving a thought to he inevitable result Midas wished that whatever he touched would turn into gold. Of course Bacchus in granting the favor foresaw what would happen at the next meal, but Midas saw nothing until the food he lifted to his lips became a lump of metal. Dismayed and very hungry and thirsty, he was forced to hurry off to the god and implore him to take his favor back. Bacchus told him to go wash in the source of the river Pactolus and he would lose the fatal gift. He did so, and that was said to be the reason why gold was found in the sands of the river.

Later on, Apollo changed Midas' ears into those of an ass; but again the punishment was for stupidity, not for any wrong-doing. He was chosen as one of the umpires in a musical contest between Apollo and Pan. The rustic god could play very pleasing tunes on his pipes of reed, but when Apollo struck his silver lyre there was no sound on earth or in heaven that could equal the melody except only the choir of the Muses. Nevertheless, although the umpire, the mountain-god Tmolus, gave the palm to Apollo, Midas, no more intelligent musically than in any other way, honestly preferred Pan. Of course, this was double stupidity on his part. Ordinary prudence would have reminded him that it was dangerous to side against Apollo with Pan, infinitely the less powerful. And so he got his asses' ears. Apollo said that he was merely giving to ears so dull and dense the proper shape. Midas hid them under a cap especially made for that purpose, but the servant who cut his hair was obliged to see them. He swore a solemn oath never to tell, but the secrecy so weighed upon the man that he finally went and dug a hole in a field and spoke softly into it, "King Midas has asses' ears." Then he felt relieved and filled the hole up. But in the spring reeds grew up there, and when stirred by the wind they whispered those buried words—and revealed to men not only the truth of what had happened to the poor, stupid King, but also that when gods are contestants the only safe course is to side with the strongest.

AESCULAPIUS

There was a maiden in Thessaly named Coronis, of beauty so surpassing that Apollo loved her. But strangely enough she did not care long for her divine lover; she preferred a mere mortal. She did not reflect that Apollo, the God of Truth, who never deceived, could not himself be deceived.

> The Pythian Lord of Delphi,
> He has a comrade he can trust,
> Straightforward, never wandering astray.

> It is his mind which knows all things,
> Which never touches falsehood, which no one
> Or god or mortal can outwit. He sees,
> Whether the deed is done, or only planned.

Coronis was foolish indeed to hope that he would not learn of her faithlessness. It is said that the news was brought to him by his bird, the raven, then pure white with beautiful snow plumage, and that Apollo in a fit of furious anger, and with the complete injustice the gods usually showed when they were angry, punished the faithful messenger by turning his feathers black. Of course Coronis was killed. Some say that the god did it himself, others that he got Artemis to shoot one of her unerring arrows at her.

In spite of his ruthlessness, he felt a pang of grief as he watched the maiden placed on the funeral pyre and the wild flames roar up. "At least I will save my child," he said to himself; and just as Zeus had done when Semele perished, he snatched away the babe which was very near birth. He took it to Chiron, the wise and kindly old Centaur, to bring up in his cave on Mount Pelion, and told him to call the child Aesculapius. Many notables had given Chiron their sons to rear, but of all his pupils the child of dead Coronis was dearest to him. He was not like other lads, forever running about and bent on sport; he wanted most of all to learn whatever his foster-father could teach him about the art of healing. And that was not a little. Chiron was learned in the use of herbs and gentle incantations and cooling potions. But his pupil surpassed him. He was able to give aid in all manner of maladies. Whoever came to him suffering, whether from wounded limbs or bodies wasting away with disease, even those who were sick unto death, he delivered from their torment.

> A gentle craftsman who drove pain away,
> Soother of cruel pangs, a joy to men,
> Bringing them golden health.

He was a universal benefactor. And yet he too drew down on himself the anger of the gods and by the sin the gods never forgave. He thought "thoughts too great for man." He was once given a large fee to raise one from the dead, and he did so. It is said by many that the man called back to life was Hippolytus, Theseus' son who died so unjustly, and that he never again fell under the power of death, but lived in Italy, immortal forever, where he was called Virbius and worshiped as a god.

However, the great physician who had delivered him from Hades had no such happy fate. Zeus would not allow a mortal to have power over the dead and he struck Aesculapius with his thunderbolt and slew him. Apollo, in great anger at his son's death, went to Etna, where the Cyclopes forged the thunderbolts; and killed with his arrows, some say the Cyclopes themselves, some say their sons. Zeus, greatly angered in his turn, condemned Apollo to serve King Admetus as a slave— for a period which is differently given as one or nine years. It was this Admetus whose wife, Alcestis, Hercules rescued from Hades.

But Aesculapius, even though he had so displeased the King of Gods and Men, was honored on earth as no other mortal. For hundreds of years after his death the sick and the maimed and the blind came for healing to his temples. There they would pray and sacrifice, and after that go to sleep. Then in their dreams the good physician would reveal to them how they could be cured. Snakes played some part in the cure, just what is not known, but they were held to be the sacred servants of Aesculapius.

It is certain that thousands upon thousands of sick people through the centuries believed that he had freed them from their pain and restored them to health.

THE DANAÏDS

These maidens are famous—far more so than anyone reading their story would expect. They are often referred to by the poets and they are among the most prominent sufferers in the hell of mythology, where they must forever try to carry water in leaking jars. Yet except for one of them, Hypermnestra, they did only what the Argonauts found the women of Lemnos had done: they killed their husbands. Nevertheless, the Lemnians are hardly ever mentioned, while everyone who knows even a little about mythology has heard of the Danaïds.

There were fifty of them, all of them daughters of Danaüs, one of Io's descendants, who dwelt by the Nile. Their fifty cousins, sons of Danaüs' brother Aegyptus, wanted to marry them, which for some unexplained reason they were absolutely opposed to doing. They fled with their father by ship to Argos, where they found sanctuary. The Argives voted unanimously to maintain the right of the suppliant. When the sons of Aegyptus arrived ready to fight to gain their brides, the city repulsed them. They would allow no woman to be forced to marry against her will they told the newcomers, nor would they surrender any suppliant, no matter how feeble, and no matter how powerful the pursuer.

At this point there is a break in the story. When it is resumed, in the next chapter, so to speak, the maidens are being married to their cousins and their father is presiding at the marriage feast. There is no explanation of how this came about, but at once it is clear that it was not through any change of mind in either Danaüs or his daughters, because at the feast he is represented as giving each girl a dagger. As the event shows, all of them had been told what to do and had agreed. After the marriage, in the dead of night, they killed their bridegrooms—everyone except Hypermnestra. She alone was moved by pity. She looked at the strong young man lying motionless in sleep beside her, and she could not strike with her dagger to change that glowing vigor into cold death. Her promise to her father and her sisters was forgotten. She was, the Latin poet Horace says, splendidly false. She woke the youth,—his name was Lynceus,—told him all, and helped him to flee.

Her father threw her into prison for her treachery to him. One story says that she and Lynceus came together again and lived at last in happiness, and that their son was Abas, the great-grandfather of Perseus. The other stories end with the fatal wedding night and her imprisonment.

All of them, however, tell of the unending futility of the task the forty-nine Danaïds were compelled to pursue in the lower world as a punishment for murdering their husbands. At the river's edge they filled forever jars riddled with holes, so that the water poured away and they must return to fill them again, and again see them drained dry.

GLAUCUS AND SCYLLA

Glaucus was a fisherman who was fishing one day from a green meadow which sloped down to the sea. He had spread his catch out on the grass and was counting the fish when he saw them all begin to stir and then, moving toward the water, slip into it and swim away. He was utterly amazed. Had a god done this or was there some strange power in the grass? He picked a handful and ate it. At once an irresistible longing for the sea took possession of him. There was no denying it. He ran and leaped into the waves. The sea-gods received him kindly and called on Ocean and Tethys to purge his mortal nature away and make him one of them. A hundred rivers were summoned to pour their waters upon him. He lost consciousness in the rushing flood. When he recovered he was a sea-god with hair green like the sea and a body ending in a fish's tail, to the dwellers in the water a fine and familiar form, but strange and repellent to the dwellers on earth. So he seemed to the lovely nymph Scylla when she was bathing in a little bay and caught sight of him rising from the sea. She fled from him until she

Glaucus and Scylla

stood on a lofty promontory where she could safely watch him, wondering at the half-man, half-fish. Glaucus called up to her, "Maiden, I am no monster. I am a god with power over the waters—and I love you." But Scylla turned from him and hastening inland was lost to his sight.

Glaucus was in despair, for he was madly in love; and he determined to go to Circe, the enchantress, and beg her for a love-potion to melt Scylla's hard heart. But as he told her his tale of love and implored her help Circe fell in love with him. She wooed him with her sweetest words and looks, but Glaucus would have none of her. "Trees will cover the sea bottom and seaweed the mountain tops before I cease to love Scylla," he told her. Circe was furiously angry, but with Scylla, not Glaucus. She prepared a vial of very powerful poison and, going to the bay where Scylla bathed, she poured into it the baleful liquid. As soon as Scylla entered the water she was changed into a frightful monster. Out from her body grew serpents' and fierce dogs' heads. The beastly forms were part of her; she could not fly from them or push them away. She stood there rooted to a rock, in her unutterable misery hating and destroying everything that came within her reach, a peril to all sailors who passed near her, as Jason and Odysseus and Aeneas found out.

ERYSICHTHON

One woman had power given her to assume different shapes, power as great as Proteus had. She used it, strangely enough, to procure food for her starving father. Her story is the only one in which the good goddess, Ceres, appears cruel and vindictive. Erysichthon had the wicked audacity to cut down the tallest oak in a grove sacred to Ceres. His servants shrank from the sacrilege when he ordered them to fell it; whereupon he seized an ax himself and attacked the mighty trunk around which the dryads used to hold their dances. Blood flowed from the tree when he struck it and a voice came from within warning him that Ceres would surely punish his crime. But these marvels did not check his fury; he struck again and again until the great oak crashed to the ground. The dryads hastened to Ceres to tell her what had happened, and the goddess, deeply offended, told them she would punish the criminal in a way never known before. She sent one of them in her car to the bleak region where Famine dwells to order her to take possession of Erysichthon. "Bid her see to it," Ceres said, "that no abundance shall ever satisfy him. He shall starve in the very act of devouring food."

Famine obeyed the command. She entered Erysichthon's room where he slept and she wrapped her skinny arms around him. Holding him in her foul embrace she filled him with herself and planted hunger within him. He woke with a raging desire for food and called for something to eat. But the more he ate the more he wanted. Even as he crammed meat down his throat he starved. He spent all his wealth on vast supplies of food which never gave him a moment's satisfaction. At last he had nothing left except his daughter. He sold her too. On the seashore, where her owner's ship lay, she prayed to Poseidon to save her from slavery and the god heard her prayer. He changed her into a fisherman. Her master, who had been but a little behind her, saw on the long stretch of beach only the figure of a man busy with his fishing lines. He called to him, "Where has that girl gone who was here a moment ago? Here are her footprints and they suddenly stop." The supposed fisherman answered, "I swear by the God of the Sea that no man except myself has come to this shore, and no woman either." When the other, completely bewildered, had gone off in his boat, the girl returned to her own shape. She went back to her father and delighted him by telling him what had happened. He saw an endless opportunity of making money by her. He sold her again and again. Each time Poseidon changed her, now into a mare, now into a bird, and so on. Each time she escaped from her owner and came back to her father. But at last, when the money she thus earned for him was not enough for his needs, he turned upon his own body and devoured it until he killed himself.

POMONA AND VERTUMNUS

These two were Roman divinities, not Greek. Pomona was the only nymph who did not love the wild woodland. She cared for fruits and orchards and that was all she cared for. Her delight was in pruning and grafting and everything that belongs to the gardener's art. She shut herself away from men, alone with her beloved trees, and let no wooer come near her. Of all that sought her Vertumnus was the most ardent, but he could make no headway. Often he was able to enter her presence in disguise, now as a rude reaper bringing her a basket of barley-ears, now as a clumsy herdsman, or a vine-pruner. At such times he had the joy of looking at her, but also the wretchedness of knowing she would never look at such a one as he seemed to be. At last, however, he made a better plan. He came to her disguised as a very old woman, so that it did not seem strange to Pomona when after admiring her fruit he

said to her, "But you are far more beautiful," and kissed her.
Still, he kept on kissing her as no old woman would have done,
and Pomona was startled. Perceiving this he let her go and sat
down opposite an elm tree over which grew a vine loaded
with purple grapes. He said softly, "How lovely they are together, and how different they would be apart, the tree useless
and the vine flat on the ground unable to bear fruit. Are not
you like such a vine? You turn from all who desire you. You
will try to stand alone. And yet there is one—listen to an old
woman who loves you more than you know—you would do
well not to reject, Vertumnus. You are his first love and will
be his last. And he too cares for the orchard and the garden.
He would work by your side." Then, speaking with great seriousness, he pointed out to her how Venus had shown many
a time that she hated hard-hearted maidens; and he told her
the sad story of Anaxarete, who had disdained her suitor Iphis,
until in despair he hanged himself from her gatepost, whereupon Venus turned the heartless girl into a stone image. "Be
warned," he begged, "and yield to your true lover." With this,
he dropped his disguise and stood before her a radiant youth.
Pomona yielded to such beauty joined to such eloquence, and
henceforward her orchards had two gardeners.

21—Brief Myths Arranged
Alphabetically

AMALTHEA

According to one story she was a goat on whose milk the infant
Zeus was fed. According to another she was a nymph who
owned the goat. She was said to have a horn which was always
full of whatever food or drink anyone wanted, the Horn of
Plenty (in Latin *Cornu copiae*—also known as "the Cornucopia" in Latin mythology). But the Latins said the Cornucopia was the horn of Achelous which Hercules broke off when
he conquered that river-god, who had taken the form of a bull
to fight him. It was always magically full of fruits and flowers.

THE AMAZONS

Aeschylus calls them "The warring Amazons, men-haters."
They were a nation of women, all warriors. They were supposed to live around the Caucasus and their chief city was
Themiscyra. Curiously enough, they inspired artists to make
statues and pictures of them far more than poets to write of
them. Familiar though they are to us there are few stories
about them. They invaded Lycia and were repulsed by Bellerophon. They invaded Phrygia when Priam was young, and
Attica when Theseus was King. He had carried off their Queen
and they tried to rescue her, but Theseus defeated them. In
the Trojan War they fought the Greeks under their Queen,
Penthesilea, according to a story not in the *Iliad*, told by
Pausanias. He says that she was killed by Achilles, who
mourned for her as she lay dead, so young and so beautiful.

AMYMONE

She was one of the Danaïds. Her father sent her to draw water and a satyr saw her and pursued her. Poseidon heard her cry for help, loved her and saved her from the satyr. With his trident he made in her honor the spring which bears her name.

ANTIOPE

A princess of Thebes, Antiope, bore two sons to Zeus, Zethus and Amphion. Fearing her father's anger she left the children on a lonely mountain as soon as they were born, but they were discovered by a herdsman and brought up by him. The man then ruling Thebes, Lycus, and his wife Dirce, treated Antiope with great cruelty until she determined to hide herself from them. Finally she came to the cottage where her sons lived. Somehow they recognized her or she them, and gathering a band of their friends they went to the palace to avenge her. They killed Lycus and brought a terrible death upon Dirce, tying her by her hair to a bull. The brothers threw her body into the spring which was ever after called by her name.

ARACHNE

(This story is told only by the Latin poet, Ovid. Therefore the Latin names of the gods are given.)

The fate of this maiden was another example of the danger of claiming equality with the gods in anything whatsoever. Minerva was the weaver among the Olympians as Vulcan was the smith. Quite naturally she considered the stuffs she wove unapproachable for fineness and beauty, and she was outraged when she heard that a simple peasant girl named Arachne declared her own work to be superior. The goddess went forthwith to the hut where the maiden lived and challenged her to a contest. Arachne accepted them. Both set up their looms and stretched the warp upon them. Then they went to work. Heaps of skeins of beautiful threads colored like the rainbow lay beside each, and threads of gold and silver too. Minerva did her best and the result was a marvel, but Arachne's work, finished at the same moment, was in no way inferior. The goddess in a fury of anger slit the web from top to bottom and beat the girl around the head with her shuttle. Arachne, disgraced and mortified and furiously angry, hanged herself. Then a little repentance entered Minerva's heart. She lifted the body from the noose and sprinkled it with a magic liquid. Arachne was changed into a spider, and her skill in weaving was left to her.

ARION

He seems to have been a real person, a poet who lived about 700 B.C., but none of his poems have come down to us, and all that is actually known of him is the story of his escape from death, which is quite like a mythological story. He had gone from Corinth to Sicily to take part in a music contest. He was a master of the lyre and he won the prize. On the voyage home the sailors coveted the prize and planned to kill him. Apollo told him in a dream of his danger and how to save his life. When the sailors attacked him he begged them as a last favor to let him play and sing, before he died. At the end of the song he flung himself into the sea, where dolphins, who had been drawn to the ship by the enchanting music, bore him up as he sank and carried him to land.

ARISTAEUS

He was a keeper of bees, the son of Apollo and a water nymph, Cyrene. When his bees all died from some unknown cause he went for help to his mother. She told him that Proteus, the wise old god of the sea, could show him how to prevent another such disaster, but that he would do so only if compelled. Aristaeus must seize him and chain him, a very difficult task, as Menelaus on his way home from Troy found. Proteus had the power to change himself into any number of different forms. However, if his captor was resolute enough to hold him fast through all the changes, he would finally give in and answer what he was asked. Aristaeus followed directions. He went to the favorite haunt of Proteus, the island of Pharos, or some say Carpathos. There he seized Proteus and did not let him go, in spite of the terrible forms he assumed, until the god was discouraged and returned to his own shape. Then he told Aristaeus to sacrifice to the gods and leave the carcasses of the animals in the place of sacrifice. Nine days later he must go back and examine the bodies. Again Aristaeus did as he was bid, and on the ninth day he found a marvel, a great swarm of bees in one of the carcasses. He never again was troubled by any blight or disease among them.

AURORA AND TITHONUS

The story of these two is alluded to in the *Iliad:*—

Now from her couch where she lay beside high-born Tithonus,
    the goddess
Dawn, rosy-fingered, arose to bring light to the gods and to
    mortals.

This Tithonus, the husband of Aurora, the Goddess of the Dawn, was the father of her son, the dark-skinned prince Memnon of Ethiopia who was killed at Troy, fighting for the Trojans. Tithonus himself had a strange fate. Aurora asked Zeus to make him immortal and he agreed, but she had not thought to ask also that he should remain young. So it came to pass that he grew old, but could not die. Helpless at last, unable to move hand or foot, he prayed for death, but there was no release for him. He must live on forever, with old age forever pressing upon him more and more. At last in pity the goddess laid him in a room and left him, shutting the door. There he babbled endlessly, words with no meaning. His mind had gone with his strength of body. He was only the dry husk of a man.

There is a story too that he shrank and shrank in size until at last Aurora with a feeling for the natural fitness of things turned him into the skinny and noisy grasshopper.

To Memnon, his son, a great statue was erected in Egypt at Thebes, and it was said that when the first rays of the dawn fell upon it a sound came from it like the twanging of a harpstring.

BITON AND CLEOBIS were the sons of Cydippe, a priestess of Hera. She longed to see a most beautiful statue of the goddess of Argos, made by the great sculptor Polyclitus the Elder, who was said to be as great as his younger contemporary, Phidias. Argos was too far away for her to walk there and they had no horses or oxen to draw her. But her two sons determined that she should have her wish. They yoked themselves to a car and drew her all the long way through dust and heat. Everyone admired their filial piety when they arrived, and the proud and happy mother standing before the statue prayed that Hera would reward them by giving them the best gift in her power. As she finished her prayer the two lads sank to the ground. They were smiling, and they looked as if they were peacefully asleep; but they were dead.

CALLISTO

She was the daughter of Lycaon, a king of Arcadia who had been changed into a wolf because of his wickedness. He had set human flesh on the table for Zeus when the god was his guest. His punishment was deserved, but his daughter suffered as terribly as he and she was innocent of all wrong. Zeus saw her hunting in the train of Artemis and fell in love with her.

Hera, furiously angry, turned the maiden into a bear after her son was born. When the boy was grown and out hunting, the goddess brought Callisto before him, intending to have him shoot his mother, in ignorance, of course. But Zeus snatched the bear away and placed her among the stars, where she is called the Great Bear. Later, her son Arcas was placed beside her and called the Lesser Bear. Hera, enraged at this honor to her rival, persuaded the God of the Sea to forbid the Bears to descend into the ocean like the other stars. They alone of the constellations never set below the horizon.

CHIRON

He was one of the Centaurs, but unlike the others who were violent fierce creatures, he was known everywhere for his goodness and wisdom, so much so that the young sons of heroes were entrusted to him to train and teach. Achilles was his pupil and Aesculapius, the great physician; the famous hunter Actaeon, too, and many another. He alone among the Centaurs was immortal and yet in the end he died and went to the lower world. Indirectly and unintentionally Hercules was the cause of his dying. He had stopped in to see a Centaur who was a friend of his, Pholus, and being very thirsty he persuaded him to open a jar of wine which was the common property of all the Centaurs. The aroma of the wonderful liquor informed the others what had happened and they rushed down to take vengeance on the offender. But Hercules was more than a match for them all. He fought them off, but in the fight he accidentally wounded Chiron, who had taken no part in the attack. The wound proved to be incurable and finally Zeus permitted Chiron to die rather than live forever in pain.

CLYTIE

Her story is unique, for instead of a god in love with an unwilling maiden, a maiden is in love with an unwilling god. Clytie loved the Sun-god and he found nothing to love in her. She pined away sitting on the ground out-of-doors where she could watch him, turning her face and following him with her eyes as he journeyed over the sky. So gazing she was changed into a flower, the sunflower, which ever turns toward the sun.

DRYOPE

Her story, like a number of others, shows how strongly the ancient Greeks disapproved of destroying or injuring a tree.

With her sister Iole she went one day to a pool intending to make garlands for the nymphs. She was carrying her little son, and seeing near the water a lotus tree full of bright blossoms she plucked some of them to please the baby. To her horror she saw drops of blood flowing down the stem. The tree was really the nymph, Lotis, who fleeing from a pursuer had taken refuge in this form. When Dryope, terrified at the ominous sight, tried to hurry away, her feet would not move; they seemed rooted in the ground. Iole watching her helplessly saw bark begin to grow upward covering her body. It had reached her face when her husband came to the spot with her father. Iole cried out what had happened and the two, rushing to the tree, embraced the still warm trunk and watered it with their tears. Dryope had time only to declare that she had done no wrong intentionally and to beg them to bring the child often to the tree to play in its shade, and some day to tell him her story so that he would think whenever he saw the spot: "Here in this tree-trunk my mother is hidden." "Tell him too," she said, "never to pluck flowers, and to think every bush may be a goddess in disguise." Then she could speak no more; the bark closed over her face. She was gone forever.

EPIMENIDES

A figure of mythology only because of the story of his long sleep. He lived around 600 B.C. and is said as a boy when looking for a lost sheep to have been overcome by a slumber which lasted for fifty-seven years. On waking he continued the search for the sheep unaware of what had happened, and found everything changed. He was sent by the oracle at Delphi to purify Athens of a plague. When the grateful Athenians would have given him a large sum of money he refused and asked only that there should be friendship between Athens and his own home, Cnossus in Crete.

ERICTHONIUS

He is the same as Erechtheus. Homer knew only one man of that name. Plato speaks of two. He was the son of Hephaestus, reared by Athena, half man, half serpent. Athena gave a chest in which she had put the infant to the three daughters of Cecrops, forbidding them to open it. They did open it, however, and saw in it the serpent-like creature. Athena drove them mad as a punishment, and they killed themselves, jumping from the Acropolis. When Ericthonius grew up he became King of Athens. His grandson was called by his name, and was the father of the second Cecrops, Procris, Crëusa, and Orithyia.

HERO AND LEANDER

Leander was a youth of Abydus, a town on the Hellespont, and Hero was Priestess of Aphrodite in Sestus on the opposite shore. Every night Leander swam across to her, guided by the light, some say of the lighthouse in Sestus, some of a torch Hero always set blazing on the top of a tower. One very stormy night the light was blown out by the wind and Leander perished. His body was washed up on the shore and Hero, finding it, killed herself.

THE HYADES were daughters of Atlas and half sisters of the Pleiades. They were the rainy stars, supposed to bring rain because the time of their evening and morning setting, which comes in early May and November, is usually rainy. They were six in number. Dionysus as a baby was entrusted to them by Zeus, and to reward them for their care he set them among the stars.

IBYCUS AND THE CRANES

He is not a mythological character, but a poet who lived about 550 B.C. Only a very few fragments of his poems have come down to us. All that is known of him is the dramatic story of his death. He was attacked by robbers near Corinth and mortally wounded. A flock of cranes flew by overhead, and he called on them to avenge him. Soon after, over the open theater in Corinth where a play was being performed to a full house, a flock of cranes appeared, hovering above the crowd. Suddenly a man's voice was heard. He cried out as if panic-stricken, "The cranes of Ibycus, the avengers!" The audience in turn shouted, "The murderer has informed against himself." The man was seized, the other robbers discovered, and all put to death.

LETO (LATONA)

She was the daughter of the Titans Phoebe and Coeus. Zeus loved her, but when she was about to bear a child he abandoned her, afraid of Hera. All countries and islands, afraid for the same reason, refused to receive her and give her a place where her child could be born. On and on she wandered in desperation until she reached a bit of land which was floating on the sea. It had no foundation, but was tossed hither and thither by waves and winds. It was called Delos and besides being of all islands the most insecure it was rocky and barren. But when Leto set foot on it and asked for refuge, the little isle welcomed her gladly, and at that moment four lofty pillars rose from the bottom of the sea and held it firmly anchored forever. There Leto's children were born, Artemis and Phoebus Apollo; and in after years Apollo's glorious temple stood there, visited by men from all over the world. The barren rock was called "the heaven-built isle," and from being the most despised it became the most renowned of islands.

LINUS

In the *Iliad* a vineyard is described with youths and maidens singing, as they gather the fruit, "a sweet Linus song." This was probably a lament for the young son of Apollo and Psamathe—Linus, who was deserted by his mother, brought up by shepherds, and before he was full-grown torn to pieces by dogs. This Linus was, like Adonis and Hyacinthus, a type of all lovely young life that dies or is withered before it has borne fruit. The Greek word *ailinon!*, meaning "woe for Linus!" grew to mean no more than the English "alas!" and was used in any lament. There was another Linus, the son of Apollo and a Muse, who taught Orpheus and tried to teach Hercules, but was killed by him.

MARPESSA

She was more fortunate than other maidens beloved of the gods. Idas, one of the heroes of the Calydonian Hunt and also one of the Argonauts, carried her off from her father with her consent. They would have lived happily ever after, but Apollo fell in love with her. Idas refused to give her up; he even dared to fight with Apollo for her. Zeus parted them and told Marpessa to choose which she would have. She chose the mortal, fearing, certainly not without reason, that the god would not be faithful to her.

MARSYAS

The flute was invented by Athena, but she threw it away because in order to play it she had to puff out her cheeks and disfigure her face. Marsyas, a satyr, found it and played so enchantingly upon it that he dared to challenge Apollo to a contest. The god won, of course, and punished Marsyas by flaying him.

MELAMPUS

He saved and reared two little snakes when his servants killed the parent snakes, and as pets they repaid him well. Once when he was asleep they crept upon his couch and licked his ears. He started up in a great fright, but he found that he understood what two birds on his window sill were saying to each other. The snakes had made him able to understand the language of all flying and all creeping creatures. He learned in this way the art of divination as no one ever had, and he became a famous soothsayer. He saved himself, too, by his knowledge. His enemies once captured him and kept him a prisoner in a little cell. While there, he heard the worms saying that the roof-beam had been almost gnawed through so that it would soon fall and crush all beneath it. At once he told his captors and asked to be moved elsewhere. They did as he said and directly afterward the roof fell in. Then they saw how great a diviner he was and they freed and rewarded him.

MEROPE

Her husband, Cresphontes, a son of Hercules, and king of Messenia, was killed in a rebellion together with two of his sons. The man who succeeded him, Polyphontes, took her as his wife. But her third son, Aepytus, had been hidden by her in Arcadia. He returned years later pretending to be a man who had slain Aepytus and was kindly received therefore by Polyphontes. His mother, however, not knowing who he was, planned to kill her son's murderer, as she thought him. However, in the end she found out who he was and the two together brought about Polyphontes' death. Aepytus became king.

THE MYRMIDONS

These were men created from ants on the island of Aegina, in the reign of Aeacus, Achilles' grandfather, and they were Achilles' followers in the Trojan War. Not only were they thrifty and industrious, as one would suppose from their origin, but they were also brave. They were changed into men from ants because of one of Hera's attacks of jealousy. She was angry because Zeus loved Aegina, the maiden for whom the island was named, and whose son, Aeacus, became its king. Hera sent a fearful pestilence which destroyed the people by thousands. It seemed that no one would be left alive. Aeacus climbed to the lofty temple of Zeus and prayed to him, reminding him that he was his son and the son of a woman the god had loved. As he spoke he saw a troop of busy ants. "O Father," he cried, "make of these creatures a people for me, as numerous as they, and fill my empty city." A peal of thunder seemed to answer him and that night he dreamed that he saw the ants being transformed into human shape. At daybreak his son Telamon woke him saying that a great host of men was approaching the palace. He went out and saw a multitude, as many as the ants in number, all crying out that they were his faithful subjects. So Aegina was repopulated from an ant hill and its people were called Myrmidons after the ant (*myrmex*) from which they had sprung.

NISUS AND SCYLLA

Nisus, King of Megara, had on his head, a purple lock of hair which he had been warned never to cut. The safety of his throne depended upon his preserving it. Minos of Crete laid siege to his city, but Nisus knew that no harm would come to it as long as he had the purple lock. His daughter, Scylla, used to watch Minos from the city wall and she fell madly in love with him. She could think of no way to make him care for her except by taking her father's lock of hair to him and enabling him to conquer the town. She did this; she cut it from her father's head in his sleep and carrying it to Minos she confessed what she had done. He shrank from her in horror and drove her out of his sight. When the city had been conquered and the Cretans launched their ships to sail home, she came rushing to the shore, mad with passion, and leaping into the water seized the rudder of the boat that carried Minos. But at this moment a great eagle swooped down upon her. It was her father, whom the gods had saved by changing him into a bird. In terror she let go her hold, and would have fallen into the water, but suddenly she too became a bird. Some god had pity on her, traitor though she was, because she had sinned through love.

ORION

He was a young man of gigantic stature and great beauty, and a mighty hunter. He fell in love with the daughter of the King of Chios, and for love of her he cleared the island of wild beasts. The spoils of the chase he brought always home to his beloved, whose name is sometimes said to be Aero, sometimes Merope. Her father, Oenopion, agreed to give her to Orion, but he kept putting the marriage off. One day when Orion was drunk he insulted the maiden, and Oenopion appealed to Dionysus to punish him. The god threw him into a deep sleep and Oenopion blinded him. An oracle told him, however, that he would be able to see again if he went to the east and let the rays of the rising sun fall on his eyes. He went as far east as Lemnos and there he recovered his sight. Instantly he started back to Chios to take vengeance on the king, but he had fled and Orion could not find him. He went on to Crete, and lived there as Artemis' huntsman. Nevertheless in the end the goddess killed him. Some say that Dawn, also called Aurora, loved him and that Artemis in jealous anger shot him. Others say that he made Apollo angry and that the god by a trick got his sister to slay him. After his death he was placed in heaven as a constellation, which shows him with a girdle, sword, club and lion's skin.

THE PLEIADES

They were the daughters of Atlas, seven in number. Their names were Electra, Maia, Taygete, Alcyone, Merope, Celaeno, Sterope. Orion pursued them but they fled before him and he could never seize any of them. Still he continued to follow them until Zeus, pitying them, placed them in the heavens as stars. But it was said that even there Orion continued his pursuit, always unsuccessful, yet persistent. While they lived on earth one of them, Maia, was the mother of Hermes. Another, Electra, was the mother of Dardanus, the founder of the Trojan race. Although it is agreed that there were seven of them, only six stars are clearly visible. The seventh is invisible except to those who have specially keen sight.

RHOECUS seeing an oak about to fall propped it up. The dryad who would have perished with it told him to ask anything he desired and she would give it. He answered that he wanted only her love and she consented. She bade him keep on the alert for she would send him a messenger, a bee, to tell him her wishes. But Rhoecus met some companions and forgot all about the bee, so much so that when he heard one buzzing he drove it away and hurt it. Returning to the tree he was blinded by the dryad, who was angry at the disregard of her words and the injury to her messenger.

SALMONEUS

This man was another illustration of how fatal it was for mortals to try to emulate the gods. What he did was so foolish, however, that in later years it was often said that he had gone mad. He pretended that he was Zeus. He had a chariot made in such a way that there was a loud clanging of brass when it moved. On the day of Zeus's festival he drove it furiously through the town, scattering at the same time fire-brands and shouting to the people to worship him because he was Zeus the Thunderer. But instantly there came a crash of actual thunder and a flash of lightning. Salmoneus fell from his chariot dead.

The story is often explained as pointing back to a time when weather-magic was practised. Salmoneus, according to this view, was a magician trying to bring on a rainstorm by imitating it, a common magical method.

SISYPHUS was King of Corinth. One day he chanced to see a mighty eagle, greater and more splendid than any mortal bird, bearing a maiden to an island not far away. When the river-god Asopus came to him to tell him that his daughter Aegina had been carried off, he strongly suspected by Zeus, and to ask his help in finding her, Sisyphus told him what he had seen. Thereby he drew down on himself the relentless wrath of Zeus. In Hades he was punished by having to try forever to roll a rock uphill which forever rolled back upon him. Nor did he help Asopus. The river-god went to the island but Zeus drove him away with his thunderbolt. The name of the island was changed to Aegina in honor of the maiden, and her son Aeacus was the grandfather of Achilles, who was called sometimes Aeacides, descendant of Aeacus.

TYRO was the daughter of Salmoneus. She bore twin sons to Poseidon—but fearing her father's displeasure if he learned of the children's birth, she abandoned them. They were found by the keeper of Salmoneus' horses, and brought up by him and his wife, who called one Pelias and the other Neleus. Tyro's husband Cretheus discovered, years later, what her relations with Poseidon had been. In great anger he put her away and married one of her maids, Sidero, who ill-treated her. When Cretheus died the twins were told by their foster-mother who their real parents were. They went at once to seek out Tyro and discover themselves to her. They found her living in great misery and so they looked for Sidero, to punish her. She had heard of their arrival and she had taken refuge in Hera's temple. Nevertheless Pelias slew her, defying the goddess's anger. Hera revenged herself, but only after many years. Pelias' half-brother, the son of Tyro and Cretheus, was the father of Jason, whom Pelias tried to kill by sending him after the Golden Fleece. Instead, Jason was indirectly the cause of his death. He was killed by his daughters under the direction of Medea, Jason's wife.

PART SEVEN

The Mythology of the Norsemen

Introduction to Norse Mythology

The world of Norse mythology is a strange world. Asgard, the home of the gods, is unlike any other heaven men have dreamed of. No radiancy of joy is in it, no assurance of bliss. It is a grave and solemn place, over which hangs the threat of an inevitable doom. The gods know that a day will come when they will be destroyed. Sometime they will meet their enemies and go down beneath them to defeat and death. Asgard will fall in ruins. The cause the forces of good are fighting to defend against the forces of evil is hopeless. Nevertheless, the gods will fight for it to the end.

Necessarily the same is true of humanity. If the gods are finally helpless before evil, men and women must be more so. The heroes and heroines of the early stories face disaster. They know that they cannot save themselves, not by any courage or endurance or great deed. Even so, they do not yield. They die resisting. A brave death entitles them—at least the heroes—to a seat in Valhalla, one of the halls in Asgard, but there too they must look forward to final defeat and destruction. In the last battle between good and evil they will fight on the side of the gods and die with them.

This is the conception of life which underlies the Norse religion, as somber a conception as the mind of man has ever given birth to. The only sustaining support possible for the human spirit, the one pure unsullied good men can hope to attain, is heroism; and heroism depends on lost causes. The hero can prove what he is only by dying. The power of good is shown not by triumphantly conquering evil, but by continuing to resist evil while facing certain defeat.

Such an attitude toward life seems at first sight fatalistic, but actually the decrees of an inexorable fate played no more part in the Norseman's scheme of existence than predestination did in St. Paul's or in that of his militant Protestant followers, and for precisely the same reason. Although the Norse hero was doomed if he did not yield, he could choose between yielding or dying. The decision was in his own hands. Even more than that. A heroic death, like a martyr's death, is not a defeat, but a triumph. The hero in one of the Norse stories who laughs aloud while his foes cut his heart out of his living flesh shows himself superior to his conquerors. He says to them, in effect, You can do nothing to me because I do not care what you do. They kill him, but he dies undefeated.

This is stern stuff for humanity to live by, as stern in its totally different way as the Sermon on the Mount, but the easy way has never in the long run commanded the allegiance of mankind. Like the early Christians, the Norsemen measured their life by heroic standards. The Christian, however, looked forward to a heaven of eternal joy. The Norseman did not. But it would appear that for unknown centuries, until the Christian missionaries came, heroism was enough.

The poets of the Norse mythology, who saw that victory was possible in death and that courage was never defeated, are the only spokesmen for the belief of the whole great Teutonic race—of which England is a part, and ourselves through the first settlers in America. Everywhere else in northwestern Europe the early records, the traditions, the songs and stories, were obliterated by the priests of Christianity, who felt a bitter hatred for the paganism they had come to destroy. It is extraordinary how clean a sweep they were able to make. A few bits survived: *Beowulf* in England, the *Nibelungenlied* in Germany, and some stray fragments here and there. But if it were not for the two Icelandic Eddas we should know practically nothing of the religion which molded the race to which we belong. In Iceland, naturally by its position the last northern country to be Christianized, the missionaries seem to have been gentler, or, perhaps, they had less influence. Latin did not drive Norse out as the literary tongue. The people still told the old stories in the common speech, and some of them were written down, although by whom or when we do not know. The oldest manuscript of the *Elder Edda* is dated at about 1300, three hundred years after the Christians arrived, but the poems it is made up of are purely pagan and adjudged by all scholars to be very old. The *Younger Edda*, in prose, was written down by one Snorri Sturluson in the last part of the twelfth century. The chief part of it is a technical treatise on how to write poetry, but it also contains some prehistoric mythological material which is not in the *Elder Edda*.

The *Elder Edda* is much the more important of the two. It is made up of separate poems, often about the same story, but never connected with each other. The material for a great epic is there, as great as the *Iliad*, perhaps even greater, but no poet came to work it over as Homer did the early stories which preceded the *Iliad*. There was no man of genius in the Northland to weld the poems into a whole and make it a thing of beauty and power; no one even to discard the crude and the commonplace and cut out the childish and wearisome repetitions. There are lists of names in the *Edda* which sometimes run on unbroken for pages. Nevertheless the somber grandeur of the stories comes through in spite of the style. Perhaps no one should speak of "the style" who cannot read ancient Norse; but all the translations are so alike in being singularly awkward and involved that one cannot but suspect the original of being responsible, at least in part. The poets of the *Elder Edda* seem to have had conceptions greater than their skill to put them into words. Many of the stories are splendid. There are none to equal them in Greek mythology, except those retold by the tragic poets. All the best Northern tales are tragic, about men and women who go steadfastly forward to meet death, often deliberately choose it, even plan it long beforehand. The only light in the darkness is heroism.

22 The Stories of Signy and Sigurd

*I have selected these two stories to tell because they
seem to me to present better than any other the Norse
character and the Norse point of view. Sigurd is the
most famous of Norse heroes; his story is largely
that of the hero of the* Nibelungenlied, Siegfried. *He
plays the chief part in the* Volsungasaga, *the Norse
version of the German tale which Wagner's operas
have made familiar. I have not gone to it, however,
for my story, but to the* Elder Edda, *where the love
and death of Sigurd and Brynhild and Gudrun are the
subject of a number of the poems. The sagas, all prose
tales, are of later date. Signy's story is told only in
the* Volsungasaga.

Signy was the daughter of Volsung and the sister of Sigmund.
Her husband slew Volsung by treachery and captured his sons.
One by one he chained them at night to where the wolves
would find them and devour them. When the last, who was
Sigmund, was brought out and chained, Signy had devised a
way to save him. She freed him and the two took a vow to
avenge their father and brothers. Signy determined that Sigmund should have one of their own blood to help him and
she visited him in disguise and spent three nights with him. He
never knew who she was. When the boy who was born of their
union was of an age to leave her, she sent him to Sigmund and
the two lived together until the lad—his name was Sinfiotli—
was grown to manhood. All this time Signy was living with her
husband, bearing him children, showing him nothing of the
one burning desire in her heart, to take vengeance upon him.
The day for it came at last. Sigmund and Sinfiotli surprised
the household. They killed Signy's other children; they shut
her husband in the house and set fire to it. Signy watched them

with never a word. When all was done she told them that they had gloriously avenged the dead, and with that she entered the burning dwelling and died there. Through the years while she had waited she had planned when she killed her husband to die with him. Clytemnestra would fade beside her if there had been a Norse Aeschylus to write her story.

The story of Siegfried is so familiar that that of his Norse prototype, Sigurd, can be briefly told. Brynhild, a Valkyrie, has disobeyed Odin and is punished by being put to sleep until some man shall wake her. She begs that he who comes to her shall be one whose heart knows no fear, and Odin surrounds her couch with flaming fire which only a hero would brave. Sigurd, the son of Sigmund, does the deed. He forces his horse through the flames and wakens Brynhild, who gives herself to him joyfully because he has proved his valor in reaching her. Some days later he leaves her in the same fire-ringed place.

Sigurd goes to the home of the Giukungs where he swears brotherhood with the king, Gunnar. Griemhild, Gunnar's mother, wants Sigurd for her daughter Gudrun, and gives him a magic potion which makes him forget Brynhild. He marries Gudrun; then, assuming through Griemhild's magical power the appearance of Gunnar, he rides through the flames again to win Brynhild for Gunnar, who is not hero enough to do this himself. Sigurd spends three nights there with her, but he places his sword between them in the bed. Brynhild goes with him to the Giukungs, where Sigurd takes his own shape again, but without Brynhild's knowledge. She marries Gunnar, believing that Sigurd was faithless to her and that Gunnar had ridden through the flames for her. In a quarrel with Gudrun she learns the truth and she plans her revenge. She tells Gunnar that Sigurd broke his oath to him, that he really possessed her those three nights when he declared that his sword lay between them, and that unless Gunnar kills Sigurd she will leave him. Gunnar himself cannot kill Sigurd because of the oath of brotherhood he has sworn, but he persuades his younger brother to slay Sigurd in his sleep, and Gudrun wakes to find her husband's blood flowing over her.

> Then Brynhild laughed,
> Only once, with all her heart,
> When she heard the wail of Gudrun.

But although, or because, she brought about his death, she will not live when Sigurd is dead. She says to her husband:—

> One alone of all I loved.
> I never had a changing heart.

Sigurd riding through the fire to Brynhild

She tells him that Sigurd had not been false to his oath when he rode through the fiery ring to win her for Gunnar.

> In one bed together we slept
> As if he had been my brother.
> Ever with grief and all too long
> Are men and women born in the world—

She kills herself, praying that her body shall be laid on the funeral pyre with Sigurd's.

Beside his body Gudrun sits in silence. She cannot speak; she cannot weep. They fear that her heart will break unless she can find relief, and one by one the women tell her of their own grief,

> The bitterest pain each had ever borne.

Husband, daughters, sisters, brothers,—one says,—all were taken from me, and still I live.

> Yet for her grief Gudrun could not weep.
> So hard was her heart by the hero's body.

My seven sons fell in the southern land, another says, and my husband too, all eight in battle. I decked with my own hands the bodies for the grave. One half-year brought me this to bear. And no one came to comfort me.

> Yet for her grief Gudrun could not weep.
> So hard was her heart by the hero's body.

Then one wiser than the rest lifts the shroud from the dead.

> . . . She laid
> His well-loved head on the knees of his wife.
> "Look on him thou loved and press thy lips
> To his as if he still were living."
> Only once did Gudrun look.
> She saw his hair all clotted with blood,
> His blinded eyes that had been so bright,
> Then she bent and bowed her head,
> And her tears ran down like drops of rain.

• • •

Such are the early Norse stories. Man is born to sorrow as the sparks fly upward. To live is to suffer and the only solution of the problem of life is to suffer with courage. Sigurd, on his way to Brynhild the first time, meets a wise man and asks him what his fate shall be,

> Hide nothing from me however hard.

he wise man answers:—

> Thou knowest that I will not lie.
> Never shalt thou be stained by baseness.
> Yet a day of doom shall come upon thee,
> A day of wrath and a day of anguish.
> But ever remember, ruler of men,
> That fortune lies in the hero's life.
> And a nobler man shall never live
> Beneath the sun than Sigurd.

23 The Norse Gods

No god of Greece could be heroic. All the Olympians were immortal and invincible. They could never feel the glow of courage; they could never defy danger. When they fought they
were sure of victory and no harm could ever come near them.
It was different in Asgard. The Giants, whose city was Jötunheim, were the active, persistent enemies of the Aesir, as the
gods were called, and they not only were an ever-present danger, but knew that in the end complete victory was assured to
them.

This knowledge was heavy on the hearts of all the dwellers
in Asgard, but it weighed heaviest on their chief and ruler,
ODIN. Like Zeus, Odin was the sky-father,

Clad in a cloud-gray kirtle and a hood as blue as the sky.

But there the resemblance ends. It would be hard to conceive
anything less like the Zeus of Homer than Odin. He is a strange
and solemn figure, always aloof. Even when he sits at the feasts
of the gods in his golden palace, Gladsheim, or with the heroes
in Valhalla, he eats nothing. The food set before him he gives
to the two wolves who crouch at his feet. On his shoulders
perch two ravens, who fly each day through the world and
bring him back news of all that men do. The name of the one
is Thought (Hugin) and of the other Memory (Munin).

While the other gods feasted, Odin pondered on what
Thought and Memory taught him.

He had the responsibility more than all the other gods together of postponing as long as possible the day of doom,
Ragnarok, when heaven and earth would be destroyed. He was
the All-father, supreme among gods and men, yet even so he
constantly sought for more wisdom. He went down to the Well
of Wisdom guarded by Mimir the wise, to beg for a draught
from it, and when Mimir answered that he must pay for it with
one of his eyes, he consented to lose the eye. He won the knowl-

edge of the Runes, too, by suffering. The Runes were magical inscriptions, immensely powerful for him who could inscribe them on anything—wood, metal, stone. Odin learned them at the cost of mysterious pain. He says in the *Elder Edda* that he hung

> Nine whole nights on a wind-rocked tree,
> Wounded with a spear,
> I was offered to Odin, myself to myself,
> On that tree of which no man knows.

He passed the hard-won knowledge on to men. They too were able to use the Runes to protect themselves. He imperiled his life again to take away from the Giants the skaldic mead, which made anyone who tasted it a poet. This good gift he bestowed upon men as well as upon the gods. In all ways he was mankind's benefactor.

Maidens were his attendants, the VALKYRIES. They waited on the table in Asgard and kept the drinking horns full, but their chief task was to go to the battlefield and decide at Odin's bidding who should win and who should die, and carry the brave dead to Odin. *Val* means "slain," and the Valkyries were the Choosers of the Slain; and the place to which they brought the heroes was the Hall of the Slain, Valhalla. In battle, the hero doomed to die would see

> Maidens excellent in beauty,
> Riding their steeds in shining armor,
> Solemn and deep in thought,
> With their white hands beckoning.

Wednesday is of course Odin's day. The Southern form of his name was Woden.

Of the other gods, only five were important: BALDER, THOR, FREYR, HEIMDALL, and TYR.

BALDER was the most beloved of the gods, on earth as in heaven. His death was the first of the disasters which fell upon the gods. One night he was troubled with dreams which seemed to foretell some great danger to him. When his mother, FRIGGA, the wife of Odin, heard this she determined to protect him from the least chance of danger. She went through the world and exacted an oath from everything, all things with life and without life, never to do him harm. But Odin still feared. He rode down to NIFLHEIM, the world of the dead, where he found the dwelling of HELA, or HEL, the Goddess of the Dead, all decked out in festal array. A Wise Woman told him for whom the house had been made ready:—

> The mead has been brewed for Balder.
> The hope of the high gods has gone.

Odin knew then that Balder must die, but the other gods believed that Frigga had made him safe. They played a game accordingly which gave them much pleasure. They would try to hit Balder, to throw a stone at him or hurl a dart or shoot an arrow or strike him with a sword, but always the weapons fell short of him or rolled harmlessly away. Nothing would hurt Balder. He seemed raised above them by this strange exemption and all honored him for it, except one only, LOKI. He was not a god, but the son of a Giant, and wherever he came trouble followed. He continually involved the gods in difficulties and dangers, but he was allowed to come freely to Asgard because for some reason never explained Odin had sworn brotherhood with him. He always hated the good, and he was jealous of Balder. He determined to do his best to find some way of injuring him. He went to Frigga disguised as a woman and entered into talk with her. Frigga told him of her journey to ensure Balder's safety and how everything had sworn to do him no harm. Except for one little shrub, she said, the mistletoe, so insignificant she had passed it by.

That was enough for Loki. He got the mistletoe and went with it to where the gods were amusing themselves. HODER, Balder's brother, who was blind, sat apart. "Why not join in the game?" asked Loki. "Blind as I am?" said Hoder. "And with nothing to throw at Balder, either?" "Oh, do your part," Loki said. "Here is a twig. Throw it and I will direct your aim." Hoder took the mistletoe and hurled it with all his strength. Under Loki's guidance it sped to Balder and pierced his heart. Balder fell to the ground dead.

His mother refused even then to give up hope. Frigga cried out to the gods for a volunteer to go down to Hela and try to ransom Balder. Hermod, one of her sons, offered himself. Odin gave him his horse Sleipnir and he sped down to Niflheim.

The others prepared the funeral. They built a lofty pyre on a great ship, and there they laid Balder's body. Nanna, his wife, went to look at it for the last time; her heart broke and she fell to the deck dead. Her body was placed beside his. Then the pyre was kindled and the ship pushed from the shore. As it sailed out to sea, the flames leaped up and wrapped it in fire.

When Hermod reached Hela with the gods' petition, she answered that she would give Balder back if it were proved to her that all everywhere mourned for him. But if one thing or one living creature refused to weep for him she would keep him. The gods dispatched messengers everywhere to ask all creation to shed tears so that Balder could be redeemed from death. They met with no refusal. Heaven and earth and everything therein wept willingly for the beloved god. The messengers rejoicing started back to carry the news to the gods. Then, lmost at the end of their journey, they came upon a Giantess —and all the sorrow of the world was turned to futility, for she refused to weep. "Only dry tears will you get from me," she said mockingly. "I had no good from Balder, nor will I give him good." So Hela kept her dead.

Loki was punished. The gods seized him and bound him in a deep cavern. Above his head a serpent was placed so that its venom fell upon his face, causing him unutterable pain. But his wife, Sigyn, came to help him. She took her place at his side and caught the venom in a cup. Even so, whenever she had to empty the cup and the poison fell on him, though but for a moment, his agony was so intense that his convulsions shook the earth.

Of the three other great gods, THOR was the Thunder-god, for whom Thursday is named, the strongest of the Aesir; FREYR cared for the fruits of the earth; HEIMDALL was the warder of Bifröst, the rainbow bridge which led to Asgard; TYR was the God of War, for whom Tuesday, once Tyr's day, was named.

In Asgard goddesses were not as important as they were in Olympus. No one among the Norse goddesses is comparable to Athena, and only two are really notable. Frigga, Odin's wife, for whom some say Friday is named, was reputed to be very wise, but she was also very silent and she told no one, not even Odin, what she knew. She is a vague figure, oftenest depicted at her spinning-wheel, where the threads she spins are of gold, but what she spins them for is a secret.

FREYA was the Goddess of Love and Beauty, but, strangely to our ideas, half of those slain in battle were hers. Odin's Valkyries could carry only half to Valhalla. Freya herself rode to the battlefield and claimed her share of the dead, and to the Norse poets that was a natural and fitting office for the Goddess of Love. Friday is generally held to have been named for her.

But there was one realm which was handed over to the sole rule of a goddess. The Kingdom of Death was Hela's. No god had any authority there, not Odin, even. Asgard the Golden belonged to the gods; glorious Valhalla to the heroes; Midgard was the battlefield for men, not the business of women. Gudrun, in the *Elder Edda*, says,

The fierceness of men rules the fate of women.

The cold pale world of the shadowy dead was woman's sphere in Norse mythology.

THE CREATION

In the *Elder Edda* a Wise Woman says:—

> Of old there was nothing,
> Nor sand, nor sea, nor cool waves.
> No earth, no heaven above.
> Only the yawning chasm.
> The sun knew not her dwelling,
> Nor the moon his realm.
> The stars had not their places.

But the chasm, tremendous though it was, did not extend everywhere. Far to the north was Niflheim, the cold realm of death, and far to the south was MUSPELHEIM, the land of fire. From Niflheim twelve rivers poured which flowed into the chasm and freezing there filled it slowly up with ice. From Muspelheim came fiery clouds that turned the ice to mist. Drops of water fell from the mist and out of them there were formed the frost maidens and YMIR, the first Giant. His son was Odin's father, whose mother and wife were frost maidens.

Odin and his two brothers killed Ymir. They made the earth and sky from him, the sea from his blood, the earth from his body, the heavens from his skull. They took sparks from Muspelheim and placed them in the sky as the sun, moon, and stars. The earth was round and encircled by the sea. A great wall which the gods built out of Ymir's eyebrows defended the place where mankind was to live. The space within was called Midgard. Here the first man and woman were created from trees, the man from an ash, the woman from an elm. They were the parents of all mankind. In the world were also DWARFS—ugly creatures, but masterly craftsmen, who lived under the earth; and ELVES, lovely sprites, who tended the flowers and streams.

A wondrous ash-tree, YGGDRASIL, supported the universe. It struck its roots through the worlds.

> Three roots there are to Yggdrasil
> Hel lives beneath the first.
> Beneath the second the frost-giants,
> And men beneath the third.

It is also said that "one of the roots goes up to Asgard." Beside this root was a well of white water, URDA'S WELL, so holy that none might drink of it. The three NORNS guarded it, who

> Allot their lives to the sons of men,
> And assign to them their fate.

The three were URDA (the Past), VERDANDI (the Present), and SKULD (the Future). Here each day the gods came, passing over the quivering rainbow bridge to sit beside the well and pass judgment on the deeds of men. Another well beneath another root was the WELL OF KNOWLEDGE, guarded by MIMIR the Wise.

Over Yggdrasil, as over Asgard, hung the threat of destruction. Like the gods it was doomed to die. A serpent and his brood gnawed continually at the root beside Niflheim, Hel's home. Some day they would succeed in killing the tree, and the universe would come crashing down.

The Frost Giants and the Mountain Giants who lived in Jötunheim were the enemies of all that is good. They were the brutal powers of earth, and in the inevitable contest between them and the divine powers of heaven, brute force would conquer.

> The gods are doomed and the end is death.

But such a belief is contrary to the deepest conviction of the human spirit, that good is stronger than evil. Even these sternly hopeless Norsemen, whose daily life in their icy land through the black winters was a perpetual challenge to heroism, saw a far-away light break through the darkness. There is a prophecy in the *Elder Edda*, singularly like the Book of Revelation, that after the defeat of the gods,—when

> The sun turns black, earth sinks in the sea,
> The hot stars fall from the sky,
> And fire leaps high about heaven itself,

—there would be a new heaven and a new earth,

> In wondrous beauty once again.
> The dwellings roofed with gold.
> The fields unsowed bear ripened fruit
> In happiness forevermore.

Then would come the reign of One who was higher even than Odin and beyond the reach of evil—

> A greater than all.
> But I dare not ever to speak his name.
> And there are few who can see beyond
> The moment when Odin falls.

This vision of a happiness infinitely remote seems a thin sustenance against despair, but it was the only hope the Eddas afforded.

THE NORSE WISDOM

Another view of the Norse character, oddly unlike its heroic aspect, is also given prominence in the *Elder Edda*. There are several collections of wise sayings which not only do not reflect heroism at all, but give a view of life which dispenses with it. This Norse wisdom-literature is far less profound than the Hebrew Book of Proverbs; indeed it rarely deserves to have the great word "wisdom" applied to it, but the Norsemen who created it had at any rate a large store of good sense, a striking contrast to the uncompromising spirit of the hero. Like the writers of Proverbs the authors seem old; they are men of experience who have meditated on human affairs. Once, no doubt, they were heroes, but now they have retired from battlefields and they see things from a different point of view. Sometimes they even look at life with a touch of humor:—

> There lies less good than most believe
> In ale for mortal men.

> A man knows nothing if he knows not
> That wealth oft begets an ape.

> A coward thinks he will live forever
> If only he can shun warfare.

> Tell one your thoughts, but beware of two.
> All know what is known to three.

> A silly man lies awake all night,
> Thinking of many things.
> When the morning comes he is worn with care,
> And his trouble is just as it was.

Some show a shrewd knowledge of human nature:—

> A paltry man and poor of mind
> Is he who mocks at all things.

> Brave men can live well anywhere.
> A coward dreads all things.

Now and then they are cheerful, almost light-hearted:—

> I once was young and traveled alone.
> I met another and thought myself rich.
> Man is the joy of man.

Be a friend to your friend.
Give him laughter for laughter.

To a good friend's house
The path is straight
Though he is far away.

A surprisingly tolerant spirit appears occasionally:—

No man has nothing but misery, let him be never so sick.
To this one his sons are a joy, and to that
His kin, to another his wealth.
And to yet another the good he has done.

In a maiden's words let no man place faith,
Nor in what a woman says.
But I know men and women both.
Men's minds are unstable toward women.

None so good that he has no faults,
None so wicked that he is worth naught.

There is real depth of insight sometimes:—

Moderately wise each one should be,
Not overwise, for a wise man's heart
Is seldom glad.

Cattle die and kindred die. We also die.
But I know one thing that never dies,
Judgment on each one dead.

Two lines near the end of the most important of the collections show wisdom:—

The mind knows only
What lies near the heart.

* * *

Along with their truly awe-inspiring heroism, these men of the North had delightful common sense. The combination seems impossible, but the poems are here to prove it. By race we are connected with the Norse; our culture goes back to the Greeks. Norse mythology and Greek mythology together give a clear picture of what the people were like from whom comes a major part of our spiritual and intellectual inheritance.

The Principal Gods

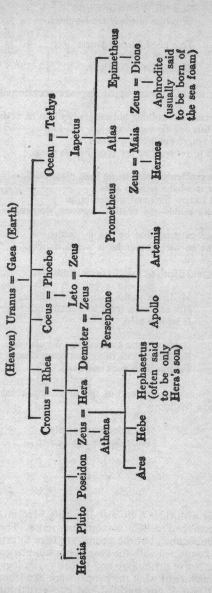

(Heaven) Uranus = Gaea (Earth)

Cronus = Rhea — Coeus = Phoebe — Ocean = Tethys

Hestia   Pluto   Poseidon   Zeus = Hera   Demeter = Zeus   Leto = Zeus   Iapetus

Persephone

Ares   Hebe   Hephaestus (often said to be only Hera's son)   Athena

Apollo   Artemis

Prometheus   Atlas   Epimetheus

Zeus = Maia   Zeus = Dione

Hermes   Aphrodite (usually said to be born of the sea foam)

Descendants of Prometheus

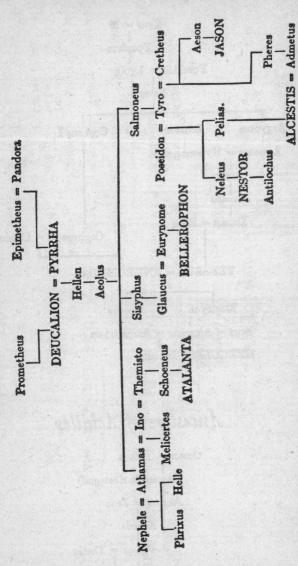

Ancestors of Perseus and Hercules

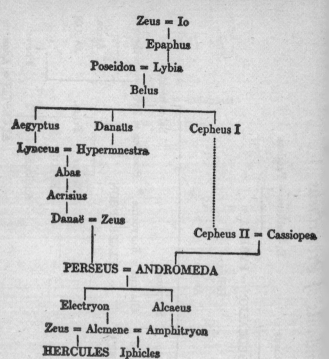

```
              Zeus = Io
                 |
              Epaphus
                 |
        Poseidon = Lybia
                 |
               Belus
     _____|_____
    |             |                   |
Aegyptus       Danaüs            Cepheus I
    |                                 :
Lynceus = Hypermnestra                :
    |                                 :
  Abas                                :
    |                                 :
 Acrisius                             :
    |                                 :
 Danaë = Zeus            Cepheus II = Cassiopea
         |                        |
         |_____|
                 |
      PERSEUS = ANDROMEDA
        _____|_____
       |                     |
   Electryon             Alcaeus
       |                     |
  Zeus = Alcmene = Amphitryon
         |
  HERCULES   Iphicles
```

Ancestors of Achilles

```
     Ocean = Tethys
           |
    Asopus (a river-god)
           |
     Aegina = Zeus
           |
        Aeacus
           |
      Peleus = Thetis
           |
        ACHILLES
```

The House of Troy

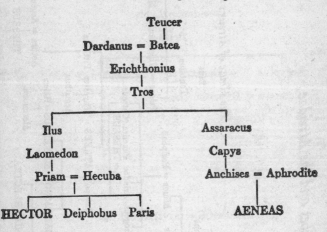

```
                    Teucer
        Dardanus = Batea
            Erichthonius
                 Tros
        ┌──────────────────┴──────────────────┐
      Ilus                              Assaracus
    Laomedon                              Capys
  Priam = Hecuba              Anchises = Aphrodite
  ┌──────┼──────┐
HECTOR Deiphobus Paris                    AENEAS
```

The Family of Helen of Troy

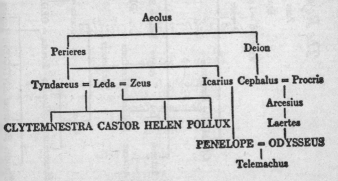

```
                        Aeolus
        ┌──────────────────┴──────────────────┐
     Perieres                              Deion
  Tyndareus = Leda = Zeus    Icarius  Cephalus = Procris
                                              Arcesius
                                              Laertes
CLYTEMNESTRA CASTOR HELEN POLLUX   PENELOPE = ODYSSEUS
                                        Telemachus
```

The Royal House of Thebes and the Atreidae

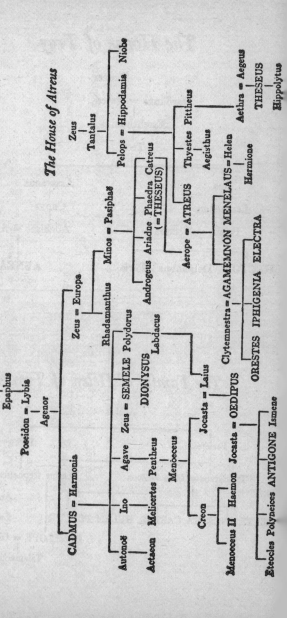

The Royal House of Thebes

Zeus = Io
  Epaphus
  Poseidon = Lybia
    Agenor

CADMUS = Harmonia — Zeus = Europa

Autonoë
Actaeon
Ino
Melicertes
Agave — Pentheus
  Menoeceus
Zeus = SEMELE
DIONYSUS
Polydorus
Labdacus

Rhadamanthus
Minos = Pasiphaë

Androgeus Ariadne Phaedra Catreus
  (=THESEUS)

Creon
Jocasta = Laius

Menoeceus II Haemon Jocasta = OEDIPUS

Eteocles Polyneices ANTIGONE Ismene

The House of Atreus

Zeus
  Tantalus
    Pelops = Hippodamia Niobe

Thyestes Pittheus
  Aegisthus

Aerope = ATREUS

Clytemnestra = AGAMEMNON MENELAUS = Helen
  Hermione

ORESTES IPHIGENIA ELECTRA

Aethra = Aegeus
THESEUS
Hippolytus

The House of Athens

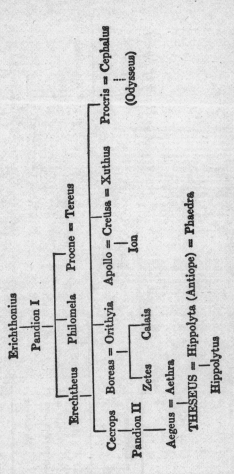

Index

*The names without page numbers
do not appear in the book.*

Abas, 282

Abydus, 293

Abyla, a mountain, one of the Pillars of Hercules, Ceuta today, *see* Calpe

Acestes, a Trojan living in Sicily, who entertained Aeneas

Acetes, pilot of the ship whose sailors captured Dionysus. He alone recognized the god

Achaeans, a division of the Greek people, said to be descended from Xuthus, a son of Hellen

Achates, friend of Aeneas, 224

Aechelous, 167, 287

Acheron, 39, 227

Achilles, 181-184, 188-192; Agamemnon angers, 187; death of, 194; Penthesilea killed by, 287; pupil of Chiron, 291; sometimes called Aeacides, 298

Acis, 84

Acrisius, 141-142; Perseus kills, 148

Acropolis, 269

Actaeon, 291

Admeta, daughter of Eurystheus, for whom Hercules got the Amazon's girdle

Admetus, 168-170, 281

Adonis, 90-91

Adrastea, a nymph who took care of the infant Zeus

Adrastus, 262-263, 265-266

Aeacides, 298

Aeacus, 296; a judge in Tartarus, 39; son of Aegina, 298

Aeaea, 211

Aegae, a place in Euboea near which was Poseidon's palace

Aegaeon, 235. *See also* Hecatonchires, 235

Aegean Sea, 252

Aegeus, 149-151; death of, 152

Aegina, 296, 298

Aegina, island of, 296, 298

Aegis, 27, 29

Aegisthus, 240; lover of Clytemnestra, 244; Orestes slays, 246

Aegyptus, 281

Aeneas, 220-235; Andromache welcomes, 221; arrival of, in Carthage, 223; descent of, to underworld, 226-230; Dido's love for, 224-225; Diomedes wounds, 185; escape of, from Troy, 200; Juno's hatred of, 222-223; Latins and Rutulians defeated by, 230-235; marries Lavinia, 235; Polyphe-

mus attempts to capture, 222; Rome founded by, 221; Turnus killed by, 235; Venus protects, 223-224

Aeneas Sylvius, King of Alba Longa, great-grandson of Aeneas

Aeolians, a division of the Greek people supposed to have descended from Aeolus, son of Hellen

Aeolus, King of the Winds, 43

Aeolus, King of Thessaly, son of Hellen, and grandson of Pyrrha and Deucalion; father of Alcyone, 106; Odysseus visits, 211

Aepytus, 295

Aero, 297

Aerope, wife of Atreus, mother of Agamemnon

Aeschylus, 22

Aesculapius, 279-281; pupil of Chiron, 291; Zeus kills, 168

Aesir, 308, 311

Ǣetes, 118, 123-126

Aethra, 265

Aetolus, son of Endymion

Agamemnon, 240-243; Achilles quarrels with, 183-184; attempts to appease Achilles, 187; member of House of Atreus, 236; permits sacrifice of Iphigenia, 182; return of, from Troy, 241-242

Agave, 255

Agenor, son of Priam

Aglaia, 35, 37

Aglauros, daughter of the half-dragon, half-man Cecrops, *see* Herse

Aidos, 37-38

Ajax, 185, 194

Ajax the Less, 203

Alba Longa, 221

Alcaeus, 161

Alcestis, 168-170; Hercules rescues, from Hades, 281

Alcides, 161

Alcinoüs, 209-210

Alcmaeon, son of Amphiaraus, who helped destroy Thebes

Alcmena, 161

Alcyone, 106-108, 297

Alecto, 40, 230-231

Alexander, a name of Paris

Alexandrian poets, 22

Alfadur, name of Odin, All Father

Aloadae, 138

Aloeus, 138

Alpheus, 116

Althea, 174-175

Amalthea, 287
Amata, 230
Amazons, 287; Argonauts avoid, 122; Athens invaded by, 154; Bellerophon conquers, 137
Ammon, identified with Jupiter, a famous temple and oracle in an oasis of the Libyan desert
Amphiaraus, 262
Amphion, 238-239, 288
Amphitrite, 28, 38
Amphitryon, 161-162
Amymone, 288
Anadyomene (rising up, usually from the sea), a name of Aphrodite
Anaxarete, 286
Ancaeus, one of the heroes of the Calydonian Hunt
Anchises, 226, 228-230
Androgeus, 150-151
Andromache, 221; Greeks capture, 200; wife of Hector, 183
Andromeda, Perseus rescues, 146-148
Andvari, a dwarf, Loki forced him to give up his hoard of gold, together with his magic ring which could create it, so that he, Loki, could pay Otter's father the ransom for Otter whom he had slain. Andvari gave them, but put a curse upon them. Thereupon Fafnir, Otter's brother being refused part of the gold by his father, slew him and seized it all, assuming the shape of a dragon and guarding it. His brother Regin urged Sigurd to slay Fafnir. This he did, but being warned by birds that Regin was a traitor to him, he slew him too. He took the ring and from that time on it was fatal to all who possessed it.
Anemone, 90
Angerbode, mother of Hela, the Fenris wolf, and the Midgard serpent
Antaeus, 167
Anteia, 135
Anteros, 36
Antigone, 261-264
Antilochus, 189, 193
Antinoüs, the worst of Penelope's suitors
Antiope, 154, 288
Aphrodite, 32-33. See also Venus; Adonis loved by, 90; aids Aeneas to escape from Troy, 200; anger of, at Hippolytus, 156; attempts to save Aeneas, 185; Harmonia receives necklace from, 255; loved by Ares, 34; mother of Eros, 36; Paris awards golden apple to, 179; wife of Hephaestus, 35
Apollo, 30-31; Alcestis served by, 168; anger of, at Greek Army, 183; Arion rescued by, 289; birth of, 294; Cassandra loved by, 202; Coronis loved by, 279; Creüsa abducted by, 273-274; Daphne loved by, 114-115; directs Cadmus to found Thebes, 254; gives Midas asses' ears, 279; Hercules quarrels with, 160; Hyacinth killed by, 88-89; Marpessa loved by, 294; Marsyas challenges, 295; oracle of, at Delphi, 256; receives lyre from Hermes, 103; sides with Hector in Trojan War, 184; slave

of Admetus, 168, 281; slays children of Niobe, 239
Apollodorus, 23
Apollonius of Rhodes, 22
Apples of Hesperides, Golden, 165
Apsyrtus, 126
Apuleitus, 22-23
Aquilo, see Boreas
Arachne, 288
Arcady, 40, 232
Arcas, 291
Archer-god, see Apollo
Arcturus, see Boötes
Ares, 34; father of Amazons, 122; imprisoned by Otus and Ephialtes, 138; role of, in Trojan War, 184-186
Arete, 209
Arethusa, 116
Arges, a cyclops, see Brontes and Steropes
Argo, voyage of, 123-127
Argonauts, 119-126; adventure of, with Harpies, 120-122; Amazons avoided by, 122; encounter of, with Scylla and Charybdis, 126-127; escape of Symplegades, 122; Hera asks Aphrodite's help for, 123; Lemnos visited by, 120; Medea saves, from Talus, 127; Phineus aids, 120-122; return of, to Greece, 127
Argos, 28, 281
Argos, dog of Odysseus, 216
Argos, statue of Hera at, 290
Argus, 77
Argus, the man who built the Argo
Ariadne, 151-152; Dionysus rescues, 56; sister of Phaedra, 156
Arimaspi, according to Aeschylus, one-eyed horsemen living near a stream which flows with gold, guarded by the Griffins
Arion, 289
Arion, the first horse, offspring of Poseidon
Aristaeus, 289
Aristophanes, 22
Arne, daughter of Aeolus, ancestress of the Boeotians
Arsinoë, sometimes said to be the mother of Aesculapius
Artemis, 31-32. See also Diana; and Hippolytus, 156-158; anger of, at Greeks, 182; Arethusa rescued by, 116; Actaeon, 255-256; causes death of Actaeon, 255-256; comes to dying Hippolytus, 158; Iphigenia rescued by, 249; Orion killed by, 297; sends boar to ravage Calydon, 174; slays children of Niobe, 239; Trojans aided by, 184; vengeance of, on Otus and Ephialtes, 137-138
Aruns, slayer of Camilla
Ascanius, 231
Asgard, 300, 308; goddesses unimportant in, 311
Ask, the name of the first man (Norse Mythology)
Asopus, 298
Astraea, daughter of Zeus and Themis (Divine Justice). During the Golden Age this star-maiden, which is what her name means, lived on earth and blessed mortals. After it ended she was placed among the stars as the constellation Virgo.
Astyanax, 186, 200-201

Atalanta, 173-177; Calydonian Hunt joined by, 174-175; childhood of, 173-174; Melanion wins, 177; Meleager falls in love with, 174; Peleus conquered by, 175

Ate, goddess of mischief, author of all rash actions and their results

Athamas, 118

Athena, 29-30. See also Minerva; anger of, at Greeks returning from Troy, 202-203; Bellerophon aided by, 135; flute invented by, 103; grows olive tree on Acropolis, 269; Iphigenia, Orestes, and Pylades rescued by, from Taurians, 253; Odysseus welcomed by, in Ithaca, 215-216; opposes Paris in Trojan War, 184; Paris bribed by, 179; Perseus aided by, 144-146; removes curse from House of Atreus, 248; Telemachus aided by, 205-206

Athenians, 265-266

Athens, 30; Minos demands tribute of, 150-151; Poseidon sends flood to, 269; Royal House of, 268-276; Theseus King of 152

Atlas, 25; fate of, 66; father of Maia, 33; Hercules visits, 165

Atli, the Norse form of Attila, who marries Gudrun and is finally slain by her after he slays her brothers

Atreus, 239

Atreus, House of, 236-253

Atropos, 43

Attica, 154, 287

Audhumbla, a cow formed from the vapor, whose milk fed the giant Ymir. She fed on the salt in the ice and as she licked it a living being emerged, from whom sprang Odin's father, Bor.

Augean Stables, 164

Aulis, 182, 242

Aurora, 289-290; bears Cephalus away, 271-272; Orion loved by, 297

Auster, 43

Autonoe, 255

Avernus, 227

Axine see Euxine

Babylon, 101

Bacchantes, see Maenads

Bacchus, 278-279. See also Dionysus

Balder, 309-311

Battus, a peasant who broke his promise not to tell Apollo Hermes had stolen his cattle, and was turned into stone

Baucis, 111-113

Bear, Great, 291

Bear, Lesser, 291

Bellerophon, 134-137, 287

Bellona, a Roman war-goddess, see Enyo

Belus, grandfather of the Danaïds

Benignant Goddesses, see Erinyes

Beowulf, 301

Bifröst, 311

Bion, myths related by, 22

Biton, 290

Black Sea, see Euxine

Boeotia, 254

Boötes, a star just behind the Dipper; also called Arcturus and the Wagoner who drives the Dipper, called the Wain or Wagon

Bor, see Audhumbla

Boreas, 43, 273

Bosphorus, 78

Bragi, Norse god of poetry

Breidablik, Balder's home

Briareus, see Hecatonchires

Briseis, 184, 187

Bromius, a name of Dionysus

Brontes, a Cyclops, see Arges

Brynhild, 304-307

Cabeiri, magical beings connected with the island of Lemnos where they protected the fruits of the field. Herodotus says they were dwarfs and that there were mysteries celebrated in their honor.

Cacus, a giant who stole some of Geryon's cattle from Hercules, dragging them backward by their tails to his cave so that Hercules could not track them down. In the end the trick was discovered and Cacus killed

Cadmus, 118, 254-256

Caduceus, 33

Calais, 273

Calchas, 182, 183

Calliope, 37

Callisto, 290-291

Calpe, one of the Pillars of Hercules, Gibraltar today, see Abyla

Calydon, 154-155, 174

Calydonian Hunt, 154-155, 174-175

Calypso, 204-205, 208

Camenae, 46

Camilla, 231, 234

Canace, 138

Capaneus, 266

Capitol, 232

Carpathos, 289

Carthage, 222-223

Cassandra, 202-203, 242-243; death of, 240

Cassiopeia, 146

Castalia, 30

Castor, 41-42; Argonauts joined by, 119; Helen sister of, 179

Catullus, 23

Cecrops, 269, 292-293

Celaeno, 297

Celeus, 50, 52; Demeter teaches sacred rites to, 53

Centaurs, 43; Atalanta shoots, 174; Lapithae battle with, 155

Centimanus, see Hecatonchires

Cephalus, 271-273

Cepheus, 146

Cephissus, 30

Cerberus, 39; Hercules captures, 165; mollified by cake, 227, 228

Cercopes, gnomes who stole Hercules' weapons

Ceres, 284-285. See also Demeter

Cerynitia, 164

Cestus, Aphrodite's girdle

Ceyx, 106-108

Chair of Forgetfulness, 156, 165

Chaos, 63-64

Charites, Greek name of the Graces

Charon, 39, 227-228

Charybdis, 126, 214, 221

Chimaera, 136

Chios, 297

Chiron, 43; Aesculapius reared by, 280; death of, 291; dies for Prometheus, 73

Chrysaor, a horse that sprang from the blood of Medusa

Chryseis, 183-184

Chrysothemis, according to Homer

and Sophocles one of the daughters of Agamemnon
Cimmerians, 67, 107
Cinyras, father of Adonis
Circe, 211-212, 284
Cithaeron, 162
City, Goddess of the, see Athena
Clashing Rocks, see Symplegades
Cleobis, 290
Clio, 37
Clotho, 43
Cloud-gatherer, see Zeus
Clymene, 131
Clytemnestra, 240-248; Agamemnon slain by, 243; daughter of Leda and King Tyndareus, 41; death of, 246; slays Cassandra, 240; wife of Agamemnon, 41, 236
Clytie, 291
Cnossus, capital of Crete, city of Minos, 292
Cnosus, see Cnossus
Cocytus, 39, 227
Coeus, 294
Colchis, 118, 122
Colonus, 262
Commerce and the Market, God of, see Hermes
Cora, see Kora
Corinth, 17, 127; previously called Ephyre, 134
Cornucopia, 287
Coronis, 279-280
Corybantes, see Cybele
Cottus, see Hecatonchires
Cow, 22
Crab, 132-133
Cranes of Ibycus, 293
Creon, 262-264; Oedipus sends, to Delphi, 260; regent of Thebes, 261, 266
Cresphontes, 295
Cretheus, 299
Creüsa, 273-276
Cronus. See also Saturn, 24-25, 65-66; father of Demeter, 40, 47; identity of, with Saturn, 45; wounds hit Heaven, 65
Crossways, Goddess of the, see Hecate
Crow, 31
Cumae, Sibyl of, 226-230
Cupid, 36, 92-100; causes Jason's love for Medea, 123; inflames Dido with love for Aeneas, 223-224
Curetes, guards of infant Zeus who clashed their arms so that Cronus should not hear him. Later identified with the Corybantes.
Cybele, a Phrygian goddess often identified with Rhea. Her priests were the Corybantes who worshiped her with cries and shouts and clashing cymbals and drums. The Romans called her the Great Mother, also Mater Turrita because her crown was a miniature city wall.
Cyclopes, 65; Aeneas escapes from, 222; Apollo kills, 168, 280; favorites of Zeus, 81-82
Cycnus (swan), the name of three young men changed into swans: (1) son of Apollo, (2) ally of the Trojans at Troy, killed by Achilles, (3) friend of Phaëthon, placed among the stars as a swan. It is sometimes said there was a fourth, a son of Ares, killed by Hercules
Cydippe, 289

Cyllene, a mountain in Arcady where Hermes was born
Cynosure (dog's tail). (1) a name for the constellation, the Little Bear, (2) a name for the North Star at the end of the tail of the Little Bear
Cynthia, 31
Cynthus, Mount, 31
Cypress, 32
Cyprian, 32
Cyprus, 32, 108; Venus honored in, 110
Cyrene, 289
Cythera, Aphrodite born near, 33
Cytherea, 33

Dactyls, the discoverers of iron and the art of working it. Their home was usually said to be Mount Ida in Crete. They were considered to have magical powers.
Daedalus, 138-140; aids Theseus to escape from Labyrinth, 151-152; Labyrinth built by, 151
Danaäns, the subjects of Danaüs of Argos, used in the Iliad for the Greeks generally
Danaë, 141-143, 148
Danaïds, 281-282
Danaüs, 281
Daphne, 114-115
Daphnis, a Sicilian shepherd of the Golden Age whose beauty won the hearts of nymphs and muses. Different stories are told about him. In one he is the exemplar of faithful lovers and was true to the nymph he loved, although Aphrodite herself and Eros tried to make him false. In another, he broke his troth and was punished by becoming blind. See Lityerses.
Dardanus, 297
Dark of the Moon, Goddess of the, see Hecate
Daulis, 271
Day, 63
Death, 40
Deer, 32
Deianira, 167, 171
Deidamia, (1) mother of Sarpedon, (2) mother of Neoptolemus also called Pyrrhus
Deiphobus, 191
Delian, 30
Delos, 239, 294; birthplace of Apollo, 30, and Artemis, 294
Delphi, 30, 256; Cadmus visits, 254; Hercules visits, 163; Orestes visits, 244, 250; Perseus visits, 144; Xuthus visits, 274
Deluge, 73-74, 269
Demeter, 40, 47-54. See also Ceres daughter of Cronus and Rhea, 47; festival of, 48; sorrow of, at loss of Persephone, 49-53; worship of, at Eleusis, 48
Demophoön, 50-52
Deucalion, 74
Diana, 46. See also Artemis
Dictys, 143, 148
Dido, 223-226; Aeneas meets, in underworld, 228
Dike, 37
Diomedes, 185-186, 267; Hercules slays, 165
Dione, mother of Aphrodite, 32

Dionysus, 54-62. *See also* Bacchus birth and youth of, 54-55; death of, 61; dual nature of, 49; entrusted to Hyades, 293; festival of, 60-61; visit of, to Thebes, 57-59; wanderings of, 55-56; worship of, 48, 57, 60-62
Dioscouri, 41
Dirce, 288
Dis, 29
Discord, Goddess of, *see* Eris
Dithyramb, a form of poetry connected with the worship of Dionysus
Divine Herald, 33
Dodona, 27, 144
Dog, 34
Dolphin, 31
Dorians, a division of the Greek people supposed to have descended from Dorus, a son of Hellen
Doris, 38, 85
Dove, 33
Dryads, 42
Dryope, 291
Dwarfs, 312

Eagle, 27
Earth, 40, 64. *See also* Mother Earth
Earth-shaker, *see* Poseidon
Echidna, half woman, half serpent, mother of Cerberus, the Nemean Lion, the Hydra of Lerna
Echo, 86-88
Edda, Elder, 301-302
Edda, Younger, 301-302
Egeria, 46
Eileithyia, *see* Ilithyia and Lucina
Elder Gods, *see* Titans
Electra, 244-248; daughter of Agamemnon, 236; one of Pleiades, 297; wife of Pylades, 251
Electryon, 148
Eleusinian Mysteries, 48, 60-61
Eleusis, 48-52, 269
Elfheim, home of the elves, good spirits (Norse Mythology)
Elli, Old Age, who out-wrestled Thor in Utgard—Loki's palace
Elves, 312
Elysian Fields, 39, 228
Emathia, a name applied to Macedon, Thessaly, Pharsalia
Embla, the name of the first woman (Norse Mythology)
Enceladus, one of the Giants
Endymion, 113-114
Enna, Vale of, 86-87
Enyo, 34
Epaphus, 78
Epeus, the maker of the Wooden Horse
Ephialtes, 137-139
Ephyre, *see* Corinth
Epigoni, 267
Epimenides, 292
Epimetheus, 68-69; father of Pyrrha, 74; Pandora received by, 70
Erato, 37
Erebus, 39, 63; Odysseus visits, 212-214
Erechtheus, 269, 273. *See also* Ericthonius; father of Creüsa, 274
Ericthonius, 292-293. *See also* Erechtheus
Eridanus, 134
Erinyes, 40; birth of, 65; Orestes

pursued by, 246-248; sacred spot of, in Colonus, 262
Eriphyle, 262
Eris, 34, 179
Eros, *see* Cupid
Erymanthus, 164
Erysichthon, 284-285
Erythia, 165
Eteocles, 261-263
Eteoclus, 266
Ethiopia, 146
Ethiopians, 68
Etruria, 232
Etruscans, 232
Eumaeus, 215-218
Eumenides, 248
Eumolpus, a Thracian singer whose descendants, the Eumolpidae, were priests of Demeter at Eleusis
Euphrosyne, 37
Euripides, 22, 54
Europa, 78-81
Eurus, 43
Euryale, one of the Gorgons, *see* Stheno and Medusa
Euryalus, 233-234
Eurycleia, 217-219
Eurydice, 103-105
Eurynome, with Ophion ruled the Titans before Cronus, 37, 134
Eurystheus, 163-165
Eurytus, 168, 171
Euterpe, 37
Euxine, 38, 67
Evadne, 266-267
Evander, 232
Evenus, father of Marpessa

Fafnir, *see* Andvari
Farbaut, father of Loki
Fate, 27
Fates, 43, 222-223; Admetus' thread of life spun by, 168; Meleager's death foretold by, 174-175
Father Heaven, *see* Heaven
Father Tiber, 232
Fauna, Roman Goddess of the Fields, also called Bona Dea (Good Goddess). *See* Maia
Fauns, 45
Faunus, 45, 230
Favonius, 43. *See also* Zephyr
Fenris, a wolf, son of Loki and Angerbode, *see* Gleipnir
Fensalir, Frigga's palace
Fields of Mourning, 228
Fire, God of, *see* Hephaestus
Flora, Roman Goddess of Flowers
Forum, Roman, 232
Freki, the Greedy, one of Odin's wolves, *see* Geri
Freya, 311
Freyr, 311
Friendly Sea, *see* Euxine
Frigga, 309-310, 311
Frost Giants, 313
Furies, *see* Erinyes

Gaea, 64
Galatea, 84-85, 107-111
Ganymede, 36
Garm, the dog that guards Hela's gate
Gemini, 42
Genius, a Roman spirit supposed to attend every person from birth to death. Every place, too, had a genius.
Gerda, wife of Freyr

Geri, the Ravenous, one of Odin's wolves, see Freki
Geryon, 165
Giallar, Heimdall's horn
Giants, Greek, 65, 67; Norse, 308, 313
Ginungagap, the chasm that preceded the creation (Norse)
Giuki, father of Gunnar
Giukungs, 304
Gladsheim, 308
Glaucus, a sea-god, 282-284
Glaucus, grandson of Bellerophon: in the Greek Army of Troy
Glaucus, King of Corinth, 134
Gleipnir, a magic chain made of the noise of a cat's footfall, the beard of women, the roots of stones, the breath of fish, the nerves of bears, the spittle of birds. The gods bound the Fenris-wolf with it (Norse Mythology).
Gnossus, see Cnossus
Golden Age, 25, 45; no women in, 70
Golden Fleece, 41, 117-130
Gordian Knot, Gordus, father of Midas, was a farmer who became king of Phrygia because he happened to drive into the public square of a town when the people were looking for a king who an oracle had said would come in a wagon. He tied the wagon in the temple of the god of the oracle. A saying grew up that whoever untied the knot would become Lord of Asia. Many tried, but all failed. Alexander the Great also tried and failed, then cut the knot with his sword.
Gorgon(s), 43, 143-144; Perseus pursued by, 146; Perseus slays, 135
Graces, 37
Graiae, 43
Gray Women, 144-145
Greek miracle, 14-17
Greyfell, Sigurd's horse
Griemhild, 304
Griffins, called by Aeschylus "the hounds of Zeus, who never bark, with beaks like birds"; sometimes said to have had the body of a lion, the head and wings of an eagle. They guarded the gold of the North which the Arismapsi tried to steal.
Gryphons, see Griffins
Gudrun, 304-306
Gullinbursti, a boar with golden bristles who drew Freyr's car
Gunnar, 304-306
Guttorm, Gunnar's half-brother who killed Sigurd
Gyes, see Gyges
Gyges, one of the hundred-handed creatures (Hecatonchires). See Briareus
Gyoll, the river that encircled Hela's realm

Hades, 39, 212-214
Haemon, Creon's son to whom Antigone was betrothed
Halcyon days, 108
Hamadryads, 42
Harmonia, 254-256, 267
Harmony, mother of Amazons, 122
Harpies, 120-122, 221

Healer, 30
Hearth, Goddess of the, see Hestia
Heaven, 64-65
Hebe, 36, 172
Hebrus, river, 105
Hecabe, a form of the name Hecuba, wife of Priam
Hecate, 31, 227
Hecatonchires (Latin, Centimanus), three monsters with a hundred hands; Briareus, also called Aegaeon; Cottus; Gyges or Gyes
Hector, 183, 185-192; death of, 191
Hector, prowess of, 183
Hecuba, 183, 190; Greeks capture, 200
Heimdall, 311
Hel, 313
Hela, 309-311
Helen, 179-181; on walls of Troy, 184-185; returns to Menelaus, 200; Telemachus recognized by, 207; Theseus kidnaps, 155
Helenus, 194-195, 221
Heliades, 134
Helicon, 37, 133
Helios, 31. See also Sun; Phaëthon received by, 131-132
Helle, 118
Hellen, son of Pyrrha and Deucalion and ancestor of the Hellenes or Greeks
Hellespont, 118, 293
Hephaestus, 34-35; Europa's basket made by, 79; husband of Aglaia, 37; Aphrodite, 33
Hera, 28. See also Juno; Argonauts aided by, 123; causes death of Semele, 55; Echo punished by, 87-88; Greeks aided by, in Trojan War, 188; guides Argonauts between Scylla and Charybdis, 126-127; hatred of Io, 76-78; Hercules reconciled to, 172; Jason aided by, 119, 126; jealous of Aegina, 296; Hercules, 161, 162, 164, 165; mother of Ares, 34; Hebe, 36; Hephaestus, 34-35; Otus plans to carry off 138; Paris visited by, 179; plots death of Hercules, 161; protector of marriage, 28; role of, in Trojan War, 184-185; statue of, at Argos, 290; vindictiveness of, 28
Hercules, 159-172; Achelous overcome by, 167; Admetus visited by, 168-170; Alcestis rescued by, from Hades, 281; Antaeus strangled by, 167; Argonauts joined by, 119-120; character of, 160-161, 170-171; Chiron accidentally wounded by, 291; death of, 171-172; Eurytus killed by, 171; husband of Hebe, 36, 172; labors of, 164-167; Laomedon slain by, 167; marriage of, to Deianira, 167; marriage of, to Megara, 162; Minyans conquered by, 162; Nessus killed by, 171; Pillars of, 165; Prometheus freed by, 73, 167; slave of Omphale, 168; Theseus befriends, 154, 163; Thespian Lion killed by, 162; wife and children killed by, 162-163; youth of, 161-162; Zeus punishes, 168
Hermes, 33. See also Mercury; Apollo receives lyre from, 33; Ares freed from prison by, 138; Argus slain by, 77; brings Persephone from underworld, 52;

Calypso ordered to free Odysseus by, 208; father of Pan, 40; father of Silenus, 40; lyre and shepherd-pipe made by, 103; messenger of the gods, 36; Odysseus rescued from Circe by, 212; Perseus aided by, 144-146; Phrixus rescued by, 118; Protesilaus brought from dead by, 183; sent as messenger to Prometheus, 71

Hermione, daughter of Helen and Menelaus, wife of Achilles' son Neoptolemus, and also of Orestes, 221

Hermod, the swiftest of foot among the Norse gods, 310

Hero, 293

Herodotus, 22

Herse, one of the three daughters of the dragon-man Cecrops, sister of Pandrosos and Aglauros

Hesiod, 21-22, 37

Hesione, (1) the daughter of Laomedon, King of Troy, rescued from the sea monster by Hercules, (2) wife of Prometheus, a sea nymph

Hesper, the Evening Star

Hesperia, 221

Hesperides, daughter of Atlas, who guarded trees with golden branches, golden leaves, and golden apples

Hesperides, Golden Apples of, 165

Hestia, 35

Hilara (the laughter-loving), (1) daughter of Apollo, (2) one of the daughters of Leucippus in the story of Castor and Pollux

Himeros, 36

Hippocrene, 135

Hippodamia, wife of Hercules' friend Pirithoüs

Hippodamia, wife of Pelops, 238

Hippolyta, 154, 165

Hippolytus, 156-158; Aesculapius brings, back to life, 280; son of Theseus, 154

Hippomedon, 226

Hippomenes, 177

Hippotades, son of Hippotes, usually said to be Aeolus, King of the Winds

Hoder, a son of Odin, 310

Hogni, brother of Gunnar

Homer, 14, 21-22

Homeric Hymns, 22

Horace, 23

Horn of Plenty, 287

Hugi, Thought, who raced with Thialfi, Loki's servant, in the palace of Utgard-Loki

Hugin, 308

Hyacinth, 88-89

Hyades, 55, 293

Hydra, 164

Hygea, Goddess of Health, said sometimes to be daughter of Aesculapius

Hygia, see Hygea

Hylas, 119, 160

Hymen, 36

Hyperboreans, 68, 145

Hyperion, 25, 30-31

Hypermnestra, 281-282

Hypnus, Greek name of the God of Sleep (Latin Somnus), whose three sons are Morpheus, Icelus, Phantasus

Hypsipyle, 120

Iacchus, a name of Dionysus

Iapetus, 25

Iasus, 173

Ibycus, 293

Icarius, father of Penelope

Icarus, 139-140

Icelus, a son of Hypnus (Latin Somnus), the God of Sleep, who gives dreams of birds and beasts

Ida, Mount, 133, 179

Ida, one of the nymphs who cared for the infant Zeus

Idas, 41, 294

Idomeneus, leader of the Cretans in the Trojan War

Iduna, wife of the Bragi and keeper of the apples which preserve the youth of the gods (Norse Mythology)

Ilion, name of Troy, meaning city of Ilus, founder of Troy

Ilios, see Ilion

Ilissus, 273

Ilithyia, 28

Ilium, see Ilion

Illyria, 256

Inachus, 76

Ino, 255; Odysseus rescued by, 209; wife of Athamus, 118

Io, 75-78, 281

Iobates, the king who sent Bellerophon against the Chimaera

Iolaus, 164

Iolcos, a town in Thessaly where the Argo was launched

Iole, 171, 292

Ion, 273-276

Ionian Sea, 78

Ionians, a division of the Greek people said to have descended from Xuthus, son of Hellen

Iphicles, 161

Iphigenia, 248-253; Artemis rescues, 249; daughter of Agamemnon, 236; escape of, from Taurians, 252-253; sacrifice of, 181-182, 241

Iphimedea, mother of the Aloadae, 138

Iphis, 286

Iris, 36; rescues Harpies, 122, 221; Somnus visited by, 106-107

Island of the Sun, 214-215

Ismene, 261-264

Ithaca, 181, 203

Itys, 270

Iulus, a name given to Aeneas' son Ascanius

Ixion, one of the great sinners in Hades, punished for insulting Hera by being bound to a wheel which revolves forever, 104

Jana, wife of Janus

Janus, 45

Jason, 118-130; arrival of, at court of Pelias, 118-119; deserts Medea, 127-129; Hera aids, 119, 126; love of, for Medea, 123-126; Medea's revenge on, 129-130; return of, to Greece, 127; subdues bulls of Æetes, 124-126

Jocasta, 256-261; death of, 261; Oedipus marries, 257

Jomunrek, husband of Sigurd's daughter Swanhild, whom he killed, having her trampled to death by horses

Jötunheim, 308, 313

Jove, 133

Judgment of Paris, 179-180
Juno, 46. *See also* Hera; Aeneas hated by, 222-223; Alcyone aided by, 106-107
Jupiter, 25, 27. *See also* Zeus; Aeneas driven from Carthage by, 225; Phrygia visited by, 111-113; Psyche made immortal by, 100
Juturna, Roman Goddess, of Springs who had a sacred pool in the Forum
Juventus, Roman God of Youth

Kora (maiden), a name of Persephone
Kronus, *see* Cronus

Labdacus, grandfather of Oedipus
Labyrinth, 139, 151
Lacedaemon, another name for Sparta
Lachesis, 43
Ladon, the serpent that guarded the Golden Apples of the Hesperides
Lady of Wild Things, 31
Laertes, 204
Laestrygons, 211
Laius, 256-259; Oedipus kills, 259
Laocoön, 198
Laodamia, 183
Laomedon, 167
Lapithae, 155
Lar(es), 44
Larissa, 148
Larvae, *see* Lemures
Latins, 230-235
Latinus, 230
Latium, 230
Latmus, 114
Latona, *see* Leto
Laurel, 31, 115
Lausus, son of Mezentius
Lavinia, 230, 235
Leander, 293
Leda, 41; mother of Helen, 179
Lemnians, 281
Lemnos, 120, 297
Lemures, 45
Lerna, 164
Lethe, 39, 228
Leto, 294; mother of Apollo and Artemis, 30, 31, 239
Leucippus, 41
Leucothea, 38, 255
Liber, *see* Lyaeus
Liberia, a Roman name of Persephone
Libethra, place in Greece where Orpheus' body was buried
Libitina, a Roman goddess of the underworld
Light, God of, *see* Apollo
Linus, 294
Lityerses, a Phrygian harvest song, supposed to be sung in memory of a farmer, Lityerses, who forced all strangers who came to his house to reap for him. If anyone was able to do less than he, he would cut off his head, place the body in a sheaf, and sing a song. Hercules killed him and threw his body into the Meander as he was about to kill Daphnis whom he had defeated in the reaping contest.
Logi, Fire, who contended with Loki in the palace of Utgard-Loki to see which could eat the faster
Loki, 310-311

Lotis, 292
Lotus-eaters, Odysseus visits, 211
Love, 63-64
Love and Beauty, Goddess of, *see* Aphrodite
Lucian, myths related by, 23, 42
Lucifer, 106
Lucina, 46
Luna, 31. *See also* Selene
Lyaeus (he who looses, i.e., from care), a name of Bacchus, the equivalent of the Roman Liber
Lycaon, 290
Lycia, 135-136, 287
Lycian, 30
Lycomedes, 158, 181
Lycurgus, 56
Lycus, 288
Lydia, 168
Lynceus, 41, 282

Machaon, son of Aesculapius; physician of the Greeks at Troy
Maeander, a river in Phrgia with many windings
Maenads, 56-57, 105
Magna Mater (Rhea, Cybele), the mother of the gods
Maia, mother of Hermes, 33, 297
Maia, wife of Vulcan, sometimes called Bona Dea (Good Goddess), *see* Fauna
Maiden, 30
Manes, 45
Marpessa, 294
Mars, *see* Ares
Marsyas, 295
Mater Matuta, Roman name of Ino when she became a sea goddess, also of Aurora
Mater Turrita, *see* Cybele
Meander, *see* Maeander
Medea, 123-130; Apsyrtus killed by, 126; Argonauts saved from Talus by, 127; causes death of Pelias, 127; flees with Jason, 126; influence of, on Aegeus, 150; Jason deserts, 127-129; love of, for Jason, 123-126; plans death of Theseus, 150; revenge of, 129-130
Mediterranean Sea, 38, 67
Medusa, 143-146
Megaera, 40
Megara, 162, 296
Melampus, 295
Melanion, 177
Meleager, 174-175
Melic Nymphs (of ash wood), nymphs who sprang from the blood of Heaven when Cronus wounded him. They carried spears of ash wood.
Melicertes, 255
Melpomene, 37
Memnon, 193, 290
Menelaus, 181; brother of Agamemnon, 236; Helen recovered by, 200; last days of, 240-241; Paris fights with, 184-185; Proteus captured by, 206-207; Telemachus visits, 205-207
Menoeceus, 262-263
Mentor, 206
Mercury, 33. *See also* Hermes; bids Aeneas leave Carthage, 225; brings Psyche to palace of gods, 100; favorite companion of Jupiter, 111; Phrygia visited by, 111-113; received by Philemon and Baucis, 111-112

Merope, 295
Messenia, 295
Metaneira, 50-52
Metis (prudence), warned Zeus that if she bore him a child it would be greater than he, Zeus then swallowed her and later Athena sprang from his head
Mezentius, 231-232, 234
Midas, 278-279
Midgard, 311, 312
Milanion, *see* Melanion
Mimir, 308, 313
Minerva, 29-30. *See also* Athena; Arachne challenged by, 288
Minos, 39, 228; Athens invaded by, 150-151; Daedalus and Icarus imprisoned by, 139; Megara besieged by, 296; son of Europa, 81
Minotaur, 139, 151-152
Minyae, descendants of Minyas, King of Thessaly. A name given to the Argonauts
Minyans, 162
Mnemosyne, 25, 37
Moira (Fate), not a god, but a mysterious, tremendous power, stronger even than the gods. To scorn Fate was to bring Nemesis, the certain consequence of defying Fate.
Moirae, see Fates
Moly the magic herb Hermes gave Odysseus to protect him from Circe
Moon, 113-114
Mopsus, soothsayer of the Argonauts
Morpheus, 107
Mors, Latin for Death, in Greek Thanatos
Moschus, 22
Mother Earth, 38, 64. *See also* Earth
Mountain Giants, 313
Mourning, Fields of, 228
Mouse-god, 30
Mulciber, *see* Hephaestus
Munin, 308
Muses, 37; Camenae identified with, 46; daughters of Zeus and Mnemosyne, 37; residence of, 68; voices of, 103
Muspelheim, 312
Mycenae, King of, *see* Eurystheus
Myrmidons, 189, 296
Myrrha, mother of Adonis, changed into a myrtle tree by Aphrodite
Myrtilus, 238
Myrtle, 33

Naiad (s), 38
Nanna, 310
Narcissus, 87-88
Nausicaä, 209-210
Naxos, 56; disappearance of Artemis at, 139; visit of Theseus to, 152
Neleus, 299
Nemea, lion of, 164
Nemesis, 37, 88
Neoptolemus, 195-196, 221
Nepenthe (banishing pain), a drug given Helen of Troy in Egypt
Nephele, 118
Neptune, 28-29, 38. *See also* Poseidon; favors Trojans, 323
Nereid(s), daughters of Nereus and Doris, 38
Nereus, 38
Nessus, 171
Nestor, 187; father of Antilochus, 193; Telemachus visits, 205-206

Nibelungenlied, 301
Nidhogg, the dragon that gnaws at the roots of Yggdrasil (Norse)
Niflheim, 309, 312
Night, 63
Nike (Latin Victoria), Goddess of victory
Nile, 78, 133
Ninus tomb of, 102
Niobe, 238-239
Nisus, 233-234, 296-297
Norns, 312-313
Notus, 43
Numa, 46
Numina, 44
Nysa, 55
Nysaean nymphs, nurses of Bacchus in the valley of Nysa; later the Hyades

Oak, 27
Ocean, 28, 38; father of Eurynome, 37
Ocean river, 25, 38; lands bordering on, 67
Oceanids, 38
Ocyrrhoe, daughter of Aesculapius
Odin, 308-309; fall of, prophesied, 313; ravens of, 308; visit of, to Niflheim 309-310
Odysseus, 202-219; adventure of, with Polyphemus, 82-84; Aeolus visited by, 211; Athena decides to aid, 204; Calypso holds prisoner, 204-205; Circe frees, 211-212; Erebus visited by, 212-214; escapes Sirens, 214; inherits arms of Achilles, 194; Ino rescues, 208; joins Greek Army against Troy, 181; Laestrygons destroy ships of, 211; Lotus-eaters visited by, 211; Nausicaä rescues, 209-211; passes Scylla and Charybdis, 214; Penelope's suitors slain by, 217-219; Phaeacians visited by, 209; Polyphemus visited by, 211; return of, to Ithaca, 214-219; Sun's vengeance on, 214-215; Teiresias consulted by, 214; Telemachus meets, 216; wooden horse suggested by, 195-196; Zeus punishes, 204-205
Oedipus, 256-261; consults Teiresias, 259; death of, 262; driven from Thebes, 261; marries Jocasta, 257; Theseus receives, 154; youth of, 256-257
Oeneus, 174
Oenone, 179
Oenopion, 297
Oeta, Mount, 171
Oileus, father of Ajax the Less
Old Man of the Sea, 38
Olive, 30
Olympians, 25-35; replace ancient Roman deities, 43-44; Tantalus punished by, 237
Olympus, 25; fired by horses of Sun, 133; mountain of the muses, 37; Trojan War reaches, 184, 190
Omphale, 168
Ophion (serpent), *see* Eurynome
Ops, 45
Oracle(s), *see* Delphi and Dodona
Orcus, 29
Oreads, 42
Orestes, 244-248; escape of, from Taurians, 249-253; son of Agamemnon, 236
Orion, 297

Orithyia, 273
Orpheus, 103-105; Argonauts joined by, 119
Orthia (severe), name of Artemis
Ortygia, 116
Ossa, 138
Othrys, mountain in Thessaly, headquarters of the Titans when they fought the gods
Otus, 137-139
Ouranos, 64
Ovid, 21
Owl, 30

Pactolus, 279
Paean, in the *Iliad* an Olympian, physician to the gods; then a name given first to Apollo and later to Aesculapius. A paean was a song of thanksgiving or of triumph usually addressed to Apollo as the Healer.
Palaemon, 38, 255
Pales, 44
Palinurus, death of, 226
Palladium, 195
Pallas, a giant
Pallas Athena, *see* Athena
Pallas, son of Evander, 232-233, 234
Pan, 40; Midas awards musical palm to, 279; reed pipe made by, 103
Pandarus, 185
Pandora, 70, 74
Pandrosus, daughter of the first Cecrops. See Herse
Panope, a Nereid
Paphos, 111
Parcae, 43, *see* also Fates
Paris, 179; Achilles slain by, 193; death of, 195; in Trojan War, 184-185; Menelaus fights with, 184-185
Parnassus, 30, 37; escapes flood, 74; fired by horses of Sun, 133
Parthenia, 29-30
Parthenopaeus, 177, 266
Parthenope, one of the Sirens
Parthenos, 29-30
Pasiphaë, 151
Patroclus, 187, 188-189
Pausanias, 23, 66
Peacock, 77
Pegasus, 133-137
Peitho (Latin Suadela), Goddess of Persuasion
Pelasgus, grandson of river god Inachus and founder of the Pelasgic division of the Greek people
Peleus, 119; Atalanta conquers, 175; marriage of, 179
Pelias, 118-119; death of, 127; son of Poseidon and Tyro, 298-299
Pelion, 138, 280
Pelops, 237-238
Penates, 44
Penelope, 203-204; Odysseus slays suitors of, 217-219; reunited with Odysseus, 219
Peneus, 115
Penthesilea, 287
Pentheus, 58-59, 255
Perdix nephew and pupil of Daedalus. He invented the saw and the compass. Daedalus became jealous of him and killed him, and Minerva, pitying him, changed him into a partridge (perdix).

Pergamos, 185
Persephone, 49-54; Adonis loved by, 90; carried to underworld, 49-50, 86-87; character of, 53-54; daughter of Demeter, 49; Pirithoüs attempts to kidnap, 155-156; return of, from underworld, 52-53; wife of Hades, 29; worship of, 62
Perseus, 141-148; great-grandson of Abas, 282
Phaeacians, 209, 240
Phaedra, 156-158
Phaedrus, 273
Phaëthon, 131-134
Phantasus, one of the sons of Hypnos (Latin Somnus), God of Sleep, who gives dreams of inanimate objects
Phaon, beloved by the poetess Sappho. He was said, when an old man, to have ferried Aphrodite from Lesbos to Chios, in return for which the goddess gave him youth and beauty.
Pharos, 207, 289
Pherae, home of Alcestis and Admetus
Phidias, 290
Philemon, 111-113
Philoctetes, 172, 194-195
Philomela, 270-271
Phineus, 120-122
Phlegethon, 39
Phobos (Fear), attendant of Ares (Mars)
Phoebe, a name of Artemis, 31
Phoebe, a Titan, 294
Phoebus Apollo, *see* Apollo
Pholus, 291
Phorcys, 43
Phosphor, Greek for Lucifer
Phrixus, 118, 255
Phrygia, 111-113, 278; Amazons invade, 287
Pieria, 37
Pierides, the Muses, a name derived from their birthplace, Pieria, in Thessaly
Pierus, 37
Pillars of Hercules, 165
Pindar, 22
Pirene, 135
Pirithoüs, 155-156
Pittheus, King of Troezen, father of Theseus' mother
Plato, 22
Pleiades, 293, 297
Pluto, 29, 39-40. See also Hades
Plutus (Wealth), a Roman allegorical figure wrongly confused with Pluto
Poeas, father of Philoctetes. Sophocles says he, not his son, set fire to Hercules' pyre.
Poena, goddess of punishment, an attendant of Nemesis
Pollux, 41-42; Argonauts joined by, 119; brother of Helen, 179; Helen recovered by, 155
Polybotes, one of the Giants
Polybus, 257, 260
Polyclitus the Elder, 290
Polydectes, 143, 148
Polydectes (he who receives many), a name of Hades
Polydeuces, 41-42. *See also* Pollux
Polydorus, (1) son of Cadmus, father of Labdacus, (2) son of Priam
Polyhymnia, 37

Polyidus, 135
Polyneices, 261-264
Polyphemus, 81-85; Aeneas escapes from, 222; Odysseus visits, 211
Polyphontes, 295
Polyxena, 201
Pomona, 46, 285-286
Pontus, 38
Porphyrion, one of the Giants
Poseidon, 28-29. See also Neptune; Acropolis opened by, 269; Amymone rescued by, 288; anger of, at Greeks returning from Troy, 203; father of Bellerophon, 134; Otus and Ephialtes, 138; Polyphemus, 84; Proteus, 38; Triton, 38; Greeks favored by, in Trojan War, 184; husband of Amphitrite, 38; Laomedon cheats, 167; return of Odysseus delayed by, 208-209; saves Erysichthon's daughter from slavery, 285; sends flood to Athens, 269; Tyro loved by, 298
Priam, 179, 183; death of, 199
Priapus, 44
Procne, 270-271
Procris, 271-273
Procrustes, 150
Proetus, 135-137
Prometheus, 75-78; aids Zeus in war on Cronus, 66; blood of, produces magic plant, 124; father of Deucalion, 74; Hercules frees, 167; mankind created by, 68-70; revenge of Zeus on, 70-73; savior of mankind, 25
Proserpine, 29, 99. See also Persephone
Protesilaus, 183
Proteus, 38; Aristaeus seizes, 289; Menelaus captures, 207
Psamathe, 294
Psyche, 92-100
Psychopompus (conductor of souls), a name of Hermes
Pygmalion, 108-111
Pygmalion, Dido's wicked brother, King of Tyre
Pylades, 244-246, 250-253
Pylos, 206
Pyramus, 101-103
Pyrrha, 74
Pyrrhus, 195, 221
Pythian, 30
Python, 30

Quirinus, 45. See also Romulus

Ragnarok, the day of doom (Norse Mythology), 308
Rainbow, Goddess of the, see Iris
Rain-god, see Zeus
Raven(s), bird of Apollo, 280; Odin's, 308
Remus, 221
Rhadamanthus, 39, 228; son of Europa, 81
Rhea, 40, 47; queen of the universe, 65; sent by Zeus as messenger to Demeter, 53
Rhesus, Tracian ally of the Trojans whose horses surpassed all mortal horses
Rhoecus, 298
Rhoetus, one of the Giants
Romulus, 45, 221
Runes, 308-309
Rutulians, Aeneas wars on, 230-235

Salamis, Telamon of, 167
Salii, priests of Mars who guarded the shield that fell from heaven in the reign of Numa
Salmoneus, 298
Sarpedon, (1) son of Zeus and Europa, ancestor of the Lycians, (2) grandson of Bellerophon and one of the Trojan leaders in the Trojan War
Saturn, 25, 45. See also Cronus
Saturnalia, 45
Satyrs, 42
Scaean gates, 190
Scamander, 190
Scheria, in the Odyssey the country of the Phaeacians
Schoenius, 173
Sciron, 150
Scorpion, 132, 133
Scylla, 282-284; Argonauts escape, 126-127; Circe changes, into a monster, 284; Minos loved by, 296; Odysseus escapes, 214
Scyros, island ruled by Lycomedes where Theseus was killed and Achilles disguised as a girl
Sea, Lord of the, see Poseidon
Seasons, 25, 81
Selene, 31, 113-114
Selli, 144
Semele, 54-55; daughter of Cadmus and Harmonia, 255; Dionysus takes, to Olympus, 56
Semiramis, 101
Serimnir, the boar which perpetually furnishes the food for the heroes of Valhalla
Seriphus, island on which Danaë and Perseus landed
Sestus, 293
Seven against Thebes, 152-154, 264-267
Sibyl of Cumae, 226-230
Sichaeus, Dido's husband
Sicily, 116
Sidero, 299
Sidon, King of, 78
Siggeir, husband of Signy
Sigmund, 303-304
Signy, 303-304
Sigurd, 304-307
Sigyn, 311
Simois, river, 183
Sinfiotli, birth and youth of, 303-304
Sinis, 150
Sinon, 196-198
Sirens, 43; Argonauts saved from, by Orpheus, 104; Odysseus escapes, 214
Sirius, the Dog Star who follows Orion
Sisyphus, 134, 298
Skidbladnir, a magic ship made by the dwarfs for Freyr. It could be folded up and carried in a pocket. Unfolded, it was big enough to carry all the gods.
Skirnir, Freyr's servant who wooed and won for him the giantess Gerda
Skuld, 313
Sky, Lord of the, see Zeus
Sleep, 40
Sleipnir, 310
Sminthian, name given to Apollo, 30
Socrates, 273
Sol, Latin name for the sun-god, see Helios

Solymi, 137
Somnus, 106-107, *see* Hypnus
Sophocles, 22
Sparrow, 33
Sparta, 206
Sphinx, 257
Sterope, 297
Steropes, a Cyclops, *see* Arges
Stheno, one of the Gorgons, *see* Euryale and Medusa
Stone People, 74
Strife, 34
Strophius, King of Phocis where Orestes grew up
Sturluson, Snorri, 302
Stymphalian birds, 164
Stymphalus, 164
Styx, 50, 99
Suadela, *see* Peitho
Sun, 50. *See also* Helios; Odysseus' visit to island of 214-215; Phaëthon's adventure with horses of, 131-134
Sun-god, 30-31, 291
Surt, ruler of Muspelheim (Norse Mythology)
Swan, 33
Swanhild, *see* Jomunrek
Sylvanus, 44
Symplegades, 122
Syracuse, 116
Syrinx, 77

Taenarum or Taenarus, a place in Laconia where there was a descent to the lower world
Talus, 127
Tantalus, 104, 237-239
Tarpeian rock, 232
Tartarus, 39
Taurians, 249-250
Taygete, 297
Teiresias, 58; death of, 267; Odysseus consults, 214; Oedipus consults, 259; prophecy of, concerning Hercules, 161-162; prophesies death of Menoeceus, 262-263
Telamon, father of Ajax the Greater, 167, 296
Telemachus, 205-207; Odysseus meets, 216; return of, to Ithaca, 215-219; scorned by Penelope's suitors, 203
Telephus son of Hercules, wounded by Achilles, but healed by the rust on the spear
Tempe, a valley in Thessaly through which flowed the Peneus, the father of Daphne
Tereus, 270-271
Terminus, 44
Terpsichore, 37
Tethys, 25, 28; wife of Ocean, 38
Teucer, (1) son of the river Scamander and first King of Troy, (2) son of Telamon, half-brother of Ajax the Greater
Teucri, the Trojans
Thalia, Muse of Comedy, 37
Thalia, one of the Three Graces, 7
Thamyris, a famous bard who challenged the Muses to a combat and was struck blind for his presumption
Thanatos, 29
Thea (shining), name sometimes given to the moon
Thebes, 254-255; Athenians march against, 265-266; birthplace of

Dionysus, 54; Dionysus' visit to, 257-259; home of Hercules, 17; plague visits, 257-259; Royal House of, 254-267; Seven against 264-267; Sphinx besets, 257; Theseus leads army against, 154
Themis, 25, 37
Themiscyra, 287
Theocritus, 22
Thersander, son of Polyneices, one of the Epigoni
Theseus, 149-158; abandons Ariadne, 56; Aegeus receives, 150; Amazons defeated by, 154, 287; Ariadne aids, 151-152; Athens ruled by, 152-154; battles with Centaurs, 155; death of, 158; friendship of, with Pirithoüs, 154-155; Hercules befriended by, 154, 163; compared with, 159-160; joins Calydonian Hunt, 154; marches against Thebes, 265-266; marriage of, to Phaedra, 156; Minotaur slain by, 151-152; Oedipus received by, 154; Pirithoüs aided by, in attempt to kidnap Persephone, 155-156; aids Adrastus, 265; return of, to Athens, 152; sails on *Argo*, 154; youth of, 149-150
Thespian lion, 162
Thessaly, 25
Thestius, King of Calydon, father of Leda and Althea
Thetis, 38; asks Zeus to give Trojans success, 184; marriage of, 179
Thialfi, *see* Hugi
Thisbe, 101-103
Thoas, 252-253
Thor, 311
Thrace, 34
Thracians, 103
Thrinacia, *see* Trinacria
Thrym, a giant who stole Thor's hammer
Thyestes, son of Pelops, 239
Thyiades, a name for the followers of Bacchus
Tiber, Father, 232
Tirnys, city in Argolis where Hercules was educated
Tirnys, King of, *see* Eurystheus
Tisiphone, 40
Titans, 24-25, 65-66
Tithonus, 289-290
Tityus, giant slain by Apollo
Tmolus, 279
Trinacria (having three promontories), a name for Sicily
Triptolemus, 53
Tritogenea, epithet of Athena, of uncertain meaning
Triton, 38
Trivia (three roads), name of Hecate, Goddess of the Crossways
Troezen, city in Argolis, birthplace of Theseus
Troilus, son of Priam, killed by Achilles
Trojan War, 178-192; cause of, 178-179; Olympus takes sides in, 184
Troy, 178, 183; fall of, 193-201
Truth, God of, *see* Apollo
Turnus, 230-231, 234-235
Tyche (Latin Fortuna), Greek name of Goddess of Fortune
Tydeus, 267
Tydides (son of Tydeus), Diomedes
Tyndareus 41, 179-181

Tyndaridae, 41
Tyndaris (daughter of Tyndareus),
    Helen or Clytemnestra
Typhoeus, another form of the name
    Typhon
Typhon, 67
Tyr, 311
Tyro, 298-299

Ulysses, *see* Odysseus
Underworld, 39-40
Urania, 37
Uranus (sky), father of Cronus
Urda, 313
Urda's Well, 312
Utgard-Loki, ruler of Jötunheim

Valhalla, 300, 309
Valkyries, 309
Ve, brother of Odin
Venus, 32-33; *See also* Aphrodite;
    Aeneas protected by, 223-224;
    Anaxarete turned to stone by,
    286; anger of, at Psyche, 96-100;
    asks Cupid's aid against Psyche,
    92; feast day of, in Cyprus, 110;
    imposes tasks on Psyche, 98-100
Verdandi, 313
Vertumnus, 46, 285-286
Vesper, another form of Hesper
Vesta, *see* Hestia
Vestals, 35
Victoria, Latin name of Nike, God-
    dess of Victory
Vidar, one of Odin's sons
Vigrid, the field where the gods will
    be defeated (Norse Mythology)
Vili, brother of Odin
Vingolf, home of the goddesses in
    Asgard
Virbius, 280
Virgil, 23
Volsung, 303-304
Voluptas, Latin Goddess of Pleasure
Vulcan, *see* Hephaestus
Vulture, 34

War, Goddess of, *see* Enyo
Wealth, God of, *see* Hades
Wedding Feast, God of the, *see* Hy-
    men
Well of Knowledge, 313
Well of Wisdom, 308

West Wind, 43
Winds, 43; country of, 211
Woden, *see* Odin
Wooden horse, 195-199

Xanthus, 190
Xuthus, 274-276

Yggdrasil, 312
Ymir, 312
Youth, Goddess of, *see* Hebe

Zephyr, 43, 89; rescues Psyche, 93
Zetes, 273
Zethus, 238, 288
Zeus, 27. *See also* Jupiter; Aegina
    loved by, 296, 298; Aesculapius
    killed by, 280; anger of, at Pro-
    metheus and mankind, 70-73;
    birth of, 65-66; brings Perseph-
    one from underworld, 52;
    brother of Hestia, 35; Callisto
    loved by, 290; character of, 19-
    20; Cronus dethroned by, 24-25;
    Cyclopes protected by, 82; Danaë
    visited by, 142; displeasure of,
    with Phineas, 120; Europa loved
    by, 78-81; father of Aphrodite,
    32; Apollo, 30; Ares, 34; Arte-
    mis, 31; Athena, 29; Dionysus,
    54; Graces, 37; Hebe, 36; Helen,
    179; Hephaestus, 34; Hercules,
    161; Hermes, 33; Muses, 37; Pol-
    lux and Helen, 41; Tantalus, 237;
    Hercules punished by, 168;
    hounds of, 120-122; husband of
    Hera, 28; infidelity of, 27; Io
    loved by, 76-78; Leto loved by,
    294; Lycaon punished by, 290;
    Lycurgus struck blind by, 56;
    Odysseus rescued by, 204-205;
    Pleiades placed in heavens by,
    297; refuses to award golden ap-
    ple, 179; Salmoneus slain by,
    298; Semele loved by, 54-55;
    sends flood to destroy mankind,
    73-74; Sisyphus punished by,
    298; supreme ruler, 25; Tithonus
    made immortal, 290; Trojans
    aided by, 184, 187-188; walls of
    Troy built at command of, 167;
    wars on Cronus, 66-67; women
    created by, 70

MENTOR Books of Special Interest